boilerplate

boilerplate

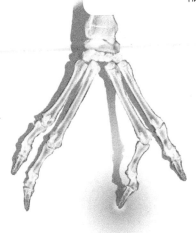

SPOT AND SMUDGE
BOOK 2
THE GLASGOW GRAY
ROBERT UDULUTCH

THE SPOT AND SMUDGE SERIES

To discover more about the books,
the real Spot and Smudge,
and the author, please visit:
SpotandSmudge.com

ISBN-13: 978-1542623728
ISBN-10: 1542623723

WANT MORE WONDERFULLY TWISTED DOGS?
GET THE **ONE PAW IN THE GRAVE** SERIES OF SHORT STORIES:

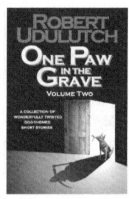

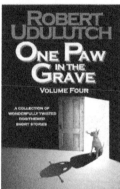
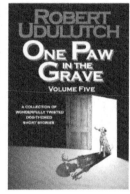

For Coal and Baloo and Boris and Panco.
Often soaked, frequently stinky, always wagging, and forever welcome.

For the strength of the Pack is the Wolf,
and the strength of the Wolf is the Pack.
— *Rudyard Kipling*

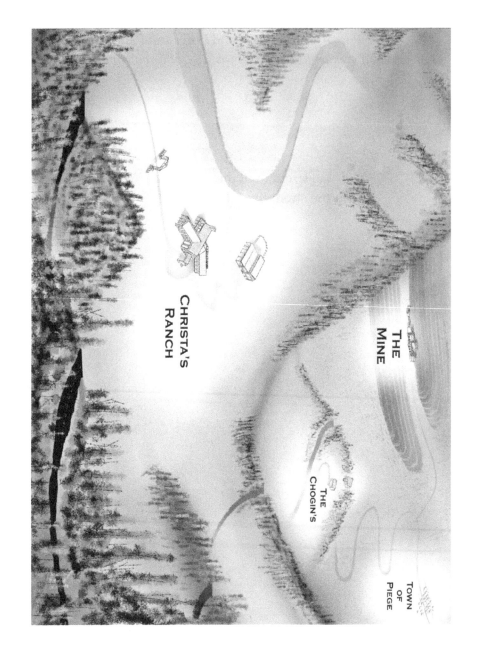

CHAPTER 1

"Your bum's out the window dear brother, he's nary a bother at all," Mimi said into the phone she had cradled against her chin. As her brother-in-law Hamish loudly droned on about kids always being a bother she pulled open the oven door and used a dishtowel to slide out a pan of hot rolls. She swapped it with a cast iron pan filled with an apple dessert, and after spinning the oven's timer she tossed the rag over her daughter's shoulder and whispered, "How we looking dearie?"

Aila dried her hands on the towel and leaned against her mom as they scanned the kitchen table. With a satisfied nod she said softly, "Enough to feed the Dragoons and have some left for stovies."

Mimi nodded and said to the phone, "Just give it some thought, the lad's dying to come up…What's that?…Aye, all of them are here, plus one. Ronnie's friend Lindsay is coming for her Christmas dinner as well."

As she rummaged through a drawer for a lighter a medium-size black dog trotted into the kitchen.

When Spot got to the back door he went up on his hind legs and deftly landed his front paws on the windowsill.

"You'd like her," Mimi said. "She's a fair bit bigger in every dimension than Ronnie was, but just as cute…Aye, I'm sure she fancies mature blokes."

She shared an eye-roll with her daughter, and Spot added his own headshake as his perked ears swiveled to listen to the soft crunching that was coming up the snowy driveway.

"She's a love," Mimi said. "She came to look after Ronnie's farm but has decided to stay, and the new clinic was happy to take her on."

Spot's tail started to sweep back and forth.

"Aye, she's a tech like Ronnie was," Mimi said as she leaned over the sink but didn't see anything through the kitchen's large window.

"Is she here?" she whispered to Spot.

He nodded, and to the phone Mimi said, "Our guest has arrived so that's me away. Give all the shaggy wee ones there a pat for us and I'll ring you later."

She heard the crunching, and a moment later a small pickup truck rolled into the farm's turnaround. Spot's tail started to spin in circles as Mimi replied to Hamish's parting comment with, "Oh, I'll certainly tell her all about you...Aye, love you too."

After going through several drawers she gave Spot's ear at tug and said, "Be a love and fetch my new lighter. I thinks it's on the mantle, and please turn down the music a little."

Spot gave her an annoyed look she read as, *But I have to welcome Lindsay*, to which Mimi's head tip replied, *If you did less crabbin' and more movin' you'd be back by now.*

He dropped down and skulked away, and a few seconds later the Christmas carols softened and he trotted back into the kitchen with a silver cigarette lighter in his mouth.

The metal zippo was a present from Aila's husband Dan, and it had the Walker family tartan on one side and the royal standard lion on the other. Mimi hadn't smoked in decades but every horizontal surface in the farmhouse had at least one candle on it.

Spot put his paws on the windowsill again, and spat the lighter across the countertop to Mimi. He'd used a little more force than intended and it sailed past her, bumped over the lip of the sink, and flipped down into a pot of soapy water.

"You dotty thing," she scolded as she rolled up her sleeve. She fished around in the bottom of the dirty pot as she received an ears-down shrugged apology from Spot.

He turned back to the window, and as Lindsay slid out of the truck's seat and bumped her door closed with a hip Spot's back end wiggled and he turned to give Mimi his best puppy eyes.

"Aye, you can go say hello," she said as she opened the door for him. She ran a hand over his head as he slipped past her and nosed through the screen door.

She couldn't be too mad. The pups had been good about sticking to the rules and not doing anything unusual when outsiders were around. Friends and neighbors stopped by the farm often during the holidays, especially as it was Mimi's first Christmas without Papa, and Spot could have easily opened the back door by himself.

As she shook water out of the lighter Aila joined her at the sink, and they watched Spot trot across the snowy driveway to welcome Lindsay with wags. She was holding a full paper bag and bent carefully to drum her free gloved hand on her knee when she saw him coming. After giving him a few scratches she detoured to the goat pen so the bleating Mr. Watt could get his required chin and horn rubbing through the fence.

At the far end of the turnaround the barn door slid open and eleven year old Ben stepped out with another wagging black dog.

When they saw their guest had arrived Ben yelled something back into the barn before he rolled the heavy door closed behind them. When he and Smudge got halfway down the ramp they hopped off the side to trudge through the knee-deep snow.

Aila watched her son kicking up white clouds and yelled at the kitchen window, "Tie your boots, you big…"

She trailed off when she realized there was no way he could hear her.

Mimi put a fingertip in her ear and worked her jaw.

"Sorry Mum," Aila chuckled as she patted her mom's shoulder. She cracked open the kitchen door, leaned out into the falling snow, and called out, "Hey Lindsay! Merry Christmas!" and to Ben she yelled, "Are they coming?"

Ben nodded, and Aila added, "Lace up your boots, you big numpty!"

As she closed the door her son shot her a big smile and a double thumbs-up.

"Gifted my ass," Aila mumbled as Ben raised his snow-filled boot and tried to tie it while balancing like a stork.

Mimi gave her daughter's backside a solid whack on her way to the kitchen table. She had to flick the wet lighter until her thumb was raw before it finally caught flame enough to light the dozen red centerpiece candles.

❧§§☙

Dan dropped his fork onto his empty plate and pushed back from the table. He gave his wife and his mother-in-law firm nods, and as he slid a hand under his waistband he said in his best hick voice, "I suuuuu-render. Women, that there was one fine damn meal."

Ben mimicked his dad as he rubbed his shoved-out stomach and added, "Ah-yep, best possum I ever et'."

"Aw shucks," Aila said as she touched her heart and tipped her wine glass to them. "Y'all's rosen' my cheeks."

Mimi's hick sounded more like country Irish, but she chimed in with, "The coon was a mite dry, but the shine made up fer' it."

"Soooo Lindsay," Kelcy said as she turned away from her family, "isn't the new vet from down south?"

"Why yes, Kelcy," Lindsay said with a smirk. "The doctor is a southern gentleman. A Texan, I believe."

"And as I understand it," Mimi said, "that tall drink of water's not hard on the eyes."

"Or the ears," Lindsay said. "The office does have its perks."

The women at the table smiled and raised a toast.

"Ugh," Ben said as he slipped Spot and Smudge another piece of turkey under the table.

"I'm sitting right here," Dan said.

Aila ignored her husband and asked, "So you're liking it, and it's going well?"

"Yes I do, and it is," Lindsay said. "Mari kept a copy of the old clinic's client list at home for her fundraisers, so she and I went through and called everyone. We tried to explain things as best we could, you know."

Aila nodded, even though she thankfully didn't know. She didn't envy Lindsay having to explain to people that she was taking the place of her murdered friend. The new clinic was right across the street from the clinic Ronnie was butchered in before it burned to the ground.

There was a long silent moment at the table.

Mimi got up with her empty plate, and as she passed Lindsay she gave her shoulder a tender squeeze and said, "Good on you dearie. Who's ready for tea and apple crumble?"

Ben raised his fork, the pups wagged, and Dan groaned.

"Jean, I can't thank you enough," Lindsay said as Mimi rose up on her toes to give the taller woman a big hug. A paper shopping bag filled with leftovers crumpled between them as Lindsay added, "I appreciate you inviting me to intrude on your holiday. You guys have been so sweet to me."

"Wasn't a bother, you're always welcome," Mimi said. As she pulled away she took Lindsay's hand and held her eyes for a moment as she said, "Listen to me when I tell you something. Ronnie was a dear friend and a big help to us, and we'll never forget her. I know settling her affairs and taking care of her farm can't be easy for you, so don't hesitate if there's anything we can do to lend a hand."

She went in for another hug, and as the paper bag complained again she noticed the pups were looking up at her from behind Lindsay.

They nodded and wagged in sync as Mimi winked down at them and added, "The whole family appreciates what you're doin' dearie."

When Lindsay turned to thank Aila for the lovely meal she was pulled into another long embrace. It wasn't lost on her that the dozen or so hugs it had taken her to exit the house were meant as much for

Ronnie as they'd been for her. A barrage of family affection wasn't something she was used to, nor was a big holiday dinner, but she was finding she could get used to both.

She turned back to the table and said, "And I wasn't kidding Kelcy, you should stop by the new clinic. I'd love to give you a tour."

To Aila she said, "The rest of you should come too. It's pretty impressive, and I don't just mean Doc Marty."

Aila laughed and said, "We will certainly stop by. I'm sure Ben would love to see it, wink wink. Thanks for the wine, and you drive carefully out there."

She pulled open the kitchen door and flipped on the floodlights that lit up the turnaround.

Spot and Smudge trotted out into snow, which had accumulated another few inches since Kelcy last plowed the farm's long driveway. She loved getting behind the wheel of Papa's Wagoneer, especially when the plow was attached and there was enough snow to make it fun. Both kids had been driving the plow with Papa as copilot for a few winters, but as Kelcy had just gotten her learner's permit Dan let her clear the driveway by herself for the first time. Aila wondered how long the novelty would last and assumed sometime before the snows stopped for the year their daughter's volunteering would dry up. Aila hated to drive the plow and made a mental note to catch Dan at the right time to convince him their son was ready to fly it solo.

Lindsay thanked Ben for warming up her truck, and she wished everyone a merry Christmas as she pulled her hood up and backed through the door. She crossed the turnaround, and before getting into her truck she gave the wagging pups a few rump rubs and ear pulls.

The dogs watched her headlights slowly move down the long snowy driveway, turn onto the road, and disappear north toward town.

When the road went dark they signaled to the large coyote who'd been patiently waiting in the barn's shadow.

The pack's new leader One Ear hopped the snow berm left by the plow and stepped into the light. Light she would have bolted from a few weeks ago.

The impressive gray and brown hunter was only half a head taller than the pups, but she was thicker through the chest and shoulders. She had sharp, bright eyes, and even with only one ear she could hear the mice moving under the barn and a squirrel rustling in a far treetop. She could also smell the turkey carcass in the house and the new chicken eggs in the coop behind her. Of course she knew better than to give the chickens a second look anymore. Her new alphas were not to be trifled with and she followed their rules without question. These odd dogs had dispatched her previous alpha, an elite killer who'd never before been bested, and they'd taken over the pack with a cunning gambit. They had also taught One Ear more about keeping a pack safe and well-fed than her old alpha ever could.

These curious dogs also had a unique relationship with their den of humans, and One Ear had grown to trust them as well. It was something she would have never thought possible, but she felt safe around them. The humans here had become an extension of her pack and she and her hunters would protect them with their lives if needed, again.

One Ear dropped a dead rabbit at Spot's feet and submissively licked his chin. She rolled onto her back in the snow and poked her nose playfully at Smudge, who pinned her and nipped gently at her tail.

She and her newly trained hunting party had just been successful in the woods to the east of the farm, and she'd sent them ahead to the den with their two other rabbits while she detoured to the farm. She wanted to see if her alphas needed dinner, or anything else from her.

Things had been peaceful since the fires so Spot only had the coyotes patrol the farm once a week or so, mostly just to keep them trained and familiar with the family.

The winter weather was starting to clamp down on the South Shore of Massachusetts in earnest, and short days of low forties were accompanied by long freezing nights. Spot and Smudge had been visiting the den in The Bogs less often but still had daily visits from at least one of the pack. Usually it was from One Ear herself, and she often brought her new mate with her. She and the other lead female had each found new males and would likely mate soon. The pups and the rest of the Hogan-Walker family were looking forward to meeting a batch of coyote puppies in the spring.

The pack was doing well, and with the training they received from the pups they were able to feed themselves well while virtually eliminating encounters with other humans. The coyotes had upped their hunting game, and they'd become expert fishers. The kettle ponds and rivers provided an endless supply of sunfish and brook trout and herring, and the younger ones were even getting adept at opening clams and mussels, and were finally learning how to avoid getting nipped by crayfish pinchers.

One Ear couldn't argue with the relatively easy supply of protein, but she wasn't a fan of standing in the cold water. Spot found that funny as the tough coyote was normally the most patient of hunters, but when it came to staring down until a fish swam by she was easily frustrated and gave up quickly. Although they didn't need to hunt fur-and-feather prey as often anymore the pups agreed with One Ear's insistence that they kept their skills sharp. She was a masterful teacher, and clearly enjoyed grooming her juveniles in the killing arts.

Smudge gestured to the dead rabbit as she said, *Great catch girl, but no thanks. You can take that with you back to the den.*

The dogs said goodbye and One Ear scooped up the rabbit and darted back into the darkness. Her wounded hip had healed well and she was back to shooting down the trails at top speed.

From inside the house Ben tapped on the kitchen window and signed to the pups, *Everything alright?*

Smudge raised a paw, split it open into two halves at the wrist, and signed back to him, *Yep, all good. She just stopped to say hello. We're coming, just gotta pee.*

Several months earlier Spot had designed the radical modifications to their front feet, and they'd coerced the old clinic's owner into doing the work. She was reprehensible person, but she was a talented surgeon and had done a bang-up job before she disappeared and was never heard from again.

When their paws were closed the hairs covered the split so they looked like normal, slightly chunky forelimbs, but when their paws were open they formed powerful and dexterous opposing appendages that were essentially two large fingers. Each finger had two toe pads, and the individual pads had been modified with a transverse split, giving them muscular flaps that extend distally, like a small fold-out fingertip.

As the pups' dexterity with their newly acquired split paws increased they'd created and mastered a modified version of sign language.

Although useful as hands, they couldn't traditionally fingerspell with only the two appendages so Spot and Ben had worked out a system that added wrist rotation to replace positions the missing fingers would normally take. Although they often held full conversations by signing, Smudge had abbreviated many of their more frequently used phrases into short, easily identifiable gestures. Some of which didn't involve their front paws at all.

Like the sign for peeing, which was obvious, and in Mimi's opinion a little crude.

Spot and Smudge took their bathroom break, said goodnight to Mr. Watt, and bounded through the snow to the house. They let themselves in and pushed the kitchen door closed, and stopped on the little rug just inside the back door.

"I like her," Ben said as he dug his spoon into his third helping of Mimi's apple crumble dessert. "She knows a lot about animals, and she could clearly beat Dad up."

Aila laughed as she grabbed the designated dog towel from a hook behind the back door.

"I like her too," she said as she bent to dry off the pups' damp backs, heads, and bellies, "but we gotta be really careful."

Spot and Smudge both nodded up at her as they lifted their front paws one at a time, and then turned so Aila could wipe their hind feet.

"The boy has a point," Dan said from the sink where he was washing a pot. "You know I loved Ronnie, but her old roommate seems quite a bit sharper. And we're gonna need a new vet we can trust for these little idjets."

The pups both nodded again

Dan flicked soap at Ben as he added, "And you cut me deep dude. I could so take her."

Ben chuckled, but after his dad turned back to the sink he shared a headshake with the pups.

"But I must say buddy," Dan said as he rinsed the pot. "Telling her the pups don't like to have strangers touch their paws 'cause of the pen fire was pretty smart."

"That was actually Smudge's idea," Ben said. "We just didn't want her poking at them until we came clean. So when do you think we can tell her?"

"I think we should hold on that a bit Ben," Mimi said. "We're getting to know her, and I like her too, but it's not something we should take lightly."

"Yeah," Kelcy said. "Mom's right, we gotta be careful."

"I know," Ben said. "I'm the one that keeps telling you guys we gotta be smart, but she was Ronnie's bud and all. And they're gonna need a checkup eventually."

Aila started to say something, thought for a second, and then straightened up.

"Why the heck am I wiping your paws?" she asked. "Wipe them yourselves."

She draped the towel over the wagging pups and returned to the table where her cup of tea was getting cold.

To the smirking humans she added, "And you lot can shut your mingin' geggies."

CHAPTER 2

In the cavernous lobby of the finishing school Brother Sacarius beckoned to a small group of young men and women as they exited one of the lifts. He spread his hands and said in his haughty British accent, "Can I trouble you to bestow the gift of a carol on our esteemed benefactor here? Give us something, fitting."

His students huddled for a second before they formed a line in front of the old Capuchin priest and the mountain of a man who was his guest.

One of the young women marked a cadence with her swinging finger, and after a few beats she started to sing with her classmates joining in one at a time, "Hark how the bells, sweet silver bells, all seem to say, throw cares away, Christmas is here…"

Semion appreciated their strong, well-trained voices, and the Russian origins of the carol they had selected. He wondered if Brother Sacarius had planted them or if it was one of the headmaster's famous little impromptu tests. Deciphering Semion's nationality by quick observation would certainly be part of the curriculum taught at this very special academy.

He guessed the group of singers were mid-twenties or a little older, and noticed most of them had tattoos peeking out from the collars and wrists of their matching suits. All of them were big and tough enough looking to be forward on a professional rugby team, even the women, although Semion still dwarfed them.

The old priest's hands danced in the air as the repeating ostinato of his students' caroling echoed around the huge lobby. It bounced back at them from the stained glass windows and carved staircase that wrapped around a large Christmas tree.

Brother Sacarius beamed proudly at Semion as he rotated in time with the song to press the lift's call button.

The carolers were still singing when the elevator doors closed and the ornate lift carried the two men down into the basement levels of the academy.

As Brother Sacarius continued to hum Semion noticed the old priest was staring at his new shoes.

In fact he was more than staring. He was almost drooling.

"Bespoke Italian split wingtips," Brother Sacarius whispered with a sparkle in his eye. "Fetal pony leather, hand cut long-wing brogueing, shark oil tanning, gold-tipped guanaco silk laces."

Semion nodded at each of the brother's correct dissections.

The priest steepled his fingers and said confidently, "Would they be from a small seaside shop in Brancadoro?"

Semion had known the priest for almost thirty years and he wasn't surprised the brother could pick out the origins of his bench-made footwear. He had worn them to their meeting on purpose.

"I go directly to their studio every spring," he said.

"That is the only way," Brother Sacarius said as he nodded his approval. "I find their fall leather selection to be a mite ashy."

As they left the lift Semion glanced at the priest's own expensive dress shoes, which knew were subtly disguised custom tactical boots.

They strolled down a long center catwalk that ran above a dozen large, well-lit rooms.

"I'm pleased to hear your daughter is prospering," Brother Sacarius said as he walked with his hands behind his back. "She's a very special young woman. On a short list of our finest accomplishments that one. When she first arrived she reminded me of a similarly ill-tempered young man from the Caucuses, but of course she was far better looking. You must be very proud."

"*Dah,*" Semion said, raising his voice over the sounds of suppressed weapons gunfire coming from one of the rooms below them. "You did a fine job with her as well, Brother. She sends her regards."

They passed above a room with a pair of very fit and very naked students on a raised platform. A circle of equally fit and naked young men and woman were huddled around them. Each held a small digital tablet and most were taking notes. An older instructor wearing the same brown robes as Brother Sacarius was pointing out various aspects of the pair's copulation with a pointer.

Brother Sacarius and Semion stopped above the next room. It was a gymnasium with padded mats on the floor and climbing ropes hanging from the ceiling.

A line of well-dressed young men and women were standing at rest attention on one side of the room. They held out their hands as a serious-looking older woman in a fitted nun's habit paused at each of them to put them in handcuffs.

As she pulled the last pair off cuffs from her belt Semion saw a hint of a slim, well-hidden bulletproof vest under her tunic. He noticed all of the students were wearing them under their suit jackets.

He also saw a flash of a pistol's hand grip in the nun's concealed shoulder holster.

She made a show of tossing the handcuff keys into the opposite corner of the room before she moved behind the students. She paced back and forth as she lectured them about patience and concentration, and then in mid-sentence she drew her pistol and tossed it over their heads. The gun bounced on the mat and came to rest not far from the keys.

The students immediately leapt, and sounds of a significant struggle rose from the room, followed quickly by several gunshots.

In less than four seconds the room was quiet again.

Three of the students were lying on the mat in the center of the room. They were in obvious pain and carefully probing under their vests with their cuffed hands for bruises that were certainly forming from the bullet strikes. The other students were on their knees with their hands raised in surrender.

Except for one.

A tall, handsome young student with thick hair and a square jaw stood over the nun, who was kneeling on the mat next to him cradling her elbow.

The student was aiming a small pistol at his classmates.

Semion saw the gun the instructor had originally tossed into the corner had not been touched. It was still lying on the floor near the keys.

Rather than chase after the tossed gun with the rest of his fighting classmates the young man had spun and dropped the nun to the mat with a seemingly effortless flip before snatching her backup gun from her ankle holster.

Semion watched as the young man helped the nun to her feet. He handed her the small pistol and then strolled past his fellow students to retrieve the handcuff keys and the other gun.

When Semion turned to Brother Sacarius the priest smiled and said, "Yes, he's the one we spoke of. Grew up in a proper slum in the north, but somehow made it into the elite Pathfinder's sixteenth brigade, where he sliced up one of his incompetent superiors. I found him working in India as a bagman. The lad was rough to be sure but is well on his way to being added to that short list I mentioned. His assignments have all been very successfully completed, and with top marks from our clients."

As the student bent to snatch the keys he noticed a smudge on his dress shoe. He removed a handkerchief from his jacket pocket and knelt to carefully polish it away.

"Of course you've noticed the boy has chosen a customized Mammut alpine boot," Brother Sacarius said as he shook his head. "A little blackguard for my taste, but I allowed it. Sometimes a roguish spirit is a good quality to have in an asset, don't you agree?"

"Dah," Semion said. "It sure is brother. I would like to meet him."

CHAPTER 3

"Three...two...one...Happy New Year!" the family shouted as the sparkling ball dropped on the television.

Aila gave Dan a big wet kiss as Mimi hugged the kids and kissed each of them on the forehead, and then did the same to the dogs. Everyone swapped positions until they all got kissed and hugged, and then they joined the red-cheeked television reporter and his glass-raising sidekick in singing, "Should old acquaintance be forgot..."

Aila tooted a shiny horn and Dan pulled apart a confetti cracker, and the small paper bits floated down to cover the swaying humans and wagging dogs.

Ben gave up trying to fully heft Spot into his arms and just danced with his front paws as Kelcy lifted and cradled Smudge like a sack with her big paws sticking out.

The family bounced around the room as they lifted their champagne glasses and got kisses from the pups. Smudge was high fiving them as Kelcy spun her around in a circle.

Mimi put an arm around Kelcy, grabbed one of Smudge's split paws, and pressed her cheek to the pup's cheek. The three of them danced around the couch like they were doing the tango.

Ben let go of Spot's paws and picked up his flute of ginger ale. He shouted, "To our pups, *Shlainte!*"

"*Do dheagh shlainte!*" the family retorted, and raised their champagne glasses to toast the dogs' good health.

"Here's to us!" Mimi shouted.

"Who's like us?" the family replied in unison.

"Not too many!" Mimi shouted, and together they all yelled, "And they're dead! More's the pity!"

After a long while of dancing, and more of their traditional toasting foolery, Aila said to Kelcy, "Turn that down for a minute love."

Kelcy muted the television, and when all was quiet Aila raised her glass and said, "To Papa."

"To Papa," they all responded.

Mimi clinked their glasses in turn and solemnly raised her glass. She winked at the ceiling and said, "I hope there's a pea under your cloud, you cheeky old bastard."

Aila hugged her mom, and after a few more toasts and rounds of dancing together they eventually turned off the television and settled down into their comfy spots around the family room.

Mimi stoked the fire as the pups cuddled with the kids on the couch under blankets.

Aila dropped down next to Dan on the loveseat, draped her legs over his, and pulled a heavy afghan over them. The sectional couch and loveseat had been pulled in close around the hearth so there was essentially one continuous pile of people and dogs under the blankets.

"I miss him," Ben said as he dropped his forehead against Spot's and gave Smudge a rub. "I wish you guys had known him," he added with a sniffle. "He was the best."

Spot reached a front leg out from under the blanket, split open his paw, and signed, *Don't cry Ben. He's here with us. We can still smell him.*

Mimi put the screen back on the hearth, wiped her damp cheek, and nestled down into the couch between her grandchildren.

"Listen my grandweans whilst I tell you something," she said as she took a hand from each of them. "I can tell you both for certain, my smart wee boy and my brave lass, your Papa would be so very proud of the both of you, as am I. And he would have loved the stuffing out of our wee pups."

Dan had a bit of a buzz on so his voice was a little thick when he raised his glass and said, "Here here."

"You guys, it's been a tough year for us," he said, "but we're here, in the place we love, all together, with our slightly larger family." He tipped his glass to the pups, who both nodded back at him.

"Ben," he said as he looked over his glasses at his son. "Man, you've done such a great job this year, with the pups, and the new school, and not being a pain in the ass all the time. I gotta hand it to you boy, you knocked the shit...snot out of anything that got in your way, literally."

He reached out to clink Ben's glass, and then looked at Kelcy.

"And to our lovely daughter," he said as he toasted her. "You're just the coolest, smartest, prettiest, toughest son of a bitch I've ever met."

Kelcy smiled at him, and hugged Smudge as she nodded.

Dan put a hand on Aila's knee and gave it a shake as he said, "This is going to be a good year you guys. A great year."

The phone rang and Ben yelled, "Uncle Hamish!" as he dove for it. He hit the talk button and said, "Hey there Unc. Wait, let me put you on speaker. Can you hear us?"

"Hallo me lovelies," Hamish said in his deep, musical voice. "Happy Hogmanay. How's it with yeh all in the lesser Americas?"

"Hail to the first foot!" Dan called out, knowing his in-laws considered it an honor to be the first visitor of the new year.

"Oh, Danny boy," Hamish sang. "Yeh haven't up and left that fucking crazy bunch yet?"

"And leave all of this lovely snow, and bitchin?" Dan said. Aila stuck her tongue out at him.

"Thanks for the puzzles," Kelcy piped up. "I figured out the first one already but the metal one's impossible."

"*Failte* Kels, good to hear yeh love," Hamish said. "Sorry they were late getting there. Yeh remember my clever Cree welder, the one who's half blind and full 'deef? Well, he says if yeh solve that one he'll get yeh a fucking honorary First Nations membership when yeh come next time. Is my wee sis-in-law about?"

"Hello to you laddie," Mimi sang out, "and watch your language. Are you up at the ranch or down in Digby?"

"I'm at the ranch," Hamish said. "The party at The Grub was pure barry, but we came home early to see the ball drop in our jammies. We're slugging it out with this current lot of huddy dogs so I have to be up early. I'll be heading down to Nova Scotia later this week."

"Hi Hamish," Aila said. "Hope you're well. The gifts are beautiful, thank you so much. Say hello to Christa for us, and Sholto of course."

"I'll do that very thing my bonnie lass," Hamish said. "Any plans for the road ahead? You poor lot have had a time of it down there this past year."

"Yeah, I think we're just going to let this one sail past us quietly, if possible," Aila said as she looked around the room.

"Good on yeh," Hamish said. "Well look loves, enjoy yer prissy version of football. Ben, I'll be waiting for yeh on the ninth. Jean, did the vests I sent for those curs arrive yet?"

A silence fell over the room as all eyes turned to Dan.

"Hamish, you daft arse," Mimi said. "We haven't discussed it with his father yet."

"Right, I'm away then," Hamish said. "Love yeh!"

CHAPTER 4

Half of the ballroom's huge monitors showed the countdown in sparkling numbers, and the other half showed the proportionally blessed hostess. She was wearing a gravity-defying dress, and she was using her whole body to call out the falling numbers into a microphone. Stage lights pulsed with each count as her band's drummer kept time. Smoke machines started up, and the fog rolled over the front of the stage and swirled among the mass of black tie and sequined party goers as they chanted in time with the hostess's bouncing.

Waitresses had circled the room with trays of champagne and glowing fluorescent necklaces and bracelets. The crowd had used them to accessorize their formalwear and were leaving trails of light as they surged up and down in the foggy dark.

The hostess raised her glass as she called out the final seconds, and beams of laser light swept through the smoke and drew red and green lines over the excited faces.

The ball dropped, and the entire ballroom erupted into a boiling sea of falling confetti, clinking glasses, and cheering and kissing. Waves of balloons dropped from the ceiling and firework fountains showered the perimeter of the room as the swaying crowd launched into a frenzy of applause.

Semion was standing at the back of the room, and he touched glasses with a stunning, athletic brunette. She stood on her toes, leaned over his considerable bulk, gave him a peck on the cheek, and whispered, "May we take what we want this year, *moy Batya.*"

Semion smiled as he looked across the ballroom to a knot of grinning penguins who'd gathered near the stage. Standing out above the black and white was a tall island of fire engine red. He nodded, and through the lingering smoke and swirling confetti the woman in the red dress almost imperceptibly nodded back.

Two men in tuxedos appeared behind Semion. One of the men was young, tall, and handsome, and he had thick hair and a square jaw. The other was older, craggy, and looked like an ugly brick wearing an ill-fitting tuxedo. He was also just plain huge, but both men were a few inches shorter than Semion.

"We're ready sir," the handsome asset said in a polished British accent.

Semion took his companion's champagne flute and placed both of their glasses on a nearby table, where they were immediately removed by a beautiful waitress wearing small angel wings. The oval logo etched into the champagne glasses was repeated on the cocktail napkins and plates, adorned the centerpieces, and was hung throughout the ballroom.

The huge man cut a wide path as he led them through the rowdy crowd. They passed the packed bar and a long buffet table overflowing with exotic appetizers that had barely been touched. They rounded a ten foot tall ice sculpture carved in the same oval logo, and a two story pyramid of champagne glasses being filled by more models dressed as scantily clad angels.

After turning down the restroom hallway they made a sharp left at the busy wait station and pushed through the kitchen doors at the end. The dark thumping of the main ballroom was replaced by the bright kitchen lights and the quiet scurrying of the army of white tuxedoed wait staff. The huge man led them between walk-in coolers and through a large dry storage area to a loading dock. At the far end they exited through a door and a blast of cold snowy air hit them.

Semion paused to put his tuxedo jacket over the young woman's bare, well-defined shoulders.

The loading dock and the little back parking area was hidden behind a discrete row of bushes, and beyond it they could see a wide cobblestone street and walkway. Both were beautifully decorated with holiday lights, and the walkway curved around the front of the large function hall and followed a stone ocean breakwater down to a large empty marina and an icy, deserted beach. The slip of sand narrowed in the distance where it ended at the foundation's private lighthouse.

To the rear of the loading dock were a row of dumpsters and an alley that led to a parking garage used by the valets.

Semion pointed out to the young woman how the fronts of the buildings in the compound were seamless expressions of the finest glass and steel and marble, but the backs were cinder block and brick. She nodded when he said the shiny veneers put on everything in the States still required the same necessary foundations, and those innards were just as ugly and utilitarian as they were everywhere else on the planet.

"This way," the huge man grunted in Russian.

They followed him off the dock and into the featureless alley that was just wide enough for a delivery truck. The alley slowly sloped down one story, where the huge man stopped at a solid metal door.

He pulled it open and held it as the handsome asset stepped through ahead of Semion and the young woman.

The underground garage was large, dark, and heated, and they saw a single light on at the far end.

Semion slipped his jacket off the young woman's shoulders, and as he put it on he turned back to the huge bodyguard and said, "Tuman and Graf."

The big man nodded, and the door closed behind him as he lumbered away up the cold alley.

Semion and the young woman followed the asset past rows of covered cars with her high heels clacking softly on the polished concrete floor. Semion noticed his own dress shoes squished along while the asset's custom tactical footwear moved absolutely silently. As he watched the man's head swiveling to scan the corners of the garage Semion remembered Brother Sacarius smiling broadly as he unabashedly quoted the small fortune it cost to hire him. "Many a mickle makes a muckle," the old priest had said, indicating all of the small details fostered in his students by his unique school added up to one formidable, and well-worth the price tool.

As they went deeper into the garage Semion inspected the covered cars. He could tell by their shapes and the Bugatti and Pagani logos they weren't just cheap Lada's, and they certainly weren't being driven by the party's guests in the snow. He guessed they were part of a private collection, and confirmed his suspicion when they approached the far corner of the garage and stepped onto a checkerboard section of floor that was surrounded by an immaculate and fully equipped automotive workshop.

As they stepped into the circle of light a silky, strong voice said from the shadows, "Good evening Semion."

The woman in the red dress came forward.

Even in medium heels she almost looked him in the eye. He saw her light but not-quite-blonde hair was short enough to mean business but long enough to still be considered pretty. Her dress was tailored just tight, low, and short enough to draw an eye, but not enough to raise an eyebrow. It was also red enough to overpower any competition. Her accoutrements were perfect, with expert yet subtle makeup and jewelry that was expensive but not overly large. She also wore a small jeweled pin shaped like a twisted ribbon that supported whatever cause was popular that month. At the center of the pin was the same oval logo from the ballroom.

Semion guessed she'd had just enough work done to turn fifty back to forty, so she appeared experienced, but not old.

He knew her to be exactly what her carefully crafted appearance screamed; she was a very successful politician.

"Gloria, so nice to see you," he said as he stepped forward to take her hand and air-kiss both of her cheeks. "Such a lovely party. You do know how to impress your guests. How is your daughter? She is at Dartmouth, yes?"

"Yes Semion, she is. Thank you for asking," Gloria said. "Her final year, God willing." She crossed her fingers for effect.

Semion beckoned behind him as he said, "I don't believe you've met my daughter. She heads up my interests here in the States." As the brunette stepped to his side he said, "Katia, this is the new Deputy National Security Advisor, Gloria Bekker-Myers."

Katia moved in very close to Gloria and took her hand firmly as she looked up at her. In perfect English with a hint of Manhattan she said, "Katia Mogevich. My father's told me so much about you."

"I'm sure he has," Gloria said as she retrieved her hand and took a half-step back. She had to work to break away from the pretty young woman's smoky stare.

When she turned back to Semion he read the slight disconnect on her face and said, "Dah, her mother was a model."

Semion didn't introduce the asset standing in the shadow behind him and Gloria didn't acknowledge him.

"It's lovely to see you Semion," she said, "but we need to be more careful."

He ignored that and asked, "Do you have it?"

"I could have arranged for you to get this tomorrow," Gloria said as she flapped her fingers in the air and an expressionless aide in a simple dress stepped from the edge of the checkerboard.

She handed Gloria a large envelope, Gloria held it out to Semion, and Katia snatched it and slid out the binder it contained.

As she flipped through its pages Semion swept his arm at the garage behind him and said, "I didn't know we shared a love for *kolymagas*, Gloria. Looks to be a most impressive collection."

Gloria smiled, touched his arm, and said, "Thank you. You'll appreciate this, in a few weeks I'm taking delivery of a custom Russo Baltique," she was careful to pronounce the Russian SUV properly.

"You and Katia should come for a ride this summer," she added, "We'll take the doors off and head out to the cape."

Semion nodded at the invite, Katia did not. She was too busy flipping pages.

"Of course, officially these are all my foundation's cars," Gloria said as she tapped her foot on the oval that was set into the center of the checkerboard floor. It was the logo of her family's non-profit organization, and she stepped on it as she leaned closer to Semion and added, "Why do you think I keep having these God-awful charity events?"

The door at the far end of the dark garage opened and closed.

"Dah, perfect," Semion said with a smile as he raised a finger to indicate this was something he'd been waiting for.

As he held Gloria's eyes he whistled two short notes.

A faint clicking started in the darkness, and as it grew louder it was joined by panting. A few seconds later a pair of enormous mounds of moving brown and black fur trotted into the circle of light with their clicking toenails echoing on the polished floor.

They were the largest dogs Gloria had ever seen.

Semion patted his hips and the two behemoths split up and stopped at his sides. With a slight flick of his wrist he ordered the dogs to sit, and when their bushy bottoms hit the floor their basketball-size heads came up to his waist.

"Gloria, these are my babies," he said. "Caucasian Ovcharka shepherds from my home in the Urals." His big hand disappeared into a deep fur that surrounded the flat face of the dog on his left, and he said, "This is Tuman." He tugged at the fluffy ear of the dog on the right and said, "And this is Graf."

The dogs didn't react. They just sat there as they panted and drooled with their shovel-size tongues bouncing.

"Fog and Thunder," Katia translated without looking up from the papers.

Semion studied Gloria's face and said, "One hundred and ten kilograms of impressive wolf-hunting aggression, are they not? They require a strong hand as they can be quite vicious, especially around strangers. The Ovcharka are notorious for not listening to a command to stop attacking. They will, on occasion, just keep biting and ripping until well after their opponent is dead no matter what their master tells them. Of course Tuman and Graf here are quite well trained, mostly."

"They are beautiful," was all Gloria could manage.

Twenty years ago she'd given a teary-eyed speech at an ASPCA fund raiser where she'd revealed a traumatic childhood event involving a large dog. She had dabbed at her eyes and politely refused the chairwoman's offer of a tissue as she patted a little golden Labrador. She had explained to the riveted crowd how she'd worked hard to overcome her fears, and had become a true dog lover. The speech had gotten play on the national news and won her first congressional election race. The tears were orchestrated bullshit, but the story and her fear of large dogs was plenty real.

She read the slight smirk on Semion's daughter, and gave the tough little bitch some credit for doing her research.

Gloria smiled, drew an even breath, and worked to keep calm. It wasn't only the dogs that were chaffing her backside. These vodka-swilling vipers were getting her ire up, but she reminded herself she had handled enough snakes to know how to put slimy serpents back into their basket without getting bit.

Still, she couldn't stop staring at the two grizzly bears watching her dispassionately with their dark oval eyes. They looked hungry, and somewhere deep inside her a six year old little girl was screaming.

"This document only covers the cleanup efforts," Katia said. "And the backup reports are heavily redacted." She waved the papers in front of Gloria and said, "Nothing of any use to us." To her father she added, "It's *govno*, Batya."

Gloria didn't know *govno* meant shit, but she got the gist from the sneer on the pretty girl's puss.

"Hold on," she objected with a raised hand. "Let us not forget who supplied you with the original report in the first place, which I procured at great risk, thank you very much. I'm the one who handed you solid proof your accelerator formula finally worked, and it had worked on someone in Pembury."

"We need the entire file, and all referenced reports," Katia said as she fixed Gloria with a hard look she had to admit was pretty good. "We need the concentrations, timelines, aliasing components, environmental factors. Thoroughness is essential, Madam Deputy."

Gloria noted with some satisfaction that a little Russian accent had crept into Katia's voice.

"I can't get anything deeper than summary reports without it being noticed," she said flatly, "I work in the West Wing for Christ's sake, we don't trifle with details like that."

Gloria dug into her mental toolbox of carefully crafted hard-ass looks and pulled out one of her classics to use on Katia.

After enduring a long moment of the women's posturing duel Semion said, "I think we need a better understanding of our relationship."

He raised a finger, and in one fluid motion the handsome asset pulled a silenced pistol and fired. There was a small snap and a simultaneous thunk from one of the metal tool closets behind Gloria, followed by the tinkling of the empty shell bouncing on the polished floor.

Gloria's aide clutched her throat with both hands and made faint convulsive sucking sounds as she dropped to her knees. Her elbows flapped as if she was trying to fly away, or pump the blood out of her drowning lungs. She was staring up at Gloria with surprised eyes, and as she mouthed something a dark stain spread down the front of her dress.

Tuman licked his chops loudly.

Gloria looked down at the line of splatter that ran up her own dress. On the red material the blood looked black.

She held out her hands as if to catch the aide but she didn't move when the woman fell forward. She hit the floor with a thump, and as blood flowed from under her body it spread over the checkerboard and covered the foundation's logo.

Semion stepped over the woman and took Gloria's shaking hands. They looked small wrapped in his.

The normally polished politician looked at him with wide eyes that were unable to look away.

"Gloria, my little *reebyohnuk*," Semion said. "You have no idea what you're dealing with. My accelerator formula is poised to be the defining leap forward in the evolution of warfare, and quite possibly our own evolution. It will eclipse any invention before it, and will ensure peace and order for generations to come. My government lacks the vision to see its true potential, and yours lacks the will to see it through to completion. Both have become ineffective. I built this program through shed blood and plundered fortunes the depths of which you can't even conceive. I've brought in the best and have given them everything they need, and we're ready to unlock the formula's secrets. We just need to GET THE FUCKING THING TO WORK!"

Gloria continued to stare at him as she winced at the pain from her crushed hands.

Semion took a breath, and with the red slowly fading from his face he let go of her hands and fixed an errant strand of her hair. "A spoiled, ungrateful little ex-senator who fancies herself a glorified security guard isn't even a small *shiska* in the road," he said calmly. "I put you into this new position you love so much, and I can just as easily remove it and everything you hold dear."

The asset knelt to retrieve his spent shell casing. He noticed a drop of blood splatter on his custom boot, and he took out his handkerchief and carefully wiped it clean before he stood up.

Semion waved him forward, and gave him Gloria's arm as he said to her, "Have no fear my dear, the Deputy will soon be dropped from your title. Perhaps as National Security Advisor you'll have the latitude to be more helpful. In the meantime you will continue to be smart and careful, but I need that file."

Katia took her father's arm, and before they turned to leave Semion said, "My comrade will make sure you get home safely, and don't worry about this mess."

The asset led Gloria away into the darkness as the huge bodyguard came into the circle of light with a folded tarp, a spray bottle, and a roll of paper towels. He smiled an ugly smile as Tuman and Graf started to lick up the blood.

CHAPTER 5

Mimi and Ben made it to two in the morning before they couldn't keep their eyes open and stumbled off to bed, leaving the parents, Kelcy, and the pups to tend the fire.

The snow had started again after midnight and the wind had picked up. It whistled through the eaves and produced a low creaking from somewhere in the old farmhouse. The wintery sounds gave Aila a chill, and she pulled the blanket up to her nose as she spooned her hips back into her husband.

She reached out from under the blanket and carefully picked up her wine glass. It had been filled and emptied often during the evening and she was seeing it through slightly fuzzy eyes. After downing what remained she set the empty glass a few inches out of the way on the coffee table so she could stare into the slowly dwindling fire. She was mesmerized by a bright spot at the bottom, just under the last intact piece of firewood where the shifting white heat slowly cut squares out of the log. She stared, and tried to guess the temperature at that very spot.

From deep in the loveseat Smudge groaned and readjusted, and poked her head out from under the blanket. She dug around for her little chicken plush toy, and in the process uncovered Aila's feet.

"Chilly," Aila whined as she wiggled her toes.

Smudge grabbed the blanket and carefully covered her feet again, making sure to tuck it in under her heels. She gave the swaddled feet a pat when she was done.

"So," Dan said as he shook his head at the two of them and finally broached the subject everyone had been avoiding. "Ben wants to go up to Hamish's?"

Kelcy stretched her feet out from under her blanket to flex her new tartan slippers in front of the fire as she said, "You should let him go Dad."

After a few seconds of quiet Dan said, "That's it? Oh, okay, he can go, thanks Kels."

"Mimi says he's ready," Aila said.

Another few seconds of silence ticked by.

"Okay, thanks dear," Dan said. "Wow, Hogan woman short on chin wagging. That's a first."

"It's beautiful up there," Aila said dreamily as the last log collapsed on itself and a hot ember rolled to the front of the fire screen. "Do you remember our honeymoon, dear heart? That was back when we had nothing but time and each other."

"So our eleven year old is going off to find love in the romantic great white north?" Dan asked.

"We all rave about how awesome it is up there," Kelcy said as she rotated in her blanket to face him. "Mimi's stories about Hamish are his favorites, so of course he wants to go. It's a friggin' dog lover's paradise, and in case you haven't noticed he's totally into everything canine. The pups would love it too."

Both dogs nodded.

"The canny canine cop caught the cagey criminal," Aila whispered to the fire. "We've been telling him we'll get up there when we have the time...Time, time, time. Never enough time."

Kelcy smiled at her slightly slurry mom, and then grimaced as Spot settled against her side.

"Your bony elbow's digging into me," she said as she moved the grumbling dog over a few inches.

He cocked an eyebrow at her, and she said, "I'm good, you good?"

His shrug indicated he'd been more comfortable before she'd decided to disturb him, but the current position was acceptable.

She grabbed his snout and gave it a shake as she said to her dad, "There's a bunch of reasons you should let him go."

"Yes there is," Aila added, and then fell silent again.

Dan looked down at his tipsy wife and shook his head again as he asked, "How's that Kels?"

"He really misses Papa," she said. "They used to do all kinds of things together. Hike, fish, build stuff, break stuff. Papa taught Ben a lot. You've been awesome about that lately, but no offense Dad, you didn't do much with him before we moved here. They were attached at the hip for all those summers, and Uncle Hamish is a bigger, louder, swearier Papa."

"All good points," Dan said. "But send him by himself? Sorry pups, you know what I mean."

Spot's combination nod-shrug indicated he understood, but he was still offended.

"You guys let me go up there alone when I was a kid," Kelcy said.

"You were hardly a kid," Dan said. "You were thirteen." As he wasn't too far behind his wife in the emptying wine glasses department he counted carefully on his fingers as he said, "Which was only two summers ago."

To Spot he added, "Hey useless dog number two, put another log on the fire."

When Spot gave him a look indicating he'd just gotten comfortable Dan pretended to sign by wiggling his fingers as he said, "You're closest, and don't give me any of that 'dogs are afraid of fire' crap."

Kelcy pushed Spot's rump off of her. She got up from the couch, and as she scratched her backside and headed off toward the bathroom she asked, "Does anyone want anything?"

Smudge shook her head, and Aila held her wine glass up but Dan took it from her.

"No, we're good," he said as he set it down on the end table, and then added "Hey, bring me a water please."

"Every party has a pooper that's why we invited yoo-per," Aila sang to the fire. She turned to look up at her husband as she said, "Both of your kids were created up there Daniel, or don't you recall our summer get-aways? It's a magical place, and a boy that's been through a year like he has should get to go to a magical place for a little while."

Spot nosed open the screen and carefully placed a few logs on the fire using his paw-hands. He adjusted an uncooperative log a few times to get it to stay where he wanted it, and in the process ended up lingering too long above the hottest part of the fire. He quickly pulled back his paw and licked his pads as he bumped the screen closed again with his rump and gave Dan a perturbed look.

"Fire bad," Dan grunted at him with a smile as he accepted a water bottle from Kelcy.

The gesture Spot made would normally require a middle finger but Dan clearly understood it.

"Very nice," he said as Spot hopped back onto the couch. "Good thing your Mimi's not here, she'd wash that paw out with soap."

Spot wagged, and turned in a full circle before he dropped into Kelcy's lap.

"Look," Dan said, "I want him to go, really I do. I just don't know. It's not like going to Plymouth. And since when did you stop pitching fits about Ben getting to do stuff we wouldn't let you do 'til you were older?"

"Dad," Kelcy said, "the same reason I don't pitch fits anymore is the same reason Ben's ready to go up north. You must have noticed this year's done something to us. With these pups, and what we've been through together. We're older, or smarter I guess. Sometimes I think whatever happened to these little guys has rubbed off on us. I don't care about stupid things anymore, and neither does Ben. When's the last time you had to remind him to shower, or brush his hair, or do his homework, or pulled me off of him?"

Dan caught Aila's stare, and although it was a little foggy he read is as, *She's right. We've seen it, haven't we?*

Kelcy was trying to figure out if it was the wine and champagne, or if they really hadn't noticed how far her brother had matured. She had started out the conversation thinking she was laying a foundation of the obvious to prep for the big pitch, but her parents weren't around Ben as much as she and Mimi were.

"You guys should see him at school," she said. "He's the most popular kid in his grade and no one messes with him anymore. I can't believe I'm saying this, but my little brother has actually turned into a non-loser. He's always been book smart in a massively geeky kinda way, but now he's ten times sharper than most of the kids in my grade even. His teachers have pretty much given up and let him work as far ahead as he wants to. And it's not just book smarts. He kinda just, I don't know, gets stuff."

Dan nodded, but Kelcy wasn't sure he was really picking up what she was putting down yet.

"I walked in on Smudge telling him a dirty joke the other day," she said. "Sorry Smudge."

Dan and Aila both looked at Smudge, who raised her head, shrugged, and dropped back down on Aila's feet.

"And not only did he get it," Kelcy said, "but he fired off one of his own, and it was pretty damn funny. I'm not sayin' it wasn't a little odd, but the point is he's not a normal kid, in a good way, mostly."

She pulled Spot closer and gave his chin a scratch as she said, "Ben's so far ahead because he loves doing homework with Spot, we both do actually. He reads with both of the pups every night, and I can hear him talking about what they're reading. It's not sixth grade stuff, trust me."

Spot nodded his agreement.

Kelcy tipped her head at Smudge and said, "Smudge even broke the ice for him with this really cute girl he likes. She dropped her chicken in the girl's lap, and when Ben went to retrieve it they ended up chatting for like five minutes, which is basically like getting married when you're eleven. Based on the girl's hair twisting and feet shuffling I could tell she was diggin' it. It was hilarious, but it was also pretty smooth."

Smudge raised her paw and blew on her knuckles as she waggled her eyebrows.

"Hashtag world's best wingman," Aila said as she reached out from under the blanket to hunt for Smudge's head.

Dan mulled the 'it was pretty smooth' comment for a moment as he hid his proud smile by taking a drink. He wasn't at all smooth at eleven, or seventeen, or twenty. Aila had been the one to ask him out on their first date, and she'd moved his barstool closer, and had unbuttoned his shirt when they rounded third base.

"Okay Kels," he said. "I got it. And I have noticed. We all have."

"So proud," Aila said. "Making good choices."

Kelcy glanced down at Spot, and the subtle nod they exchanged agreed it was time to move to the next phase of the conversation.

"We need to think about the pups too," she said.

"We do," Aila said as she pulled up Smudge's muzzle so her teeth showed, and then made growling noises. "His little body guards need to watch over him."

Smudge gave her a flat stare.

"Sure," Kelcy said. "But the pups need to see more of the world too."

"What do you mean Kels?" Dan asked and he sat up a bit. He was intrigued by where this was going, and by his daughter.

"Think about it," Kelcy said. "Ben and I are going to leave the nest at some point. We'll head off to do whatever we end up doing, and we can't keep Spot and Smudge down on the farm forever either. The pups' path may not be Ben's path, or mine, and they may have a larger role to play. They aren't just pets. With their gifts they can contribute much more than just taking over the local coyote pack and dispatching a few bad guys, right?"

She had directed that question to the pups, and they nodded in sync.

Dan chugged a long draw from the bottle as he thought about his quickly maturing boy, and their smart pups, and how his daughter might be growing up faster than any of them. She'd always been pretty sharp but lately she was hitting a lot of nails on the head, and she had also recently dived down a flight of stairs to pounce on a homicidal maniac four times her size to save her family. As he smiled at her beautiful face, the one that looked more and more like her pretty mom every day, he figured most parents probably felt their children turned into little adults almost overnight. But he couldn't help thinking it really was happening to his kids. He also thought his daughter's logic was sounding a lot like Spot's.

She was also right about the pups' future. He and Aila had spent more than a few late nights discussing their special family members' potential. They'd both engaged in a little wild speculation, but the sobering truth was some of it probably wasn't all that far from the realm of possibility given their brains and talents.

Spot and Kelcy shared another tiny nod when they read the acknowledgement on her father's concentrating face.

"Their sign language was a big step," she said, "but these guys have a lot more to learn to operate in the real world. One of us may not always be around to help and it could be really tough out there for them. We've been smart, but also very lucky so far. If the pups' secret gets out before we've had a chance to get them ready, well, we could lose them. Honestly Dad, that's the one thing I worry about most."

Us too, Smudge signed as her brother nodded.

"You're right Kels," Dan said. "I guess we always thought about it but none of us has ever taken it to the hoop like that."

"Mimi thinks Uncle Hamish could be just what the pups need," Kelcy said. "Depending."

Aila rose up on an elbow and asked, "On what hun?"

"Well, it's a gamble," Kelcy said. "Bringing anyone into our circle is a risk. I love Uncle Hamish, and according to Mimi he's near the top of a very short list of the best dog trainers in the world, but she's also quick to point out her brother-in-law can be a daft arse."

CHAPTER 6

Mimi's hands danced over the controls of her well-worn portable sewing machine. She worked the foot pedal, and the unit whined and thumped and the needle raced up and down as she looked down through her reading glasses. She moved the fabric carefully back and forth to go over the same place several times before she slid it out and cut the trailing thread.

She gave her work a test tug before holding up the service dog vest so Spot could inspect it. He was sitting in the kitchen chair next to hers, and he'd been scrutinizing every stitch.

Spot had wanted to try the sewing machine himself but Mimi said, "You just went through all that to get your paws separated, why would you want to sew them shut?"

Spot hadn't found that nearly as funny as Smudge had.

Mimi was pretty impressed with the construction of the service vests Hamish had sent. The body pieces were tough quilted fabric and a sturdy zipper ran around the perimeter so they were reversible, with fire engine red on one side and desert camouflage on the other. They had black trim and thick adjustable nylon straps for the neck and abdomen, and a snap-in quilted chest piece. The support straps connected to a central back piece with a heavy woven handle and a leash ring.

There were soft black squares on the body pieces, where removable 'Service Dog' and 'Search and Rescue' Velcro patches had been applied.

Spot carefully scanned her work, and when he gave Mimi a firm nod she tossed the vest down the long kitchen table to Smudge, who was waiting patiently in a chair at the opposite end.

She slipped into the vest and closed the black collar and chest strap, but she fumbled with the belly strap.

"Come to your Mimi lass," Mimi said as she waved her over.

Smudge jumped down and came around the table with the end of the strap dragging on the floor.

Spot was already wearing his modified vest, and he jumped down and walked to the hall mirror to check himself out, again. The vest fit perfectly and covered him from the base of his neck to the curve of his rump, and it didn't get in the way of his legs or his tail.

When he bounded back into the kitchen he struck an action pose, pantomimed pulling a pistol from under his vest, and finger-shot Mimi and Smudge. He blew off the end of his smoking finger gun and spun it before holstering it.

"That's enough television for you for a while Mr. Bond," Mimi said with a chuckle as she and Smudge shook their heads. She finished adjusting Smudge's strap and stood to admire her handiwork. Both of her dogs looked up at her with their chests out and heads back.

"Well, aren't you two handsome," she said as they wagged in sync at her. "You look like proper working dogs. Come to think of it, you can probably start doing some more chores around here."

Their tails stopped wagging.

Ben came through the back door stomping snow from his boots. He kicked them off and hung his jacket on a hook behind the door in one move, and as he slipped off his backpack he said, "Whoa, you two look so cool!"

Mimi tipped her cheek out for a kiss as she clicked off the reading lamp and started to pack up the sewing machine.

The pups spun in slow circles in front of Ben.

"Meem, they fit great," he said as he grabbed the back handle on Smudge's vest with both hands and leaned back to lift her off the floor with a groan.

"Mmm," Mimi agreed as she downed the remains of her tea. "I trimmed Spot's straps and added some give to Smudge's so when our wee girl here goes Cu Sith she won't split her drawers."

Mimi had shared with Ben and the pups the story of Cu Sith, the fearsome mythical Scottish hell hound. It was said to have a massive bark, and was tasked with bearing away souls to the afterlife, so it had become synonymous with Smudge's gift for transforming herself.

"Awesome," Ben said. "Did she try it yet?"

Before Mimi could tell them to wait until they were outside Smudge snapped into an attack posture. Her head was low, her front legs were spread apart, her back was slightly arched, and her tail stuck straight out. The hair on her back stood up from the crown of her head to the tip of her tail.

Her eyes narrowed and she fixed Ben with an unblinking stare, and when she growled it was far too loud and deep for a dog her size. Ben and Mimi felt it rattle their guts more than they heard it.

Her front paws split open, her nails extended out onto the kitchen floor, and her ears stood up as they rotated forward.

She bared her teeth and shook her head like she was shaking off water.

And then she just inflated.

Her neck and shoulder muscles grew to twice their normal size. In an instant she went from a normal, medium-size dog to a deranged Rottweiler on steroids. She shot forward at blinding speed, hopped onto the table, and pinned Ben against the kitchen cupboard before he could blink. Her split paws held him firmly by the shoulders as her quivering fangs hovered an inch from his face. She turned her head away and let out a bark that shook the dishes in Mimi's china hutch on the far side of the kitchen.

"Jeez, okay okay," Ben said as he raised his hands. "I'd hate to be on the receiving end of that for real."

"Hold your wheesht you bloody cur," Mimi admonished as she took her fingers out of her ears. "I will never get used to that. One of these days you're going to give someone a heart attack doing that, and I don't want it to be me."

Smudge gave Ben a lick before she let him go. She had already begun to shake as she jumped down, and starting with her snout she twisted herself all the way down to her tail. Her muscles relaxed as her fur rippled, and in an instant she was back to normal size.

She sat down and Ben dropped to his knees to inspect the vest. "Looks good," he said as he tugged at the thick elastic straps that had flexed with Smudge's bulging muscles and had shrunk back when she'd deflated.

Smudge rolled her shoulders back, pushed out her chest a little, and waited for Ben to notice something.

He didn't, so she pointed at her chest.

He leaned closer, and ran his finger over the small symbol Mimi had embroidered in the center of the vest's chest piece.

"No way," he whispered. "That's so cool."

Smudge wagged, and nodded as she stared down at the small gray zig-zag lightning bolt. It was the symbol of her favorite animated movie hero, Bolt.

CHAPTER 7

Ben dropped into a kitchen chair at the Hogan's cottage, and as the pups sat next to him he stole a big bite from his mom's bagel. Around a mouthful he asked her, "Where's Paw?"

She lowered her paper and gave him a little scowl before she answered with, "Dad had to run into the office but he'll be home by three or so. Did you need something?"

"No, was just wondering," Ben said as he nodded secretly to Spot and Smudge, who returned the nod.

"Is your sister up?" Aila asked as she slid the plate closer to him. "It's her turn to run to the grocery with me, and she needs to get in some driving time."

"No idea," Ben said after taking another huge bite.

He looked down at the pups, and even though they hadn't moved he said, "What's that Spot? No, I don't think pulling Kelcy out of bed is a good idea. In fact I'm going on record now as having told you two *not* to go upstairs and yank her out of bed."

As the dogs raced down the hallway in sync and bounded up the stairs together Aila said, "So what's on your plate this fine Saturday mister man? Any homework?"

He didn't answer the homework question as he knew it was meant as a joke. Kelcy had been right about him being so far ahead on his assignments even his teachers didn't bother checking anymore.

"We'll probably run over to Meem's," he said.

After taking another bite he added, "Soooo, has Dad made a decision yet?"

"He's still thinking about it buddy," Aila said. "But he's been really busy. We'll talk about it when Mimi comes for dinner tonight, okay?"

"Sure," Ben said with a shoulder shrug.

He slid the plate back to her and got out of the chair.

Aila watched him skulk away as a thud came from upstairs, followed by Kelcy shouting.

An hour later Ben and the pups were in Kingston, the next small town over from Pembury. They were boarding the commuter rail train that ran from the South Shore to Boston.

As they passed the smattering of yawning, coffee-sipping riders the pups' proud trots were almost prances, and their heads were held high as their tails swiped behind their new vests.

Hamish had included a variety of different patches, and Ben had selected the ones that read, 'Service Dog in Training - Please Do Not Pet'.

The train wasn't very full and he chose the empty seats in the middle of the car, where they transitioned to rear facing rows so they had plenty of leg room.

As the train made its stops on the way into the city the pups sat at Ben's feet and watched the people flow by. A few younger kids veered over to pat them but they were quickly corralled by their parents. Most of the passengers smiled at the pups as they walked past, but otherwise they were left alone until a chatty man planted himself in the seat across from them. He was talking to himself before he sat down, and when he saw the dogs he asked Ben a constant stream of monotone questions about them until he got up and walked off the train a few stops later in Weymouth.

In Braintree an old man got on the train with his granddaughter. She was maybe seven, and had thick glasses and long brown hair that was neatly braided into pigtails. When she stopped to pat the pups her grandfather nudged her softly away with an apology smile and nod to Ben.

She chose the seat opposite them so she could watch the pups, and after they settled in her grandfather asked her quietly if she liked the dogs.

The girl used sign language to respond.

Ben and the pups watched their conversation, which consisted of the little girl signing a thousand questions about the dogs, the train, the snow, and whatever other subjects jumped into a seven year old girl's head. Eventually Ben got distracted and turned back to watching the city flow past the windows, but the pups were fascinated with the girl. They had learned to sign from the internet and had never seen another live human signing outside of their family, and the little girl was very good at it. She even had the slang signing down pat.

Sometime later Smudge poked Ben and nodded at the little girl. Her grandfather was holding her hands together and he was telling her to slow down as he couldn't follow along when she was going so fast. The more he tried to stop her the quicker she signed, and as the little girl's frustration grew so did Smudge's agitation. She kept looking from Ben to the girl as she shifted on her paws, and when the little girl started to cry Smudge stood up.

Ben hugged her and whispered, "Okay girl, okay."

He leaned forward and said, "Excuse me," loud enough for the man and the little girl to hear.

She looked up, and Ben gave her a warm smile. He touched his chin with a flat hand and moved it away, and then touched his elbow and raised the opposite hand to sign, *Good morning.*

The little girl buried her face into her grandfather's arm but kept eyeballing Ben and the pups.

"What is it she's asking?" Ben asked.

"I'm not sure," the exasperated old man said. "She goes too fast for me, and then she uses signs I don't recognize."

Ben signed to the little girl, *Do you like my dogs?*

The pouting little girl straightened in her seat and freed both of her hands from behind her grandfather's coat.

She smiled, and signed, *Oh yes sir I do, very much so, but I have a question…*

The next twenty minutes was a barrage of back and forth that left Ben's arms tired and his fingers cramped. Even he had to ask her to slow down at one point, and he couldn't believe that many questions about the pups and their vests were even possible. She wanted to know why he didn't paint their toenails and why they were all black and why they wagged at the same time and why one was a boy and why one had a lightning bolt and why they had brown eyes and why they stared so much.

The pups were glued to the conversation, and at one point Smudge stuck out her tongue when the little girl asked how long their tongues were. That got them all laughing and Ben scrambled to explain there were some signs the pups could recognize.

Spot gave Smudge a dirty look, and she shrugged an *Oops* back at him.

Other than Smudge's little slip Ben thought the pups were doing great. The train had filled up at each stop, and they were enjoying people-watching and the impressed looks they received while pretending to be important, albeit simple, working dogs.

The train pulled into Boston's South Station, and after sending the giggling girl off with wags and kisses and a goodbye sign the three of them strolled along Atlantic Avenue toward the waterfront.

Spot and Smudge stayed side-by-side in front of Ben as they navigated the slushy sidewalk. He could tell from their subtle body language they were carrying on a constant conversation as they padded along and took in the sights and smells.

The sun was out and it was melting the dirty snow piles into little rivers. For early January it was a mild Saturday and the streets near the tourist attractions were busy. It wasn't as packed as it would have been in June or July, but there was still enough hustle to be a good test for the pups and their vests. Ben took them past the aquarium, where they exchanged barks with the sea lions who were swimming in their outdoor habitat, and then through the Faneuil Hall outdoor mall and the Quincy Market food court.

All of their stomachs complained as they passed a hundred different sweet and savory vendors. "Not yet," Ben said when they paused to stare up at a shop with hanging sausages and whole roasted turkey legs. He was speaking to himself as much as the pups.

They stopped to watch a mediocre street performer who was far better at tricking the crowd into clapping than she was with the actual juggling. Ben noticed the pups weren't nearly as fascinated by her as they were the tourists. As the families moved in knots and argued over their maps and mugged for pictures in front of anything that looked old Spot and Smudge watched them with tipped heads and perked ears. Ben explained the red stripe on the sidewalk the packs of tourists were following was the Freedom Trail, and Spot looked up at him with a confused look that indicated he thought it was just the opposite.

Ben laughed, and then raced them up the steps of City Hall Plaza and led them down a side street to avoid the slower mobs that were clogging the main sidewalks.

None of the narrow streets in Boston were straight for very long and navigating them was famously a challenge, but having grown up in the nearby Back Bay neighborhood Ben knew the downtown streets and shortcuts well.

He led them west and cut north a few blocks where the buildings gave way to the trees and open spaces of the Boston Common. As they walked past statues and fountains and wandered the paved paths that spider-webbed between the snow-covered fields they were greeted by a constant stream of dogs. As the pups said hello to a small terrier and a massive Great Dane, Ben fielded questions from their curious owners. He had practiced his story on the ride into town and seamlessly slipped in details about the pups' service dog school and how he was helping out his uncle who was their trainer. When he added how a walk in the city was a good test of navigating an unfamiliar urban environment he received smiles and nods.

Spot and Smudge were enjoying the attention but were also experiencing a bit of sensory overload. Aside from the parking lot at the kids' school they weren't immersed in throngs of people often, and the closest they had come to walking in a city was a few blocks on the quiet sidewalks of downtown Plymouth. The streets of Boston were a different thing altogether for them. There was an endless array of noises, smells, and sights, and there was an infinite variety of humans. Pembury, like the rest of the small towns on the South Shore, wasn't exactly a melting pot. On Boston's crowded streets they discovered how different and distinctive the layers of human smells could be. They also heard an assortment of new languages, and although there were some truly foreign speakers most of the words they heard were still a form of English. Thanks to Kelcy, Smudge was a bit of a trash TV junkie and considered herself pretty slang-savvy, but even she had to work to keep up with most of the urban vernacular they heard. She gave up trying to decipher all of it, and noticed even Spot had also abandoned trying to follow the hundreds of conversations happening around them. She noted with some satisfaction they'd finally found a place with too many inputs for his scary parallel processing brain to handle. They had to filter out half of what they took in just to keep walking in a straight line.

The people and the sidewalks seemed to go on forever. The buildings also seemed far too tall. Spot wondered why humans felt the need to be so vertical when there was so much open horizontal space.

When Smudge huffed that he was only afraid of the buildings because dogs can't look up she received a head shake, and a very little wag.

They were also surprised by the sheer volume of dogs. They could detect a hundred of them within a few blocks, and a thousand hints of pee lingering on any given light post.

And behind the smells of far too many humans and dogs were a million other scents. Endless layers of man-made smells crashed into distorted environmental ones. They felt assaulted by scents that ranged from pleasant to interesting to not so great.

The distractions were limitless, and they were having a blast.

When Smudge gave Spot a little poke to get his attention Ben noticed it.

She nodded at a man dressed in a suit holding a fistful of napkins. He was waiting for his chubby black Lab to finish doing her business as the big dog crouched right in the middle of the sidewalk. She looked at the pups with bored detachment, and when the pups looked at each other Ben could tell they were a little confused. Neither of his dogs were overly prissy about such things and there were few taboos in the Walker-Hogan households, but the dogs wouldn't just stop and drop anywhere they could be easily seen either.

Spot looked away to give the Lab some privacy, but Ben could hear Smudge and the dog were having a softly huffed chat. The dog's hind legs shook and her owner waited patiently for her to finish as she and Smudge happily grumbled and huffed away.

Spot looked up at Ben and shook his head.

"Alright Magellan," Ben said as he nudged Smudge forward. "Let's go."

He checked the time on his phone, and then looped them back toward the financial district, where they crossed over Washington Street into a seedier area of Chinatown. The cracked sidewalks were uneven and the streets were very narrow even by Boston standards, and in the shadows the piles of snow hadn't melted much so they were forced to walk single file.

As they rounded a blind corner they ran smack into a pair of large German shepherds, and their even larger cop handlers.

"Hey there, how are yah little man?" one of the huge cops asked in a thick South Boston accent. Ben could barely see their eyes under the brim of their hats, and both men had big ruddy cheeks and a circle of goatee and mustache. They could have been twins if one wasn't much darker than the other. They both took drinks from their steaming coffee cups as they watched the four dogs getting to know each other.

"Hi," a flustered Ben said. "Nice Alsatians."

Both of the cops burst out laughing.

"Alsatians?" the second cop said. "Kid, I haven't heard that word in a friggin' fort-night."

Choking back a laugh the first cop asked, "Where yah headed with these guys?"

Ben stumbled through his story as casually as he could muster.

"Yah, well they gotta be on a leash son," the first cop said.

Ben never had the pups on a leash.

He didn't need to. They never went where they weren't supposed to, especially in public. Even when they trotted off to play or chase after something they always came right back when asked.

"Oh yeah, right, sorry," Ben said as he fished in his backpack and the pups left the shepherds to stand in front of him. The leashes he clipped to their vests still had the store tags attached to them, and as Ben straightened up he noticed his pups were looking up at the cops with tandem looks that said, *You satisfied?*

The cops stared down at the dogs, and the dogs continued to stare up at the cops.

"Well," Ben said as he rubbed his shoulders like he was cold. "You officers take care. Be safe, keep up the good work."

He led the pups away.

"Hey kid," the second cop called after him.

Ben stopped.

"Stay warm, Govenah," the cop said with a laugh and a raise of his coffee cup.

Ben could still hear the cops chuckling as he and the pups rounded the next corner and moved out of sight.

He knelt and pulled them to him as he unclipped their collars and said, "Crap that was close, but you guys did awesome!"

Smudge looked around to make sure no one was paying attention before she raised her split paw and signed, *We totally got you B. Five-O just wanted to sweat us for ridin' dirty. It's a good thing they didn't get me angry. They wouldn't like me when I'm —*

Spot rump checked his sister hard and looked at Ben as he signed, *Can we have her put down, please?*

Ben laughed and booted them both forward.

Two blocks later they jogged up a short flight of steps and entered the lobby of the State Street Financial Center. As they crossed the gleaming marble floor Ben got a little nervous when he saw a pretty but serious woman wearing a fitted uniform and a headscarf step out from behind the reception desk. He was just about to turn around when she clasped her hands and beamed out a big smile as she bent down and opened her arms.

She was careful to stay a few steps away from the working dogs as she said, "Oh my, aren't they the most handsome animals?"

Ben read her nametag and said, "Hello Nelly, I'm Ben. This is Spot and Smudge." To all of them he said, "It's okay, you can say hi."

The pups stepped forward and accepted Nelly's vigorous scratching welcome.

"What are they in training for?" she asked.

"Truffle detection," Ben said.

"That's amazing," Nelly said, and then stopped scratching and cocked an eye up at him.

Ben smiled broadly at her.

"Funny," she said with a smile as she straightened up. She nodded toward the elevators as she gave the pups a final pat and said, "Go ahead."

The elevator doors slid open and Ben and the pups stepped in, and as the doors closed he looked around for a camera but he didn't see an obvious one. It was possible the ornate ceiling tiles hid one, but he just shrugged and said to Spot, "Yeah okay, you can do it."

Spot wagged, put a front paw up on the brass handrail, and with a little jump he reached up with his other paw to tap the button for the thirty-fourth floor. As the elevator started to rise he hopped down to give his sister a proud nod.

Smudge didn't appear to appreciate his sense of accomplishment.

They all faced the front of the elevator to watch the numbers counting up.

After a few moments Ben noticed his pups' heads had started to nod up and down together. The nodding turned into full-on tandem head bobs, and Ben began to nod in time with the piped-in music as well. It was a soft, lyric-less version of a heavy metal song they knew well, and as the floors continued counting up his humming turned into quietly singing, "I'm your eyes while your away...I'm your pain while you repay...You know it's sad but truuue...Sad but truuuue..."

The song was one of his dad's favorites, and he played the whole Metallica album on repeat whenever he got a bug up his backside about a mess in the house and felt a cleaning marathon was needed. The album was usually preceded by his dad saying something like, "We are going to give this entire damn kitchen a good scrubbin'."

The pups turned in circles and wagged at Ben as he started to sing louder, "Pay-ay, pay the price, pay for nothins' fairrr!" By the time he reached, "I'm your pain when you can't feeeel," his arms were spread out wide and he was exaggerating James Hetfeld's breathy grumbling inflections to the pups' happy wiggling.

When the smoothly rising elevator slowed to a gentle stop on the twenty-eighth floor the pups felt it, but Ben didn't.

Two seconds before the doors opened the pups' tails stopped and they turned to face forward.

A woman in a jogging suit looked at them, and then at the imaginary microphone Ben was holding in one hand and the devil horns he was pulsing at her with the other as his head pounded up and down.

He opened his eyes as he trailed off, "Sad but truuuuu…"

The doors closed again between them without her stepping into the elevator.

Spot and Smudge looked back at Ben.

"Nice," he said.

The pups wagged, and head bobbed to the music for the rest of the ride.

When the doors opened again Ben walked into the small lobby with the pups following behind. There was no one at the reception desk, and all of the office's low-walled cubicles were empty. They passed the glass offices on an outside wall, and as they turned a corner the pups stopped him.

"Yeah, alright," he said as he followed them into the huge conference room.

The pups trotted around the long table to the far corner, where they put their paws up on the low windowsill. Panoramic windows ran the length of both corner walls, giving an incredible view of the Boston skyline.

Ben pointed out the landmarks as they scanned the city. From the north window they could see Boston Harbor and Logan airport, and past the famous Italian neighborhood of the North End to the Longfellow Bridge. From the west facing window they could see Beacon Hill, the Charles river, Harvard, MIT, and all the way south to the Prudential Tower and Fenway Park.

"Pretty cool, eh?" Ben asked.

Smudge nodded and signed, *This must be what birds see.*

So now I understand your fascination with building vertically, Spot signed. *Impressive.*

They continued down the hall to the next corner, and when Ben stopped short to peer around a doorway the pups almost ran into his backside.

His dad was working at his desk with his back to the open office door.

Ben crept into his office and dropped silently into one of the contemporary chairs that were set around a small coffee table in the middle of the room.

The pups did the same, and Ben said gruffly, "Hogan! I think we need to recheck these quarterlies. What do you think lads?"

Spot and Smudge both gave a quick yap of agreement.

An hour later father and son were finishing up lunch at Dan's favorite spot in the financial district, where he knew enough of the staff so the dogs weren't going to be an issue on a quiet Saturday.

"You still peeved?" Ben asked as he palmed another roll from the basket on the table and split it in half in his lap.

"Gonna use the big D word on you Ben," Dan said.

"Dummy, daft, dipshit?" Ben asked.

"You're on thin ice boy, and it's a hot day," Dan said, and then he added to no one, "And I'm disappointed in you two as well. Would have thought you had more sense. Gifted my ass."

The quiet munching that was coming from under the table stopped.

"Sorry Dad, really," Ben said. "But you gotta admit, we're ready to be out and about on our own."

"We'll talk about this when we get home," Dan said as he fought back another smile and noticed the third empty bowl of rolls on the table. "Let's go, the pups gotta be full by now."

CHAPTER 8

"Thanks for that," Aila said dreamily as she wove her fingers into her husband's hand.

"No charge," he said as he found her lips in the dark and they shared another deep kiss.

He drew the covers up and around her shoulders as Aila moved her hips off him and lay against his side. She slid a leg between his and they lay there for some time, letting their heartbeats slow and their body heat spread into a comforting, all over glow.

His fingers found the bullet wound scar on her upper arm. It had healed into a two inch creased dimple that he often traced when she was stretched out against him.

She nibbled on his shoulder and enjoyed the saltiness of his sweat, and the firmness of the muscle under his warm skin. She hadn't mentioned it to him, but she'd been appreciating his rough hands and more pronounced contours. He'd been doing a lot of work around the farm and the cottage since they moved to the South Shore, and he'd even started doing his own car maintenance again with the kids' help.

He'd enlisted the pups as well, and apparently Spot had bet Dan ten bones he could change the Wagoneer's front brakes faster. According to Mimi's spies the smart pup had beaten him by a large enough margin to hover over Dan and give him pointers as he finished his side.

Aila didn't mind the bruised knuckles he'd earned in that loss, or the little scrapes and bruises that came with his menial labor. She had always loved her handsome husband's lean shape, but he had firmed up in the butt and put on some real muscle in his arms and chest. He looked good, and he looked tough, and she was enjoying running her hands over the curves of his harder body.

She wondered if he had started spending a little time in the gym at his office as well. She also wondered if maybe the attacks by the deranged thugs had him questioning his ability to protect the family, but he hadn't indicated it in any other way that she'd noticed.

She let the thought drift away as it was a discussion for another time.

"You are the sweetest man I know, Daniel Hogan," she said to his chest.

"And you are the most conniving woman I know, Aila Hogan," Dan said to her forehead. "Well, maybe the second most."

"Guilty, but that's one excited little man," she said, and then she chuckled as she moved her leg out from between his. "Ben I mean, and in his eyes you are the best dad on the planet."

"Well, you guys were right," Dan said. "He's ready, and he deserves a break. Hamish and Christa will take good care of him, and the ranch is going to be a wonderland for a boy like him."

Aila lowered her voice and said, "And by a boy like him I trust you mean our new Ben?"

Dan nodded into her hair.

"It was Kels who was right," Aila said as she traced a fingertip around his ribs. "I'd like to think it's been my amazing parenting skills that's turned our significantly introverted, overprotective, aggression-issued son into a well-adjusted, super-sharp kid, but just between us previously borderline helicopter parents we have to face facts. More than a few of the kudos gotta go to those curs of ours. I mean, there's no doubt moving down here has helped, with me working from home, and him spending more time with Mom, and you working around the farm, but it's the hot-housing from those damn dogs that has our children ready to skip grades for fuck sakes, and those mutts did it in a few short months."

Aila put her chin on his chest and looked up at him, and said what they were both thinking, "The big question is should we be concerned? Is it too much, you know, with the pups and all?"

"Honestly I'm not sure what to make of it," Dan said, "but we can't argue with how far they've come. Ben's transition has been more obvious, but Kels is operating at a much higher level as well."

"Mom's noticed that too," Aila said, "and she thinks the kids are doing just fine. She said they still do normal kid stuff, and she wondered why I was bitchin' about them finally having fun in school and bringing home straight A's. I guess I agree, but it's still damn odd to see them buried in their tablets with the pups for hours on end, especially when they're up super late. I know they've pulled a few all-nighters."

"You never did that at their age?" Dan asked.

"Sure, I had some pretty crazy sleep-overs," Aila said, "but we weren't having in depth conversations about plate tectonics and natural selection with a pair of smart dogs as the sun was coming up."

"Would you rather they play video games and get baked?" Dan asked.

"I suppose most parents would be thrilled," Aila said.

"Be careful what you wish for I guess," Dan said.

Aila nodded.

"The other night I got sucked into an argument they were having about Orwell's Animal Farm," Dan said. "It was something about the pigs' seven commandments and should the animals be walking upright. I didn't recall enough of the story to contribute much but watching the four of them beating the issue to death was fascinating. It felt like a bunch of stuffy college professors going at it. The really bizarre part was Ben giving his scarily astute opinion while translating for the pups who were signing way too fast for Kels or me to keep up with, especially once they got agitated. It was a bizarre scene, but mostly I was just proud of them. All of them, oddly enough. Spot's logic and Smudge's empathy are definitely resonating with our kids, and the pups have certainly picked up Ben's humor and Kels' insights, and more than a little of their slang. I asked Ben about the book and he said it normally gets assigned to tenth graders. He said the pups tried following the normal high school curriculum so they could use the same books, but they got bored with the pace, and now so have our kids apparently. I knew they were way ahead on the reading, but I wasn't aware they've been doing the same thing with physics, and chemistry, and biology, and—"

"Yeah, about that," Aila said as she twisted a finger around in his chest hair. "They made me promise not to tell you how much we're spending on book downloads. But I can tell you it's less than two additional college educations."

"That's not even a little bit funny," Dan said.

He thought for a moment, and said, "I guess the answer to your question is I don't know if we should be concerned, but my gut tells me they're fine. They laugh more than they used to, and they're usually doing it together, which wasn't often the case before. They seem very happy, and the four of them certainly are thick as thieves. All five of them are, actually."

Aila nodded.

They laid together for a long while in silence, mulling, stroking, and listening to the wind.

Eventually she asked, "Are you surprised our daughter wants to be a vet?"

"I was at first," Dan said. "I figured it was just a reaction to having the pups around, but she's really thought it through and has a plan. And she's a lot more excited about being a doctor than she ever was about fashion or music, thank God. "

Aila chuckled, and Dan said, "She's also right that it makes sense to have someone in our inner circle who can care for the pups. It's not like we can take them to just any vet if they get sick, and I think she'd be good at it."

Aila raised up on an elbow and said, "I think it goes deeper than that for her. She's obsessed with finding out what makes them tick. She making Spot take her through all of his paw modification designs. She says there's diagrams she can't begin to understand yet, but he's explaining them to her in little bits and pieces."

"Are we sure that was her idea?" Dan asked. "I wouldn't be surprised if it was Spot who lit the vet fire under Kels."

"Fucking probably," Aila said as she stifled her chuckle into his shoulder. "And you call me calculating. I gave up playing chess with that adorable little freak weeks ago."

Dan decided to not explore that comment. He had never beaten his wife at chess.

"Regardless of who got the ball rolling," Dan said, "I wish I'd had that level of passion when I was her age. I was only concerned with being cool and trying not to get caught playing with myself, which Ben has started to do by the way. I got him all straightened out on that front so, you know, make noise before you walk into his room or open the bathroom door. I noticed Spot deliberately bumps his hip on the loose baluster when comes upstairs so it appears the pups have also figured it out."

"Lovely," Aila said. "I'll make sure Mum clues in Hamish. I must say, I am surprised you caved so quickly on the Quebec trip after that train-ride-into-town stunt."

"It's always been hard to stay mad at him," Dan said, "and it's damn near impossible lately. I mean seriously, what do we have to complain about? When you add those pups into the mix, and Kelcy, and Meem, well, I was sorely outgunned. You know how that feels, right?"

Aila bit his neck and whispered, "I was outgunned a few minutes ago."

She took his hand and wrapped his arm around her as she turned her backside to spoon into him. "I had very little to do with this one," she said. "Mom and Kelcy got everything lined up."

"And those two really did have an answer for everything," Dan said. "The train, the bus, the border crossing, parental letter, passport, and I'm guessing Mimi called in a favor and had Mari fill out their rabies certificates. And don't get me started on those damn vests."

"Oh God, the vests," Aila chuckled into his shoulder. "They love those bloody things. Did I tell you Spot was jealous of Smudge's lightning bolt so Mimi embroidered the Underdog 'U' on his? He showed it to me three times."

Dan laughed into her hair as he said, "If that dog ever meets Polly Pureheart we're in big trouble."

"Dear Jesus," Aila whispered. "Can you imagine?"

They continued to laugh about their odd pups and their loving mother and their unique kids until Aila turned to face him again and asked, "So, what's with Ben's early birthday presents?"

"I knew you were nervous about him being in the middle of nowhere," Dan said, "and Hamish has no problem disappearing into the woods for weeks at a time with no word."

"The satellite phone was a fantastic idea," Aila said, "and that mini-tablet for the pups was dead brilliant. But I'm more interested in when you bought them."

Dan traced a line down his wife's back and took a full handful of her bottom as he said, "I picked them up the day after Ben's visit to my office. I was just enjoying all the special meals and sex you've been serving up this week, so I wasn't in a rush to tell you."

"Mmmm," Aila purred as she pushed herself back into his growing firmness. "That was just selfishness on my part."

Twenty feet down the hall Spot and Smudge were cuddled up together at the foot of the Ben's bed.

He was snoring quietly, and the pups were planning their trip and ignoring the parents' second round of love-making.

Spot had one of his toe flaps extended and was scrolling around a map of Canada on their new small tablet. He'd connected the satphone's USB tether to test out the satellite internet connection.

This thing is super cool, Spot signed. *We should get one for One Ear. She could track the weather, learn about tick-borne illnesses. Maybe even research dental hygiene.*

Smudge huffed a quiet laugh, and looked up from Mimi's tablet where she was researching the wild animals of Canada.

One Ear's not overly interested in anything she can't chase, eat, or pee on, she signed as she tapped the shut off the tablet.

She rolled onto her side, looked up at the full moon, and signed, *You sure this trip is such a good idea?*

Are you kidding? Spot signed. *Without new experiences something inside of us sleeps. The sleeper must awaken.*

Isn't that from Dune? Smudge signed.

It still applies, Spot signed. *And we're a bit like Paul Atreides, no?*

You're a total nerd, Muad'Dib, Smudge signed.

Spot gave her a single tail wag, and signed, *So, what's on your bucket list?*

Not to get lost in the great white north, Smudge signed.

Ha ha, Spot signed. *No, really.*

I'd like to see a Moose, Smudge signed, *and an elk, and a brown bear, and a snowy owl, and a pine marten.*

Spot gave her a sideways glance.

It's a weasel-like mustelid, Smudge signed.

And I'm the geek, Spot signed. *How about a wolf?*

Not much chance of that, Smudge signed. *They're super rare, and based on what I've been reading we'd barely be a snack for even a medium-size Canis lupus.*

But it'd cool, right? Spot asked.

Oh, it's going to be plenty cool, Smudge signed. *It's negative seven up there right now.*

Good thing we've got our vests, Spot signed.

Smudge gave him a flat look, and then fluffed her chicken plush toy under her chin and closed her eyes.

I'm not so sure about this trip brother, she signed. *Most dogs don't like to hear they're going to a farm up north.*

CHAPTER 9

Mimi had trouble remembering the last time she'd been to Papa's old factory, which was now the new vet clinic. She paused on the front walk to look past the plowed lot and across the road to the snowy woods of her farm, and then to the south, where her husband's grave lay on top of the cemetery hill.

She looked to the north and saw the remains of the old vet clinic. Ronnie had been killed there just a few short months ago, and all that remained was a charred slab and the parking lot. There was a real estate banner bolted over what had been the clinic's sign.

Seeing the scorched foundation always brought up a mix of memories for Mimi. There was the horror of that terrible night, but also years of Ronnie's welcoming smile. A lovely smile on a far too thin girl who's heart was warmer than a dog's wag.

Mimi turned to face the large glass doors that were set into the new clinic's curved glass front wall, and they whisked open as Ben beckoned for her to follow him and Aila. They crossed a plush doormat with the clinic's logo as they walked into the open, airy lobby. There were two rows of sleek curved wooden benches flanking the center aisle that led to a matching curved reception counter. The artwork on the walls was modern and tasteful, the lobby colors were bright but subtle, and everything was crisp and clean and new.

Mimi was impressed, and a little sad. The building had been her husband's printing factory for several decades. She was glad to see it had been cleaned up and put to good use, but she still missed the noise and the dirt and the hustle and the friendly faces of the shop. She recalled watching her ruddy-cheeked, handsome Duncan shaking hands, laughing, and clapping backs with his close-knit family of workers.

"Looks a sight better in here than the old days, doesn't it just?" she whispered to Aila.

Aila took her mom's hand and conveyed everything she needed to with just a small squeeze.

"It's lovely," she added.

She'd ridden her bike around the warehouse as a kid, and jousted with empty paper rolls with the workers, and sat on her dad's desk as he punched numbers into his ancient adding machine.

As she and Mimi crossed the lobby behind Ben they nodded and said a polite good morning to a woman who was sitting on one of the benches.

She replied with a grunt that questioned what was so damn good about the morning.

The woman didn't look nearly as cheery as the very large and very bright Christmas tree on the front of her very round sweater. She was slouched and bow legged, and the tongues of her unlaced boots were flopping out. She scowled at Ben and gave the nicely put-together women following him a sour look as they passed. When the fat cat in the small pet carrier next to her growled it sounded just like her.

"Hey sis," Ben called out as he jogged over to the reception counter.

Kelcy and Lindsay were standing together behind it, and they were looking over Carol 'Mari' Marinson's shoulder as she squinted through her reading glasses at a computer screen. Lindsay and Mari were dressed in crisp white tailored wrap-around tunics, and Kelcy wore a fitted pink smock that tied at the side.

Aila was instantly proud. Her daughter looked as professional as she was adorable.

"Let's move all of these to next Tuesday," Lindsay said as she tapped her pen on the screen. As the women stepped up to the counter she said cheerily, "Hello ladies. You guys come to see Dr. Kelcy save the world one grumpy cat at a time?"

The Christmas tree lady didn't find that overly funny, nor did her grumpy cat.

"Hey Mom, hey Meem," Kelcy said as she shot them a little wave.

Mari looked up from her computer screen and said, "Good morning Jean, hey Ben, and hello there Aila. Feels like I haven't seen you in a coon's age. How're you getting on over there at the Morgan's place?"

Mari had worked part time at the old clinic, and she'd baby sat for Mimi more than a few times. She had changed the kids' diapers, and Aila's before them.

"Peachy," Aila said with a smile. "It's good to be home. How's the family?"

"We've got too many grandkids to remember their names," she said. "I love them all, but it's nice to be back at work again. What do you think of our new digs?"

"Amazing," Aila said as she scanned the lobby. "All of this in a few short weeks?"

"I know," Mari said. She leaned forward and whispered. "Those benches cost more than my car."

The phone on the desk tinkled pleasantly, and Mari raised a finger to excuse herself as she picked it up.

"Come this way," Lindsay said as she waved for them to follow her and Kelcy down the counter. When she stepped in front of a pair of sliding glass doors they opened automatically, and she said, "Okay Kels, this is your tour. I'll catch up with you in a bit."

Kelcy looked a little surprised, but she nodded and led her family down the bright exam hallway as the doors whooshed closed behind them.

She selected one of the exam rooms and pushed its large paddle handle to open the wide door. The lights came on automatically, and she showed them the motorized multi-position table and exam lights that could be positioned with a remote.

Every surface was clean enough to eat from, and the gallery-quality artwork looked nothing like the ancient faded posters for heartworm and dewormer that had adorned the old clinic's wood-paneled walls.

Aside from the small counter with a sink the room was otherwise Spartan. Kelcy went to the feature-less back wall, waggled her eyebrows at them, and then pulled on a recessed handle. A cart that fit seamlessly into the wall rolled out, and she demonstrated to a cowering Ben that it was a high speed dental unit. Other carts held ultrasound and EKG units, and she swung out a long arm that had an x-ray device on its bulbous end.

Mimi picked up on Aila's pride, and they shared a nod as Kelcy described each piece with confidence before tucking them back into their alcoves.

They followed her out of the room and she led them to the far end of the hallway. She paused at a frosted set of doors that were tastefully marked PRIVATE, and when she raised her hands and moved them apart as she stepped forward the doors magically opened.

She turned back with a smirk to show Ben there was a key fob attached to the lanyard she wore around her neck.

They followed her into a large treatment room. Its ceiling, walls, and floors were pristine white, and Aila couldn't find any seams. It was one continuous piece of some kind of subtly dimpled material that curved in the corners of the room. There were islands of tables surrounded by low counters that she guessed held more of the same sleek, recessed equipment. Each table could be sectioned off with opaque sheets that hung from tracks in the ceiling.

Kelcy led them to the back corner of the room and waggled her eyebrows again before holding up her lanyard. A frosted glass wall slid aside to reveal a surgical room. The hardware that surrounded the gleaming table made the exam room equipment look like toys. There was every conceivable manner of high tech medical device built into one uninterrupted console with a curved row of monitors above it.

Mimi had been a nurse in her earlier years and she knew how to use most of the equipment at the old vet clinic, but she couldn't identify half of the kit in the room. Everything had a touch screen, and sleek curved lines, and every attachment and accessory fit neatly into its own recess.

"Yowsers," Ben said. "You could *build* a dog in here."

"I was just thinking that exact thing lad," Mimi said.

"I have no idea what half of this stuff does," Kelcy said. "But it's aww-soooome"

Aila high fived her daughter and said, "Oh man Kels, looks like you fell into the right job."

The wall slid closed when they left the room, and she led them past rows of shiny cages and neatly stacked supply shelves. When they passed through another whooshing doorway the floor changed from white to light hardwood, and the walls took on an upscale office feel. The room was a large circle, the high ceiling was a single round skylight, and there were a half dozen sets of frosted glass doors spread equally around the perimeter. In the center of the room was a low round table ringed with sleek chairs.

As they were taking the tour Mimi had been trying to orient herself inside the building. She quickly lost track after they left the huge glass lobby, which hadn't been part of her husband's factory. Somewhere in this back area had been rows of thumping, dirty printing presses and equally dirty men scurrying around them, but there were no signs of the old shop floor now. It looked like they had stepped into a downtown architect's office.

Kelcy crossed the room and waved her lanyard at a set of doors. They slid open and she led the family into a large conference room.

Running down the middle of the room was a long dark table ringed by padded chairs. In the center of the table was a sleek gray stalk that housed what Aila took to be a multi-camera video conferencing system. Next to the door was a small touch screen that controlled everything in the room. Motorized shades covered the windows on the opposite wall, and built into the cabinets at the rear of the room was a glass front beverage cooler, fully stocked. On the other wall two huge displays were flanked by dark glass racks that held towers of audio-visual equipment.

"Jesus Christ," Aila mumbled, and then shrugged an apology.

Kelcy laughed and said, "Yeah, you'd expect to see something like this in Dad's building, not so much in Pembury."

The doors slid open and Lindsay walked in ahead of an equally tall man in a white physician's coat that looked more like a sports jacket.

He strode up to Mimi and Aila and presented his hand.

"Marty Osipoff," he said. "We drop the doctor thing around here. It's great to finally meet you guys." He gestured to the chairs and said, "Please, sit," and to Ben he added, "You must be the famous parvo puppy life saver I've been hearing so much about. Can I buy a hero a drink?"

Ben accepted a soda, as did the rest of the family, and Lindsay brought over a tray of cookies.

For the next hour they sat and drank and snacked as they chatted.

Marty was charming, and Lindsay had been absolutely right that his slight southern accent was as easy on the ears as he was on the eyes. He immediately picked up on Mimi's accent and asked about her roots. When he heard she'd grown up in Inverclyde he said he'd been to Greenock, and remembered it as a place you could get homesick for after only a single visit. That was received with nods, and a big smile from Mimi.

Marty asked most of the questions as he hadn't been in town long and was curious about Pembury, and the South Shore in general. He was also curious about the farm and asked about their family's history in the States, and he even asked about Mr. Watt and the pups. When the somber subject of the old vet clinic came up he expressed his deep condolences. The family accepted that with nods, but then Mimi quickly brightened the mood and complimented him on the renovation. She and Aila said they couldn't believe it was the same place.

"There's no high-end animal care outside of Boston," Marty said. "For the really complex stuff you have to go to Tufts. It's a great place but it's a teaching college and they sometimes move like a herd of turtles. I think we can make a go of it offering an alternative for the rest of New England, but we need energetic and talented people. That's why we're excited to have Kelcy here." He touched her arm and added, "This one's quicker'n a scalded cat, and even the mean dogs like her."

He smiled, and the woman in the room were quite sure Dr. Martin Osipoff left a trail of fluttering hearts everywhere he went. He was a very good looking man. Aila was pretty sure most women wouldn't hesitate to tell him their bra size if the doctor smiled when asking.

He was fair skinned, Mimi guessed German, with a flawless complexion and powder blue eyes. They assumed he was pushing forty as he had just a touch of gray creeping into the temples of his short blonde hair, and he had the first few toes of crow's feet scratching at the corners of his eyes. He held a pair of stylish framed glasses but Mimi never saw him actually put them on, even when he checked his phone. She wondered if they were just to complete the outfit.

He also just happened to not be married. "Too busy," he had said with a smile.

Aila thought she might be lingering a little long staring into his eyes as he spoke so she forced herself to stare at Ben, who sipped his soda and bugged his eyes back at her as if to ask, *Why are you staring at me?*

She smiled, and fixed his bangs, and moved on to smile at Lindsay, and then at Kelcy, and then at Mimi, who totally busted her.

Aila ignored her mom's broad, knowing smile as she turned back to Lindsay, who was explaining, "Officially we can't hire Kelcy until she's sixteen. We'll just consider her a volunteer for these first few weeks, with her hiring bonus coincidentally equaling her back pay."

"I can't tell you how much we appreciate this," Mimi said. "She's got her heart set on animal science, and she's been going on about this place non-stop."

Marty's phone chirped, and when he rose from his chair everyone else followed suit.

"I'm sorry gang but I gotta run," he said as he clasped his hands. "It sure was nice meetin' y'all, and I hope you come back real soon to see us again. Kelcy, quit your lolly-gagging and get back to work.

It's a safe bet there's a fresh poop somewhere in this building that needs warshin' up."

They laughed and thanked Marty, and he paused in the doorway to say to Ben, "Have a great time in Canada. When you get back bring those dogs of yours in for a checkup, on the house of course. I'd love to meet them."

CHAPTER 10

The director of the FBI's Boston field office, Douglas 'VB' Barton, rarely had to raise his voice or state his position more than once, but he was losing an important argument.

"We're not having this conversation again," he said as he folded his arms across his chest to signify a finality that rarely worked against the tough, stubborn guy he was facing off with. "It's simple, you take the proper gear or you don't go."

"Dude, that helmet's the lamest thing on the planet," his son said as he folded his arms across his chest.

VB looked to his wife for help. She was corralling their waddling daughter and her two little friends before dragging them over to the tow rope for another run down the bunny slope. He wasn't sure why she kept calling it a 'run' as the bunny slope was essentially flat and they didn't move unless she shoved them on their little foot-long skis.

She gave him her signature *have fun with that* look before she turned away with the three little ones. They both knew she could get the kid to slam on the helmet with any one of a dozen of her mom looks, but she didn't like to interrupt when he was flexing his dad muscles. She was also clearly enjoying seeing him get his balls busted for a change so there was no way she was going to step in.

"You gotta wear the helmet," VB pleaded after his wife moved out of ear shot. "When you smack into a tree and your three brain cells leak out all over that new jacket your mom'll have my ass."

The boy started a fresh round of protests but VB stopped him with a raised finger as he pointed to his Bluetooth earpiece. His son wasn't well trained when it came to helmets but there was no confusion when it came to his dad having to take a phone call.

He stomped off to join his buds as he slammed on the helmet and shot his dad some parting venom.

"That may have been the worst excuse for parenting I have ever seen," Special Agent in Charge Dr. Loyal Comina said as she appeared at VB's side.

She took a knee in the snow and pretended to tie a boot as she checked to make sure no one was listening. The bottom of the bunny hill wasn't overly busy and she assumed the seven year old savant shooshing past them with perfect form wasn't an eavesdropper.

"Taking a nonexistent phone call is one of my patented managerial tools," VB said as he waved to his scowling son, who was in line for the chair lift. "And it's works equally well on arguing wives and annoying agents."

Comina stood up and put her gloves back on.

"Boss, are we okay?" she asked.

"Well, that really depends on you, Loyal," he said. "You've got two choices. I can tell you about the problem we have, and in doing so I'd be violating a direct order from my superior as well as seven bureau charters and a few codes of conduct. I'd also be putting both of our careers in significant jeopardy. Or, I can *not* tell you our problem. Our case disappears faster than a skydiver's fart, and we move on to the next crusade."

Comina nodded, and said, "Just so I'm clear here, if we shutter the case the very fabric of our mission to protect good from evil comes crashing down and anarchy will ensue. Dogs and cats will live together, and the forces of Mordor will rise to swallow Middle Earth. And it'll get buried so no one will ever know?"

"Right," VB said as a tiny tike executed a perfect power-stop in front of them and flicked off the straps of her snowboard in one fluid motion. She flip-kicked the board into her hand and trotted off to the lodge.

To answer Comina's unasked question VB said, "It's very possible they'll get harmed."

He didn't need to look at her to know she'd raised a skeptical eyebrow.

"Okay, it's probable," he conceded. "And if I tell you our problem you'll likely be in more danger as well."

She gave him a sideways glance he didn't see, but he corrected himself, "Certainly be in more danger."

A gust of wind knocked snow from the pines, and the skiers on the lift swayed as the hanging chairs crawled up the mountain. Comina zipped up her jacket as she said, "I like them VB. They're good people and we can't see them harmed. This is what we do, right? Protect people."

"Yes it is Loyal, and I like them too," VB said. "And they have an important role to play. I took a gamble leaving them out in the open as I thought it would be the best way to keep them safe."

"Has that changed?" Comina asked.

"Yes," VB said.

"Tell me," Comina said.

"I'm pretty sure Daddy Mogevich and psychotic mini-Mogevich already have their claws sunk into Pembury," he said. "They have at least one of their people there, or maybe a local ally, or both."

Comina nodded.

"And someone in Executive accessed my accelerator formula incident report through a back door leak," VB said. "I'm not exactly sure how much they were able to pull before I got wind of it, but I buried my report and all of the related files."

"You lied," Comina said. "That's two problems."

"Actually there's three," VB said. "I've been ordered to let it go and look the other way. Sam doesn't know who's behind it, but it's gotta be coming from pretty high up."

They sat in silence for a while as they watched the brightly colored ants zig-zag down the slopes.

VB hated putting her in this position. Continuing to work a case after they'd been ordered to pull the plug isn't something to be done lightly. Of course he wasn't sure she'd listen even if he did try to reassign her. She was like a dog with a bone when a bad guy needed dealing with or an innocent needed saving, and she worked the really tough ones. The ones Sam gave only to him, and he gave only to her.

He'd met Loyal Comina by chance fifteen years ago, when she was just a grunt. She had appeared like a heavily armed angel out of the dark and pulled him from a burning helicopter that wasn't supposed to be where it was. As hell rained down she disobeyed her superiors, and him, and kept him from bleeding out while she single-handedly held off a rabble with helo-fuel Molotov cocktails. She was the smartest, toughest person he'd ever met, and he'd convinced her to join the bureau while she was still finishing her first doctorate. He pulled strings to get her assigned to his Boston undercover team, and for a decade he's watched her deftly morph into housewives and hookers and heart surgeons without a slip. She was as good as they came, and he'd be working for her by now if she didn't have an irrepressible need to be honest at all times.

Which was ironic as she was the best liar on the planet.

She also had no family and no significant attachments, which was great for a field agent but often kept them from being promoted. As screwed-up as his organization could be, they understood to effectively lead you had to know how to compromise, and you had to have experienced loss.

Those skills really only came from having a family.

Regardless, he was a huge Loyal Comina fan, and admitted to himself that he was probably a little bit in love with her to boot.

"Jesus VB, you weren't kidding," she said. She turned to study his face for a second before she added, "Tell me the rest of it."

He cursed her ability to read him. He was never sure if it was their years together or her double degrees in medicine and psychology that allowed her to so easily uncover his tells, but it was really damn annoying.

He turned away from her to watch his wife. She was walking backward down the flat white hill ahead of a train of pink and blue and orange gnomes.

As if she'd felt him looking she turned and waved, and then cupped a mitten over her eyes, recognized Comina, and waved again.

They both returned her wave, and VB said, "Another barrel of accelerator formula is missing from Orthus, and this time it wasn't the Tiandihui triad who took it. It's been wiped off the company's books from the inside."

"And you know this how?" Comina asked.

"I have someone inside Orthus," VB said.

"You have someone inside Orthus' headquarters?" Comina asked. "As in you're running your own op in New York City?"

"As in way, way outside my approved purview," VB said with a nod.

"As in the NYC field office is in the dark?" Comina asked.

"As in the New York office had already been given orders to pull out anyone even close to Orthus," VB said.

"As in we're screwed," Comina said.

CHAPTER 11

Ben paused behind a large tree to catch his breath and scan the steep ridge he was trying to scramble up. He'd moved up the hill as fast and as quietly as he could in the deep snow, and sweat soaked his thermal underwear from the effort. As he worked to stifle his gasps he cupped his gloves over his mouth to hide his steaming exhale from the shafts of afternoon light filtering through the trees.

As he thought through his options he crouched against the trunk of the tree, and his snow suit scraped loudly on the bark.

He froze, and cringed, and cursed himself.

C'mon you numpty, he thought. *Gotta be smarter than that to get out of this one.*

If he continued up the ridge he'd have to trudge through deeper snow and pick his way through the dense deadfall. If he went down toward the river bank he risked running right into his attackers. Cutting across the slope would be tough as it was steep and slick. Climbing was an option. He could disappear into the thick pine canopy of the trees but he'd be stuck, and it would be dark in a few hours. He tried to remember everything the pups had taught him about evading hunters, and he really wished they were by his side to help him.

He heard a rustle to the left and tried to meld further into the bark as he thought, *Please please please don't see me.*

When the sound didn't get any closer he risked a peek around the tree and his shoulders slunk with relief. It was just a squirrel picking loudly through the frozen leaves.

Shut it! he thought, but then he remembered something Spot had said about squirrels being effective alarms and he leaned out to watch the critter for a few long breathes. It wouldn't hang around if a threat was nearby, unless of course the hunters were very stealthy.

And these hunters were.

He decided to not wait around to be attacked so he shoved off the tree and made it two steps before he covered his face with his arms and screamed.

The silent coyote pup had dived from his upslope hiding spot, and he slammed into Ben with enough momentum to send both of them tumbling a few yards down the hill.

The pup was ten months old and almost full height, but he wasn't as thick through the neck and chest as his adult pack mates. He was just as accurate with his attack however, and he'd been careful to knock Ben over without hurting him.

As Ben giggled and pushed the young hunter away the pup feigned a lunge for his neck and clamped down on his boot. The little wild dog paused, and wagged, and before Ben could protest the coyote started yanking him down the hill. Ben wrapped himself around the pup as they tumbled. With the snow and leaves flying around them another pup pounced on them and wiggled her way into Ben's arms.

At the bottom of the ravine the three of them rolled onto the snow covered stream bed in one big ball, and as Ben was getting licked from all angles he sputtered and squealed, "Okay you bawheeds, you win!"

Spot and Smudge and One Ear were watching them from the top of the opposite ridge.

The pups are getting pretty good, Smudge said with a huff and a complimentary shoulder shake. *You're doing a fine job.*

One Ear thanked her with a proud head-butt before she dropped over the lip of the slope to join her successful young hunters.

A dozen other coyotes slipped silently out of the woods and started a game of tag with Ben. The yearlings had been in on the hunt as well, but they hadn't been able to zero in on Ben as quickly as the talented younger hunters.

One Ear kept a watchful eye on them as they leapt and dodged just out of reach of the human boy. After a few minutes of Ben always being 'it' she let him tag her.

Smudge and Spot shared a wag and a satisfied nod, and he huffed, *Follow me, I have something to show you.*

They left the laughing Ben and the yipping coyotes to trot together along the ridge toward Cape Cod Bay.

As they were swallowed up by the thick evergreens Spot huffed, *She'll probably be pregnant when we get back.*

You sound a little jealous, Smudge huffed as she nudged her brother. *Sure you don't want to be a dad? Of course your pups would probably come out looking like Mr. Peabody.*

That's funny coming from Ms. Bruce Banner, Spot huffed as they came to a fork and he nodded for her to take the beach trail.

All kidding aside brother, you wanna have kids? Smudge asked. *I mean, I gotta admit I do think about it sometimes.*

What is it with you women and your damn clocks? Spot asked. After receiving a curt growl he added, *I don't know sis, I wouldn't want to be a helicopter alpha with my pups.*

I've been wondering about that, Smudge huffed. *Why does an alpha have to be a male? Why can't a female lead the pack? And if you roll your eyes I'm tossing you down this hill.*

I suppose that cold bitch Mother Nature has her own answer for the equality of the sexes issue, Spot huffed. *And she's not too PC about it. But we sure can't argue with the bang-up job One Ear's doing as our pack's leader. She's got my vote.*

I think we need to change the traditional order of things, Smudge huffed. *I mean, you and I are kinda turning that cold bitch on her head.*

Spot agreed with a nod, and they walked together in silence for a few minutes enjoying the salty air and the growing sound of the rolling waves.

As the thick snow of the forest trails became icy sand Smudge huffed, *Kels asked me if I ever wanted to be a mom.*

She asked me the same thing, Spot huffed. *Well, what she actually asked was did we ever think about getting fixed. It's funny, she immediately felt bad for asking it. She said the family would love to see us with puppies of our own and all that, and quickly assured me they thought we'd be good parents. I think she was stumbling around the larger question of should we have offspring. Aside from the obvious unknowns, and potential risk to the mother and babies. Who knows what our kids would be like?*

All true, my overly analytical brother, Smudge huffed as the grassy dunes ended and they trotted along the shoreline, *but you didn't answer the question.*

I know, Spot said as he hip-bumped his sister.

They paused to take in the picturesque little frozen beach, and the rolling swells that were being pushed by the stiff wind to break at almost a right angle to the shore. Beyond the waves the expanse of angry blue-green water stretched away unbroken, aside from the tiny dark slip of Provincetown that jutted out twenty miles distant.

They continued down the beach for a bit until Spot ducked into a small clearing that was hidden from view by a ring of dunes choked with beach heather.

He stopped and turned a slow circle with his nose twitching and his ears perked, and Smudge could tell he was making sure they were alone.

So, this is a lovely spot, she huffed as she pawed the snow and looked around at the desolate and kinda ugly little clearing. *Thanks for showing it to me on this cold and windy afternoon.*

Spot raised a paw to silence her, and then closed his eyes.

He raised his head and pointed his snout away as if he had picked up a scent.

Smudge checked but there was nothing in the wind that shouldn't be there.

Spot wiggled his paws into the snow like he was getting ready to jump, but then he just froze in place.

When he opened his eyes a few moments later Smudge's mouth dropped open.

She blinked, and blinked again to make sure her eyes weren't playing tricks on her.

What in the bleeding hell? she growled.

⚜ §§ ⚜

Smudge circled her brother slowly. She sniffed and poked, and lifted up his tail and ran her paw up his back to fluff up his fur.

That's the second strangest thing I've ever seen, she grumbled. *The first being that thing One Ear does when she regurgitates birds.*

Pretty cool, eh? Spot huffed with a little wag.

I'll say, Smudge huffed. *How'd you do it?*

I think you can do it too, Spot huffed. *Come here, let me show you.*

He had her assume the same position and close her eyes. He moved in close to her ear and huffed and grumbled so low she could barely hear him. What followed from her brother was an unbroken stream-of-consciousness narrative that guided her to seek out and control specific autonomous processes, similar to those she uses to pump herself up, and the ones they use to speed-heal themselves.

His flow of instructions washed over her like the constant rumble of the rolling waves, *The white of the snow color white find your xanthophores white move them into your guanine nanocrystals white snow find your organelles flood your biochromes white snow white have them drop your phaeomelanin white snow pull your eumelanin white snow no color white…*

Spot continued to fill his sister's head for several minutes before he slowly backed away and then huffed softly, *Open your eyes.*

Smudge opened one eye and looked at her brother.

When he nodded at the ground she looked down at her feet.

Her paws were white. Stark white. As white as the snow, and so were her legs, and chest. She turned and saw the rest of her was white too, down to the tip of her wagging tail.

Just like her brother.

CHAPTER 12

Katia sipped from her tumbler of kvass as she leaned on the glass wall of her office.

The beating blades of a helicopter thumped past the building and faded away as it turned in a long slow arc over the Hudson. It dropped down over the river to eventually land at the Thirtieth Street helipad far below. In this weather, and from this high up, the red and white lights from the cars creeping along the wet West Side Highway were just blurry strings. Her normally sweeping views of Ellis Island and the Jersey skyline were lost in the night's fog and freezing drizzle.

There were two quick raps on her office door, and after a pause a well-dressed young man in horn-rimmed glasses stepped halfway through the threshold.

In a soft voice flavored with both British and Baltic accents he said, "She's downstairs. Two minutes, ma'am."

Katia's wave was both acknowledgement and dismissal, and as her assistant left she tapped the tablet on her desk.

The bar on her office's back wall split in two and slid open to expose a very large monitor. The Orthus company logo appeared with a small padlock icon and a green status bar that circled around it.

A second later her father's bulk filled the screen.

He was leaning against his large desk in his office in Orenburg, and the morning sun was lighting the tops of the Ural Mountains in the panoramic windows behind him. He was dressed in a running suit, there was a towel around his neck, and he was holding a big plastic bottle in his meaty hands.

In the bright morning light his age showed more than usual, but Katia thought her father still looked as solid as the granite mountains behind him.

"I hope that's just water," she said in Russian.

"Sadly it is," Semion said with a little smile as he held up his large bottle.

Katia tapped her tablet to bring up her reception room's security camera, and as she watched her guest exit the elevator she said, "She'll be here in fifteen seconds."

Semion's smile dropped as he said, "We need her for a while longer, so play nice."

Katia shrugged to indicate she wasn't making any promises as her assistant rapped again and opened the office door.

He held it for a small Asian women and a very large black man. The woman nodded to Katia as she stopped just inside the doorway so her bodyguard could remove her coat. She eyed the office quickly, handed her gloves to the big man, and dismissed him with a nod.

Katia tapped her tablet, and subtly looked down to check the results of the weapons detector that was built into her office door frame.

She nodded slightly to her assistant to indicate both of her guests had been carrying pistols when they entered but both guns had left with the black man and the woman's coat.

As the woman crossed the office Katia's assistant backed out and closed the door.

"Good evening Jia," Katia said warmly in English as they shook hands. "We very much appreciate you coming down to the city on such a night."

"I had business in town anyway," Jia said curtly with a very slight Chinese accent. She let Katia's hand go after a brief but firm pump, and added, "So it wasn't a completely wasted trip."

She was a full head shorter than Katia and easily twice her age, and as usual she was dressed in all black. Where Jia's late sister Mina had been very fashionable, Jia always wore utilitarian clothes and no makeup. That alone was enough for Katia to not trust her.

"Hello Jia," Semion said warmly from the monitor. "As my daughter said, it's a pity to have to summon you so late on a night like this. Completely my fault, I have an opportunity for you that couldn't wait."

Katia motioned to the contemporary couch and chairs in the center of her office. "Can I get you something?" she asked as she retrieved her tablet and tumbler from her desk.

"What do you have there?" Jia asked, attempting a cordial smile that didn't seem to fit her face.

Katia held up her glass and said, "Kvass? It's similar to beer, but made from bread and—"

"I know what it is," Jia said, and then reminded herself to remain courteous. She sat down and said, "We have it in Hong Kong too. A Russian import our kids pollute themselves with. Just water please. What is it you have for me Semion?"

"A gift," he said with a broad smile. "Jean Walker has a brother-in-law in Canada. You can do whatever you want with him, as long as you help me out with a bit of business up there, quietly."

Jia stared at him for a long moment before she asked, "Is that why I'm here tonight?"

Semion straightened and stepped away from his desk, and the automatic video conference system adjusted to keep him in frame.

"I thought you'd be pleased," he said. "I know how you feel about the Hogan-Walker family. I completely understand your desire to go to Pembury with some of your Tiandihui and a flamethrower, and I appreciate your agreeing to not do that very thing based on my request that you wait."

Jia accepted the glass of water from Katia, thanked her with a nod, and said, "Semion, those monsters killed my son, and I'm convinced they're responsible for my sister's disappearance, and Larry's, and that doctor. Not to mention the loss of a very profitable business for my family. I want justice, not some distant relative."

Semion took a step closer and said, "Jia, you know I respect family above all else, but I have reasons for keeping Pembury isolated, for now. There are too many prying eyes and too much is at stake. We can't yet make any trouble there. Your continued cooperation in this regard is appreciated, and it has been rewarded, has it not?"

"Nothing can compensate me for what I've lost," Jia said. "Larry's businesses are not replacement for my son, or my sister."

Katia tapped the rim of her glass, and flashed a hand sign to her father that asked permission to end the old bat's bullshit. She was growing impatient and couldn't understand how her father could be so accommodating of this rude *suka*.

Semion told her to stand down with a finger twitch.

"I want to have a chat with the Hogan family," he said. "We can't touch them in Pembury, but we can certainly touch the boy in Canada, and we know he's going to visit his great-uncle in Quebec. Are you interested in being a part of this, or are you not?"

Katia could tell her father was finally getting close to his limit as well. He rarely raised his voice. Typically he just raised his finger instead, and things were resolved quickly.

She smiled at him, and when she put her arm over the back of the couch her fingers rested on the hidden panel's release catch.

She casually looked down at her tablet to check the video feed from her reception room. Her assistant was sitting at his desk, and Jia's bodyguard was sitting across the room in one of the padded chairs. Her foppish man-Friday was a drama queen and not great at taking messages, but he was deadly with the pistol that was less than an inch from his fingertips.

Katia let her mind wander a bit as she stared at the dark man. He couldn't look more like a bodyguard if he tried, which she knew was by design as most of his job was intimidation. He was big, and handsome in a hard way, and had a shiny bald head and a full-length black leather coat. She wondered what would happen if her assistant failed. What if everyone's guns jammed? How would she fair against such a large man? Could she disable him and then toy with him, or would her hands be full just trying to kill him? And what if they were naked when they fought?

As amusing as her train of thought was she put down her glass of beer and willed herself back to the present. Maybe Jia had been right about the kvass. *Or maybe my father has me working too many late nights,* she thought.

"What I'm interested in is going to Pembury and killing everyone on that farm," Jia said.

Semion considered his next move as he folded his large arms across his barrel chest and looked from Jia to his daughter.

He knew the silenced MSP assassin's pistol that was three inches from his daughter's fingertips would have a round in the chamber, the safety would be off, and the hammer would already be pulled back.

Semion finally pressed his massive hands together as if in prayer as he said, "Jia, please trust me when I tell you that I am just now giving you a gift. Speaking frankly, and with all due respect, your son was an idiot. He and some of your Tiandihui gang *mudaks* stole my accelerator formula, and then had the balls to try to sell it back to me. I should have castrated all of them. Also, that was some really unsavory shit you and your sister had going on in Pembury, and I can't blame that family for torching your son and his moronic comrade. And I can't fault them for somehow taking out Mina and Larry, if they did, which I still doubt, at least not single-handedly. You've been handed Larry's very lucrative dealings worth at least—," his eyes darted to Katia, who held up four fingers, "—four million a year. More than fair by any measure. And let us not forget, you are still in business because you are useful to me."

Semion saw his daughter shift in her seat. He knew she wanted him to succeed, but wouldn't be too upset if the meeting went off the rails. A part of him wanted it to fail as well. He enjoyed watching her work out a little frustration.

Soon enough my lovely lethal daughter, he thought. *Soon enough.*

Jia was smart enough to keep quiet, so he continued, "I want you to go to Canada and retrieve young Ben Hogan for me. You have to be discrete and you can't bring an army. Just you and my best asset, and your associate in the lobby if you wish. Use your snakehead's northern border crossing so there won't be any red flags raised."

Semion was suitably impressed that he couldn't read Jia's pretty, stone pale face. She was probably older than her smooth skin let on, and she was obviously experienced at not giving away much. As he took a drink from his bottle he checked with his daughter, who wasn't picking up which way their guest was leaning either.

"This Quebec job has to be done with local talent," he said. "And I need your gift for motivation and creative problem solving up there. We can't draw attention to this. It absolutely has to look like an unfortunate accident. Beyond that, what you do with the uncle is your business. Do this for me and I will hand you Pembury on a platter when the time is right, which should be soon after your successful return home."

Katia massaged the button on the back of the couch as she stared at Jia. She wanted her father's persuasion to work of course, but it had been a while since he'd allowed her to get her hands dirty. She picked the triangle-and-tree triad tattoo just below Jia's left ear as her target. As she thought more about it she decided to forego the gun altogether and just snap the rude Chink bitch's neck with her bare hands.

Jia gave Katia a little smile and a nod as she was warming up her response to the slut's boorish father. She wasn't anyone's errand girl, and she certainly had no interest in chasing off to the cold north in January to kidnap a kid and murder an old man.

She felt her temper rise, and she was just about to deliver her less than pleasant reply when she looked up and saw something she didn't like on Semion's face.

He was telling her she was in no position to bargain, and he was absolutely right. As she cursed her senses for letting her down she hoped it wasn't too late. She really didn't want to kill the whore right in front of her father, but if it came to that the flexible ceramic knife hidden in the hem of her skirt could be in her talented hands in an instant.

"Mr. Mogevich," she said with a respectful bow. "I must apologize. This business with my family has affected my judgement, and my manners. When I found out about the theft, and that you were behind Orthus, we immediately told my son to return your property. I was as shocked as you to find out he hadn't. I'm convinced it was the doing of that American scum-bag he was running around with, but regardless, we take full responsibility for that unfortunate situation. You have been nothing but fair with us. I would be honored to carry out this task for you, and for Katia."

She put her water glass on the table and smiled at Katia as she planted her back foot and picked a target just below the slut's chin.

"Pembury shall wait as long as you deem it necessary," she added as she smoothed an imaginary wrinkle from her skirt.

Semion exhaled loudly and smiled at his daughter.

Katia returned his smile with a slightly disappointed one of her own, and tapped around on her tablet.

"*Velikiy*, that's great to hear," Semion said to Jia with a nod. "And there is no need for apologies. It's been a stressful time for all of us. I truly appreciate your being accommodating, and I'm happy we could reach an agreement. Katia has the details. Good hunting."

Semion bid the women a final good evening, and when he tapped a button on his desk he faded out and the Orthus company logo appeared on Katia's monitor.

Katia trailed her hand away from the back of the couch, stood up, and took her tablet to her desk. As the bar closed in front of the monitor she nodded toward the door and said, "He'll make sure you have what you need. You leave tomorrow."

Jia turned to look in the direction of Katia's nod and was surprised to see a handsome young man smiling down at her. He was close enough to touch but she never heard him enter the room or approach her side. She gave him a quick looking over, from his chiseled jaw to his expensive suit with its almost imperceptible shoulder holster bulge, to his custom looking tactical boots that could be mistaken for dress shoes when casually viewed.

She was impressed. The young man was a professional.

CHAPTER 13

Dan hefted the Wagoneer's rear gate and gently shoved it closed. He climbed into the driver's seat, turned the heat up, and rolled down his window as he watched his wife and son.

Aila was giving Ben his third goodbye kiss and another stream of do's and don'ts as he flapped his arms under her tight embrace.

"Mum, can't, breathe," he gasped.

"Turn the boy loose mother," Dan said. "He's gonna miss his train." He pounded on the side of the jeep and whistled to the pups, who were hanging out with One Ear and a few of the smaller coyotes on the far side of the goat pen.

Spot and Smudge said their goodbyes, bounded around the rear of the jeep, and leapt through the open back door together.

Kelcy came over to give them a last kiss. "Take care of Ben," she said as she closed the door, and a little louder through the window she said, "And each other!"

Ben twisted out of Aila's grasp, swatted Kelcy on the bottom, and ran around the Wagoneer to jump into the passenger seat.

The Hogan women stepped up to the driver's window as Mimi came out of the house carrying a small plastic grocery bag.

"Some sammies for the road," she said as she handed the bag to Dan and pointed at Ben, "Now listen to me whilst I tell you something, all of you."

The dogs came forward and jammed together over the center console as she punctuated each of her instructions with her finger stab, "Keep your wits about you, and never leave each other's side. There's to be no carrying on for Hamish. Do as you're told and don't be a crabbit, but also don't listen to a word he says, especially the four-letter ones. Don't let him drive like a madman, call home every day, and wash your bums so you're not boggin'."

She paused for a moment before she leaned in a little closer and said, "Look here you lot, be careful with your gifts. Protect them, and don't be flippant with whom you trust, and only use them if you have to. You'll need to decide if and when to show them to Hamish."

She gave Ben and the pups a long look, blew them each a kiss, and said, "Trust yourselves, and you'll know."

As Dan started to roll down the driveway he sent a wink to his misty-eyed wife.

"I'll be back before Burns' Night!" Ben shouted. "Love you guys!"

CHAPTER 14

Spot poked Ben awake as the train pulled into North Station. He stuffed his water bottle into his backpack's side mesh pocket, shouldered the heavy bag, and nodded for the pups to exit the train.

The dogs kept close as they wound their way through the morning crowd. Aside from there being more people on the train, the ride into town had gone pretty much like their last one. Most commuters just gave the boy and his service dogs a friendly nod and a curious smile. The pups were already bored with train travel so they mostly napped clustered at his feet.

Ben had been in North Station a few times. It was located under the iconic Boston Garden sports arena and he had been to concerts and Celtic's basketball games there. The station wasn't nearly as nice as South Station, but the lobby had the same basic food kiosks, self-serve ticket machines, waiting area, and small ticket counter. Announcements droned from crackly speakers, but they were almost impossible to decipher.

Ben needed to transfer to Amtrak's Downeaster, and according to the hanging monitors the train was waiting on track nine. It didn't leave for an hour but they walked onto the covered train platform just to make sure. The huge hissing gray engine was head-in to the station and was hard to miss as it had 'Downeaster' plastered across its front in large white letters.

"Guess that's it," Ben said, and received tandem nods of agreement as he rummaged through his backpack and pulled out the first of four rubber-banded envelopes. It was labelled 'North Station' in Mimi's perfect scroll, and she'd written a name and a telephone number below it.

He hoisted his bag and led the pups to the Amtrak ticket window, where a round man with round glasses leaned into his microphone and grumbled in a dripping Boston accent, "What can we do for yah?"

"Hi," Ben said. "May I speak to April please?"

"Yah must be Ben Hogan," the man grumbled, and then shouted over his shoulder, "April!"

A nearby side door opened and a pretty, very curvy young woman walked through it. She wore a crisp blue Amtrak jacket with a matching tight blue skirt, and swinging from her neck was a lanyard with two dozen keys. She walked toward Ben with her hips swaying, but her feet only moved a few inches with each step so it seemed to take her forever to get to him.

When she was halfway the pups looked up at Ben but he ignored their raised eyebrows.

She was a little winded by the time she stopped in front of them, but she smiled a full white smile when she asked in a musical voice, "Hey hun, you Ben?"

Ben nodded.

"I'm April. You ready for your adventure?" she asked. Her head of thick, cascading shiny black curls shook with each word.

Spot and Smudge nodded that they were ready, but April didn't notice.

"We sure are," Ben said.

April took the paperwork from his envelope, scanned it, and led them to another ticket window that was manned by a short blonde woman with really pink cheeks.

"Hey girl," April said as she slid the paperwork through the slot. As the woman smiled at Ben and riffled through the papers April leaned on the window's little metal counter. Her ample hip cocked out and almost completely obscured Ben from the pups' view.

The dogs leaned far to the side and raised their eyebrows again at Ben from behind her curves.

Ben gave them a tiny headshake.

The woman behind the window typed a blinding barrage of keystrokes, and after a printer whined she folded something back into the paperwork and slid it through to April.

"Thanks love," she said, and then made sure Ben tucked the envelope safely back into his bag.

She led them to the center of the terminal where she pointed to the large overhead board. "Ben, you're on the Downeaster," she said. "Track nine. You can board in about a half hour. We'll announce it. Do you want me to wait with you?"

"No thanks," Ben said. "So that's it?"

"That's it," April said with a big smile. "You're all set. Did you call your grandmother?"

"No, but I will," he replied.

"Don't forget now," she said as she wagged a colorful fingernail at him. "You need anything else? Bathroom?"

Ben looked down at the pups, and then said, "Nope, I think we're good."

"Somethin' to drink?" April asked. "Or a snack maybe?"

Ben patted his bag and shook his head, but the pups nodded.

April noticed the dogs' synced nods, and when she chuckled her curves and curls shook. She touched Spot on the nose with a fingernail and said, "You sure you don't want me to wait with you?"

"No thanks," Ben said. "We're fine."

"Okay hun," April said. "I'm right over there if you need anything. Stay in the station, and don't get sidetracked, okay?"

Ben smirked at the pun, and the pups wagged.

April winked, and Ben said, "We won't. Thanks again."

As April walked away Smudge huffed that her caboose looked to be smuggling a bag of shar-peis.

Spot shook his head, and turned away from his sister to hide his chuckle.

They found a secluded bench at the back of the station, and Ben poured a little water into a bowl and split one of Mimi's sandwiches with the pups. He unzipped his jacket, pulled out his cellphone, and scrolled down to tap the farm's number.

"Hey Meem," he said, and then fielded her rapid-fire questions. "Yes, we're fine...No, I didn't lose the pups...Yep, she's very nice...Yep, she's waiting with me...Yep...Yep...Yes, I know...Yep...Okay...Okay...I will, I promise. Love you too, bye."

He shared a headshake with the pups as he texted with his sister and his parents, and received a thumbs-up, a string of Xs and Os, and a big heart and a smiley face.

He put away his phone, packed the water bowl back into his backpack, and settled back onto the bench with the pups curled up at his feet.

When he let out a yawn they exchanged tongue-curling ones of their own.

It had been a busy few days. In addition to just being super excited he'd had to figure out exactly what to bring and not bring from the mountain of clothes and gear he'd stacked up on his bed. The family had offered their often-conflicting suggestions, but at the same time they'd suddenly clammed-up about any details related to the ranch.

"You'll see," was their stock answer to all of his questions, which was followed by a big grin.

It was maddening, but also kind of fun. They'd made sure he packed plenty of warm clothes, and his mom had been pushing him to take a rolling bag but he hated that idea so Kelcy borrowed a really cool backpack from a bud. It had a single wide sling strap and large pockets for everything, and it even had a padded section for his tablet and satphone. It looked a little big on him, but everything fit and it wasn't too heavy.

Mimi had added zippered pockets inside the pups' vests so they were able to carry some of their own gear. Spot insisted on carrying their little tablet and Smudge carried her little stuffed chicken. It was the first thing she took out and put away whenever they stopped.

§§

Forty-five minutes later a commuter in a crisp business suit sat at one of the station's benches with a plastic spoon hanging from her mouth and a very confused look on her face.

Her bench was directly across from the one Ben and the pups had just darted away from, and she was trying to wrap her head around what she'd just seen.

Three minutes earlier she'd grabbed a yogurt from the snack kiosk and found a quiet bench to enjoy it. While she licked the tear-off lid and stabbed at the cup with the spoon she'd noticed the cute young man and the two adorable service dogs that were cuddled up at his feet. He was leaning against his backpack and the dogs had their chins on his feet, and they were all sawing lumber.

The overhead speakers screeched, and a garbled voice announced last call for the Amtrak Downeaster.

One of the dogs sleepily raised its head and cocked an ear toward the ceiling.

The announcement came again, and this time it ended with, "All aboooooard!"

The dog shot up and urgently pawed the boy a few times on the knee. The other dog woke up, and the first dog pointed angrily at it with its paw. The second dog shrugged its shoulders and shook its head, and then both dogs put their paws on the young man's knees and vigorously shook him awake. He sat up, rubbed his face, and looked down as one of the dogs quickly shook its paw like it was broken.

"What?!" the young man hissed. "Why the heck didn't you wake me up?!"

The woman stared with the spoon hanging out of her mouth as the young man grabbed his coat and backpack, and bolted through the lobby with the dogs running behind him.

When she turned back to her yogurt she noticed there was something on the floor under their bench.

It was a faded stuffed chicken.

She was thinking about getting up and chasing after them when one of the dogs tore back through the station, weaved through the crowd, and scooped up the toy at a run without slowing.

The dog disappeared through the doors as she licked the spoon and crinkled her confused brow.

CHAPTER 15

It took Ben fifteen hushed minutes on the phone and a dozen texts to convince his family everything was fine and they had made the train with no harm done.

Kelcy texted that he had exceeded the train's duh-nage limit, and Ben admitted with a winking smiley face that had been a pretty good one.

An old ticket taker wearing a smart blue uniform and red tie took a shine to the pups and had escorted them to a big curved seat at the front of one of the train's upper decks. He'd even asked some older teens to clear out and give the service dogs some room.

As he looked at Ben's ticket he asked, "So you gonna be with us all the way to Pahtland?"

Ben and the pups nodded, and the man said, "Well, you might as well make yourselves comfortable. If you have something to spread out on the seats the dahgs can hop up. I whant tell if you dan't."

There was something in the man's kind smile that reminded Ben of Papa.

The conductor checked back with them every so often, and even smuggled the dogs a few hotdogs from the snack car.

The Downeaster ran north from Boston and through the tip of New Hampshire before angling east to follow the coast into Maine. Ben and the pups followed their progress on the little satphone-tethered tablet and took turns reading little blurbs about the coastline, and how Downeast was the nickname for that area. The trip included stops at the oceanfront towns of Wells, Saco, and Old Orchard Beach, and the conductor paused as they pulled into each to explain the towns' charms, which had a lot to do with lobster. He explained in the summer months the train would be packed and those stops would be thick with sunburnt vacationers.

They arrived at the station in Portland, where Ben and the pups were met by the Hastings. Carl had worked for Papa at the printing factory and Mimi and Rebecca had kept in touch. Ben was starting to realize that everyone Mimi knew tended to stay in touch. His grandmother bought stamps by the roll for her Christmas cards.

As he and the pups jumped into the back of the minivan Rebecca told him they'd met before, and she launched into a very long story about how she'd taken care of Kelcy when Ben was getting born.

Ben and the pups stayed with the Hastings for a total of fourteen hours, and aside from the seven hours they were asleep Rebecca talked the entire time as she doted on them. Spot confirmed she actually did stop talking at some point after she turned out the bedroom light and closed the door, but Ben wasn't so sure as she was still talking when she came into their room the next morning. She'd even told the pups all about the dang squirrels eating her suet cakes while the pups were peeing in the back yard.

Rebecca prattled on about the factory and the Hastings' days in Pembury as Ben ate dinner, fed the pups, called home, washed up, went to bed, woke up, donned fresh drawers, ate breakfast, fed the pups, got resupplied with snacks, and was delivered on time to the Portland bus station.

Rebecca told Ben every detail of Kelcy's stopover when she'd gone up to Hamish's while Carl reviewed Ben's tickets with the bus driver. The driver gave them both a nod, and Ben stuffed the 'Portland' envelope back into his bag.

Carl gave the pups a pat and Ben's shoulder a gentle squeeze, and Rebecca was still saying goodbye as they climbed onto the bus bound for the Canadian border. He and the dogs took a seat, and as he waved down to his hosts he realized Carl hadn't uttered one word the entire visit.

Even with a full night's rest Ben and the pups were exhausted, partly from the trip and partly from trying to keep up with Rebecca's running dialog. So shortly after they settled into their seats they dropped back into a deep sleep.

Spot and Smudge were wrapped around each other on their fleece blanket, with the chicken plush toy sandwiched between them. The dogs took up the window seat and half of Ben's seat, but he was half laying on them so they were all comfortable.

Aside from the odd stretch or yawn they didn't move until the bus pulled into Bangor two hours later. A cold front had moved in overnight, and when they jumped off the bus for a bathroom break they were right back on it a minute later shaking like the last three leaves on a tree, as Mimi would have said.

CHAPTER 16

Two and a half hours later the bus pulled into the circular drop-off at the border crossing near the small town of Calais, Maine. The cheery bus driver announced the easternmost point in the United States was just a few miles down the road. He also announced the bus would pick up its disembarking passengers in Canada, on the other side of the lot after it had been inspected and the passengers had cleared border control.

Where the train had hugged the Maine coastline and offered intermittent views of rocky shores and the Atlantic, the bus had travelled inland, cutting through the rolling hills of the snowy Maine countryside. The land had started to stretch out into long uninterrupted spaces as they neared the border and moved away from the suburbs and strip malls. Ben texted a few pictures of the more interesting things he saw along the way, and at one stop he sent Kelcy a selfie of him and the pups peeing on a moose crossing sign.

He stepped off the bus with the pups, and as he was taking a pic of the huge side-by-side US and Canadian flags he walked right into a wall.

The wall was a massive dark man, and he was dressed in a sharp brown uniform with a matching puffy jacket. His reflective sunglasses looked down from under the brim of his US Border Agent baseball cap at Ben, who barely came up to the badge on his chest.

The pups stood perfectly still, and their eyes slowly climbed the man's body as their heads craned to look up at him.

The agent folded his thick arms across his chest and eyeballed Ben and the pups. At least Ben assumed he was being eyeballed, he couldn't tell through the man's sunglasses.

The agent looked up at the flags, and in the deepest voice Ben had ever heard said, "Ugly damn flags. Sicily has the best flag. It's a face between three women's legs."

Ben looked at the pups, and they wagged a single wag.

When the agent looked down at Ben again he asked, "Just where do you think you're going?"

"The great white north, sir," Ben said.

The agent boomed out a laugh that made the other bus passengers turn and stare.

"You wouldn't happen to be Ben Hogan, would you son?" he asked.

"Yes sir, I am," Ben said. "Are you Mr. Coleman?"

"I am not," the agent said as he held out his hand and flashed a huge white smile. "My dad's Mr. Coleman. I'm Ollie, and that useless bag of bones over there is Snyder." As Ben's hand disappeared into Ollie's massive mitt the agent nodded to a black and white border collie who was sniffing the snow at the far end of the parking lot.

In a normal voice that was louder than most peoples' yells, Ollie said, "Get over here and say hello, you lazy Frenchman."

When Snyder looked up Ben saw the dog's handsome black face was perfectly split by the iconic white blaze stripe. It started on his forehead, narrowed between his ice-blue eyes, flared around his nose, and created a diamond on his chest. He was about the same size as the pups, and he was wearing a vest as well. His was black, and it had large white POLICE patches on the sides.

Snyder trotted along a well-worn path in the snow until he got to the curve of the bus turnaround's sidewalk. When he joined them below the flags he sniffed a hello to the dogs and paused for a pat from Ben before he went to Ollie's side.

"Here, let me take that," Ollie said as he flipped Ben's pack over his shoulder like it was a purse. "Let's grab a quick bite before we kick you out of the country."

As the three dogs fell in line behind them Spot eyeballed the badge that was pinned to Snyder's chest.

Spot turned to Smudge and huffed, *We gotta get some of those.*

Smudge nodded, and Snyder wagged.

They walked into the bright lobby of the border crossing building, passed the gawking travelers queued at the inspection islands, and went through a set of side doors to a hallway that led to a small cafeteria.

Ollie dropped his hat, coat, and glasses onto one of the tables, and crossed the room to grab a cooler from the countertop.

"Give your Mimi a quick call," he said as he set out a lunch of fruit wedges and ridiculously thick sandwiches. He held out two cans to Ben, who tapped the can of ginger ale.

As Ben munched and chatted with Mimi, Ollie nodded to a large empty dog bowl on the floor.

Ben nodded, and Ollie filled it with kibble from a plastic tub.

The dogs lined up and ate together with their tails wagging. Spot and Smudge's swiped like wiper blades, and Snyder's randomly thwapped into them.

Ben handed the phone to Ollie so Mimi could thank him, and Ollie joked that the bill's in the mail before he said goodbye.

Between bites Ben asked Ollie how he knew his great-uncle, and Ollie told Ben he'd met Hamish Walker a long time ago when the big idiot had tried to bring his first team of sled dogs through the border crossing without any clue as to the correct paperwork.

After a few more sandwiches and several stories Ben was pretty sure he shouldn't have heard, Ollie nodded to a row of monitors on the break room wall and said, "Well, we should probably finish up. The line's moving pretty good out there."

Spot and Smudge stopped eating and came around the table to stand next to Ben.

When they looked up at Ollie he gave them a curious look, and noticed the lightning bolt and the U embroidered on their vests.

"You can finish if you want to," he said to them. "We're not in that big of a rush."

The pups looked at Ben, and then went to slurp water from another bowl with Snyder.

Ollie gave Ben a long sideways look as he took another enormous bite and chewed slowly. He swallowed, downed his can of soda, and then said, "When you see your great-uncle tell him he still owes me fifty bucks."

They packed up and put on their coats, and Ollie stuffed a big paper bag filled with snacks into Ben's backpack. They went back outside to the turnaround, and as Snyder introduced the pups to his bathroom area Ollie checked the paperwork from Ben's third envelope.

When the dogs came back Ollie led them inside to the islands of inspectors. He steered them to an empty lane, and a pert young woman smiled as they approached her.

"Once the beautiful Maria here is done with you just go through those doors," Ollie said as he pointed past her to a wall of windows. "Your bus is right there in lane six."

Ben saw it, and as he thanked Ollie he held out his hand.

Ollie smiled broadly as they shook. "You have a good time up there with that *foufolle* uncle of yours," he said. "He's a solid pain in the ass sometimes, but a better man I've never known."

Ollie and Snyder paused at the terminal's side door to watch Ben heft the backpack and walk to the bus. Spot and Smudge were trailing behind him, and they were trotting and wagging in perfect sync.

When the bus doors closed behind them Ollie pursed his thick lips, nodded to himself, and winked a thanks to Maria. He put on his sunglasses and kicked Snyder playfully on the behind to scoot him toward the vehicle inspection lot as he said, "Why couldn't Hamish make you that smart?"

The travelers at the other islands had thinned to a trickle, and at the last empty island a slight, pock-faced Asian customs agent watched Ollie and his dog cross the lot.

The man gently scratched the collar of his turtle-neck sweater, which hid the triangle-and-tree tattoo below his left ear.

He turned to watch Ben's bus pull away, and then typed into his phone, THEY HAVE LEFT CALAIS.

CHAPTER 17

A few hours later Ben flipped up his hood and spread his feet to steady himself on the treacherously icy sidewalk. He blew into his hands as he patiently waited for his pups, who were taking care of their business behind a tree.

The bus roared away, and with it no longer blocking the wind they were blasted by the stinging spray that was blowing in sideways from the Bay of Fundy.

As is the case with most girl dogs, Smudge crouches when she pees. Her brother is a boy, so he goes high-and-proud with a raised back leg.

When the gale hit them it caught Spot's stream and whipped it into a mist that swirled around both of them, and Smudge happened to be in full yawn at that exact moment.

Spot quickly cut off his stream and lowered his leg, and shrugged an apology to his sputtering, headshaking sister.

With a tandem shoulder-twitch they agreed never to discuss it as they trotted over to join Ben, who gave them a pat and just assumed it was sleet that wetted his hand.

He baby-stepped backward through the gale across the ice-rink parking lot with the pups shuffling flat-footed behind him until they stepped into the Saint John's ferry terminal.

Ben noted how all transportation hubs pretty much looked the same, although this one's signs were in English and French. He did a quick scan as he slipped his backpack off his shoulder to note the ticket window, the bathrooms, and the vending machines.

Bathroom first please, his lower region suggested.

He backed through the restroom door and held it for the pups. Once inside he set his backpack on the floor well away from the dirty triangle of slush that ran from the door to the urinals to the sinks.

The pups took up station on either side of his bag, and Ben bellied up to one of the urinals.

He had just opened the tap when someone loudly booted the bathroom door open. A big old codger in well-worn coveralls shuffled in and rubbed the knit skull cap off his head. His boots squeaked noisily on the wet tile floor as he stepped up to the urinal next to Ben. He unzipped, let out a long exhale, and unleashed a loud flow.

Out of the corner of his deeply weathered eyes he gave Ben a look.

Ben tried to stare straight ahead but couldn't help himself. He looked up at the man's thick white beard and wind-reddened cheeks.

"*Salut,*" the salty coot said with a slight nod as he studied Ben's face.

"Hello," Ben said. He wondered if the standard 'you don't look at me and I don't look at you' urinal etiquette didn't apply north of the border.

"*Comment vas tu?*" the man asked.

"Um, sure," Ben said as he looked back at the pups and shrugged.

The man turned to see what Ben was looking at and did a double take.

"*Ce que l'enfer?!*" he asked with a start. "Give me *crise cardiaque.* Where'd they come from?"

He'd turned his hips a little too far when he swung to look at the dogs, and then a little too far the other way when he turned back to Ben.

"They're with me," Ben said as he moved his foot away from the yellow the man had added to the slush.

The man looked down and noticed his stream had missed.

"Oh my friend, *vraiment desole,*" he said as he straightened his hips.

"S'okay," Ben said.

The man carefully craned back to take another look at the dogs, who were staring up at him with identically tipped heads. He turned back to scrutinize Ben's face for a moment before he asked, "You wouldn't be Hamish Walker's *petit-neveu?*"

After they finished and washed up the man offered Ben his hand and a broad smile as he said, "Emile Sain-John, this city was named after me."

Emile took Ben's backpack and escorted him to the ticket window. He spoke to the woman behind the counter in a mix of French and English as he handed her Ben's last envelope. When she was done Emile walked them through the lobby and got them settled by the wall of windows.

Beyond them was the large blue and white ferry that was tied up at the dock, and the whitecaps on the boiling, wind-whipped bay beyond it.

Emile insisted on buying at the vending machines, and as he and Ben returned to the pups with a coffee and a hot chocolate he said, "Known your *grand-oncle* for going on thirty years. You look like a miniature version o' him, only nowhere near as hairy, or as ugly. Buy him a *biere* or six when he passes through sometimes, and then he crashes on my canape when he misses the last ferry. Man's snores can raise *les morts*. Met your *grand-mere* and *grand-pere* a few times too. Fine people them."

Ben told him about Papa's passing, and Emile gave his shoulder a tender squeeze as he expressed his condolences in a quick string of French.

They chatted for a while longer, with Emile feeding the dogs pieces of sandwich from the bag lunch as he told Ben more Hamish stories he definitely shouldn't have heard.

Eventually Emile stood and said, "*Eh bien*, back to work for me. Ferry will start to board in a few minutes."

He shook Ben's offered hand, and said with a smile, "You tell that *fou renard* I said *salut*."

"I will sir," Ben said. "Thanks for the cocoa."

Emile saluted him with a wave, gave the pups a final pat, and pulled on his gloves and hat.

As he pushed through the doors to the docks he said with a laugh over his shoulder, "*Faites attention* in those north woods, Ben. And beware the *loup-garou!*"

Once they were hunkered down on the ferry and out of sight of anyone Spot looked it up on the mini-tablet.

He spun it around so Ben and Smudge could read it; WEREWOLF.

CHAPTER 18

The ferry's four-lane wide deck held dozens of cars and trucks, and above them was a large lounge with tables and rows of connected, comfortably padded seats. Windows ran around the lounge's perimeter, and Ben could see the slowly receding New Brunswick shoreline behind them and the angry, mist-shrouded bay in front of them.

He and the pups were camped out in a far corner of the front row, where the windows looked down on the bow of the ship and the whitecaps they were pushing through.

Smudge was sitting in the seat next to Ben on their fleece blanket.

She was facing him, and she'd been staring at him for the last five minutes.

Ben was facing forward, and he'd been ignoring her for the last five minutes.

She poked him on the shoulder with her snout again.

He continued to ignore her.

She poked him again. And again. And again.

"I don't care how bonnie she is," Ben whispered without looking away from his tablet.

Smudge looked casually at the ceiling, and then out the window, and then over her shoulder to the very pretty young girl who was sitting with her family a few rows back on the opposite side of the aisle.

The girl looked at Smudge with big brown eyes and smiled an adorable little smile.

Smudge turned back to Ben, double checked to make sure no one could see, and signed, *She just waved to you.*

"She did not," Ben whispered. He was hunkered down in the seat with his feet stretched out in front of him on his backpack.

Just go say hello, Smudge signed. *We've got another two hours on this tub. Who knows what can happen in two hours? We might hit an iceberg and you'll be sorry you didn't steal her away to fog up some car in the cargo hold.*

"Shut it," Ben grumbled, but then he snuck another quick look over Smudge's shoulder at the girl, who shot them an equally quick glance as she fixed a strand of her lovely long brown hair that wasn't out of place to begin with.

Ben quickly returned to pretending to look at his tablet, and she did the same to her phone.

What's the big deal? Smudge signed. *Do I have to show you how this works again?*

"I hate to break this to you," Ben whispered without looking up, "but binge watching 'Sex and the City' with Mimi does not make you a relationship expert."

Smudge let that go and signed, *Just go over there and sniff her bum, head-butt her, and then woo her with tales of your good grades and the upcoming science fair.*

Ben shook his head, and Smudge snuck another look at the girl.

On second thought, maybe you're right, Smudge signed. *By the looks of her I'd say she's been to band camp a few times, and she looks French, or maybe even Irish, may the saints preserve us.*

Ben ignored her.

Spot lifted his head off Ben's lap, looked around, and signed, *If you two don't quit it I'm gonna barf on both of you.*

The ferry was a big boat, but it still rocked a little in the stiff crosswind as it crawled across the bay, and Spot had gotten a little green around the jowls after they cleared the breakwaters.

He plunked his head back down onto Ben's lap with a groan.

Smudge stuck her tongue out at her brother as she tapped Ben on the shoulder and signed, *Or, if you need to use the men's room for some, you know, young man private time we can watch the stuff for three minutes.*

Ben successfully let that go after a deep breath.

Smudge continued to stare at him.

Ben continued to stare into his tablet.

Smudge very slowly leaned in closer to him until her snout was right next to his ear.

And she then exhaled heavily into it.

Ben did nothing.

Smudge slowly yawned, and extended her tongue as she uncurled it noisily. She gave his ear a long slow lick as she looked back at the girl, who saw it and smiled.

Ben patiently moved Smudge's snout away from his ear.

Smudge rested her chin on his shoulder, looked back at the girl, and signed, *I'd ride that into battle.*

Ben jerked his shoulder hard enough to almost knock Smudge off the seat, and in the process he bounced Spot's head off his lap.

Spot growled at them before he snatched Smudge's chicken and hopped down.

He trotted to the middle of their row, turned down the center aisle, walked right up to the girl, dropped the chicken in her lap, and wagged at her.

An hour later Ben was sitting with the pretty girl at a small round table near the windows. They had split a plate of chicken fingers and were laughing as they quietly compared French and English swear words.

The pups were playing on the floor with the girl's eight year old brother as they eavesdropped. They were getting a little sick of sit, shake, and roll over, but they were keeping the unimaginative kid suitably occupied.

The girl's parents stayed near the front of the boat but wandered back every few minutes to check on their daughter and her cute, if a little odd suitor. They made lame excuses about needing to use the bathroom or grab a beverage which caused the girl to roll her eyes and shoo them away.

Ben found her eye roll to be mesmerizing.

The next hour flew by, and as the ferry docked at Digby, Nova Scotia, they walked together to the terminal. Her parents had taken her younger brother with them to get the car, having reluctantly agreed to let her catch up with them in the parking lot after she threatened to murder both of them if they ruined her life again.

Inside the lobby of the terminal she and Ben exchanged contact info, and she stood dangerously close to him as they did so. She leaned in to make sure he spelled her name correctly as his thumbs struggled to type.

He could smell her hair.

And so could the pups, who were wagging as they stood in front of them and stared. They could also hear Ben's heart hammering in his chest.

He helped her with her coat after Smudge told him to.

She zipped up, patted the pups, touched Ben's sweating hand, and then said goodbye with the best smile he'd ever seen.

He watched her float away, and the pups exchanged proud nods as they watched him hover a few feet off the floor.

The girl bounced through the glass doors and out into the parking lot, and the way she pulled her fingers through her long hair as the wind whipped it made Ben's grin broaden into a simpleton's smile.

Before she disappeared into the rows of cars she shot him a final small wave.

And then she was gone.

"I'd ride that into battle," Hamish said from behind them.

Ben jumped a mile.

CHAPTER 19

Ben groaned and spun to point his backside at the fire. He was sharing a big comforter with the pups, who were sleeping at the far end of the couch. Smudge had her chin on her stuffed chicken, and Spot had his head on his sister's back.

Their slight snores were drowned out by the lumber-sawing German shepherd who was sprawled out on a blanket in front of the hearth.

When Sholto let out something that wasn't a snore Hamish shook his head at his ancient dog.

He'd paused at the back of the couch to look down at his snoozing grandnephew before he continued on down the creaking hallway and slipped into his office.

He slowly sunk into his chair, being careful not to spill his scotch or loose a ginger snap from the small plate he had balanced on top of the glass.

"Alright lass," he said to the phone that was pressed to his ear, "hauld yer wheesht. I'm sure you're doing your best. They're bawheeds, every last one of them. I wouldn't have picked them but we're stuck with them, and you'll just have to manage until I get there. How yeh getting on with the other two?"

As Hamish listened he stared out through his office windows to follow the lights of a creeping ship. It was a big freighter, which it had to be as the meter-high swells it was cutting through in the bay would be three times that when it hit the Atlantic.

His saltbox house had originally belonged to a ship captain's, and it sat high up on a bluff above the shoreline. From the top of the ridge he couldn't see the white tops of the waves below, there was just the dark of the water meeting the dark of the sky at the black line of the shore on the horizon. A few twinkling lights along that line struggled to poke through the fog and snow.

"Of course I'm glad to have 'em," he said, "I've nae' been down that way since the funeral, and I love that he's here. It's just we're under the gun now with this current lot. We're gonna be busier'n a one-armed pimp in a whore-skelping contest."

He tapped on his laptop to wake it up as he said, "I canae' say that? Fine, how about a one-legged cat in a litterbox?"

A gust of wind rattled his office windows and produced a low groan from somewhere in the old house. What had been a stiff breeze in the afternoon had turned into a gale after sundown and the constant wind was pounding up the cliffs and howling through the eaves. The snow wasn't heavy but it was blowing sideways as it flashed in the roving light from the lighthouse on the point.

"No, I donae' think he'll be any help," he said. "I'm guessing the kid's about as useful as a knitted condom."

He brought up the weather forecast, and dragged the map to the north with the tip of his finger until it showed central Quebec.

"Guess we'll find out soon enough," he said. "Jean says he's gotten to be right brilliant lately, and she's pretty truthful about such things, but I donae' know. He's always been a bit of a Nancy for my liking. His city parents spoiled him rotten. Still, he seems to have grown a foot, and he did manage to pick up a minty on the ferry. Maybe he's got a little squirt of Walker in him after all."

Hamish took a sip and a bite of cookie, and nodded to the weather report as it showed they should have good weather for the long drive north.

"By the way, yeh were wrong about your Sholto," he said. "The old bitch barely raised a hackle when his dogs came strolling in like they owned the bloody place. The wee curs seem smart enough, and they're bigger than I would have thought based on Jean always calling them her pups. Truth be told, they're plenty solid for nonworking dogs."

He wiped crumbs off the keyboard and closed the laptop as he said, "The boy does handle them well, maybe yeh can find something to keep him busy with after all."

After another long pull from his drink and another bite of cookie he said, "Yeh can always tell him all about yer sex life, that'll keep the pain in the arse occupied for six seconds. Of course four of those seconds will be him rolling on the pitch laughing. And speaking of depressing failures, when's our next conference call?"

They chatted and insulted each other for a few more minutes, and after Hamish hung up he drained the last of his glass and stood up.

He noticed one of Ben's black pups was watching him from the hallway.

The dog stared up at him, and he stared down at the dog.

"Are yeh needing to pish again wee girl?" he asked.

CHAPTER 20

Hamish kicked the end of the couch for the third time in fifteen minutes. "Let's go lad, drop yer knob and forget her gob," he said as he put on his tam. "We've got lots of road to chew on, and yeh can dream about her in the truck."

His heavy feet thumped away and he slid a heavy cooler off the kitchen table before tapping open the back storm door with his boot.

As the door banged shut behind him Ben dangled his feet over the couch and rolled to a barely upright position.

Spot dragged his backpack over and signed, *Come on Hef, he's starting to get annoyed.*

"What time is it?" Ben groaned as he squinted at the windows flanking the fireplace and saw only black outside.

Four-fifteen, Spot signed.

"Jeez," Ben said as he grabbed the comforter and let his head fall back onto the pillow.

Spot watched the back door as he unzipped the backpack and started pulling out a change of clothes.

He huffed across the room, *Sis, little help here.*

Smudge was laying back to back with Sholto on her blanket, after having just shared a snack and a morning pee. Hamish had said Sholto was getting up there in years, which was obvious, but he'd also told Ben she'd been through a lot for a dog and she was getting a little bit daft and a lot bit ornery. The pups had found all of those things to be absolutely true, and the crotchety ex-army dog and Smudge were getting along famously.

Smudge excused herself and went over to the couch. In one move she flipped the comforter onto the floor, grabbed Ben by the ankle, and pulled him off the couch. She returned to the blanket and plopped down next to an amused, wagging Sholto.

Before Ben could protest Hamish yanked open the storm door and strode into the kitchen.

"It's alive," he said as Ben pulled on his socks and shot Smudge a dirty look. "Grab some grub and give yer fizzog a quick splash, we're off in ten."

When he grabbed another large cooler from the kitchen counter Ben offered to help but Hamish grumbled something about almost being done, and how the coolers were bigger than the useless lad anyway.

A few minutes later Ben was standing at the kitchen sink wolfing down a bowl of cereal as he watched Hamish load his big pickup. The truck had four doors, double rear wheels under wide flared fenders, and a matching top over the extended bed. It was a deep maroon with chrome trim, and it had leather seats and a sunroof and a cool nav system. Ben had expected Hamish to be a bit of a slob based on Mimi's description, but aside from fresh mud behind the tires the truck was as nice as his house.

As Ben rinsed his bowl he watched Hamish carry a medium-size engine across the driveway. It wasn't big enough to have come from a car, but looked to be larger than a lawnmower. When he dropped it onto the tailgate the suspension creaked and the whole back end lowered a few inches.

Ben had forgotten how big his great-uncle was. Hamish came to Mimi's just about every summer for a visit, and the kids had always stared up at him like he was a tree. Ben's dad was pretty tall, and Papa had been as well, but Hamish was bigger still and a lot wider. Seeing him toss the engine around Ben realized his uncle was truly a redwood of a man. With his tight gray beard, buzz-cut hair, and tam hat he looked like a story-book lumberjack. Ben's mom said Hamish was a very handsome bloke, and Mimi said in his ruttin' days he had a lass in every port and two waiting in the lighthouse. Kelcy said he looked like every hipster *thinks* they look, and their dad added that Hamish had been rocking that look since before those hipster's fathers were able to grow fuzz.

CHAPTER 21

Ben raised his head only once during their drive east through Nova Scotia, when they stopped for a quick bathroom break just outside of Halifax. The sky had just started to lighten and he nodded right off again before they pulled out of the gas station parking lot and headed north.

Hours passed as he slept. At some point they left Nova Scotia and crossed into New Brunswick, where they hugged the coastline. The road wound around inlets and took them through a dozen fishing villages, but he snoozed through them all.

He eventually returned to the living as the sun rose above the trees, and as he rubbed the sleep from his eyes Hamish explained they had entered the Acadian region. He said it had originally been a French colony and was still thick with French speakers, and their bloody odd culture. He also told Ben to keep his eyes peeled as it was also full of really easy girls.

Hamish's weather report had been correct and the sun beat back the northern Atlantic's spiteful January chill. By mid-morning it was almost warm, and the kilometers flew by in a blur of sunny snow fields and quick stops for food and gas.

Hamish drove like someone was chasing him, and Ben wondered if the truck only had an on and off switch. They'd go from a dead stop to whiplash speed as the truck's big v-ten engine roared, and then back to a screeching halt with little variation in between. It took a bit of getting used to but they were making great time, and the pups had learned to follow Sholto's lead as she'd mastered the cadence of leaning and digging in to avoid getting toppled off the back seat.

Ben followed their route on his tablet using the satphone tether, chatted a bit with his family and friends, and sent a few pix to his teachers. When he'd told them he was going to Canada for three weeks most of them didn't even mention homework as he was already months ahead. They'd pretty much stopped checking his assignments anyway, and his math teacher had said she'd give him an A if he held off raising his hand in class so the other kids could answer a question.

But he had no such arrangements with Mr. P.

His social studies teacher had forbade Ben from working ahead, and he'd actually used the word forbid. In his lilting, effeminate voice he'd explained to Ben that the experiential benefits of collaborating with his classmates to uncover the mysteries of social studies was far too important a life lesson to be rushed.

Mr. P had reluctantly agreed to *let* Ben leave school for three weeks only after he promised to send frequent updates to the class about his 'Kerouacian odyssey', including one video call per week. When Ben told Spot about it he'd rolled his eyes, and suggested they take Mr. P on a journey out to The Bogs to introduce him to One Ear and the pack.

The pups were content to chill in the back of the truck with Sholto. They had plenty of room and alternated between napping and checking out the smells and the scenery. Ben hopped over the seat a few times to hang with them and sneak in a quick signed chat when Hamish wasn't paying attention.

The pups were also getting to know Sholto. Ben could tell they were having full-blown dog conversations, and whenever they stopped the three of them trotted off together as they rubbed and bumped one another. He'd didn't need the pups to interpret how much Sholto was taking a shine to Smudge. The old shepherd leaned on the pup when she slept, which was most of the time.

Ben could also tell his sensitive Smudge was worried about Sholto. Whenever anyone in the Hogan-Walker house was even a little off Smudge was usually found lying on top of them, and she pitched a tent on Sholto. She even shared her stuffed chicken when they napped.

Sholto moved a little slowly, and she wheezed and panted a bit, but she seemed happy enough. She wagged a lot and clearly adored Hamish, even when he was cursing at her for being the last one in or out of the truck. As he held the door for her he'd say things like, "Always at the coo's tail, aye?" or, "Yer slowr'n custard when it's *snellin'*, yah daft arsepiece."

He also said she had one paw on a banana peel and one in the grave, and that he'd stopped buying the big bags of dog food, and everything was Sholto's last thing, as in, "C'mon Sholto, time for your last bloody truck ride," or, "Yeh enjoyin' your last biscuit Sholto?" or, "Sholto, finish your last jobby so we can go."

Ben and Spot found it to be hilarious, Smudge not so much.

They also figured out Hamish drove like a madman partly because he liked to stop more often than they needed to. The truck had a huge gas tank and they didn't need to pee that often, but they still jumped off the highway almost every hour to say hello to someone, and to eat.

Hamish liked to share at least a snack with everyone they ran into. There were plates of fried bacon at pubs, and sliced deer sausage shared over tailgates, and more than a few lobster rolls shared over boat gunwales as all of the towns had fishing fleets nestled in cliff-protected coves. Bouctouche, Loggerville, Bathurst, Tide Head, all offered a quick meal of lobster bake, or fricot, or smoke meat sandwiches, and Ben stopped counting at five kinds of poutine. Fricot was similar to Mimi's stovies, a stew of potatoes and onions and whatever meat was available. Ben fell in love with the poutine rapees, which was a pork-stuffed potato dumpling that Hamish dunked into maple syrup.

There also seemed to be a direct connection between what they ate and Hamish's habit of destroying the inside of the truck mere minutes later, loudly. Ben and the pups were thankful it was a warm day as they rode many miles with the windows cracked open. Sholto didn't seem to notice the smell, in fact the pups confirmed Ben's suspicions that she was responsible for more than a few of the vile affronts to their environment.

Sholto went everywhere Hamish did, and was given a bite of everything they ate, and Ben was happy to see his pups were just as welcome. Whether it was tossed to them or handed over with a pat, everyone they met fed the dogs.

After the first few stops he noticed Spot was studying Hamish, and the warm reception they received by the people they were sharing food with. He told Ben to watch carefully as there was real power in eating together. *If you want to feel that power in its primal form come have a meal with a pack of coyotes*, Spot signed to him. *But the effect is no different than that captain handing you a piece of the cod he'd just smoked.*

Spot also pointed out the people they met definitely got stranger the farther north they went, which also seemed to be directly tied to their affection for Hamish. His great-uncle had driven the route from his home in Digby to the Quebec ranch hundreds of times and had shaken a thousand hands, and Ben was beginning to understand if you met a Walker once you met them forever, especially Hamish.

He also noticed his great-uncle and his odd mix of friends communicated mostly through insults. Their banter was a constant barrage of subtle and not-so-subtle abuse. Ben knew the Scots had raised cube-cracking to high art centuries ago, but he'd never seen such virtuoso performances in public. The French they met were pretty good at it, as were the First Nations people and the Danes, but Hamish trumped them all, even other Scots. There were some women who gave him a run however, and Ben noticed flirting played a role in their ball-busting as well. By the end of the day he fully understood the respect, deep connection, and love that could only come from telling someone their mom's got balls and their dad loves it.

He didn't see how a mere compliment could ever compete.

Hamish had also fallen into a cadence of flinging insults at Ben every time he climbed in or out of the truck. There was always some small chore to be done and Hamish spouted some classics like, "Hey, Skippy McArsemuncher, that bag's not going to toss itself out," or, "There'll be no milquetoast mollycoddling here lad."

Ben had silently laughed them off until he was struggling to put one of the heavy coolers back into the truck, and Hamish had watched from two feet away with his arms folded.

"We pull our own around here, Nancy," he'd said, to which Ben had responded not quite under his breath, "I'm sure you do Unc."

Hamish had looked down at him, roared with his head tossed back, and clapped him hard enough on the shoulder to almost make him drop the cooler.

The names of the towns and even some of the people sparked memories for Ben. He was finally experiencing the places he'd only heard about in his family's best stories, and nearly every stop triggered a memory of Papa's rollicking tales. Many of them were about Hamish, but plenty of them included his grandparents as they'd all lived in the region. It was no coincidence Nova Scotia meant New Scotland, and Ben had seen enough pictures of the rolling hills and wild flower covered pastures of eastern Canada to know it reminded his family of the old country.

Of course he remembered every word of those stories, but he goaded Hamish into retelling them simply by starting them off wrong.

"Bah! Yer bum's oot the window lad," Hamish would say as he cut him off. "That's what they told yeh? Well, 'snot what happened at all. Yeh see Duncan, yer Papa, was getting his arse handed to him by a yocker of a sailor when I strolled in and..."

Hamish's colorful and massively embellished versions certainly wouldn't be Mimi-approved, which meant Ben and the dogs were absolutely riveted.

They were having an incredible time and it wasn't just the stories and the sensory flood that comes with travelling through new and amazing places. The best part was he and his dogs were experiencing it together, and their quick signs and wags and eye rolls just made every joke, vista, and taste seem all the more vibrant.

As they crossed into Quebec and left the Acadian coast the highway narrowed to one lane. They continued north along the inland route until they came to the Gulf of Saint Lawrence, which

Hamish explained was the head of the mighty river that took ships all the way to the Great Lakes.

The hills had been getting larger throughout the day and the shore road was hugging steep cliffs that were hinting at proper mountains.

Exhausted from the excitement of the drive, and from eating twice his body weight, Ben napped again as the late afternoon sunlight picketed through the trees.

Later, as the sun was starting to set, Hamish aimed the truck down an exit and cut the corner at the end of the ramp without slowing. Gravel crunched under the truck's skidding tires and pinged loudly in its wheel wells.

Ben shook awake and spun around to check on the pups. He suspected they'd been snoozing as well as they were both staring at him wide-eyed as they gripped the front edge of the seat. If black fur hadn't covered their paws he was pretty sure their knuckles would have been white.

Sholto hadn't stirred and was out cold between them.

Hamish caught the pups staring at him in the rear-view mirror.

"Don't watch me drive," he said with a smile. "It makes me nervous."

He moved the wheel back and forth and the truck swayed sideways as it careened down the country road. The pups were tossed around in the back seat as something heavy thumped loudly in the truck's bed.

Hamish pulled the wheel hard and they roared into a small tree-lined parking lot. He stomped the brakes and the truck skidded to a stop on the crushed seashells the lot used for gravel.

When the dust cleared Ben saw they were facing a vine-covered walkway with an ornate carved sign that read, 'LA FALAISE DE CHIENS - Bed and Breakfast'.

Hamish opened the back door to let Sholto out, but he held up his hand to stop Spot and Smudge.

"Hold yourselves," he said. "Ben, can yer pups behave in a restaurant?"

Spot and Smudge looked at Ben with eager eyes. They could smell a hundred great scents coming from the large house at the end of the path. Ben thought about letting Smudge stay in the truck for the couch stunt she had pulled that morning, and he paused just long enough to make the point before he said, "Yeah, they're fine."

It had been fourteen hours since they'd left Digby and they were all a little stiff. Hamish groaned as he removed his tam, and the five road-weary travelers all stretched out their kinks as they entered the house.

The floorboards creaked under Hamish's weight as they walked down the stately Victorian home's ornate central hallway. It took them to an amazing sunroom that was perched high above a rocky inlet. The inlet led to a cove, and they could see the swells of the gulf beyond its breakwaters. On the far curve of the cove a cluster of white fishing boats were huddled together in the calm water, and a few dozen colorful houses dotted the hills behind them.

There was a row of cafe tables along the sunroom's windows, and a long dining table with two dozen chairs running down its middle. Other than Hamish, Ben, and the three dogs, the place was empty.

"What's a bloke gotta do to get some scran in this dump?" Hamish asked.

From behind a narrow set of double doors they heard a silky, French-infused woman's voice say almost in a whisper, "Call the constables, there's a sheep-shagging Jock in the house."

Sometime later Ben wiped his mouth with a white cloth napkin after finishing his milk. He drew a big breath and said, "Miss Rene, that was by far the most incredible cheeseburger I've ever had, and I've had them all."

Miss Rene chuckled a nearly silent, tinkling laugh, and tipped her cigarette into a crystal bowl as she ran her red fingernail around the rim of her china cup.

"My handsome Mr. Ben," she said in a voice that was barely louder than a breath. "You are welcome to visit me any time, provided you come alone. Well, they can come too." She nodded to the three dogs who were lying on a blanket happily munching on chunks of shoulder bone.

Miss Rene wore a flowing, low-cut dress that matched her nails, and she smelled like the good soaps Mimi kept in the bathroom but never used. She swung a shoe from the painted toes of a slender foot that connected to a shapely leg that seemed to go on forever.

While her guests had been devouring dinner Miss Rene told Ben the history of her house, and of Anticosti, the island across the strait that sat at the mouth of the St. Lawrence River.

As her story unfolded Ben had been whisked away. Her intoxicating accent was like a warm soft pair of hands holding his face, and the tip of her cigarette moved like a snake charmer.

Miss Rene told them her great grandfather had sailed across the Atlantic from Bayonne, and when he landed in Acadia he'd run afoul of the local crooked magistrate on Anticosti. He was tossed into the local jail, which was guarded by savage dogs. Those dogs were fed by the magistrate's beautiful indentured niece, who also fed the prisoners. She fell in love with the charming French sailor, and one night she broke him out of jail. They were discovered as they fled, and a fight ensued. The guards shot at them, and she shot back. Her bullet found her wicked uncle, whose dying command to his men was to kill them both. The lovers escaped into the river, but their little skiff had been shot full of holes. The boat sank in the dangerous currents of the strait, and just as they were about to drown, and share their last kiss, the guard dogs she had fed since they were pups leapt into the water and pulled them to the safety of the far bank. The lovers scaled the cliffs, and built their house on this very spot.

"And so this is Hound's Cliff," Miss Rene said as her exhaled smoke curled out of her red lips. She gave Ben a sultry smile, and whispered, "Some say they never left, so be mindful when you roam my halls. The lovers still like to slip out for a swim with their dogs."

As Hamish watched Ben melt in Miss Rene's silky clutches he smiled, and thought, *Vive la femmes Francaise.*

He noticed Spot and Smudge's heads were identically tipped, and they seemed to have the same dreamy look on their little black faces as Ben. They had stopped gnawing on their bones and hadn't looked away from Miss Rene for several long minutes.

They caught Hamish looking and lowered their heads back down to lick their bones, but they still watched Miss Rene.

After dinner Hamish took Ben and the dogs for a stroll down to the marina, and then Miss Rene got him and the pups settled into an upper room. She placed a small plate of chocolates and a bottle of water on the night table, turned down his covers, and paused to take his chin in her hands and tip it up until their eyes met. When she asked her handsome Mr. Ben if he needed anything else it was almost a whisper.

Ben was transfixed by the feeling of her long nails on his face, and by her stare, and her perfume, and he barely managed to shake his head.

Miss Rene smiled and softly kissed him on the forehead after bidding him *bonne nuit.*

She glided out of the room and pulled the door closed behind her, and Ben noticed his pups were staring at the door with their heads tipped. Their nostrils were flaring, and when they blinked and looked up at him it was like they'd just woken up from a trance. Whatever the heck that had been apparently worked on dogs too.

The room had a small covered veranda with a bench that overlooked the gulf. Ben and the pups wrapped themselves up in an impossibly thick comforter and cuddled on the bench to watch the ships go by. Smudge held her little plush chicken toy in her split paws as she and her brother rested their chins on Ben's knees.

It was a clear night and they could make out the crewmembers moving on the decks of the huge ships that slipped by in the dark.

As they took turns picking out the constellations in the billions of overhead stars they laughed about the characters they'd met, and about Hamish telling Sholto that if she passed tonight she could spend eternity swimming with the lovers and their dogs.

When they finally turned in Ben immediately fell into a hard sleep but the pups watched the ships for a while from the foot of the bed.

They also heard Miss Rene's soft whispering approval of whatever Hamish was doing to her in one of the lower bedrooms.

"I'm not sure this would fit their definition of subtle," Jia's big bodyguard Lucy whispered with his breath rolling out as fog. "And didn't you say she wanted us to wait until we met up with their asset in Piege?"

He was following Jia across the crushed seashell driveway, and although they were creeping quietly each footstep felt like it was making a loud crunch in the still, frozen air.

"It's called initiative," Jia whispered as they slipped around the big maroon pickup truck. "You should try it sometime."

She blew into her balled fists, and mist rolled out from between her fingers as she added, "An empty bed and breakfast couldn't be more perfect. They're frequent targets for robberies, and sometimes those robberies go wrong."

The shrug of Lucy's huge shoulders indicated he wasn't convinced.

"It's subtle enough," Jia said, "because I'm done freezing my yellow buns off chasing these two around this shitty little country."

"Canada is actually the exact same size as the US," Lucy said. "They're both three point eight million square—"

Jia cut him off with a glare. The steam from her exhale exited her nostrils like a mad bull's.

Lucy found that really funny but decided to hold his cartoon joke.

The moonlight broke into shafts as they walked under the arched trellis and stopped at the ornate carved glass front door. In an alcove next to the door was a statue of a small dog holding a lantern. In its glow they saw a doorbell and a hand painted sign that read "PLEASE RING AFTER HOURS" in both English and French.

Jia stepped aside to let Lucy pass her.

He didn't. He just stared at the door handle.

"Well?" Jia asked.

"I don't like dogs," Lucy said.

Jia put her hands on her hips and said, "Didn't you say the old geezer and his decrepit shepherd looked like they were about to fall over when they dragged their asses in here?"

Lucy shrugged.

"The shaggy old thing's likely to have a heart attack when it sees your big black ass," Jia said. As she pinched a hunk of his leather jacket at the elbow and steered him toward the door she added, "And the boy's runts are barely north of being puppies."

"Remember," she added, "don't kill them. We need the boy unscathed."

Lucy nodded, turned to face the door, and slipped his huge pistol from his shoulder holster. He spun the gun in his hand, brought the butt close to the glass, and picked a spot next to the lock.

"Wait," Jia hissed as she reached out and held his arm. She leaned past him to thumb the paddle on the door's big brass handle. The latch clicked softly, and when she pushed the door it swung open with a soft whisper.

Lucy took two steps into the house, stopped, and turned back around.

Without a word he walked right past Jia and continued down the covered walkway. He stepped into the moonlight and kept on going with his boots crunching softly on the parking lot's shells.

Jia stared at her bodyguard's broad back with a questioning look until he disappeared into the dark. She shook her head and reached into her pocket for her own pistol.

And then she heard the growl.

She turned slowly back to the doorway, and silhouetted against the moonlit windows at the far end of the hall was the old man's

German shepherd. The fur on its neck was puffed up, its ears were laid back on its head, and its upper lip quivered above an impressive set of fangs.

Its low growl rolled down the hallway and crept up Jia's spine, and she thought the dog didn't look very decrepit at all. In fact it looked rather formidable, and really pissed off.

It took one step toward her.

Jia slowly reached out, grabbed the door handle, and gently swung it closed between them until it clicked shut.

In the little bedroom on the fourth floor Spot felt Smudge stir against him.

You okay? he huffed softly.

Yeah, Smudge replied as she rotated her perked ears. *But Sholto's not happy about something.*

Spot dropped his head onto his sister's back and closed his eyes as he huffed, *Miss Rene's ghost dogs are probably trying to steal Sholto's last bone.*

The next morning Ben watched through the windshield as Miss Rene rose up on her toes to put Hamish's tam on his head. She gave him a long hug and a slow kiss on both cheeks, and her fingers trailed off his back as he walked away. She flicked a goodbye to Ben with her cigarette and wistfully ran her hand along the trellis as she strolled back into the house.

Hamish fired up the truck and spit gravel shells as they flew into the street without him looking in either direction for traffic.

As they pulled back onto the highway he tipped his head toward Ben and said with a smile and a waggle of his brows, "Dodged a bullet with that bird a few decades ago lad. Might have been a bloody mistake."

CHAPTER 22

They took the Matane-Comeau ferry across the St Lawrence River and continued north through Quebec.

An hour later Hamish announced he needed a break for, "A single fish and crisps," which Ben knew was a stop for a piss and potato chips, not to be confused with, "A jobby and a poke," which was a crap and French fries.

Ben and the pups were in the back seat sharing a bag of flame-grilled Aberdeen Angus crisps, while Sholto sat up front and Hamish fed her crisps infused with whisky. Ben had been astonished by the variety of potato chips available in even the smallest store, including haggis flavored, which he had to try and Hamish had to finish. They had a dozen half-empty bags in the truck at one point before they both groaned and agreed to a crisps-ercism.

When the snow-covered pine forest parted at the banks of a wide river Hamish looked in the rear-view mirror and said they were seeing something very rare, and it was the largest of its kind in the world.

Ben brought up their location on the little tablet's mapping app, and saw the river was actually a huge ring lake. It was a perfect circle with a round island in the middle.

"Manicouagan Reservoir," he read as the pups book-ended him and stared down at the tablet. "Why's it round?"

"It was made by an asteroid that was larger than Manhattan," Hamish said as the road followed the gentle curve around the ring. "It's called an annular lake, and you can see it from space."

Smudge subtly signed that it looked like someone had shot a hole in Quebec.

"It's the great white north's arsehole," Hamish said with a chuckle from the front seat. "Complete with a turtle head poking out."

From the ring lake they turned northwest, and the low mountains started to build into proper ones. The pines got taller and crept closer to the road, and every curve brought them higher and rewarded them with breathtaking views whenever they broke through the trees.

The hours came and went, and all signs of civilization fell away as they wound their way deeper into the remote mountains of central Quebec.

Ben had drifted off again, and he woke with a start when the truck braked hard before it rumbled loudly over a grid of cattle guards. He was in the front seat, and when he turned around to check on the pups Spot nodded at the windshield.

Ben turned back forward, and his mouth dropped open when he saw the massive timber archway they were heading toward. It topped the hill they were climbing, and its complex grid of foot-thick logs sat on fieldstone abutments that flanked two huge iron gates.

As they passed beneath it he read the large iron sign that hung from the lowest row of timbers, "Amaruq Irriq."

"Aye lad," Hamish said as the road fell away over the crest and a beautiful snow-covered valley spread out below them. "Welcome to the third largest timber ranch in Quebec."

The road snaked back and forth down the mountain, disappeared into the thick forest, and reappeared again at the bottom of the valley where it followed a narrow river to a small clearing. In the middle of the clearing was a small log house and a red barn. On the other side of the river the dense pine forest returned and climbed the slopes of the mountains in the distance.

Ben noticed their tops were hidden in clouds and the gray of the oncoming night, and when he looked at the clock on the dashboard he was surprised to see it was only half past three. It was already getting dark and the truck's headlights were faintly lighting up the snow that had started to fall.

It took another half hour to pick their way down the valley's switchback road before they came to the icy banks of the river.

Ben was surprised by its size. What had looked to be a stream from the top of the ridge was a wide tumultuous river when they got up close.

Hamish read his confused look and said, "The first lesson you gotta learn is distances can be deceiving up here. The low sun and blue-shifted light can shrink kilometers, making the vast snow fields look like little backyards and the peaks seem closer than they really are. Errors in visual perception have caused the end of more than a few poor buggers above the fiftieth parallel, and it gets worse the farther north you go. We've found a few corpsicles who saw a camp twenty clicks away and thought, 'I'll just stroll on over to the neighbors for a wee cuppa'."

"I bet", Ben said. "I woulda' bet the river was just a hop, skip, and a jump from the entrance. Papa had tried to teach me how to use trees to judge distance but I never got the hang of it."

"Aye," Hamish said. "Duncan was always a canny bastard when it came to that sort of thing. Mature trees of the same species tend to grow to the same height, depending on their location on the mountain. I'll show you how to judge it proper when we're on the trail, and I'll show you how to trust the dogs' sense of distance. They don't have red cones so they aren't fooled by the blue shift as much as we feeble blokes are. They also haven't lost their appreciation for that cold fucker old man death like some of us idjet humans. A good dog won't let you do something stupid."

Spot and Smudge nodded to each other in the back seat.

Ben smiled at his great-uncle. He was excited, and at the same time he was also very sad. He'd been dreaming about this ranch since he was five and finally seeing it was an amazing payoff, but Hamish was too much like Papa.

Not that there weren't some differences. Papa rarely swore, and his insults had been far subtler, and although his voice had been just as powerful it was half the volume of Hamish's. But their teaching and storytelling voices had the exact same musical firmness, and when Hamish was describing reading the trees and relying on the dogs it could have been Papa speaking.

With that same voice Papa had taught Ben a million things, and he'd promised to take him up to this ranch when he was ready.

Smudge picked up on the change in Ben's breathing and she stepped through the gap in the front seats. She nudged his arm up to force him to give her a rub as she tenderly licked his face.

Hamish had also noticed Ben's brow was working overtime, and he had a pretty good idea what was tugging at the lad.

He wasn't surprised the dog was trying to lift the boy's spirits. Sholto did the same thing to him when he got to grumping about something.

As Smudge got Ben smiling again Hamish said cheerily, "So who's hungry?"

Smudge's tail thwapped her brother and Sholto, and she gave Hamish a quick lick on his fuzzy cheek.

The truck passed through a smaller version of the same gate, and clanged over another row of metal cow guards. As they entered the clearing on the valley floor Ben realized he had also been wrong about the size of the barn and the ranch house. They were both huge. The red post and beam barn was three stories tall, and the all-glass entrance to the log and stone house was even taller.

The circular driveway brought them under a timber portico, and as they rolled to a stop one of the giant front doors opened and a young woman stepped out. She was wearing camouflage pants and an army-green thermal top, and she waved enthusiastically at them.

Sholto was up and scratching at the rear door, and Hamish asked Ben to reach back and let her out.

Ben didn't know the old dog could move so fast. She wobbled and faltered a little when she hit the pavement but quickly got her feet under her and shot across the walkway to the porch. The woman knelt as Sholto got close and they fell into a pile when the wagging shepherd hit her.

"Know each other?" Ben asked.

"Aye, I suspect so," Hamish said with a laugh.

The pups' tails were thumping against the back of his seat so Ben said, "Sure, go say hi."

They jumped down and raced off, and as Hamish got out of the truck he said, "Whatever you do, don't bloody stare when you meet her."

"Wait, don't stare at what?" Ben whispered, but Hamish had already shut the door.

Ben grabbed his pack from the back seat, and as he slid out of the truck the woman put a hand on his shoulder and said, "Hey there young man."

Ben turned and was pulled into a crushing hug.

When she pushed him back to arm's length she scanned his face and said, "God, you look just like your handsome dad. I'm Christa."

Ben held out his hand, and Christa smiled as she shook it.

"I'm Ben, Ben Hogan, ma'am," he said as he scanned her face looking for some hideous deformity but found nothing but a warm smile. "Thanks for letting me and my pups come here. Your house is ginormous, I mean awesome."

"Drop the ma'am shit son," Christa said. "How's your family?"

"They're fine ma'am, um, sorry," Ben said. "They send hugs and kisses, and I'm supposed to tell you thanks from Mimi."

Ben gave the rest of her a quick looking over and didn't find any lumps or extra appendages that shouldn't be there. She was about his mom's height, and maybe a little younger, and she was pretty. Her skin looked to be snow-tanned and her long black hair was braided tight to her head and pulled back into a ponytail. She was slim, but based on her curvy shoulders and arms, and that hug, he guessed she was pretty strong.

"Tell her she's very welcome," Christa said. "And I already got enough kisses from these two."

She looked down at the pups, who were standing at her sides wagging in sync.

"Your Mimi said they're a handful," Christa said, "but they don't look so bad to me."

"Spot, Smudge, this is Christa," Ben said. He had a flash of worry that they were going to offer to shake her hand with a split paw but they settled for a tandem head bow.

Christa laughed, and as she grabbed an ear on each dog she correctly guessed which was which, "Hello Spot and Smudge."

The dogs wagged, and from the back of the truck Hamish said, "When you Skippy McArsemunchers are done playing grab-ass come be useful."

They joined him at the tailgate, and when he tossed Christa a duffle bag that was almost as big as Ben she snatched it and slung it over her shoulder in one smooth move.

Hamish tossed a smaller bag to Ben, shut the tailgate, and booted Sholto on the backside as he said, "C'mon most useless, let's get yeh yer last meal."

"That's not funny," Christa said as she tried to catch the shepherd's wagging tail. "You'll be paying the boatman long before Gunny does."

Christa noticed Ben's confused look, and said, "Gunnery Sergeant Sholto, the hardest charging, loudest barking, ass-bitingest bitch in the history of the Royal Canadian Dragoons."

Ben looked down at the gentle, thin-in-the-hips, slightly hunched old dog and struggled to picture her fighting anything other than slick floors and icy driveways.

Hamish led them toward the house, and Ben noticed Christa walked with her feet slightly apart. It gave her and odd rocking gait, but it was subtle and he wouldn't have noticed it if he wasn't studying her for things not to stare at.

As they strolled down the covered walkway Christa asked him about the trip, and noticed he'd stopped looking at her.

She leaned forward and smacked Hamish hard on the back of the head as she said, "You told him not to stare? What is it with you Jocks and your sick humor?"

A chuckling Hamish caught his flying hat and hunched in anticipation of another blow as he pulled open the door and held it for them.

"He did the same thing to your sister," Christa said as they passed Hamish and she punched him in the gut.

When they entered the huge front hall she dropped the duffle bag, turned to face Ben, and pulled up her camouflage pant legs to expose titanium shins and ankles that fit into normal tennis shoes.

Ben stared, and Spot and Smudge leaned in to give the prosthetics a sniff.

Spot reached out with a paw and tapped her ankle, and then her shin, and then her knee.

He looked at his sister, they identically tipped their heads, and then both of them looked up at Christa.

"If you want to go any higher I'll expect some wine first," she said with a smile.

She dropped her pant legs and straightened up, and said to the still-staring Ben, "I picked them up overseas. Most women fawn over new shoes, I get to buy new legs. Any questions?"

"They're incredible," was all Ben could come up with.

CHAPTER 23

The next morning Ben rummaged through the duffle bag they'd left in the front hall and returned to Christa's side at the kitchen stove.

"This what you wanted?" he asked as he looked down into the gently bubbling pot she was stirring. It looked like she was getting ready to fry chicken, but it smelled like Mimi's bathroom, and Miss Renee.

Christa took the small yellow bricks from Ben and said, "Perfect, thanks."

Lined up on the counter next to the stove were a dozen unlabeled mason jars filled with various liquids and thick pastes. He picked up a white one, gave it a sniff, smiled, and raised his eyebrows at her.

As she carefully slipped the beeswax cakes into the pot she said, "That's coconut oil. I'm making foot wax. My secret recipe."

"Uh-huh," Ben said with a non-understanding nod.

He returned to the large fieldstone hearth and picked up his bowl of oatmeal and half-eaten banana. The pups and Sholto were munching away happily at their bowls in the corner. Spot and Smudge had never had venison, and they both agreed with Sholto that the little cubes were meaty bits of heaven.

Sitting next to Ben on the hearth was a two-foot tall brain teaser puzzle. He'd gotten it from a side table where a dozen others were neatly arranged by size. Each one was unique, and had intricate loops of ropes wound between various shapes of beautifully carved wood and chrome metal and ornately tooled leather pieces. They all had a common theme in that the object was to manipulate the puzzle to remove the parts that were trapped within the structure. Hamish sent smaller versions of these puzzles to the Hogans and Walkers for birthdays and Christmas gifts, and Ben thought it was cool to see the originals.

Smudge thought it was cool too. She stopped chowing long enough to nudge Spot, and they shared a nod as they recognized the puzzle Ben had selected. The first night the pups had their new paws Mimi had given Smudge a smaller copy of the same puzzle to test out her dexterity. She'd solved it in just a few minutes while her brother played with and solved a Rubik's cube. Spot had teased his sister into trying to bend the chrome ring with her paws, and she had folded the strong ring almost in half.

The chrome ring on the puzzle next to Ben was three times as thick, and with a snort Spot challenged her to try to bend that one.

As Christa stirred the pot she watched the curious kid and his dogs study the puzzle, and she saw Ben was admiring the fireplace's large andirons.

"Those were a gift from Hamish to my parents," she said. "They were made in Glasgow."

The large black iron figures were shaped like sitting dogs. They looked just like the pups, and were about the same size.

Nestled among the many overlapping frames on the big mantle was a picture Ben had seen before. A very young Mimi and Papa were sitting on a sled behind a team of fluffy dogs, and a brown-bearded Hamish was standing next to them holding Ben's five year old mom.

A box frame next to that picture also caught Ben's eye. It held a photo of Sholto and Christa standing with a stiff-looking woman in a pillbox hat. Christa was wearing a dress uniform brimming with medals and there wasn't even a hint of gray in Sholto's muzzle. She wore a desert camo service vest that looked like a beefier version of the pups'. Mounted on a field of blue velvet next to the photo was a round bronze medal with the cursive words 'For Gallantry', and below the medal was a small brass plate engraved with 'SGT. SHOLTO'.

Christa watched as Ben took it down and showed it to his dogs. When he looked across the room at her she gave him a smile, but turned away without saying anything.

Ben put the picture back, and turned in a slow circle again to look at the huge atrium they were standing in. He and the pups had explored the ranch house and were awed by its scale. It was just so big, and seemed to go on and on.

His wise-ass family had told him the ranch house was, "A nice little place."

Ben understood their reluctance to tell him more, and figured even if they had tried to accurately describe it they couldn't have done it justice.

The fireplace was three stories tall, and was flanked by windows that spanned the entire back wall. The house sat up on a rise, and beyond the wrap-around deck Ben could see the river and the big red barn. Behind the house and the barn was a pristine snow field that led to a pine covered bowl valley. The trees stretched up and away to meet the bald white peaks of the mountains.

Ben had stood in the center of the house with the pups for a full five minutes staring up at the complex framework of soaring timbers. The vertical logs were huge and rough-hewn, and they met framing that was cut square and formed a grid to support the massive ceiling beams.

There was another whole wing of the house that connected to the front hallway and seemed to be newer. It had a dozen bedrooms, including several with bunks, and a fully equipped rec room, large laundry room, supply room with a car-size generator, and a huge garage. All of the bedrooms had sliding glass doors that connected to the wide deck.

Hamish came down the log stairs from the second floor. He was pulling on a sweater, and as he walked into the kitchen and poured himself a cup of coffee Christa answered Ben's questions about the ranch.

"It was just a small hunting lodge when my crazy great-grandmother came here," she said. "She was a tough old bird, and the first woman lumberjack in Quebec to start her own company. As her logging business grew she kept buying more of the surrounding forest land, as did my grandparents, and my parents when they took over. Which is kinda funny as Mom and Dad never really liked the business, or the cold. They aren't into hunting or skiing or fishing, but our guests sure are. We just seem to always be adding onto our little shack here to make room for them, and sometimes this place feels more like a hotel than a house."

Hamish tipped his coffee at Christa as he said, "Her poor parents retired and move away because this disappointment has refused to provide them with grandchildren, thusly breaking their fragile hearts. Their tears kept freezing up here so they had to move to Florida."

"This from a man with no children," Christa said.

"That I claim as mine," Hamish said as he put on his tam. "Right, let's get to work."

They put their coats on and followed him out onto the back deck, and as they walked to the stairs Christa swept a hand to the right and said, "Now we lease the southern half to the logging companies, except for this valley of course." She swept her left hand past the barn and the river to point up at the mountains as she said, "The northern half we've recently trusted to the National Park Service."

As Ben and the pups followed her and Hamish down the stairs she added, "But we're still working through the details of keeping our wolf sanctuary secure."

Ben and the pups stopped on the steps.

They exchanged a quick and very animated secret chat, and then continued down the stairs as Ben said, "Excuse me Christa, did you just say you had a wolf sanctuary?"

CHAPTER 24

Ben grabbed a stack of empty five gallon buckets from the back of the pickup truck and followed Hamish onto the covered front porch of the huge red barn. The barn's frame was a mix of round logs and square timbers, much like the ranch house. The broad porch was supported by foot-wide hewn posts set on fieldstone pillars. The top of each tall post had curved braces pegged to equally large timbers that made up the interior framework of the barn. Ben and pups couldn't help but stare at the way everything fit together, it was like a huge version of the puzzles.

Ben mimicked Hamish and stomped the snow off his boots on a metal grate set in the porch floor before they stepped into the barn.

Spot and Smudge had been following behind them and Hamish hadn't notice them until they were inside.

He grabbed a moving blanket from a shelf and tossed it on the floor as he said, "Leave them here."

He continued into the barn, and Ben motioned for the pups to hang back. They nodded and sat like Sphynx's as they watched him jog off.

He caught up to Hamish, and as he followed him through the barn he spun in slow circles and let out an impressed whistle.

He had always thought Papa's barn back home was big, but it seemed like a dozen would fit inside Christa's. It was absolutely huge, and bright, and super clean. The thick support posts from the porch continued in rows down the center and divided the barn into large bays. The same posts outlined its many sliding garage doors, and the large transom windows above them. Curved wooden braces connected the posts to a grid of rafters. They supported a wide central loft and the pitched roof, where the morning sun streamed in shafts through windows set high above the loft. Heaters hung from chains on every other support beam, and big dome-shaped work lights dropped down from the high rafters.

In the first few bays were a half-dozen shiny snowmobiles and a quad with huge balloon tires. There was a workshop with islands of equipment and workbenches for metal fab and woodworking, and an entire wall of rolling tool cabinets. Ben noticed everything in the shop was immaculately clean and well-organized.

They passed shelves stacked with dry dog food bags, and several large empty chain link kennels. The middle bays of the barn held a dozen dog sleds of different sizes.

Ben took a detour around one of them.

"Whoa," he said as he ran his hand over its sleek black rails. He noticed the handlebar was being repaired and had thin strips of a shiny woven fabric hanging from it.

"Kevlar?" he asked.

Hamish paused and scratched his head under his tam,

"Aye," he said. "What do you know about Kevlar?"

"Mimi got me a phone case made out it and we looked up how they make it," Ben said. "With all the layers and binders and stuff, very cool. They've even woven it into a fabric with zinc-oxide nanowires to generate electricity."

"You and your Mimi looked that up?" Hamish asked as he looked down at Ben.

"Yeah," Ben said as he glanced at the door where the pups were sitting. "She's, you know, into stuff like that."

They continued on to the far side of the barn where there was a large fieldstone fireplace and timber stairs that led to the loft. There was also a large pegboard with packs, leather harnesses, and a bunch of other gear Ben couldn't identify.

Next to the door was a huge shiny steel vat. There was gas fire ring below it that was hissing blue flame, and Ben could feel the heat coming off it. A dozen small animal carcasses hung next to it that he guessed were rabbits. They'd been gutted and skinned and their heads had been removed, and there was a long tray on the floor to catch the drippings.

Hamish removed his work gloves and put them in his mouth. He ran his hand up the side of the vat and then tested the manhole-size lid for heat before lifting it off.

He slid over a small crate, and Ben used it as a stool so he could see down into the drum. It was half full of a chunky brown liquid, and the contents were steaming slightly. It smelled like soup.

Hamish took the largest ladle Ben had ever seen from a hook on the wall and stirred the mixture before he scooped some of it into one of the empty buckets. He handed the ladle to Ben and nodded for him to fill it and the two remaining ones.

As Ben carefully scooped and poured Hamish went to a rack that held cans of lard and various large white plastic tubs. He pulled one down, spun the lid off, and scooped equal amounts of powder into the buckets as Ben stirred them.

Hamish put his gloves back on, grabbed one of the full buckets, and backed through a door as he said, "Ready to meet these backward bloody weegies?"

Ben waddled behind Hamish with the other two buckets, and followed him outside to a corral.

Eight identical gray and brown, medium-size fluffy dogs with black faces and curled tails immediately went nuts. They barked and yapped, and wagged, and leapt against their chains.

"No way," Ben said as he put down his buckets and went up to the first dog. He let it smell the back of his hand before he bent down and let the dog deliver a face full of licks.

"These guys rock Unc," he said between sputters. "They're so cool!"

"Aye, they sure think so," Hamish said. "Ben, say *gud morgen* to the Norwegian elkhound. They're insanely loyal, protective to a fault, and thrice stronger than their size should allow. They can smell a moose at seven clicks and they don't know how to quit, but this useless lot are the biggest group of chancers, scunners, and numptys as ever wagged or woofed. That girl there sniffing yer giblets is T'nuc. She's the head idjet."

"Can the pups meet these guys?" Ben asked as he playfully pounded on the sturdy dog's side.

"Aye," Hamish said, "but let's ease into that as these arse-hats can be a might..."

He trailed off as the pups came trotting through the door.

They walked into the corral, and then something happened Hamish had never seen before.

Their greeting had started off normal enough. Spot and Smudge made the rounds to each elkhound to say hello with the standard head-butting and rear sniffing. Hamish wasn't too concerned as the sled dogs were chained up and Ben's pups had been fine with the dozen other dogs they'd met on the trip up, and even if things turned hairy the elkhounds were only slightly larger than the pups, and most of that was fur.

Ben was making the rounds as well. He was patting and scratching each dog as he knelt in front of them and checked out the names on their collars.

When Hamish was satisfied everyone was getting along he grabbed a bucket of the game soup, but as he walked around the circle filling bowls he couldn't take his eyes off Spot and Smudge. They had finished their hellos and were standing in front of T'nuc as they wagged slowly in sync and took turns gently chin-rubbing her and delivering subtle body language cues.

T'nuc watched them intently, and from time to time would respond with similar gestures. That alone was only a little odd, but what really gave Hamish pause was the rapt attention of the rest of the team.

He knew the pain-in-the-arse young elkhounds to be a flighty lot. They had almost no attention span when food was around, but all seven of the dogs were sitting upright and staring at their leader as she huffed and snorted with the black pups. The team would give a quick head shake or body shift when Spot or Smudge turned to look at them, but otherwise they were still and silent, and they hadn't touched their bowls.

Hamish stopped pouring the soup and stared.

Ben was suddenly at his side holding his own bucket.

"So Unc, we just dump a little in each bowl, right?" he asked loudly.

Spot looked at Ben, and then at Hamish.

He wagged and bumped Smudge, and they trotted away from T'nuc. They bounded around and played with the other dogs, and then Spot glanced back at Hamish.

"Unc?" Ben repeated louder as he bumped Hamish with the bucket.

"Aye lad, just a little in each bowl," Hamish said as he continued watching the pups play with the dogs, who had started to eat.

"They don't look so stubborn," Ben said as he stepped in front of his uncle to get his full attention.

"They're stubborn as your Mimi," Hamish said. "And likely to turn gee when I say haw."

Ben furrowed his brow and cocked his head.

"Gee and haw?" Hamish asked. "Right and left? Oh we've got leagues to go to turn you into a proper musher lad."

With the bowls filled Hamish and Ben tossed the empty buckets toward the back door and watched the sled dogs burying their noses in the steaming soup. Spot and Smudge sampled some from the dogs' bowls, and Hamish again raised a curious brow. These uppity dogs wouldn't normally let another dog stick its nose in their bowl, especially a dog they just met, but the elkhounds didn't seem to mind and they even moved over a little to let the pups in.

Eventually Hamish looked down at Ben, folded his big arms across his chest and asked, "So, dog whisperer Ben, what do yeh make of the team?"

Ben folded one arm under the other and rubbed his chin as Spot and Smudge stopped to watch him.

"You named them as pups?" Ben asked.

"Aye," replied Hamish. "After I got to know them."

"Good," Ben said, "just like Dr. Herriot suggested. Although I don't know what their Norwegian names mean."

As Hamish watched Ben's concentrating face work he had a flash of his brother from sixty years ago.

Ben pointed around the circle with his finger, and starting with the dog next to the leader he said, "K'cuf there, I guess she's the second in command, then S'ufud, and the triplets K'naks, T'sohg, and T'raf, at least I assume they're littermates, they all seem to be a little younger and I guess those are your swing dogs. And then those two powerhouses R'ekcuf and E'sra are your wheels, right? What exactly is the problem you're having with them?"

Hamish laughed a booming laugh and slammed Ben on the back with his huge mitt.

"Okay grandnephew," he said. "We'll get to that, you annoying little bastard."

He turned to kick the empty buckets back into the barn and said, "Your Dr. Herriot was not officially a doctor, nor was he really named James Herriot, although he was a sight quicker than any doc I've ever known. A right genie-arse Scot that one. His true name was Alf Wight."

"You knew him?" Ben gushed as he followed behind his great-uncle. "He sure was a genius, and I've read everything he's ever wrote!"

"Written. And he'd be happy about that," Hamish said as he pointed to a large sink.

Ben started to rinse out the buckets, and Hamish leaned back against a workbench to watch him.

"I know yeh was just having me on with that 'gee' and 'haw' thing," he said. "I bet you've read everything yeh can get yer little mitts on about mushing, Aye?"

Ben smiled but didn't look up from his bucket.

"Okay lad," Hamish said, "But just so you've been warned, I serve revenge up cold. Finish that up and come out front when you're done."

Hamish crossed the cavernous barn, and as he stepped through the front door he took out his cellphone.

≈≈$$≈≈

Ben finished up with the buckets and called the pups. They joined Hamish on the barn's front porch just as Christa pulled up in a pickup. She parked it next to Hamish's truck, and Ben noticed the two were virtually identical.

As Christa went to the back and rummaged around in the bed Hamish patted his pockets like he was searching for something.

"Ach," he grumbled. "Be a lad and run up to the house for me, I left my phone on the kitchen counter. Be double quick about it. You can leave the pups here with me."

Ben signaled for Spot and Smudge to stay, and saluted Hamish before he sprinted off across the small gravel lot. He slid and danced to keep his balance when he hit the packed snow of the path that led to the back deck of the house.

The pups exchanged a look. They were smelling something that made their noses twitch, and hearing something that made their ears perk

Smudge started to stand up but Spot stopped her.

Wait a sec sister, he huffed. *This should be interesting.*

He could see the lump of the phone in Hamish's hip pocket.

Christa saw the pups fidget and settle, and when she turned back to Hamish she noticed his broad grin.

He gave her an expectant head tip, and she shrugged and said, "Sure, go ahead."

Hamish pursed his lips and made a little chirping sound.

The suspension of Christa's truck creaked, and its rear end rose a little when two huge mastiffs deftly leapt from the tailgate. The identical littermates were solid muscle, and they had light brown coats, blocky heads, black faces, fleshy jowls, and very sharp eyes.

They ran to Hamish's side, and when he made a hand gesture they turned a quick circle, made eye contact with the pups, and then noticed Ben, who was halfway up the path.

Hamish flashed another gesture and the mastiffs kicked up snow as they blasted off across the lot. In an instant they'd shot up the path and closed the gap to Ben.

Christa looked over at Spot and Smudge to make sure they were staying put, and noticed they were wagging.

Ben never saw the two huge dogs coming, and he screamed when they knocked him off the path and sent him tumbling down the snowy slope.

The mastiffs snapped to attention and their alert heads turned back to look at Hamish. He flashed another hand sign and the dogs bounded off the rise and waded into the deep snow. They dragged Ben by his jean cuffs and jacket hood back up to the path and started pulling him toward the barn.

The flailing Ben was beating at them as he used words Mimi would not have approved of.

Hamish whistled and the dogs turned Ben loose and casually trotted back down the path to his side.

"I'd say that was a belter of a test," Hamish said with a big smile as he patted the mastiffs' proud heads.

"Seems to have been," Christa said with a chuckle as she headed up the path to help the still-cursing Ben straighten his jacket and brush himself off.

Hamish flashed another hand sign and the mastiffs trotted over to get acquainted with the pups, which they did in the same odd way as with the elkies. His typically dominant police-dogs-in-training were three times the size of Ben's black pups but the mastiffs were cueing slightly submissive with their tails flat and their heads lowered.

As Hamish scratched under his tam he said, "Spot and Smudge, meet Vuur and Rook."

CHAPTER 25

"Hello Mr. Preston, I got you," Ben said. "Can you guys see me?"

"Yes we can Ben," his social studies teacher said as he put the tablet on a stand on his desk.

He plugged a monitor into it and Ben appeared on a large screen in front of the class.

Ben saw them on his tablet, and as he waved to them he said, "Hey guys!"

The class waved back. There were a few hoots and whistles, and some of the boys started a low chant of, "Ben, Ben, Ben…"

The teacher hushed them with a wave, and said, "So tell us Mr. Hogan, what have you learned about Quebec so far?"

He exaggerated the pronunciation of the province as 'Ca-beck', and Christa rolled her eyes as she took the tablet from Ben so he could take a few steps back.

"I learned it's friggin' cold!" he said as he breathed out a puff of steam for effect, and got laughs from the class. "Mr. P, the average *high* here at the ranch in January is minus fifteen Celsius, or about four degrees Fahrenheit. As you can see I'm wearing just about everything I own." He showed them he was wearing a tattered one-piece quilted coverall with two heavy sweaters underneath.

He introduced Christa, and when she toggled to the front camera briefly to wave the class waved back.

She made sure to keep Ben in the shot as she panned slowly so they could see the ranch house and the barn. He described both of them with some historical background and stats tossed in, and then said, "As you can see we're up in the mountains, well, in a valley in the mountains. It's about four thousand feet up, which is higher than mount Greylock, the tallest point in Mass."

He knew he'd have to pepper the call with facts if he wanted to get a good grade from Mr. P. The teacher was all about facts, and stats, and data, and if you didn't insert them he certainly would.

Mr. P added some random Greylock Mountain facts of his own, apparently not wanting to be upstaged. Ben knew enough to hang back as Mr. P liked to be adored by his audience.

Christa followed Ben as he walked backward toward the barn and described the different types of trees in the forest behind him.

When Spot and Smudge trotted into the shot half the class yelled their names. The pups turned to look at the tablet and wag, and the kids laughed.

"Where exactly are you?" Mr. P asked.

"I have no idea," Ben said, and got more chuckles. "You guys down there in Pembury are about two hundred miles from the Canadian border, and I'm about six hundred miles north of that. By road it was way more than a thousand miles, partly because I came through Nova Scotia and New Brunswick first, but the roads bend and twist a lot up here once you're in the mountains. Everything is in kilometers, so the thousand miles we travelled was about sixteen hundred kilometers, or clicks as my Uncle calls them. There's a tiny mining town twenty minutes down the road, but beyond that we're a hundred clicks from the nearest anything."

Mr. P added some distance facts that seemed a little unrelated, and even a little incorrect, but Ben let that slide.

"How was the trip?" the teacher asked.

"It took two trains, a bus, two ferries, and two days driving to get here," Ben said. "On the way up we drove through the Acadian part of Canada, where most of the people speak French but also eat British food for some odd reason."

As Ben tried to keep the class interested by describing the more colorful highlights of the ranch Mr. P kept asking him boring social studies questions. Ben had correctly assumed his teacher would be firing them at him as the man seemed obsessed with any topic designed to bore a preteenager to tears. Christa had helped him to prepare so he was able to quickly blow through details about the local mining and logging industries. He tried to steer the discussion back to the more engaging topics of fishing and hunting and Nordic skiing, but every time he was just warming up a good story Mr. P swept in with a stream of questions about parliament or free health care and the class would immediately glaze over.

Ben answered a question about iron ore by pivoting to some of the ranch's more colorful logging history, and then quickly moved on with, "Let me show you what we do here today."

As he walked into an open bay in the barn he said, "There are three things my Uncle Hamish and Christa are working on."

"The first is this," he said as he held up a large plastic dog collar with a black bump in the middle, and in the other had he held up what looked like a thicker version of a smartphone.

"This is a radio collar," he said. "And this is a radio telemetry receiver. They're used to track the gray wolves my uncle is reintroducing into this part of Quebec. Gray wolves are common in northern Canada and Alaska, so common they aren't protected in some places, but they were driven out of these mountains years ago. Mostly by over-hunting and mining and logging encroaching on their homes. The habitat here will still support them, and now the people are starting to understand the importance of bringing the wolves back here. So my uncle and Christa are doing it, with help from the community."

There were a million questions about the wolf reintroduction, and wolves in general. A cute girl in the front row raised her hand and smiled when she said hello to Ben. As she tugged on her hair she waved to Smudge, and then asked Ben how wolves reproduced. The class laughed and Ben's hands and face got hot, but thankfully Mr. P moved them along to the rest of the questions which ranged from the astute to the downright stupid.

Ben answered them all and was a font of knowledge about all things Canis lupus. Whenever Christa thought she'd have to jump in Ben would come up with the answer, even if he had to think about it for a second, which he usually did while looking at Spot.

Mr. P was pretty silent for this part. Apparently wolves were a little out of his social studies wheelhouse.

The questions dried up, and before the teacher could jump in Ben said, "And this is the second reason we're here."

Christa panned again and Ben took the class around the circle of Norwegian elkhounds. He introduced each one, and explained their role on the team. He also showed them the sleds and the steel soup tank, complete with decapitated rabbits, which drew the typical sounds kids make when they're grossed out.

There were a million more questions about the sled dogs, including how fast can they pull the sled, and does T'nuc fart in S'ufud face.

Mr. P was now dead silent and looking a little annoyed. Apparently he didn't know crapola about sled dogs either.

Christa gave Ben a wave to indicate they were getting near the end of the class period.

"Mr. P," he said, "if we have time I'd like to show you guys the third thing we're doing here at the ranch."

"That's fine Ben," Mr. P said, clearly not meaning it. "We have a few minutes left, but I'm sure the class has questions about the plight of the local indigenous people."

Ben gave him a wave and turned away from the camera as he pulled up his hood and put on his heavy gloves. He walked out of the barn and into the snowy corral, and Spot and Smudge trotted with him for a bit before they walked off camera.

Ben turned, put his hands on his hips, and stood stone still.

The class watched, and waited.

The confused Mr. P was just starting to ask a question when two huge brown dogs charged into the picture at full speed and knocked Ben off his feet. They attacked, and Christa zoomed in on the action. There was an explosion of barks and growls as they ripped and tugged and Ben pounded and kicked. The muscular dogs each had fifty pound on him, and they tore into him like a sack of fresh meat.

The class gasped and one girl started to cry as Mr. P's mouth dropped open.

Christa pulled back a bit to show a big man with a gray beard was calmly watching the attack with the equally calm Spot and Smudge. He whistled a short double-toot and the massive dogs immediately let Ben go and calmly trotted over to the man's side. They sat down next to the much smaller pups, and they all wagged.

Ben slowly rolled to his knees with the old coveralls in tatters.

He pushed the hood back from his red face as he stood up on wobbly legs and put his hands on his knees.

Between panting breaths he said, "That was Vuur and Rook. They're police dogs my Great-Uncle Hamish over there is custom training for his friend in the Kwazulu-Natal. It's also called Zululand, that's in South Africa. Their names mean fire and smoke in Afrikaans, which is kinda like an abbreviated form of Dutch. Say hi Unc."

Hamish pinched the brim of his tam at the class.

"Rook and his brother Vuur are boerboels," Ben said as Christa zoomed in on the dogs. "They're also called South African mastiffs. Their breed is part of a category of strong dogs called Molossers. These guys are a hundred and seventy-five pounds, or about eighty kilos, and as you can clearly see they have big bones, big necks, big teeth, round floppy ears, and short snouts. Bulldogs and pit bulls are Molossers too. Unc says these boerboels make great security dogs 'cause they're way smarter than they look, protective as hell, and real bad asses. Luckily, they were just playing with me. He coulda' had them remove my head and limbs with a simple hand sign."

Hamish concurred with a nod, and so did Spot and Smudge.

As Ben straightened up with a groan Christa panned back to him.

"So, who wants to go on a field trip?" he asked.

Mr. P stared with his mouth open, and the class erupted in applause.

Ben heard the period bell ring behind his friends' hoots and chants, and as he waved goodbye Hamish sent the wagging mastiffs at him again with a flick of his wrist. Spot and Smudge joined in, and Ben was knocked to the snow with each growling dog taking a limb and tugging. As he laughed and kicked Christa ended the video call.

CHAPTER 26

"Hand me an Allen wrench please," Christa said. "The one with the white handle."

Smudge put her front feet up on the rolling tool cart, split open a paw, grabbed the wrench, and froze.

It had been a long day and they were all a little tired, and she had forgotten she was supposed to act like a normal dog.

Ben quickly slid off the workbench, took the tool from her, and leaned down to slap it into Christa's waiting palm.

"Thanks," she said from under the dog sled.

Her prosthetic legs were leaning against the workbench, and her leg stumps were pressed against the jack stands that were holding up the ends of the sled. She grunted as she torqued down on some out-of-sight thing, and then swore as whatever it was thumped loudly.

Smudge and Ben let out a relieved breath, and she shrugged an apology before padding over to curl up with Sholto, Vuur, and Rook. The dogs were snoozing on a pile of moving blankets under the closest heater.

Aside from the light over their bay and the work light Christa had with her under the sled the rest of the large barn was dark. There was a slight glow coming through the transom windows from the corral where Hamish was working late with the elkhounds.

The barn was mostly quiet except for an intermittent yap from outside, the dogs' snoring, Christa's tinkering and frequent cursing, and the occasional hoot from the snowy owl who was nesting somewhere high up in the rafters.

Ben continued to hand Christa tools, and she continued to curse from under the sled, and sometime later the glow from the transoms went dark and they heard the back door of the barn slam closed.

Hamish stomped the snow from his boots before he walked out of the shadows with Spot following him.

"I give up," he said as he pulled the cap off his head. "I'm throwing in the bloody towel."

He stood over the napping police dogs and turned his face up to the blast from the heater.

Ben noticed his face was ruddier than normal and suspected it wasn't all from the cold.

"I told him not to use that breeder," Hamish said. "I told him, and the stupid fool wouldn't listen. I've trained fifty teams of weegies and never have I seen a lot so damn *glaikit*."

He ran his hands over his buzzed head a few times, and said, "I've only spent the last thirty five years plottin' bloodlines and hand-selectin' my teams, but why listen to me?"

Ben got the sense it wasn't a question he should try to answer.

Christa rolled out from under the sled and sat up on the creeper. As she examined a scraped knuckle she said, "I know you know this, but we have a call with him in a week. You promised they'd be ready by then, and you've never missed a deadline. Not ever. I've been working with you since I could spit, and if anyone can find a way, it's you."

"Your arse and parsley," Hamish grumbled as he stomped off into the dark of the barn. A moment later they heard the front door slam closed.

Spot waited for Christa to drop back under the sled before he signed to Ben what he'd seen transpire between Hamish and the elkies.

When he was done he nodded at the sled and signed, *Ask her.*

"Christa, what's the issue with the dogs?" Ben asked. "I mean, I'm no expert, but they seem to listen and obey commands alright."

"They do, and they do," Christa said as she rolled out from under the sled and sat up.

She nodded at the cart and Ben tossed her a bottle of water. After she took a long pull from it she said, "Ben, you have to understand we're talking about a very elite team here. They're not just runners that blindly follow a musher's orders. Hamish doesn't train dogs to run in a fancy race where they have corporate sponsors and a support team. These dogs are the real deal. They will probably run some races and be used for a bit of show, knowing their owner, but he came to us because dogs that graduate from Hamish's training are reliable in a way that gives new meaning to the word. They will pull a sled through a blizzard up the side of Everest and back down again. Emphasis on the back down again. They simply won't quit you, not ever. When you're air-dropped a thousand clicks from the nearest research station they'll make sure you make it back, or none of them will. Hamish understands his dogs could very well mean the difference between living and pushing up daisies."

Before Christa rolled back under the sled she looked at the metal legs leaning against the workbench and said, "I know, believe me."

From the time Ben was a little kid he knew Hamish worked with dogs. His parents and grandparents had always said Hamish was a top dog trainer, but Ben just assumed he was like those guys with a stapled-up sign with tear-out numbers at the bottom who taught cocker spaniels not to crap on the rug.

He and the pups silently chatted about it for a long while as the other dogs' snored, and Christa cursed, and the owl hooted.

Eventually Spot tipped his head at the sled and signed, and Ben asked, "Christa, what's the issue with the elkies?"

She rolled out from under the sled, and motioned for her legs.

Ben handed them to her as she said, "Our client insisted we use his breeder. Which we're pretty sure was a cousin, or a concubine, or both, despite his assertions of their provenance."

While Christa was slipping her legs on Spot quickly signed to Ben what the words concubine and provenance meant.

Christa finished strapping on her legs and sprung to her feet far quicker than Ben or the pups were ready for. They shared a subtle impressed nod, and a relieved head tip. Had she been looking in Spot's direction she could have caught him with his paw split open.

As Christa wiped her hands on a rag she said, "Essentially, Hamish is seeing the signs that these dogs lack heart, and it's preventing them from gaining the confidence they need to work as an effective team. Good trainers can teach a team to make decisions about their environment, but Hamish pushes them to make decisions about themselves, the rest of the team, and even their handler. Decisions that indicate what would happen when amplified a hundred fold in a real emergency situation, and that's why he's the best. He looks at dogs like they're one of his complex puzzles. He enjoys figuring out how they're put together, and he's happiest when he unlocks their secrets. The ones no one else could."

She started cleaning up the workbench, and as Ben organized the wrenches he shared a nod with Spot.

"Take Vuur and Rook," Christa said. "When Hamish trains a security dog they aren't just specialists in drug detection or guard duty. He hand selects them as pups and raises them for as long as it takes. When he's done they can perform every possible duty a service or police dog is capable of, and with a high degree of autonomy when needed. Did you know Rook and Vuur can sniff out a flash memory stick hidden in a wall?

Ben didn't, and neither did Spot or Smudge.

"Yeah," Christa said. "Hamish flies in a guy from Connecticut who specializes in canine detection of the polycarbonate adhesives used in the chip manufacturing process."

"You wouldn't have thought that possible if you saw those two lanky dolts when they came here as puppies," she said. "Truth be told I didn't see it at first. Rook and Vuur come from great stock but were passed over by the first few people who looked at them. Every trainer has their own little trait tendency tests, like flipping the puppy over, and putting it in a corner, and other kinds of Schutzhund and dominance bullshit. They would have failed those tests, and it was probably the reason they were left behind until Hamish got a look at them. He could see what the others couldn't. Those two lumps over there have a rare gift, and the rest we do with our training."

She leaned against the bench and gave Spot's staring little face a scratch as she said, "Not easily mind you. Half of the battle is the education we provide here, and they're far from perfect. With Hamish spending so much extra time with the elkies we're behind on the boerboels' training. Vuur can't cross a high beam and Rook is afraid of some types of gunfire, and he couldn't find a cadaver if he tripped over it. Those things aside, they'll be a pretty unstoppable force when we're done with them. But we can't get a dog to perform at this level unless they have that special something. That unquantifiable gift. The dog has to have heart."

Christa snapped the bench lights off, and put an arm around Ben as they walked toward the front door with the pups in tow. She whistled for Sholto and the boerboels, who rolled off their blanket and padded along behind them.

"Can heart be learned?" Ben asked.

"Sometimes," Christa said, "but sadly it's often learned in the last few seconds."

Ben clicked off the switches for the light above their bay and the overhead heater before they all walked out into the cold.

"The crazy part is Hamish knows he could sign off on the elkies and no one would probably ever know," Christa said. "There's a one in ten-thousand chance it would ever make a difference. When he's done they'll be fine sled dogs. They'll work hard for their human partner and out-perform any other team around. But it's that one time, that one unforeseen event that happens in a split second and everything changes. If that ever happened to this group and he had let them go without knowing they were absolutely solid he could never live with it."

They entered the path to the ranch house, and they could see Hamish was in the kitchen starting dinner.

Christa slid a little in the snow, and as she steadied herself on Ben's arm she said, "He has trouble living with it even when he knows he did his best work."

CHAPTER 27

"*Igjen* to me boys!" Hamish yelled as the sled moved up an embankment and started to slide sideways on its crest.

He made a kissing sound and the team dug in and pulled harder, and the sled straightened as it drove through the deep snow. The dogs were wearing leather boots tied to their feet that made soft smacking noises as they pounded through the drifts. Spot and Smudge were riding in the sled with Ben, and the pups were wearing the same boots to keep their feet warm when they stopped and walked around in the snow.

At the bottom of the slope Hamish called out, "Whoa, *stoppe*."

He set the foot brake when the team came to a stop, got off the sled, and walked past Ben and the pups. As he stomped past the team they eyeballed him with their tails down and their heads lowered and their ears lying flat. They'd done something wrong and they certainly knew it.

When Hamish reached the front he knelt and grabbed T'nuc by the muzzle and looked her dead in her eyes. He said something sternly in Norwegian, and then, "Yer going to do this until yeh get it right. I don't care if yeh freeze yer mingin' fud off. Yeh know to pull them hard and ease before the crest, not on it, and have those lazy fucking wheels do the work on the tip. They rely on yeh to know when to let on, so do it right, yeh dozy cunt."

He stood and pressed his mittens into his back as he stretched and said, "Yeh lot okay in there?"

Ben lifted his goggles and twisted his head out from under the fur covering. He smiled and said, "This is the single coolest thing I have ever done Uncle Hamish. Thanks for taking us out here."

Hamish didn't notice Spot and Smudge were nodding in agreement. Their noses just poked out past the blanket.

"Aye," Hamish said as he puffed out steam in the chilly air. "You're helping me out too lad. They gotta learn to pull people steady."

He mounted the sled and they did the same quarter mile loop a few more times until they were blasting over the ridge smoothly and he was happily yelling, "*Meget gud!*" to the team of panting dogs.

Ben could see the change in the dogs' demeanor. He had witnessed enough of his pups and the coyotes to tell the sled dogs' head bobs were the equivalent of high-fiving each other.

That lasted a full minute until they made another mistake and Hamish ripped into one of the guilty-looking wheel dogs in the back for missing a turn.

He took the team farther north along the river until they entered the national park. He drove them hard, sometimes diving off an obvious path at the last second to race up an almost vertical slope, or slamming through thick pines that whipped at the dogs and the sled.

Ben wasn't sure what the next problem was but Hamish stopped the team again in a small clearing and had another chat with E'sra, the same wheel dog in the back who'd messed up earlier. He was one of the strong pullers and Hamish took him to task in both English and Norwegian.

As he scowled down at the dog he said to Ben, "Watch this numpty closely lad. Yeh can see he loses focus when he gets distracted. His legs get out of sync and it puts the whole team off. Remember, it's a game of conservation of energy, and every errant tug and wasted step costs precious horsepower." Hamish read the skepticism on Ben's face, and said, "It wouldn't matter over a few kilometers, but when they're in the middle of the great white nowhere and that cold fucker old man death is chasin' them, running together is the only thing that's going to save them, and the poor bastard at the helm."

Ben nodded, and asked, "What distracted them?"

Hamish nodded to a spot behind the sled.

Ben and the pups turned to look, and hidden in a stand of pines just off the trail they'd come down was a huge bull moose. When it turned to look at them Ben thought its antlers were wider than a car.

"Yikes," he said. "He's huge! Pups, you seeing this?"

The pups were seeing it, and they'd had pulled off their front boots so they could communicate under the blanket by feeling each other's signs.

I'd like to see One Ear try to take that down, Smudge signed.

I'd like to know how E'sra noticed that thing at a full run in deep snow from the rear of the team, Spot signed. *I've been watching for wildlife and missed it. We could learn a thing or two from these guys sis.*

As they went deeper into the park they were also climbing out of their valley. Some of the high trails took them inches from precarious drop-offs and under walls of rock and ice.

Hamish brought them into a clearing on a high plateau. He stopped the sled and unpacked some food and gear while Ben let the elkies off the harness.

The pups snacked on hard-tack jerky with the sled dogs, who inhaled the strips of meat with quick head jerks.

When Hamish waved for Ben to follow him to the edge of the ridge Spot tagged along.

The view was breathtaking. They were high above the convergence of two snowy valleys, and they could see for tens of kilometers in both directions. A wide river wound back and forth down the bottom of one valley, dropped at a set of rocky falls, and snaked away around the curve of the mountain.

Hamish explained where they were in relation to the ranch as he unfolded a small antenna and connected it to the radio tracking handset. He held out the antenna and swung his arm in a slow arc as he showed Ben how to read the display.

Ben nodded, and Hamish handed the devices to him.

After a few long sweeps Ben swung the antenna in smaller arcs until the signal pegged at a spot just above the falls.

"Aye lad," Hamish said with a nod as he looked over Ben's shoulder. "Pack that up and let's hit it."

He slogged back toward the sled, and Ben showed the device to Spot.

With his deft toe-pads Spot quickly clicked through the screens and noted how the ranging and signal level metering worked.

Hamish paused when he saw the team hadn't finished woofing down their jerky. The elkies were having some kind of carry-on with Smudge. She was animatedly posturing, and a few of the sled dogs were responding in kind. It wasn't aggression, but there was definitely something heated happening and it made Hamish rub his frost-covered beard as he watched them.

He'd trained his first pup to sit and stay when he was eight, and had trained hundreds of dogs since, but he'd never seen dogs communicate the way Ben's pups did. Smudge was having some kind of canine discussion with the weegies, and he'd seen Spot do the same strange thing with Vuur and Rook.

"Yer pup's got her knickers in a twist about something," he said.

Ben and Spot turned and saw Smudge was bobbing her head and twitching her ears.

"Oh, she's just excited about the moose," Ben said.

Hamish looked back and gave Ben a curious look.

Ben whistled and called out to the sled, "Settle down you."

Smudge looked at them and stopped her grumble-with-shoulder-shake in mid conversation.

She waited for Ben to distract Hamish with a question about the tracker before she turned back to the elkies.

We'll continue this later, she huffed to K'naks and T'sohg, *but there's no way you two Nancies can pull more than me. And you certainly can't pull more than E'sra.*

E'sra agreed with a snort.

CHAPTER 28

On the trip down from the ridge Hamish told Ben to be absolutely quiet, and then he switched the team to some kind of stealth mode. The sled dogs trotted at half speed, and every dozen meters T'nuc glanced quickly over her shoulder to get flashed hand signs from Hamish for course corrections.

The pups watched from under their blanket in stunned awe. The coordination and silence of the sled team was truly impressive.

Spot and Smudge had learned to stalk with the coyote pack, and One Ear had taught them a vocabulary of non-verbal cues to coordinate hunts. She had also taught them how to move silently over dry leaves and muddy trails and icy stream banks. She showed them how to detect and avoid even the smallest obstacles at a full run, or anything that might make noise and give away their position and direction. Eventually the pups had taken over and expanded on those tactics. They had turned their coyote hunters into a truly silent machine, but this sled team took noiseless movement and communication to another level. The pups were fascinated by the dogs' ability to pick up on each other's signals with lightning speed, and use each other's footsteps to move as one quiet body. Being tethered feet apart and moving quickly through the snow was hard enough, but to do it absolutely silently they had to be flawlessly coordinated. The set of their harnesses, angle to the sled, foot placement, and pull timing all had to be perfect to avoid slapping lines and crunching snow.

They had to be in sync, almost as in sync as the pups.

Hamish was equally as impressive. The pups could carry on entire conversations with Ben from a distance, but for another human to convey instructions and read feedback with eight regular dogs while racing silently through the snow was pretty amazing.

Ben's hands covered the pups' paws under the fur blanket so they could have their own silent conversation.

Christa was right, Spot signed.

Yeah, Smudge signed. *He is truly very good at what he does.*

The three of them shared a look, and to answer the unasked question Ben signed, "*Soon, maybe.*"

The pups nodded their agreement as Hamish brought the team to a silent stop.

He quietly slid a rifle out of its holster, and then leaned in close to Ben and whispered for him to have the pups stay in the sled.

After slowly chambering a round Hamish motioned for Ben to follow in his footsteps.

They walked past the team and disappeared into the trees, with Ben stretching his gait to step in the holes left by his great-uncle's boots.

After a few minutes of weaving through the towering trees Hamish turned and pressed a fingertip to his lips before he slipped under the boughs of a huge pine.

The open area under its snow-filled branches was tall enough for Ben to stand up in. They skirted around its trunk and crept up to the narrow gap between the branches and the drift that surrounded the tree. It made an effective blind, and afforded them a sweeping view of the falls and the river. The softly gurgling water tumbled down the thirty-meter jumble of ice-covered rocks and spread out into a wide basin at the bottom.

Hamish scanned the river for a few long minutes, and then he moved Ben slowly in front of him and crouched to point over his shoulder.

Ben followed his finger to a spot just below the falls where the basin widened.

Standing on a boulder at the water's edge was a huge wolf.

Hamish whispered almost inaudibly in Ben's ear, "Lad, meet the Glasgow Gray."

⌘§§⌘

Hamish brought the rifle up, pressed the butt to Ben's shoulder, and pointed for him to look through the scope.

After a few cycles of lifting his head and lowering it again to get his bearings he found the wolf, and silently gasped when she filled the scope.

She was an impressive animal. Her body was as big as Rook or Vuur's and her legs were much longer. Ben guessed she was well over a meter tall at the shoulder.

She was also just plain beautiful. She was indeed all light gray except for the white patches above her eyebrows and on her cheeks, chin, and chest. The way the white flare of her jowls perfectly framed her elegant snout reminded Ben of One Ear, although the wolf's head was twice as big as the coyote's.

Glasgow was slowly scanning the river and the woods as she sampled the air and rotated her ears, but otherwise she stood perfectly still. If Hamish hadn't pointed her out Ben would have never seen her as she blended into the mottled colors of the snow and rocks perfectly.

Her head rotated away, and he saw the black curve of the radio collar in her thick neck fur.

When she turned back to stare in their direction Ben was sure she was looking right into his eyes. Even from two hundred meters away he could see the confidence and intelligence in them. He'd become a bit of an expert on smart canine stares, and Glasgow's chilled him.

"Aye," Hamish whispered when he felt the quiver in Ben's shoulders. "That look'll give you a pucker. Still does for me too lad, every bloody time."

Ben nodded. He could hear the nervous excitement in his great-uncle's deep whisper.

"I call her Glasgow 'cause she's a big, tough, cold bitch," Hamish whispered. "And yet I can't help but love her. Yer lookin' at a million years of amazing evolution in those eyes Ben. The most effective large predator on land, second only to the painted wild dogs of Africa. A bear or a bull moose might take her on, but with her pack she's almost unstoppable. The only thing that can fuck with her is us, but don't let her calm demeanor fool yeh. Look at her big feet, and the muscles under that fur. In deep snow she can hit forty miles an hour in less than three strides, so don't blink if yeh ever have to pull the trigger. Yeh likely won't get a second shot."

The rest of the wolf pack slipped from the woods behind her and came to the water's edge. There were several juveniles and two pairs of adults who were a little smaller than Glasgow.

Hamish explained the youngest of the pack were born in the spring and had just turned nine months old. After two recent growth spurts they were almost full height, and would bulk up over the summer. The mating females, including Glasgow, would probably get pregnant again soon if they weren't already.

"Just like coyotes," Ben whispered. "Ours mate in January and pup in March. Sixty three day gestation?"

Hamish nodded. He was impressed Ben knew those facts but he wasn't sure what he'd meant by 'ours'.

He pointed out two yearlings who'd been pupped the summer before last, and explained they would probably venture off in the next year or so. He told Ben he'd slowly been introducing other wolves into the park from varied bloodlines. Those Casanova males had split off some of the young females from this pack to establish two smaller packs farther to the north and east.

The wolves waded into the river up to their ankles, and when they started slapping at the water Ben noted with some pride that they weren't as good at fishing as the coyotes his pups had trained.

He smiled when he saw the younger wolves were just as impatient as One Ear's juvenile students. They charged into the water and pounced at the splashes, and always came up empty.

Glasgow must have huffed to get their attention as they all stopped to watch her.

She stood motionless in the frigid water for a full minute as she stared down without so much as an ear twitch, and then in a flash she swatted a large fish out of the water and up onto the bank.

As Ben watched the excited juveniles pull the fish apart Hamish wrapped a big hand around his chin and turned his head upriver to the top of the falls.

Barely fifty meters away from them was another massive gray wolf. It was standing on the far bank with its head lowered and its ears laid back on its head.

It was staring right at them, and Hamish slid the rifle silently from Ben's hands.

CHAPTER 29

Alpha stood motionless at the top of the falls as he stared across the river and into the dark space below the tree's branches.

He could see there were two humans hiding there, one grown and one young. He'd smelled the larger human many times before, and his captive dogs who were waiting further up the draw.

They'd never been a threat, but there were strange things in the woods these days and Alpha was suspicious of everything.

Normally he would have been fishing with the pack but he was on constant watch duty now, and the moose carcasses they'd come across earlier bothered him. They had been taken down by wolves, but not any wolves he was familiar with. There had been Casanova wolves in the forest earlier in the season but they'd formed packs with some of his young adults so there shouldn't be any rogues hunting nearby.

The odd wolves had just appeared out of nowhere, and they smelled very wrong. They left their scat and pee and drool everywhere, and their scent wasn't like any animal he'd ever encountered before.

And the most troubling thing was they had torn apart an entire moose family and hadn't eaten a thing.

Alpha stared at the humans for a few long moments. They had a weapon but they weren't making any aggressive moves, and he guessed they'd just come to watch as the big human had always done in the past. He saw there was fear in their eyes, but also the proper level of calm and respect. Agitated humans were unpredictable, and Alpha had learned in his old range how to spot humans who came to hunt. They had disrespectful looks, and they stomped around like the arrogant bears.

These two weren't hunting, but they were still humans and they had a weapon, and a little warning never hurt.

Alpha stiffened and lowered. He straightened his tail and curled his upper lip slightly as he fixed them with his best warning stare. He held it for moment, and when he was satisfied his point had been made he turned away and picked his way deftly down the icy rocks to join his pack.

Glasgow had seen her mate posturing at the top of the falls, and she could tell he wasn't worried about whatever it was he had detected across the river. She hadn't been able to make out exactly what was hiding in the trees but she doubted the dangerous wolves they were keeping an eye out for had the ability to wait patiently.

She was concerned about the senseless violence they'd seen. It was too human for her liking, and taking down a healthy bull moose wasn't easy, or advisable. Nor was taking on a moose mother. They'd come across these rogues' vile scents several times, and she was convinced the dangerous creatures were circling in toward her pack.

She was also afraid they weren't normal rogues.

Lone males were just part of wolf life, and she'd dealt with them before in their old home range. Her own mate had been a rogue once himself, and when he'd knocked their old alpha from the top spot it was over quickly and the new order was established in seconds.

Protecting and teaching the young was primary for all wolves, even rogues looking to take over the pack or Casanovas looking to mate. Turf wars and dominance challenges took a back seat when it came to the pups, even if the top females like Glasgow had to remind the males of it once in a while. Her current Alpha, the one she'd been with since before they'd been moved to these woods, was the strongest she'd ever known. He's a talented hunter and good with the pack, and he'd handily sent more than few lone males packing.

Still, she was worried about these new rogues. She couldn't help wondering if they were looking for something different than just a new pack to claim as their own.

Her mate joined her at the water's edge, and she welcomed him with a quick muzzle-lick.

What's in the trees? she asked with a head nod toward the falls.

Humans, Alpha indicated. *The big one who watches, and a new younger one from his pack. Their captive dogs are beyond the ridge.*

Anything else? she asked with a nervous tail swish.

Nothing more from the rogues, Alpha indicated. *I think they're somewhere over the south draw, but it's hard to tell for sure. They're running in circles.*

Come, eat, Glasgow nudged as she sensed his frustration. *I fear we're all going to need our strength.*

CHAPTER 30

The truck's headlights lit up a bullet-hole ridden road sign.

"Town of Piege," Ben read. "Gateway to the north. Population five hundred and ten."

He noticed the population had been crossed out with spray paint and a new total with two fewer people had been painted in below it.

"That's pretty funny," Ben said.

"Probably wasnae' so fuckin' funny to five hundred eleven and twelve," Hamish said. "They both must have been good shots."

Hamish slowed the truck just long enough to prevent the bottom from being torn out as they rumbled over a horrible pair of railroad tracks.

"Goes to the ore mine," he said when he noticed Ben was looking at the rusty tracks and the lights in the distance. "They're not used as often now as back in the mine's heyday. Cheaper steel from overseas been biting them hard for a long time now."

They raced on for another half kilometer before veering off the paved road to speed down a deeply rutted gravel path. It ended at an open gate and a well-lit parking lot, and Hamish brought the truck to a sliding stop in front of a two story corrugated metal and cinderblock building. It had a dozen small windows just below the roofline, and they were covered with heavy black rebar grates. The building looked to have been newly painted, and there were small evergreens planted in neat stone raised beds along its front. It also looked to be very secure. Ben noticed three cameras covered the lot, and it was surrounded by a high chain link fence. There were two other pickup trucks and a Land Rover parked in front of the building, and a big white utility truck with red stripes and two orange light bars on top.

"Piege Tournage Club," Ben said as he read the sign mounted above the formidable metal front doors.

Spot and Smudge poked their heads into the front seat, and Smudge gave Hamish's cheek a quick lick.

"Aye, you're coming in," he grumbled, and then swatted away her thank-you kiss.

Sholto led them up the stairs and slipped through the door when Hamish pulled it open. He held it for Ben and the pups, who saw the building was one big room.

It was also dark, except for a single light at the far end.

As they walked toward the light they moved past a long glass counter. There were dozens of neatly arranged handguns and knives inside the case, and a hundred rifles hung on the slat wall behind the counter. They ran the length of the front of the building, and Ben could only identify some of them. The further down the counter they got them more exotic and lethal-looking the weapons got. Opposite the counter was a dozen display tables with folded clothes, gun cases, scopes, and some high-tech stuff Ben didn't recognize.

As they approached the light he saw it hung above a large round table with four people seated at it.

"Hamish!" they called out as they saluted with held up beer cans and glasses.

One of the men tossed Sholto a pretzel, and she snagged it out of the air with a quick snap before she dropped her head into his lap and received firm neck and rump scratches.

As Ben walked up to the table an older woman with mahogany skin and a camouflage baseball cap smiled a big smile and said, "God, you look just like your dad."

Hamish introduced him around the table as one of the men pulled up chairs and the woman got them drinks from a fully stocked bar. The group took turns conveying their condolences about Ben's grandfather, and then launched into several rounds of stories about his parents, and his grandparents, and his sister's visit.

The pups made the rounds to receive friendly pats and a few pretzels, and then headed off with Sholto to sniff and explore.

What they had initially thought was the back of the building turned out to be a thick wall of glass that looked out over an indoor shooting range. They guessed the far wall was further than a football field away, and they could see tiny targets mounted to it.

Ben watched the dogs zig-zag around an offset glass panel and trot off into the dark of the range. He figured out the panel created an overlapping doorway so any stray bullets from the range couldn't hit anything or anyone in the front.

He turned back to the table when Lissa Chogin, the woman in the cap, asked Hamish if he'd heard about the wolf incident yet.

Lissa had a thick French accent, but based on her round face, broad nose, caramel skin, and slightly hooded eyes Ben guessed she was of First Nations ancestry. What would be Native American south of the border.

Hamish's bushy brow raise indicated he hadn't heard about the wolf incident, so Lissa said, "You should try to catch Willie before he leaves town. He says one of his party, some woman from Chicago, or was it Ohio?" She turned to her husband, who just shook his head. "Not important," she said. "She snuck off to water the snow and came running back screamin' about being assaulted by an enormous wolf."

"Assaulted?" Hamish asked as the other brow went up.

"That's what I asked," Lissa said. "Willie said she used that exact word. Apparently a lunatic wolf of incredible proportions rushed her from across the river and displayed every intention of ripping her face off. It growled and barked and snapped at her, and dove into the water a few times but the current kept it from crossing. It would get out, shake off, go nuts, and try to assault her all over again. Allegedly."

"Aye," Hamish asked. "Sounds like there was a two-legged lunatic in the glen."

The table nodded in agreement.

Ben learned the shooting club was a big supporter of Hamish's wolf project. They had initially been lulled by the sanctuary's potential economic value for their struggling town, but when they got their first look at Glasgow and her pack in the wild they'd become wolf-saving zealots, which Ben could absolutely understand.

But not everyone in town was as understanding, and the club had been dealing with exaggerated stories of wolf encounters since the first days of the reintroduction.

"And that's not the only weird animal happening," Greer Nellis said.

He and his wife Ellena were retired lawyers from Ottawa. They owned a sporting ranch on the opposite side of Christa's valley and specialized in custom excursions into the park. They were avid fishermen, but their real passions were shooting and getting a little sloshed.

Both of which they conveniently did at the same time at the gun club they'd founded.

Ben had never been in a shooting range before, or in a bar, but combining the two seemed like the kind of thing that would be frowned upon south of the border.

The Nellis' had been out-pacing the table two-for-one with drinks, but it was hard to tell if they were actually tipsy. They spoke in a Canuk-laden flat English, which as Hamish had pointed out to Ben on the trip up could even make sober people sound a little pie-eyed. Especially when the daft bastards added 'eh' to the end of a sentence.

The two couples were clearly from a different backgrounds, and at one point Lissa had referred to the Nellises as blocheads, which had prompted Ellena to fire back at Lissa's aboriginal roots by calling her a chug. Ben could tell the slurs would be extremely derogatory anywhere outside of the love shared around the table, where Hamish fit right in.

"Our daughter was out on her snow machine early this morning," Greer said. "She spotted a winter bear on the pike trail above the mine, just past your valley's high ridge. It was a big female, and the poor thing had a geezly chunk taken out of its shoulder. She didn't see any cubs, but she didn't wait around too long to find out, if you know what I mean."

To answer Ben's curious look Lissa said to him, "A winter bear is one that's been woken up from its hibernation slumber. They can be dangerous, especially if it's a momma with cubs. She'd be hungry, and there isn't much food to be had this time of year. Winter bears are often behind the worst unprovoked attacks, and brown bears can be downright ornery anyway."

"What wakes them up?" Ben asked as the dogs returned and spread out around the table to receive scratches and pats, and more pretzels.

Smudge put her head in Lissa's lap and was quickly in heaven. The woman had strong hands and she'd found the spot behind Smudge's ears that got her back leg quivering.

"There aren't many things that are dumb enough to wake up a bear," Lissa said. "Especially a big old mother grizzly. They usually find a secluded den and sleep deeply, so a winter bear like that is thankfully pretty rare."

Her husband, Hurrit 'Harry' Chogin, agreed with a nod.

They had the same round brown face and broad nose, and Ben guessed they were from the same tribe. He'd initially thought they were brother and sister until Lissa had introduced him as, "My worse half."

Harry hadn't said a thing during the entire conversation. He'd just sat quietly with his chubby arms folded over his oval body as he watched attentively through his comically thick glasses. His only reaction had been the slight shaking of his bulk whenever anyone told a joke or hurled an insult.

He leaned forward in his chair, tapped his wife on the arm to get her attention, and then signed a quick message.

Ben took a drink from his soda can to hide his surprise, and he could tell from his pups' flat stares and still tails they were controlling their reactions as well.

The three of them had easily read Harry's pudgy twisting fingers.

They'd also noticed he was missing a few digits on each hand.

When Ben saw Spot glance at the bar he guessed they were thinking the same thing. On a shelf above the bottles were a dozen of same kinds of puzzles they'd seen at the ranch. Lissa had said Harry made them his workshop, including the ones Hamish had sent down to Ben's family.

Spot turned to look at Ben, and their exchanged head tip wondered how a man with five total fingers could fabricate such intricate works of art.

"Harry says there's weather coming in," Lissa said. "That's gonna make it even tougher for that bear to find food."

"Aye," Hamish said. "We're heading into town and I'll tell the captain if we cross paths."

"Is it possible the crazy woman thought the bear was a wolf?" Ben asked.

Harry's bulk bounced with a chuckle, and he signed to his wife.

Lissa smiled and shook her head as she dismissed her husband with a wave.

Ben turned to Harry and signed, *I may be an idiot kid, and we Yanks do sometimes have trouble telling a brown bear from a brown streak in our shorts, but maybe the grizzly had just scared the crap out of her.*

Lissa burst out laughing, and translated for the benefit of the rest of the gaping table.

The Nellises pounded the table and broke into braying cackles, and Hamish smiled a broad smile as he clapped Harry on the back.

The pups wagged, and Sholto joined them as she looked around the table with her gray old unsure brows peaked.

Harry saluted Ben with a raise of his bottle, and then signed, *Touche, you little shit.*

He followed it up by raising his one remaining middle finger and giving the rest of the table a universal sign.

CHAPTER 31

When Ben commented that the shooting club was on the outskirts of Piege, Hamish pointed out the whole town was an outskirt.

He told Ben when the ore mines were booming thirty years ago there'd been four thousand workers in the valley. Most of them had lived in company-provided housing so they'd only came to town to shop, drink, fight, and patronize the brothel. At one point the place had gotten so busy you had to take a number, at least that's what Hamish had heard.

There were still some abandoned buildings and a few slab foundations left, but most traces of the boom were gone. Downtown Piege had been reduced to a handful of shops and offices surrounded by three blocks of shabby houses, and four light poles with one traffic light that had been disconnected a decade ago.

When they reached the main drag Hamish suddenly stomped on the brakes and brought the truck to an ice-scraping stop in the middle of the street.

He shoved his door open and jumped out, and Ben watched him through the side mirror as he walked past the red glow of the taillights and disappeared into the dark. He returned a few seconds later holding up a frozen, furry, slightly flattened roadkill animal by its tail. He opened and closed the tailgate, climbed back into the truck, and waggled his eyebrows at Ben before speeding off again.

Ben looked back at the pups, who shared his shrug.

Hamish hit the brakes again and cranked the wheel to pull up to a small combination grocery-hardware store.

Parked next to them was a medium-size motor coach that looked to be brand new, aside from the muddy snow packed in it wheel wells. Through its tinted windows Ben could see it would seat about twenty people, and it was empty.

Hamish told the dogs to say put as he and Ben got out of the truck.

They'd made it three steps toward the store when the front door flung open and a young man in a brightly colored and very tight one-piece ski outfit quickly closed the distance between them and stopped in front of Hamish.

There were two thin strip of hair on his jawline that met at a little patch on his chin, but he didn't have a mustache. He wore square sunglasses and a striped hat that looked Jamaican, but he was whiter than Ben and not much taller.

He fist-bumped Hamish, adjusted his thinly covered package, looked around, and then excitedly whispered, "So, did you hear?"

Before Hamish could answer he fist-bumped Ben and said with a nod, "Willie Cooke, whaz' up dude?"

He didn't wait for Ben's answer either before he turned back to Hamish and said, "The group's over at The Grub, let's go."

Willie started to walk off without waiting to see if Hamish was following him.

Before Ben could ask who the heck had just happened the grocery store door opened again and a tall young woman with long blonde hair backed through it. A skin-tight white ski suit clung to her thin curves, and she finished pushing the door open with a bump from her perfectly formed rear. She was struggling to hold two overflowing paper grocery bags, and when she twirled away from the door she was so focused on not dropping them that she ran smack into Hamish. He didn't budge, and when she bounced off of him and took a tottering step backward a loaf of sandwich bread fell from a bag and landed at Ben's feet.

He quickly snatched it out of the slush, stood, and stared with his mouth open.

Between the paper bags was a zipper that was low enough to expose a generous amount of lace pink bra. The bra was struggling to hold back the largest pair of breasts Ben had ever seen. They were tan, moved slightly as she wiggled to hold the bags, and were right in line with his wide eyes.

She smiled a too-white smile at Ben as Hamish took the bread, nestled it back into a bag, and took it from her.

She started to thank him, but when she noticed Willie her whole smiling face instantly morphed into some horrible raging thing.

"Hey, lazy midget!" she yelled at his back. "Am I like, your fucking pack mule?"

Willie stopped in the middle of the street, threw up his hands, and spun around on one planted foot.

"Sorry, geez," he said as he slunk back to take her remaining bag. "Get off my back, you're hurting it."

As he tossed the bags onto the passenger's seat of the motor coach he called out introductions, "Hamish, and little guy, meet Valerie."

"Oh mi-God," Valerie said with her whole body as she reached out to grab the tips of Hamish's fingers. When she shook his hand everything on her shook.

"So, like, you're that big bad wolf-guy Willie's been rambling about?" she asked as she gave Hamish an appreciative head-to-toe looking over. When she spoke her head rolled on her shoulders and her voice went up and down like a rollercoaster.

Before Hamish could answer her Willie said, "I'll tell you about the wolf if my group gets to meet the local legend."

When Hamish declined Willie pulled him aside and said not very quietly, "Hey man, you and I both know they aren't here for the skiing. We got the only accessible wild wolves in a thousand kilometers, and it's all they talk about. This whole 'grow the economy through furry tourism' thing was your idea, but until you loosen up on that tracker policy the chances of actually catching a glimpse of one is slim to none. So you gotta help a brother out and press the flesh a little, Paul Bunyan."

"Aye lad," Hamish conceded with a nod. "But you're buying the first three rounds."

Willie sealed the deal with a fist bump, Hamish waved for Ben to get the dogs, and they all headed across the street to the only remaining bar in town; The Grubbery.

§§

An hour and three scotches later Hamish was standing in front of the riveted table of tourists.

His lined, bearded face was warmly lit from the dim antler chandelier above the table, and he was deep into a story about getting stranded in Nord Du Quebec after losing his sled. He had crashed through a hidden patch of *sikuag*, or thin ice, and had only been able to cut three of his dogs loose before the rest of the team and his sled slipped into the black depths of Clearwater Lake. He'd managed to snatch his emergency pack, and he'd found a suitable spot on the bank to make a fire and dry out. He explained the sun barely rises that far north in winter and it was already setting by two in the afternoon, so he put up a snow shelter and settled in with the dogs for the night.

And that's when the wolves came.

Ben and the rest of the table were hooked. Not only was it a captivating story and one he'd not heard in his family's rich oral histories, but Hamish was a world class storyteller, just like his Papa had been.

Hamish held his audience in the palm of his hand as he toyed with them, and led them down dead ends, and then bit them on the backside with a surprise ending. He seamlessly wove in French and Inuit phrases to enhance the exotic surroundings, and deftly worked in their translations where needed. The rich textures of the foreign words and the flowing descriptions of the cracking ice and the northern lights and the howling wolves mixed with his animated facial expressions and deep voice to create an immersive experience. Even the wind whistling through the tavern's old eaves rose just as he reached the climax of his story like he'd planned it.

The table erupted in gasps and laughter after Hamish formed his big hands into claws and finished the story clamped down on Valerie's shoulders.

When she finally stopped jiggling and the group finished their toasts Hamish nodded for Willie to join him at the bar. As they left the table he told the elated tourists that Ben was a Canis lupus expert, and they unloaded a million wolf questions on him.

While Hamish drank with Willie he watched Ben from across the room and noted he wasn't a stranger to spinning a good story himself. He smiled as the boy told the group about their encounter with Glasgow and her pack's alpha, and was pleased to see Ben didn't let a silly thing like accuracy get in the way.

"Hamish, I just don't know what to make of it," Willie said quietly after the bartender left them to check on his table of tourists. They were the only ones in the place.

"The woman was a pain in the ass the whole trip," Willie said. "Just one of those idiots from down south who thought Nordic skiing was going to be like Nordic Track with scenery. Still, something spooked her pretty good. She came running back from the river screaming her fool head off, and it took me ten minutes to get her to calm down enough to tell me what happened. She looked like someone had just gutted her cat in front of her, and she couldn't wait to get the hell out of the woods. And she didn't say word one about a refund."

Hamish made Willie tell him the woman's story twice, once forward and once backward. He didn't see any inconsistencies, but it still didn't make any sense. Wolves just didn't randomly attack people who stopped to take a pee by a river.

As far as Hamish knew the only wolves in central Quebec were the ones he had brought in. Every so often he'd get wind of some idjet who thought it'd be cool to have a wolf, and some other idjet would hook them up with a smuggled wolf pup. The idjets and their wolves usually surfaced pretty quickly and the poor things got confiscated.

The good news was if the woman's story was even remotely true it wasn't likely to have been one of his wolves. They were all healthy and doing well. They had plenty of game and they weren't being harassed in the park, so there wasn't anything that would force them to attack. There was also no way the wolf felt trapped as it could have just walked away from the river. Wolves were far more skittish than most people realized. Part of their success was their reluctance to engage with humans, and Willie was right about seeing them in the wild being a rare treat. They can sense humans at great distances and are usually long gone before people see any signs of them.

"No, of course not," Willie said in response to Hamish's question, "You and the guys at the club are the only ones who know."

The bartender came back and asked if they wanted another. Hamish didn't recognize him but that wasn't surprising as he rarely stopped at the bar. The Grubbery was mostly a logging and miner dive and they were a transient bunch, but he immediately picked up on the fit young man's accent.

He also noticed there was a piece of a tattoo sticking out from under his rolled-up sleeve. It was a blue curve with the word "Club" visible, and Hamish assumed the rest of the tattoo would be a blue circle with the red royal standard lion in the middle.

He downed the last of his scotch, and started to sing lowly, "Hallo, hallo, you'll know us by our noise."

Willie looked up at him like he was nuts.

The bartender didn't stop washing a glass, but he responded by singing, "We'll give anything to see our team."

"At Ilbrox or away," Hamish sang a little louder.

"For we are," they sang together as the bartender looked up and smiled.

"The Glasgow Rangers Boys!" they shouted together at the top of their lungs, which sounded like ten booming men.

Ben, the dogs, and the table of confused tourists stared.

"Well that was weird," Willie mumbled as he slipped off his stool and took his drink back to the table.

"Hamish Walker," Hamish said as he extended his hand over the bar.

"Tavish McLendon sir," the bartender said as he quickly wiped his hand on his shirt and slapped his palm into Hamish's. "Glad to know yeh."

An hour and two additional scotches later Hamish and Tavish were loudly agreeing, or disagreeing, Ben wasn't sure which. The topic was the virtues and failings of the Old Firm, which Ben knew had something to do with Glasgow's Celtics and Rangers.

Even though he was fluent in tipsy Mimi-speak he was struggling to keep up with the men's abbreviated, bar-pounding Scottish, so he and the pups decided to explore The Grubbery.

The tavern was one big open space, and it looked like two separate buildings had been smashed together. Where the rear third had ancient wide-plank walls and log ceiling trusses, the front two thirds had painted plywood walls and metal rafters. It looked like someone had sliced the front wall off a cool old cabin and stuck on an ugly new warehouse. The ornate carved-wood bar was part of the back third, and the entire rear wall was fieldstone with a built-in fireplace Ben could stand up in. The hearth was charred black, and there was a rusty old pellet stove set in the center with a vent pipe that disappeared up the flue. Several large round tables were spread out around the bar and the stove, and there was a newer but equally dingy jukebox on the wall between them.

Ben read the scrolling titles on its display and noticed the most-played song was 'Bark at the Moon'.

Two dusty pool tables separated the tables and the bar from the newer front of the tavern, which was empty, unused space. Light from the dim antler chandeliers barely reached past the pool tables, and none of the utilitarian hanging fluorescents in the front were on. The heat didn't travel past the pool tables either, so it was a long cold walk through the dark to the front door.

Hamish pointed out to Ben that The Grub was far bigger than its current patronage justified. He said the front abomination had been added in the seventies, when it had been packed to the seams on any given Saturday night.

And then the blood and beer and a few condoms and tabs of LSD would get mopped up on Sunday mornings.

Next to the bar was a stone archway and a short hallway that led to the one bathroom, a tiny combination kitchen, a storage room, and the back door. Cardboard boxes and plastic crates with dry goods and paper products were stacked up in the hallway.

Ben thought the bathroom was pretty neat. There was a long stainless steel urinal trough running down the center of the floor, and a pipe with faucets hung down right above it. As Spot pointed out, it was a one-stop pee-and-wash. He lifted his leg to try out the trough and Smudge wagged when Ben turned on the water above him.

There was no women's bathroom, but Smudge noticed the one stall had the iconic ladies room symbol scratched into its door. Someone had added breasts and a triangle patch of pubes.

The walls of the bathroom were covered in graffiti of every type and skill level, and had been written in a dozen types of ink, or just scratched in. Quips and swear words and pornographic images were scrolled over life-size renderings of wildlife in action poses. They'd been done by a pretty talented artist with a black marker, and the eight-foot bear with outstretched forelimbs and bared teeth was good enough to be a little creepy. Ben held his hands up to its dinner-plate size paws and hoped its finger-length claws had been exaggerated for effect.

Every inch of free wall space in the rest of The Grub was covered with pictures and posters. There was a huge variety of photos ranging from large framed ones mounted with screws to small Polaroids tacked up with a staple. Most of the pictures in the back third of the tavern were older, and some were ancient black-and-white photos that had yellowed to sepia tones. Most of them showed men in groups who were either standing with massive pieces of logging or mining equipment or holding big fish or large dead animals.

Ben noticed Smudge had stopped near the juke box to stare at faded poster of a buxom, windswept blonde woman. She was wearing lederhosen and a big smile, and held three beers in each hand. A mustache, penis, and nipples had been added to her, and based on their realistic perspective and proportions Ben assumed them to have been drawn by the same marker artist from the bathroom.

With a head-tip Spot asked Smudge what was so interesting about the poster, and she shook her head and nodded at the old framed photo it was partially obscuring.

Ben slid over a chair and stood on it to get a better look. He lifted the poster and saw the photo was of a group of bearded, grim-faced men with rifles. They were pretty cool, but he and the pups had passed dozens of the same kind of pictures.

Smudge nodded for him to take a closer look, and Ben noticed one of the men didn't have a beard. In fact he wasn't a man at all, she was a tough-looking woman. She held a big rifle, and she was standing between the men below an archway made from logs.

The woman looked a lot like Christa, and above her head was a carved wooden sign that read 'Amaruq Irriq'.

She had one foot on a big dead wolf, and there were a dozen more wolves lined up in the snow in front of the men.

Ben and the pups shared a curious head tip before he hopped down from the chair and returned to the bar.

Ben was slowly rotating on his stool to avoid looking at Hamish. He was lying to his great-uncle about having learned sign language in school, and he hadn't figured out yet if Hamish shared Papa's radar. His grandfather's lie-detector hadn't been nearly as precise as Mimi's, but it was still capable of breaking a fibbing grandchild with just a look.

With each turn Ben picked at his burger and fries, which weren't bad, but weren't Miss Rene quality.

The pups were sitting on the floor next to his stool. They were listening to the conversation and snapping up the fries and burger chunks Ben was dropping.

After scarfing down two burgers Sholto had crashed out next to the pellet stove. She was spread out on Hamish's jacket, and alternating between snoring loudly, passing gas, and chasing something in her dreams.

Valerie had come up a few times to buy rounds for the tourist's table, on Willie's tab. She found excuses to lean against Hamish while she laughed and wiggled and flirted with Tavish. As she played with her hair she asked for a string of drinks with odd, suggestive names that had never been made in this bar, and weren't about to get made just because she was batting her eyes when she asked. Hamish was pretty sure by her third trip Valerie was inventing drinks so she could linger at the bar as Tavish politely shook his head at her.

The bartender was a rather striking bloke. He was sturdy and imposing as a Scot should be, with a chiseled chin and confident smile. Hamish thought the lasses of Edinburgh were likely missing him.

"Away and raffle your arse," Tavish said quietly to Hamish after Valerie returned to her table with a tray of beers. "That aviation blonde's fanny has had enough graffiti sprayed on it to make Banksy jealous."

Ben looked down at Smudge with a questioning raised eyebrow.

Smudge looked around to make sure no one was watching, and then used Spot's body to block her split paw from view as she subtly signed to Ben who Banksy was.

And an 'aviation blonde' is a blonde whose carpet doesn't match the drapes, she added.

Ben's head tip indicated he didn't understand, and Smudge added, *She's got a black box.*

Ben nodded and hid his smirk with another stool rotation as Smudge wagged and Spot gave them both a headshake.

"Aye," Hamish said to Tavish as they watched Valerie swaying in front of the jukebox. "But she puts up a good front and is well-reared. She's twice the woman wee Willie could possibly handle. Poor boy would need a helmet and a safety net."

He nudged Ben as he asked, "What do yeh think lad?"

Ben rotated to watch Valerie.

She was bending far forward and singing into an imaginary microphone along with the jukebox, "Mother told me, yes she told me, I'd meet girls like you. She also told me stay away, you'll never know what you'll catch…"

Ben looked down at the pups, and then turned to Hamish and Tavish and said, "I'd ride that into battle."

The men boomed out laughs, Valerie playfully shook her backside at them as she crooned on, Willie and the table of tourists shook their heads at her, and at the far end of the cold dark tavern the front door opened.

A large man in a big fur coat walked in. He stomped his feet, and initially Ben thought he was stomping off snow until he realized that's just how the man walked. He crossed the empty space, scowled at the tourists as he skirted the pool tables, and stomped up to the bar next to Hamish.

"Hamish," he grumbled without looking at him.

"Vic," Hamish said without looking at Vic.

As Ben rotated he gave Vic a quick looking over. He was a little shorter than Hamish but he was even wider. Where Hamish was thick in the chest and arms Vic was thick all over. He was the same girth all the way down to his knees. When he pulled off his fur cap Ben saw a narrow scar ran down the side of his bald head, curved in front of his ear, and ended just above his jaw.

Vic shot Ben a cold look, and he rotated away as he grabbed a fry and dropped it to Smudge.

She didn't catch it.

She was giving Spot an uneasy look, and he was agreeing with a nod.

"Breton," Vic grumbled at Tavish.

The bartender had already started to pour a few fingers of the single malt into a glass.

Vic leaned past Hamish and pushed him some as he reached over the bar to take the glass.

Hamish leaned back to give him some room, and Ben found that very odd.

Vic took his drink to a table in the corner near the stove and kicked a chair back so he could drop his bulk into it.

To answer Ben's curious look Hamish said quietly, "Victor LeClerc. He runs the ore mine, and pretty much everything else in this town. What's left of it."

"Including The Grub," Tavish said quietly.

Barely above a whisper he added, "The jobby-jabbing bawbag."

Hamish smiled into his glass as he nodded.

Ben saw his pups were staring at each other and he could tell something was wrong. He reached down to give Smudge a quick pat and felt she was shaking a little.

"I'm taking the pups for a pee break," Ben said as he slid off the stool.

"You know where the back door is, aye?" Hamish asked.

"Take them out through the front," Tavish said.

He looked in Vic's direction and Hamish added, "Right, the boss may not want them tracking through the kitchen."

Ben nodded, and the pups followed him across the big dark room and out the front door. They went around to the side of the building and checked to make sure no one could see them.

"What's up?" Ben asked as he rubbed his hands together.

I don't know, Spot signed. *He's just, wrong. But it's not something I can put my paw on.*

Agreed, Smudge signed. *We both felt it. It's a bad smell, but I can't zero it either.*

"Well that's helpful," Ben said as he tried to make light, but he knew to trust his pups' instincts. "So what do you want to do?"

Let's find a way to leave, Spot signed, and his sister agreed with a firm nod.

Ben added his own nod and started back to the bar with Spot padding behind him.

Smudge stopped them with a yap.

"What is it girl?" Ben asked as he and Spot turned around.

I really do have to pee, Smudge signed.

A minute later Ben was leading the pups up The Grub's stairs when the front door swung open.

Vic stomped out, scowled at Ben, and almost knocked him over as he pushed past him.

Spot angled himself in front of Vic, and Ben watched with wide eyes as the big man booted his dog down the stairs.

As Spot tumbled down the icy steps Vic stomped behind him and grumbled, "Watch where the fuck you're going."

Spot hit the snow bank and spun to his feet, and Vic ignored him as he stomped away.

Ben balled his fists, and he was about to shout at the bald arsehat's back when Smudge tapped his leg and shook her head for him to hold off.

Spot trotted back up the stairs and signed, *Anything?*

Smudge shrugged and gave him an unsure headshake, and Ben realized she must have snuck a big sniff of Vic's fur coat when Spot was distracting him.

"You two need to clue me in before you to pull that crap," Ben said as he yanked open the door and followed the pups back into the tavern.

As Vic stomped away through the slush he pulled out his cellphone.

CHAPTER 32

"Aye, let's call it," Hamish said.

"Sorry Unc," Ben said.

"No bother lad. Sholto's away for sawdust anyway," Hamish said as he stood up and stretched. "But yeh might have to drive."

Willie saw them getting ready to leave and came over to say goodbye. As he and Hamish were shaking hands the front door opened and several men walked in.

Their silhouettes filled the open doorway, and a few of them had to duck.

They spread out as they walked across the dark open space, and Ben wondered if stomping was just what big men did in Quebec. It was as if their feet had trouble holding up their hulking bodies.

When Spot poked Ben on the knee he nodded, and whispered, "Yeah, I see it."

There was a dog with the men, but calling it a dog didn't do it justice. It was a big walking furry muscle. The animal was as tall and wide as the boerboels, and it had an odd shaggy coat that looked familiar but Ben couldn't quite place. It wasn't a breed he recognized, and he thought he'd pretty much studied them all. The lanky dog had strange folds of extra skin around its thick neck, and its black and gray face had distinct light brown eyebrow and muzzle markings.

Once the dog entered the light of the bar Ben understood why he hadn't been able to identify it. He realized it wasn't a breed, it was two breeds.

A mix of Rottweiler and wolf.

The pups immediately thought something was off about the dog, in addition to his strange mixed lineage. He had a vacant look on his face and was completely disinterested in his surroundings. Spot guessed the big dog was mentally challenged.

The men took over the table closest to the pool tables, and as a short muscular Latino man with huge biceps sat down he backhanded the Rotty-wolf hard on the side of the head. The dog barely seemed to notice, but walked in a tight circle a few times and plunked down at the man's feet.

A massive First Nations man Ben assumed was the leader stepped up to the bar and stood next to Hamish.

Spot and Smudge exchanged dire looks and tried to get Ben's attention. This guy smelled worse than Vic. Something was wrong with these men and their scent was firing the pups' radar. They were both fighting the urge to grab Ben and run.

"Yo Tav," the big man said. "Blues."

"Evening Ty," Tavish said with a nod. He was already pulling six bottles of beer from the cooler.

Ty summoned the short Latino guy with a wave, and as he walked to bar Ben noticed a large, jagged number thirteen was tattooed across his thick neck. As he got closer Ben saw the number was made out of skulls that curled into horns behind his ears. The rest of his head was bald except for a small center strip of jet-black hair that was pulled back into a short pony tail. His chest was so wide his ballooned arms stuck out when he walked, but he was the only thug who was light on their feet.

When the man nodded at Tavish he nodded back and said, "Jero."

Jero looked up to eyeball Hamish as he reached for the beers, and gave him another long slow look as he left.

"A'right then," Hamish said as he extended his hand over the bar. "Tavish, yeh glaikit whore, it's been pure magic. I was serious about that invite. Come up to the ranch tomorrow for dinner. We'd love to have yeh."

"I'll do just that Hamish, thanks," Tavish said as they shook. "G'night Ben."

As Ben gave him a wave Hamish put his hands on Willie's shoulder. He gently pointed him in the direction of his table of tourists and whispered in his ear, "Time to wrap it up lad."

Willie nodded but hadn't really heard him. He was staring at Jero with his mouth hanging open, and he kept staring at the table of big men as he crossed the room.

When Hamish turned back to the bar Ty was standing right in front of him.

"Hamish?" he asked. "Hamish Walker? You the wolf-fucker who's got the whole town wrapped around his dick? I heard you were three meters tall. Guess not."

Ty was looking Hamish right in the eye, which not a lot of people were tall enough to do, and it was pretty clear to Ben that his insults weren't warm ribbing between friends.

Willie hadn't heard exactly what Ty had said, but he'd caught the tone, and he could tell by the other men's smirks they had as well.

This was the last shit he needed. It was hard enough convincing tourists to choose the unknown dirt speck that was Piege instead of the traditional getaways like Tremblant or Quebec City. He didn't need the local Neanderthals scaring away the money.

Still, some Wild West shit could add a little flavor to the evening that he could market, if that shit ended well, and soon.

And if anyone could end shit quickly, it was Hamish.

But Hamish was thinking the exact opposite. He normally wouldn't have let this big fop get past the first syllable of fucker without a tooth-loosening attitude adjustment, but with Ben in the bar he couldn't just haul off and deck the guy.

Jean would kill him.

"Aye, I am he," he said with a smile as he held Ty's stare. "But as there's lovely ladies and wee bairn currently in this establishment you and I will have to get to know each other at a later date."

He took a step back, and subtly motioned to Sholto.

Ben saw the old shepherd was on her feet, and she was scanning the room with an alert stare he'd never seen before. He realized, as did the pups, that Hamish's quick hand signal to her wasn't *Come here*, it was *Don't tear this guy's throat out, yet*.

Sholto stayed where she was.

Spot desperately wanted to risk a paw sign to Ben. The smell from the thugs was so bad he was starting to panic a little, but he still couldn't figure out exactly what it was. It was right there but his mind just couldn't grab it. He was also worried about his sister as she was looking like she was ready to do something drastic.

Hamish put his hands on Ben's shoulders as he took quick stock of the room. He didn't want to walk past the table of men so he pointed Ben toward the rear hallway and said, "Head on out the back door lad. Take your pups to the truck. I'll be there in a tick with Sholto, just gotta pay the tab."

Ben put on his jacket as he walked to the end of the bar with Spot at his side, but when they got to Sholto he stopped.

He decided to give her a pat, and wait for Hamish.

No, don't stop, Smudge thought as she watched her boy scratch the shepherd's shoulders.

She had hung back with Hamish, and she was pretty sure she'd figured out the smell. Not that it helped them any.

Spot looked up at Ben, and then at Sholto, and then down the hallway, and then he turned back to Smudge.

With shoulder shakes and head tips he told her what he was planning to do if things went balls-up.

That's the second worse plan you've ever had, she replied with twitches and bobs. *Let's hope we don't need to try it. We just need to leave, and if this old lump moves any slower I'm dragging him outta here by his beard.*

Hamish had paused to down the last of his drink, push in Ben's stool, and leave some money on the bar. As he pretended to count the change in his hand he wished eleven year old boys listened as well as Sholto. As much as he wanted to just grab Ben and go he needed to get Willie's attention first.

Look over here, Hamish thought as he fumbled to put on his tam. *Please see that it's time to go. No, don't sit down yeh daft arse.*

Willie sat down. He put a hand on Valerie's shoulder, whispered something to the group, and the whole table laughed as they looked at the men.

Bugger, Hamish thought as he shook his head. *Bloody idjet.*

The jukebox wailed, "For those about to rock, we salute you..."

Spot read Hamish's face and saw he was certainly tuned into what was going on.

When Spot tried to give Ben a nudge toward the back hallway Ben just shooed him away and continued to pat Sholto as he watched Hamish adjust his cap.

"Something funny over there?" Ty called over to Willie's table.

"Ty, be nice to our visitors," Tavish said as he picked up Hamish's money.

"Sure Tav," Ty said as he noticed Valerie for the first time and licked his lips. "I'll be real nice to them."

Jero smiled and rolled his massive shoulders, and Smudge noticed he'd unclipped the big Rotty-wolf's leash from his collar ring.

She looked back at Spot, who had noticed it too and indicated, *Oh great. Adding a step to the plan sister.*

Chairs screeched on the floor as all of the thugs stood up.

Rotty-wolf barely lifted his head, but for the first time he seemed interested in what was going on.

Smudge got Sholto's attention with a wag, and she gave the big old shepherd a few commands as subtly as she could. She couldn't tell for sure if Sholto understood them as she just turned her hard stare back to Hamish and Ty, but she did move closer to Ben.

Smudge wagged again, and with a head tip she asked Sholto if she got it.

The ex-army sergeant shot her a hard look, and when she shifted her posture and flared her nostrils Smudge read them as, *I'm old but I'm not stupid, and I've been doing my part since before your great-great-grandparents suckled a teat. I'll execute your stupid plan, but if Hamish gets hurt you two are answering to me.*

Smudge thought she was maybe reading a little into it, but the veteran's ferocity was clear and the message was easy enough to get the gist of.

Ty and Jero slowly walked toward the tourists.

Willie stood up and put himself between the men and his table. He certainly didn't want to face off with the big morons but he couldn't have them getting close to his paying guests.

Valerie sat up straighter in her chair with her zipper straining as she licked her glossy lips. She didn't want to miss any of this.

Hamish waved one last time at Ben for him to leave, grimaced as the boy ignored him, and walked over to stand at Willie's side.

Ty and Jero stopped a few steps away when they saw Hamish step up.

"Isn't this rich Jero?" Ty asked as he put his hands on his hips. "A *pede* and a dog fucker. I don't know which is worse."

Willie couldn't look away from Jero. They were about the same height but Jero's neck was bigger than both of Willie's thighs.

Tavish casually put one foot up on the beer cooler, tossed his towel over his shoulder, and grabbed the cut-off axe handle that was hidden just below the counter.

"Listen gentlemen," Hamish said calmly. "There's nae' need for unpleasantries here, and nae' need for our guests to see such nonsense. We donae' want to give them the wrong impression of our welcoming little hamlet."

Ty eyeballed Hamish as he clenched his jaw.

A big, terrible smile crept across Jero's face as he flexed his fists, which caused his cannonball biceps to jump.

He winked at Willie and puckered his lips like he was kissing him.

Smudge played the clueless happy mutt and wagged her way across the room to come up between Hamish and Willie.

Her tail slowed to a stop, and as she looked up at Jero's big arms she thought, *Not bad ese, but this chiquita has a little surprise for you.*

Ty locked eyes with Hamish and said, "My grandfather hunted the wolves out of these mountains so our families could cut trees and dig ore without worrying about their kids or cows or pigs getting fucking slaughtered. Wolves are just rats with bigger teeth. They're a nuisance, and we don't want them here Jock. I thought Mr. LeClerc had been pretty clear about that with you and your circle-jerk club out there at the range."

Spot was watching Ty closely and knew he'd be the one to strike first. He could also tell it was coming soon as he read his darting eyes, his deep breathing, and the way he set his shoulders. Humans were still animals, and they prepared to attack the same way. Just a lot slower.

When Ty lifted his heel to take the first step Spot was already halfway down the back hallway.

Hamish saw Ty move as well and had already balled his fist. He'd also reached out to shove Willie out of the way.

Sholto angled her body in front of Ben.

Tavish grabbed the ax handle and reached for the far lip of the bar as he pushed off with his foot.

Smudge crouched, closed her eyes, twisted her head slightly, and recited her internal dialog to fire up her muscles.

She went Cu Sith and leapt just as the lights went out.

.

CHAPTER 33

Spot had shot down the tavern's back hallway in a few big bounds. He'd jumped onto a stack of crates and launched himself high to fly into the kitchen. In one fluid motion he'd opened his split paws, flung open the electrical panel, and flicked off the main breaker to plunge the bar into darkness.

The pellet stove clicked off but it still gave off a little glow through its front grate. Far across the room at the front of the bar some light from the street made it through the small dirty window in the door. For the humans it was pitch black, but the dogs could see well enough to do what they had to do.

Sholto knocked Ben down onto Hamish's coat, and she pinned him to the floor as she stood over him crouched and ready.

Spot crashed onto the small kitchen counter, spun, and struggled to get his footing as pizza pans and dirty dishes clanged to the floor. He pulled himself off the counter with his split paws and rocketed back down the hallway.

When the lights went out Tavish was in mid-air over the top of the bar, but he landed like a cat and changed direction. He dodged bar stools and shot down the dark back hallway with his outstretched hands following the walls. He was headed for the breaker panel, and whatever had crashed in the kitchen.

Smudge had closed her eyes an instant before the lights went out and was fully adjusted to the dark as she launched herself between Hamish and Willie. She gained height and picked her targets as she drew her feet in and pulled into a ball. She reached full muscle mass just before she uncoiled explosively and caught Jero on the chin with her hind feet and Ty in the chest with her spread front paws.

Spot barely avoided taking out Tavish as they passed each other in the dark hallway.

Hamish stopped in mid-step when everything went black. He had been loading up to throw a punch across Ty's jaw but he pulled it and took a few steps back with Willie safely corralled behind his arms.

Valerie screamed, and so did Willie. His was higher-pitched.

Ty and Jero, who had been coming forward with fists raised, were flying backward and away from each other.

Ty tottered and wobbled back a few big lunging steps until he bumped hard into an empty table.

Jero smacked into two advancing thugs, and as they all went down in a pile they crashed into their table, which knocked down the two remaining men.

Spot raced past the bar stools and jogged to come in behind the big Rotty-wolf just as the dog was starting to stand up. When Spot grabbed the leash and clipped it to the dog's collar the hairy beast reflexively snapped, but without any real target he only bit the air an inch from Spot's rear.

Spot rolled forward and slipped the other end of the leash over Jero's boot before he bolted away.

Tavish hit the breaker and the lights came back on. He looked down at the mess on the kitchen floor and at the closed back door, and as he ran his fingers through his hair he whispered to himself, "What in the bleedin' hell?"

Sholto let the struggling Ben up from the floor and stood in front of him.

Spot and Smudge were standing at Hamish's side, and they were wagging like simpletons as they controlled their panting.

Ben figured out what had happened pretty quickly. He noticed his dogs' rib cages expanding and contracting in sync while the last of Smudge's hypertrophic neck muscles were returning to normal.

The group of stunned tourists saw Jero and the thugs laying on the ground, and Ty leaning against a table on unsure feet, and Hamish protecting a very pale and rattled Willie.

Valerie smiled her best smile and squared her shoulders at Hamish as she thought, *He didn't even break a sweat.*

Jero sat up and looked around, and as he rubbed his jaw he angrily shoved away his pals. He got to his feet and started to stomp toward Hamish but the leash stopped him.

He hopped on his front foot, and looked back at his dog.

Rotty-wolf looked up at him with his vapid stare, and Jero pulled the leash off his boot and backhanded the animal hard on the side of the head.

The jukebox spun back up with Mick crooning, "I can't get no, I can't get no satisfaction…"

Willie smiled, but then caught himself and bit down hard on the inside of his cheek.

Ty drew himself up to his full height and looked around the room. He took a moment to figure out what had just happened, gave up, and nodded to Jero and the rest of the boys as he slowly reached around his back and under his jacket.

Hamish saw the move and readied a hand sign for Sholto, who had already planted her back feet and picked a target on Ty's forearm. She was ready to charge when the front door of the tavern banged loudly open.

CHAPTER 34

"Good evening gentleman," the captain said as she strode into the bar with a deputy trailing behind her.

She crossed the room and stared down Ty as she passed. He was only a tad taller than she was, and not much wider. He let go of the concealed handle of his knife and dropped his hand to his side.

The captain nodded to Tavish, who had returned to the bar and was sliding his axe handle back into its hiding spot.

The big cop scanned the room as she walked up to Hamish and removed her dark green Surete du Quebec hat. The yellow trim on her hat was repeated on her fitted jacket and along the seams of her crisp uniform pants.

Ben noticed she had large features to match her stature, and they all worked well together. She was an attractive woman with sharp, but also warm blue eyes. Her light hair was held back in a tight ponytail, and even her bulky vest couldn't hide her shapely curves and athletic build.

Her deputy took up station between Jero and Ty, folded his arms, and tapped his fingers on the butt of his holstered pistol. He wasn't much taller than Jero, and about as tough looking as Willie. His hat looked comically big on his boyish head.

"Causing trouble again Mr. Walker?" the captain asked. "What exactly is it with you Jocks?"

Valerie started to speak but the captain shot her a look that shut her up. She gave the top half of the tart a look, and then smiled at Willie before turning back to Hamish.

"No issues Blu," Hamish said. "Just lads having a pint and a dance to entertain the tourists."

Captain Blu smiled, and looked down at Spot and Smudge, and then at Ben. She nodded at Sholto, and the old German shepherd gave her a wag.

She turned back to Hamish, but said to Willie, "Those of you who are hitting the trail in the morning should get a good night's sleep, eh?"

Willie corralled the tourists, tossed a small pile of money on the table, and herded them along the far wall and out the front door. Everyone, including the dogs, watched Valerie struggle to put on her coat and walk at the same time. Willie helped her through the door and gave Hamish a thank you nod before closing it behind him.

Blu shook her head as the door banged shut. She put on her hat, took Hamish by the upper arm, and said curtly, "Okay, let's go."

The thugs started to hoot and clap, and one of them chanted, "QPP, QPP, QPP..."

"*Chido* sheriff," Jero said with a big smile. "Take that *culero* out of here."

Blu walked Hamish past the grinning men, and Ty and Jero moved aside to give them a wide path.

Ben followed in their wake with Hamish's jacket and the dogs.

The deputy gave the tough loggers and miners his best glare before turning on his heels and taking up the rear.

Blu tipped her hat at the bartender, and received a thankful nod.

Hamish locked eyes with the smiling Ty as they passed each other, and then took his coat from Ben and put an arm around him as they walked to the front door.

The deputy had parked his car so close to the front steps it was blocking them. He noticed the captain's annoyed look and pushed past the group to scramble down the steps as he fumbled with his keys.

"Swing back around in an hour Dave," Blu said. "Let me know if they're still here. Goodnight."

Deputy Dave paused with his hands on his hips. He was going to ask if she needed help with these perps, but his fifteen weeks of intensive police training and eight solid months of field experience allowed him to quickly assess his captain had the old man, the boy, and the three dogs well in hand. He climbed into his car and drove off, and accidentally hit his lights for a second as he left town.

Blu had parked her cruiser next to Hamish's truck in front of the grocery store, which was now closed. Willie's motor coach was just pulling away, and he honked a quick goodbye blast as he disappeared down the dark street behind Dave.

Ben and the dogs jumped into the back of pickup as Blu removed her hat and joined Hamish in the front seat.

The big cop turned and put her arm over the back of the center console. She looked at Ben for a moment, and then gave his knee a friendly shake as she cracked a smile and said, "Jesus, you look just like your dad. You okay?"

"Yes ma'am," Ben said.

"I'm sorry you had to see that," Blu said. "We have some bad element here but normally it's a pretty nice place."

"Yeah, I know," Ben said. "It's okay. I wasn't worried." He put an arm around all of the dogs and jostled them as he said, "Sholto had my back."

"Gunny's last bar fight," Hamish said as he smiled into the mirror.

"So what'd you do to piss them off?" Blu asked.

"Wasnae' me," Hamish said like she'd offended him.

To answer her tipped head he added, "Ask the boy."

Blu didn't notice Ben was nodding.

"Vic came in," Hamish said, "downed a drink, and left. And then the boys' choir showed up. Beyond that I truly have nae' idea what just happened."

"Huh," Blu said with a disbelieving nod. "Well, I recognize that Inuit bully, Thibault Lavoie, and the midget Conan with that half-wolf abomination is Jero. They work for Vic, but those other delinquents are from the logging camp. An odd mix. Wouldn't have thought those boys were drinking buddies. Bad guys teaming up is never a good thing."

"Did yeh hear about the winter bear?" Hamish asked.

"Yes," Blu said, "but I'd really like to hear about this alleged wolf attack."

Hamish wasn't too surprised Blu had gotten wind of it as she was very good at her job. He told her everything he'd heard from Willie about the crazy tourist and the alleged crazy wolf at the river.

"Sounds like a lot of bull...shine," Blu said. "Still, something happened out there, and it's awfully bad timing. Vic and the logging brass would like nothing better than to have an incident with your wolves."

"It wasnae' them at all," Hamish scoffed. "We were just out there and the whole pack's fitter than a butcher's dog. We even got a real close look at the alpha, right Ben?"

Blu noticed Ben's vigorous nod this time, and his wide eyes.

"He looked pretty dang healthy to me, Captain ma'am, sir," he said.

"We're so bloody close Blu," Hamish said. "We're at the tipping point. We have four established families now, a self-sustainable base for the park. If we have one more successful year the university will take over the research and tracking, and the national funding kicks in to cover their protection. Even Vic canae' fuck with them once that happens. Hell, in another few years we'll have controlled hunting, husbandry programs, managed tours—"

"And the tourist dollars that will save this place," Blu interrupted, "and stop it from being a one assho-, um, man show. I got it Hamish, you know I do, but officially I can't take a stand. I've got to pretend I represent everyone's interest and I have five municipalities and aboriginal lands to juggle."

"You've done plenty Blu, "Hamish said. "You're a right square bloke and we appreciate all the help. Including tonight." He reached into the back seat and grabbed a handful of Sholto's neck fur as he added, "Not that we needed any help mind you."

"You know the new bartender?" Blu asked.

"Tavish?" Hamish asked. "Just met him tonight. Seems a likeable enough sort of fella. Gonna have him up to the ranch tomorrow, might find out a few things. Why, yeh want the lad's digits?"

Ben laughed until he noticed Blu wasn't smiling. He thought she must be the only one of Hamish's buds who didn't play his friendly ball-busting game.

"I just like to know Vic's new staff is all," Blu said. "And bartenders tend to have big ears." She turned to the back seat and said, "Ben, I hope you enjoy the rest of your stay with us, and please tell your parents I said hello." To Hamish she said, "And you, try to stay out of trouble. Oh, and tell your nutty bunch over there at the shooting club they might want to consider renaming their upcoming 'Wounded Warrior Fun Shoot'. Christ, it's as bad as the rehab clinic's 'Baked Sale' last year."

"Aye," Hamish said, and then he turned on his best smile as he added, "You coming over later? You know Christa would love to have you up for a drink."

Blu snorted out a chuckle as she got out of the truck.

Before she closed the door she said with a smile, "Christa eh?"

Captain Bluette 'Blu' Pinard got into her cruiser and gave them a nod, and as she backed away Ben noticed thick snowflakes had started to fall.

CHAPTER 35

Ten minutes earlier Jia unzipped her jacket and fanned it as she said, "Lucy, turn down the heat back here. You're cooking my cat."

He started to tell her for the tenth time there were climate controls in the back, but he just shook his head and tapped her heater controls to low instead.

"And back up a little," she added. "I can't see the around your big freaking head."

He couldn't argue with that as he did fill the driver's side of the Suburban's front seat. He put the van in reverse and rolled back at an angle until they were broadside to the back door of The Grubbery.

From their hidden spot in the tavern's back lot they saw Vic appear on the muddy strip of snow that acted as the sidewalk. He was talking on his phone as he stomped away from the front of the tavern. He disappeared behind a long stretch of buildings, reappeared at the end of the block, scanned the deserted street, and turned to stomp toward them. He angled across the lot and climbed into the back of the van next to Jia.

"They're on the way," he mumbled as he pulled the hat off his head.

Jia nodded, and tried not to stare at Vic's scar.

Lucy went ahead and stared. He looked into the rearview mirror and gave the jagged crease a long examination as the big mine boss eyeballed him right back.

Before Jia could interrupt the testosterone-bloated silence with an insincere compliment about Vic's hideous fur coat two big beat-up pickup trucks and a rusty Jeep pulled into the lot. They parked along the side of the building, and six large men and a big dog got out. As they lumbered toward the front of the tavern Jia wondered if stomping was an inherited trait in Quebec.

A few minutes passed, and Vic grumbled, "Fucks taking them so long?"

The light above the back door of The Grub went out, and Vic was just about to open the van door when Jia said, "Wait."

She nodded to the south end of town, where they could see glimpses of two police cars through the buildings. The cars disappeared in front of the tavern, and didn't appear again.

"Shit," Vic and Jia hissed at the same time.

Lucy almost called 'jinx' on them before he caught himself, and cursed his nine year old daughter.

"I'm going in," Vic grumbled.

"No, you aren't," Jia said.

Three minutes later one of the police cars left. It hit its lights for a second before it disappeared to the south, and a few seconds later a white motor coach tooted its horn and followed in the same direction.

Four minutes later the other cruiser pulled out and headed north, and Hamish Walker's truck followed it.

The back door to the bar opened and a man slipped on a coat as he trotted through the falling snow. He pulled open the van's back door and slid into the rear-facing seat behind Lucy.

"What in the fucking shit happened in there?" Jia asked.

Before the man could answer she added, "Lucy, turn the heat up back here. You trying to freeze us?"

The asset told them what had happened inside the bar as he took out a handkerchief and wiped a little smear of mud from his custom boots.

CHAPTER 36

"Are you positive?" Ben asked.

I'm not positive, Smudge signed, *but I'm pretty sure. Ninety percent. Eighty. Definitely seventy-five.*

If you're right sis, Spot signed, *how'd it get all the way up here?*

Ben slid off the bed and paced the floor.

"If it is more of that nasty stuff from the Dorschstein's kennel we gotta to tell Uncle Hamish," he said. "It's a safe bet those Skippy McArsemunchers from the bar aren't up here doing high-tech bio-research. We gotta say something."

The pups stared at him.

"Right?" Ben asked.

Give us one night, Spot signed. *We need to know more about this thing.*

"Spot, really?" Ben asked as he threw up his hands.

He realized he'd said it a little loud so he lowered his voice when he said, "You guys want to run around in the dark out there? It's not like back home, this is the real deal. There's things in those woods that make One Ear look like a hamster. No way, we have to say something."

The pups just stared at him.

"Oh, okay," Ben said. "Don't think I don't know what you're doing. If I try to tell Unc what's going on and you two decide to be all 'regular dog' I'm gonna look like more of an idiot than he already thinks I am."

What exactly are you going to tell him? Smudge asked.

She looked to her brother, who nodded his agreement as he signed, *And what do you expect him to do about it even if he believes you?*

At the very least we'll be on the next bus south, Smudge signed. *We'll lose any chance we have of solving this thing, and do you really want to bring this problem home?*

Ben reluctantly conceded she was right with a nod.

We don't have enough info to say anything of use to him, not yet. Spot signed. *And I need you to do some more homework while we're gone.*

"You might as well paint a target on your backs if you go out there," Ben said as he walked to the window. He looked out at the heavily falling snow and the elkhounds huddled in their igloos, and added, "Your black coats are fine back home, but have you noticed everything up here is a shade of grayish white? Even at night I could see you two numpties coming from a thousand meters away."

When he turned around his pups were standing next to each other on the bed, and both of them were as white as the blowing snow.

CHAPTER 37

Early the next morning Christa tapped on Ben's bedroom door, and he groaned for her to come in.

He had only nodded off two hours earlier, which was just after the pups had crept back into the house, dried off their snowy coats, hidden their borrowed sled dog boots, and curled up on the foot of the bed together with Smudge's chicken.

Christa poked her head into the room and said, "I'm heading down to the shooting club with Rook and Vuur if you want to come."

The pups were up like a shot and stood at the door wagging in sync.

Ben rolled over, looked at his beckoning dogs, and then up at Christa as he grumbled, "Yeah, I guess we do."

A few minutes later they pulled out of the garage in Christa's pickup truck, and drove past Captain Blu Pinard's police cruiser. It was parked next to Hamish's truck in the driveway, and both were covered in snow.

Christa and Ben decided to leave Sholto at home as they didn't want to open Hamish's bedroom door to fetch her.

As they pulled out of the driveway Christa looked at Ben, and they both giggled.

"So would that be the last thing Sholto can never un-see?" Ben asked.

They exchanged snickering laughter all the way to the main gate, and as they wound down the mountain's switchback roads Ben asked her about the shooting club.

Christa explained that Hamish had formed the club with Greer and Ellena. They used to meet at the Nellis' ranch once a week, and it started as a few friends shooting a little and drinking a lot, and catching up on the local news and gossip. Membership grew, and although it was technically still just a shooting club they started to get involved in things like environmental programs and municipal improvements as the local mining operations shrunk and the town fell on hard times. Before long it became a popular forum for volunteerism and local action, along with downing a few two-fers. Blu usually stopped in for the larger month-end meetings under the guise of talking gun safety and hunting laws, and then she'd stay for a few cold ones and to keep her finger on the pulse of the town's happenings.

It didn't take long for the meetings to outgrow the Nellis' place. The club's current building had been owned by the mine, as were most of the abandoned, dilapidated properties in town. The municipality exercised their right to force a transfer of ownership when the club committed to making improvements to the land. Basically they gave it to the Nellis', and they financed the build-out. Christa told Ben taking over distressed properties was a common practice in many of the deteriorating towns in the mining belt. The companies were usually cooperative, but it sure didn't sit well with Vic.

And when Hamish started the wolf program there was more friction.

Christa explained that Vic was a very vocal opponent of Hamish's plan, and for reasons the mine boss couldn't seem to clearly articulate he didn't want the tourists coming to town. Vic also had a hatred of wolves that no one fully understood, but there was talk it had something to do with his scar.

He also didn't like that the Chogins were the sanctuary's biggest backers.

"Harry worked for the mine for thirty years," Christa said, "and when Vic was brought in as the new head rock-breaker a decade ago they immediately bumped heads. It's pretty well accepted that Vic's only talent was slashing the budget. He'd been a dock manager in Thunder Bay and knew nothing about mining. There's no doubt some belt-tightening was needed, but his cuts went too far. Harry's a demolitions expert, and he was setting blasts when Vic was getting his milk-money beat out of him in kindergarten. But all Vic saw was cost. He hamstringed Harry's safety protocols, and they argued about it right up to the morning of the accident. Harry had set a rock bench explosion, and one of the untrained workers walked right into a blast site as the first charge went off. When Harry tried to save him they both got injured."

Ben felt Smudge's shoulder slump, and he gave her a tender rub.

"There's only one thing that pisses Vic off more than Harry," Christa said, "and that's Lissa. She's the demo expert at a competing mine an hour south of town, and she's been fighting Vic tooth and nail for him to keep paying Harry's benefits. Lissa also helps me with the radio collars for the wolves, and that goes right up Vic's brown mine shaft. She keeps a few collars and trackers in her work truck, and when Vic found out about it he ratted her out to her company. Of course they promptly told Victor LeClerc to go fuc...to go pound rocks."

As Christa pulled the truck into the shooting club's driveway she said, "Everyone loves Lissa, and no one can stomach that scivey *beau cave*."

⚜ §§ ⚜

An hour later Ben was pissing lead with an Israeli made Tavor assault rifle. He was holding down the trigger as it spat fire and ripped apart a scowling plywood bad guy who was pointing a big pistol at him. The rat-tatting bolt clicked forward and stopped, and the last empty shell casing bounced on the rubber floor matt as smoke rose from the end of the muzzle.

Ben smiled a huge smile.

"Nice shootin' Tex," Lissa said as she looked at the big hole in the target's chest and groin. "I'd say he's not going to bad-guy prom this year."

She had pulled one of the ear pieces from Ben's sound proofing headset away from his head, and she let it snap back with a thump.

Harry rapped on the glass from the far side of the partition wall.

He smiled, and signed to Ben, *Not bad for a slow city kid.*

222 · ROBERT UDULUTCH

From behind Ben Christa said sharply, "Vuur, Rook, *controleren.*"

Rook ran up to the castrated bad guy and circled it as he sniffed at the splintered bits of wood on the floor. Vuur crossed behind his brother and made a wide arc to come up behind the target. He watched from a few steps away with his head low and his eyes scanning.

The target exploded just above Rook's head and bits of plywood rained down. He jumped back a few steps but immediately snapped to alert.

Christa holstered her pistol and trotted over to Rook as she cooed, "Good boy! *Goeie seun!*"

The big dog buried his huge black face into her middle, and as Christa scratched his droopy jowls she said to the other mastiff, "*Lekker* Vuur, nicely done."

The bullet had passed within a few inches of him after it ripped through the target, but neither brother had flinched.

Both dogs wagged their whip-like tails around in circles, and Lissa said to Ben, "Two weeks ago Rook would have been shitting himself in the parking lot after a shot like that."

Ben nodded, and looked over his shoulder to see the pups had watched the demonstration.

They were hanging out with Harry at the front of the range.

Harry was rubber-banding small posters for the club's upcoming charity shoot, and sharing his breakfast with them. It was thick toast smeared with a cold meat and cinnamon spread called cretons, and based on the pups' smacking and wags it was quite possibly the best thing they'd ever tasted, next to venison.

They were happy to be fueling up from their long night out, but mostly they were just fascinated with Harry. The accident at the mine had taken a good bit of his hearing, eyesight, and lung capacity, and five of his fingers. At his feet was a small oxygen tank with a clear tube that ended in a small mask. He only had to use it once in a while, usually after a good joke or emptying a clip in full auto-fire mode.

The pups were riveted as Harry and Lissa carried on conversations in sign language. He'd come up his own little modifications to compensate for the lost digits, and they weren't all that different than the pups' own shortcuts, except his sign for a pee break didn't include a leg lift.

Harry seemed just as taken with Spot and Smudge. He was usually hugging or patting one or the other while he was feeding them, and they'd caught him signing to Lissa that the pups reminded him of Fuse.

Smudge had relayed that to Ben, who'd found a subtle way to work it into a question.

Lissa told him Fuse was their old black lab, and she'd died the day of Harry's accident. She'd chased after him when he'd charged after the idiot who decided to fetch his forgotten radio from under a hundred tons of rock just as it was getting blown up.

Ben and Lissa joined Christa at the glass wall, where she was opening a cardboard box.

The box was filled with dozens of small metal containers that looked like spice cans. They had twistable lids with closed holes in the top, and each was sealed in a zip-lock bag.

They were dated and labelled in Hamish's neat printing, and as Ben picked through them he read, "Blood-Human, Kush, Raw Cocaine, Feces-Human, Cadaver Flesh-Human, BC Gold, MDMA…"

He had to ask what a few of them were, and then said, "That explains why I'm craving Unc's meatloaf."

Christa chuckled as she handed Ben a pair of blue acetate gloves, paper booties, and a paper mask. "Pick five cans," she said, "any ones you want, but only take one of the cadaver cans. Hide them around the range. Take them out of their baggies, twist the top so the holes are open, and set them down carefully. Don't shake them, and try to remember which ones you hid where."

Ben headed off into the range, and it took him five minutes to walk from the glass wall to the targets.

Harry told him the huge building had been an indoor lumber yard during the town's boom years. The racks on the side walls were stacked with sheets of plywood that the club cut into various people-shaped targets. Most of the back wall was angled down to deflect bullets into a sand pit, except for a large sliding garage door that was covered in layers of thick carpet padding.

Ben walked the inside perimeter, hiding the cans as he went, and fifteen minutes later they were all standing together in the center of the range.

They were watching intently with Vuur and the pups as Rook trotted back and forth along the back wall.

Lissa was rocking from one foot to the other as she whispered, "C'mon boy, you can do it."

It was Rook's second try, and he'd covered most of the building three times. Christa told Ben the flat noses of the South African boerboels hampered their ability to distance smell. She also said what Vuur and Rook lacked in sensing ability they compensated for by covering a lot of ground, and by pure pig-headedness. But even the stubborn Rook was clearly getting frustrated. He was running in big loops with his head, ears, and tail down.

Smudge looked up at Ben with a worried face he could immediately read. His sweet dog had too much of their Mimi in her. The grandmother would be giving Rook clues, and then she'd make him a cup of tea. When Ben shook his head a discouraged Smudge turned away from him. She was shifting almost as much as Lissa.

"Shit," Christa grumbled under her breath. "He's lost it again."

As she left the group and walked toward the front of the building she said, "Maybe he'll have better luck finding my dead body when Hamish kills me."

As they watched Christa stomp off in her odd gait Harry turned and signed to Lissa.

"No, leave it in the truck," she replied. "I doubt we'll get to the ANFO today. Take them out for a break and we'll start again in a bit."

"I'll take them out," Ben said. He wanted to have a word with Smudge outside anyway.

He called for Rook, and as the dog left the back wall and trotted toward them he asked, "What's ANFO?"

"It's a mix of ammonium nitrate and fuel oil," Lissa said. "We use it to blast at the mines. It's one of the explosives the dogs need to be able to detect. I usually reek of the stuff so they end up indicating on me as often as the hidden sample. They also need to not be afraid of explosions."

As an ashamed Rook joined the dogs his brother Vuur gave him a disappointed head-butt. Ben led the dogs out through the side door, and as soon as they were outside Smudge pulled Rook aside.

"Wait wait wait," Ben said. "Let's talk about—"

Smudge growled at him.

Ben raised his hands and said, "Okay, yep, got it. Just do me a favor and be a little teeny tiny bit subtle. Spot, help a brother out here."

Spot just wagged a laugh up at Ben.

The boerboels' whipping tails indicated they'd enjoyed Smudge's growl as well.

Ten minutes later they were walking back to the center of the range, and Smudge was still coaching Rook so Ben had to shoo her away with a boot to the backside.

"Okay kids," Christa said. "Let's give this another try. You moved the cans?"

Lissa nodded.

Christa took a few steps forward with Rook and gave the alert dog the 'be ready' hand sign. He stared up at her, and she again gave him the cadaver search command in Afrikaans, "Rook, *soek ver die kadawer.*"

When she sent Rook off to search for the can last time he'd darted off just like his brother by running in the zigzag pattern of their training. Only unlike his brother he hadn't found it after three attempts, and many painfully long minutes of hunting.

This time Rook took a few steps forward and stopped. He closed his eyes and turned his black face up to the ceiling. His nostrils flared, and his ribs expanded and contracted as he pulled in long, slow breaths.

Ben folded his arms across his chest and noticed neither of his dogs would look up at him.

Rook sampled the air as he replayed Smudge's advice in his head again, *Remove sight and sound from the equation. Take in long slow breaths and label every smell, and then cast them off one at a time. You can smell the dead human, it's just masked by other scents. You know the trail is there, just remove the clutter. Picture the body. Make a connection to the person it used to be. Feel it, it wants to be found. Sense how it wants to be returned to its family. The essence of who they were will guide you right to them.*

Rook separated the smells of the live humans and dogs around him. He pushed away the ANFO on Lissa, the residual breakfast on Harry, the spent brass shells on the floor, and the smokeless powder that hung in the air. And then he removed everything else from the range, everything but one smell. One smell that wanted to be found.

Only three odor molecules out of the billion that were flowing around him had the smell he was looking for, but those three were enough for even his mediocre olfactory receptors to latch onto.

He opened his eyes and looked back at Smudge before he trotted off toward the far corner of the range. He didn't walk in a perfectly straight line and had to stop once for a quick recheck, but when he opened his eyes again he went to a row of old metal cabinets in the rear corner of the range. As he got close he started to wag.

He sat in front of one of them, and looked back at Christa.

"What the hell?" she mumbled.

Ben shook his head, and Harry signed to Lissa.

She nodded as she said, "Freaky shit is right."

CHAPTER 38

They spent the rest of the morning working with the dogs on detecting the various cans of scents, and Vuur started to use the same techniques as Rook.

Even though Spot outwardly agreed with Ben's protests about being too obvious, he secretly couldn't help adding his advice whenever they took a break. He was enjoying the boerboel brothers' progress, and his sister's elation when they nailed a detection. Ben wasn't happy but he had to admit he was loving the show.

The pups also confirmed his suspicion that the boerboels' comical combination of muscular bulk and flat black faces belied their true intelligence.

They realized Hamish had been right to select them. Rook and Vuur were special dogs indeed, but how he could have picked up on that when they were just puppies was a mystery.

Spot wondered if Hamish had a bit of Mimi in him, and a bit of Smudge.

Before long Christa couldn't stump the police dog trainees. They went through scent cans labeled with everything from dead bodies to drugs to DVDs. There were cans for cellphones, cash, precious metals, and an array of animal smells including rhino horn. She tried confusing them with several different related scents at once, and even tried to trip them up with lion and elephant urine. Rook and Vuur could always figure out the smells and lock onto the correct can she'd asked for. When they started to do it almost immediately Ben had to step in and force his pups to cool it. Rook and Vuur had begun coordinating from opposite ends of the range to find the scents more quickly, and Ben wasn't liking Christa's raised eyebrow.

They ended up getting through all of the canned scents before lunch, and an elated Christa asked Lissa to grab her training case of explosives.

All of the Chogins' joking stopped when Lissa and Harry pulled Ben aside and delivered a serious safety lesson, complete with a graphic description of Harry's accident, and his injuries.

Harry showed Ben his mangled hands, and then lifted up his shirt to show the deep scars that ran from his ribs to his hip, and the puckered chunks of twisted flesh that radiated out from them. He looked at Ben through his thick glasses and signed, *You don't get a do-over with this stuff. Not one fucking mistake, not ever. Understand?*

Ben nodded, and so did the pups.

Satisfied Ben got the point, Lissa and Harry showed him how the tubes of ANFO and the detonators worked. Ben nodded when Harry gave him a big smile and an exaggerated sign for *Boooom.*

They started blowing up the plywood targets, and then Harry showed Ben how to mix up a small amount of Tannerite, which detonates when shot. Ben blew the head and torso off a bad-guy target with just a small caliber pistol shot.

As the explosions were going off Christa ran the police dogs through a series of basic patrolling and search drills that took them far closer to the targets than Ben and the pups had expected. Christa was pretty close to the blasts too, and was watching Vuur and Rook's every move. She was right there to coach, correct, or encourage them to ignore the spraying plywood and stay on task.

The pups were again impressed with the police dogs, and with Christa. Even though Spot and Smudge understood what Ben and the Chogins were doing, and could often tell when the detonation button was about to get pressed, they still flinched when the targets exploded. Even with the larger detonations Vuur and Rook barely seemed to notice, and remained laser-focused on completing the job Christa had given them. Their single-minded desire to please her and accomplish their objective was a little humbling. Spot had noticed the same look on Sholto at The Grub, and knew these dogs wouldn't hesitate to pounce on a hand-grenade to save their handler, or if they were commanded to do so. He also saw it was something far smarter than blind loyalty. He and Smudge had certainly jumped in front of a bullet for their family, but these dogs had a pride of purpose that transcended merely selfless acts.

Ben and the pups agreed the only word to describe it accurately was professionalism.

As they rigged up the next target Ben told the Chogins one of Papa's jokes about the suicide bomber instructor who told his class, "Pay attention, I'm only going to show you this once."

Harry pounded Ben on the back as he sucked from his oxygen bottle and signed, *That's really fucking funny kid.* It earned him a smack and a smile from his wife.

The Chogins showed Ben a variety of other explosives, and Christa made Rook and Vuur find hidden samples of each. And then a small amount would be detonated so they could identify the charred remnants of explosives like TNT, Semtex, and C4.

Spot and Smudge were logging the differences between the explosives as well, and not only their before-and-after smells. They nodded to each other often as Harry setup the charges and showed Ben how to connect the detonators.

After they finished with the explosives Christa asked for a little distracting background gunfire as she repeated some of the trickier seek-and-find exercises with the police dogs.

Ben and the Chogins lit up the range with a variety of small assault rifles. There was a disagreement at one point about what Christa had meant by a *little* background gunfire, and Lissa tried to keep the boys to intermittent rounds of pissing hellfire downrange.

Ben wasn't too bad of a shot. Papa had taught him how to shoot a small twenty-two caliber rifle, and had promised to show him how to handle his coyote-scattering shotgun. Ben was comfortable with the basics but this was his first time holding assault weapons. Based on his big smile and interest in every tiny detail the Chogins could tell he was having a blast.

Even his dogs seemed to like watching the boy shoot.

Harry was impressed with Ben's focus, and his wife noticed her normally impatient husband didn't seem to mind the kid's constant stream of questions. Harry was clearly enjoying answering them, and coaching him to narrow his spray and control his bursts. He was also enjoying having someone to communicate with by signing other than his wife, and she noticed Ben had quickly picked up their modified short-cuts.

Her Harry was by no means shy, but was often perceived that way as he was usually quiet. He didn't like to speak as his voice was squeaky and distorted. No one in their circle of wonderful friends cared of course, but she knew Harry was self-conscious about it. He was even a little shy about his signing with his missing fingers, but she noticed he'd chatted more with Ben than she'd seen in a long while. In fact, he'd barely shut up the entire afternoon.

Ben and the pups found it funny that the type of small assault rifles they were using were called bullpups. Harry pointed out that the sleek, insidious looking family of short rifles had their firing mechanism and ammo magazine at the rear of the gun, in the stock. It allowed for a longer, more accurate barrel while still keeping the overall length of the rifle short. Ben liked them as they fit his smaller frame perfectly, and they looked crazy cool.

As they blew through the plywood bad guys Harry showed him how to use the short collimator scope mounted on the guns. Once Ben grasped the concept of keeping both eyes open and using his dominant eye to follow his target he mastered using the lighted dot in the scope to take off the plywood heads at twenty-five meters.

Harry moved Ben through the bullpup guns to the more traditional rifles like the M4 and M16. He explained they had been shooting with standard NATO five-five-six ammo, and he eventually brought out the larger seven-six-two round guns like the AK-47. They were a little harder for Ben to hold, but Harry was an excellent teacher and Ben was surgically removing limbs after some more pointers and practice.

Eventually they switched to hunting rifles, and shot at a different type of target. Spread out over the range were a dozen simple iron pipe frames welded to a metal base. Hanging from the frames' horizontal pipes were small orange metal squares that pinged loudly and swung when hit. They also moved to shooting while lying down with the guns resting on moving blankets laid over sandbags that were stacked up on a large rolling platform with locking wheels.

Ben hit the little orange metal squares about half of the time at seventy-five meters, but he was getting exponentially better with each shot as they coached him. Lissa and Harry were pinging every shot at the back of the range at two hundred and fifty meters. Harry wore special glasses when he distance shot that were a quarter-inch thick and made him look even more like a frog.

They moved from hunting to sniper rifles, and after Ben was getting pretty good with those Harry scooched his bulk off the shooting table and signed to Lissa, *Time to bring out the thunder?*

His wife rolled her eyes at him, but she smiled and said, "Yeah, sure, go ahead."

Ben was surprised to see Harry could actually jog. He ran off to the front of the club and retrieved two large gun cases from under the front counter. The cases were very heavy and he had to walk slowly on the return trip, but he was smiling like a schoolgirl as he puffed toward them. He placed the cases on the platform in front of Ben and opened them slowly, like they were full of gold bars.

He sucked from his little oxygen mask and waggled his bushy eyebrows while Ben ran his fingers down the sniper rifles' long, thick barrels. He studied their insanely large scopes and heavy bolt actions as Lissa described the specs of Harry's McMillan Tac-50 and her C3A1. Although the guns were different sizes, they were a similarly customized matched pair. They were black, absurdly large, and looked to be insanely lethal. Harry signed for Ben to roll over another shooter's table and toss on a few more sand bags as he walked over to the side wall of the range and held down a big green button.

The rear door at the far end of the building slowly slid open, and Ben saw several rows of the pipe frames with more square orange targets were spread out up the slope behind the range. The farthest ones were barely visible with the haze and the falling snow dancing around them.

Lissa talked Ben through the differences between shooting the other rifles and these huge sniper's cannons. She explained to him how every micrometer of error at this end meant meters of error at the other end, where it counted. She showed him how to hold the guns correctly to his shoulder, chamber a round, let out a breath, and squeeze the trigger. He missed his first two shots but with some more coaching pinged the target just outside of the open door, at two hundred meters.

"See, it's the simplest thing in the world," Lissa said, "and there's only about three dozen people on the planet who can do it consistently when it really matters."

The secret is the ability to do exactly the same thing every single time you pull the trigger, Harry signed. *And by exact, I mean you need to have the kind of muscle memory and concentration that makes Tiger Woods look like Michael J Fox."*

Lissa frowned at that description but she was nodding at the same time.

"With this gear almost anyone can get hits half of the time in a quiet shooting range at two hundred meters," Lissa said. "It's distraction-removal that separates the real shootists from the panty-crappers when the shit's flying around you. Take any elite athlete, or an amazing artist, or even a world-class scientist or CEO, anyone who's at the top of their game, and I'll show you someone who's mastered the art of focus. It's the same discipline here."

Spot subtly gestured to Smudge with a few proud ear flicks and head bobs, *Our boy has that kind of focus on tap.*

"Shooting is a fun hobby," Lissa said, "but it can be so much more. If you can succeed at this, I mean really do it well, you can do anything you put your scary little mind to."

She tapped Ben on the forehead and he nodded, and so did Spot and Smudge.

Harry told him to find a shooting mantra, some phrase that he would recite in his head every time he shot. It could be a poem, or a song, anything with a rhythm that he knew by heart.

Lissa cautioned him to not share it with anyone as his buds and other shooters would certainly use it to fuck with him when shooting for cash, trophies, or bragging rights. She told him before snipers had learned to keep their mantras secret the enemy would share it amongst themselves and use it to mess with the snipers on the front lines. They would go so far as to have their female undercover operatives try to seduce it out of the snipers.

They took turns shooting, and when Harry fiddled with the scope after each shot Lissa read him numbers from a small card. She said her husband was 'doping' the scope, and Ben was fascinated.

What started as Lissa patiently answering a few questions turned into a class about windage, spindrift, drop, and the dozen other environmental factors that affected a shooter's accuracy. She began to realize why Harry enjoyed teaching the boy. He drank in information like water. He also grasped the math behind the scope's minutes-of-angle and reticle marks faster than anyone she'd ever taught. Ben started calling out adjustment clicks for the different distances and grain loads of ammunition, and he was doing most of the range calculations in his head before they could find it on their little reference card.

After he pinged a target far out in the field Harry signed to his wife over Ben's shoulder, *This city kid's a fuckin' savant.*

The pups had hoped up onto the back of Ben's shooting table and were sitting together behind his outstretched feet.

Spot had been checking Ben's math, and subtly correcting some of it when no one was looking. He turned to share a proud nod with Smudge, but his sister had a puss on her face. When she made a snide comment about it being okay for Ben to show off Spot dismissed her with a big wag.

Lissa and Harry were also exchanging a smile behind Ben's back.

The club offered classes to teach kids to shoot. It was a mandatory part of the Nellis' silly 'lifetime founding members' obligation that Lissa and Harry didn't much enjoy but generally supported with quiet apathy. Aside from a small handful of sweet ones, the Chogins felt kids were mostly just mean little retarded people and generally a pain in the ass. They had chosen not to have any children for that very reason, but they liked teaching on those rare occasions when the kid listened and seemed into it. As Lissa watched Ben paying close attention to her husband's pointers she recalled seeing that same look on his sister's face. Kelcy hadn't been as into the guns as Ben was, but she was just as sharp and they'd enjoyed her company equally as much.

The Chogins were also enjoying Ben's well-behaved dogs. They seemed quite content to just sit behind him and watch. And one of them seemed to never stop wagging.

When Ben showed the range card to Spot the Chogins laughed, especially when the dog pawed it gently and licked him on the chin.

Even though he was tall for an eleven year old and had little trouble holding and sighting the guns, Ben was still relatively thin in the shoulders. Lissa thought he must be starting to feel the ache after expending a few full magazines from each rifle. Her large sniper rifle kicked some but Harry's fifty caliber was a teeth-jarring beast. Even with its advanced recoil suppression it still punched hard in the shoulder with each trigger pull. The whole table shook and the ceiling rattled when it fired. Lissa suggested he take a break, and said she didn't want Hamish's wrath when he went home black and blue. Ben shrugged her off, and asked for the next pointer as he lowered to look through the scope again. Harry signed for his wife to stop coddling the lad, and directed Ben to let his breath out slower.

The police dogs hadn't been flinching at any of the other barrages of gunfire, but they looked up when Lissa's rifle fired, and they paused when the fifty caliber let loose. Vuur and Rook were back on task quickly but they still gave the big gun a sideways look whenever it chugged off another devastating round.

Harry and Lissa coached Ben with things like head position and watching the bullet's vapor trail after each shot. They kept tweaking his techniques, and explained how they were reducing micro-differences between each of his shots. Lissa smiled whenever his handsome little face screwed into a knot of concentration as he ingested the next tip. He nodded while he seemed to be locking it into his brain, which he often did while looking at one of his wagging pups.

Ben hit the five hundred meter target four times in a row with his last magazine.

Harry tapped his headphones and gave him a big okay sign with the only fingers he had on that hand.

Ben switched positions and spotted through the pair of binoculars that had been setup on a small tripod while Harry and Lissa shot. They were pinging hits all day long at five hundred meters, and still hitting more than half at the seven hundred and fifty meter target. At those distances only the dogs could hear the ping that came long after they saw the hit as the bullet travelled almost a half-mile downrange at twice the speed of sound.

Harry bitched about the wind and the snow, mostly because he was behind his wife by three hits.

He even challenged Ben's last 'miss' call.

Ben pretended to confer with his dogs, and the Chogins laughed when he said both pups agreed the shot had indeed been a miss.

Later that afternoon, after they'd packed up the guns and were having snacks at the front table, the Chogins answered Ben's questions about being demolition engineers.

Lissa told him she and Harry met at a Canadian Forces base in New Brunswick. She'd been a commissioned instructor at the ordinance and bomb disposal school there, and Harry had rotated in from deployment for update training. According to Lissa he was, "The cutest, and worst student I've ever instructed."

As she draped an arm over her husband and bent to give him a big smooch on his cheek she turned to Ben and added, "My Harry couldn't find the red wire if it was labelled and wrapped around his finger. The man was half color blind even before his accident. I wondered how he'd even made it into the boom-busters, but his colleagues said he was one of the best. Of course I didn't believe them for a second. Still don't. All of those disposal guys stick together, pardon the pun."

Harry started to sign and Lissa reached over him to grab his fingers.

"Here's the part where he tells you he was just playing dumb," she said. "He'll say it was part of his master plan to get some one-on-one instruction after class, and get into my, uh, good graces. Well, if that was the case he was a much better actor than he was a tech."

She let his hands go, and Harry signed, *I was only going to tell our young friend here to never, ever cut the red wire. And that I'm the luckiest man alive, for oh so many reasons.*

Lissa patted her husband's arm and gave him a warm smile.

"Yes indeed, my love," she said. "We've have a pretty good run."

She looked up at Ben and added, "I wouldn't recommend it as a career, but we've travelled the world, and it's an interesting damn brotherhood."

Yeah, Harry signed. *We have friends scattered all over the place.*

Lissa groaned, and Ben laughed out loud. He shook his head, and noticed Spot had found Harry's joke a lot funnier than Smudge.

They heard a bark, and Ben turned to watch Christa playing with Vuur and Rook. She and the police dogs were rolling around on the rubber mat in the range together. She had taken her legs off and was being dragged around by her flopping pant legs by Rook as she held out a rope toy to fend off Vuur's frontal assault.

As Harry fed Smudge a bite of sandwich Ben walked to the glass wall and asked the couple, "What happened to Christa's legs?"

Lissa paused in the middle of making them another sandwich.

"Ben, maybe you should ask her yourself," she said. "Or maybe that's a conversation you and Hamish should have first."

"I asked him," Ben said. "He made a joke, and then didn't answer me. I would ask her but, I don't know. I get the feeling she wouldn't want to talk about it."

Harry rapped softly on the table, pointed to Ben, and signed to his wife.

"Alright," Lissa said as she patted her husband's arm.

She turned to Ben and said, "When Canada joined that ridiculousness in the Middle East our Christa told her parents she was going off to join the army. They fought her tooth and nail but she wanted to serve, and she wanted to go in as a sniper. Remember when I told you three dozen people in the world can pull the trigger right every time? Well that girl rolling around over there with those big ugly mutts is one of them."

Harry looked at Ben over his thick glasses and nodded his firm agreement.

She's lethal out to a mile and a half, he signed, *and can wing you pretty reliably at two.*

"Hamish had been there when Christa took her first steps," Lissa said, "raced her first sled, shot her first gun, and kissed her first boy. Her parents are lovely people but I think Hamish has played a bigger role in her life. He can be a bit like a big magnet, as I'm sure you've noticed."

Ben had, and so had the pups.

"It was Hamish that finally convinced her to go into the military police as a canine trainer instead of a sniper," Lissa said. "Our Christa's pretty stubborn, but I think Hamish could convince a nun to give up her panties."

Ben nodded, and so did the pups.

"She reluctantly agreed," Lissa said, "and while she was in basic training Hamish moved to Medicine Hat. That's in Alberta. He wanted to be close to the base at Suffield where the army's dog training school is. He was a contractor there back in the day and still has friends among the brass. While Christa was in basic Hamish visited his preferred breeders to select a pup to be her partner. He flew to Colorado, and then to Germany, and Ireland, and Israel. Eventually he saw whatever magic he looks for in a puppy at a ranch in Sweden. He brought her to Alberta and started to train her, and named her Sholto after some knighted Royal Air Force hero of his. As expected, Christa was assigned to Suffield after basic and Hamish went on base every day to help her work with their new super-pup."

Lissa paused to sip her coffee, and then said, "Ben, you know how he is, right? I've known him almost thirty years and as intensely passionate as he is about training dogs today, picture him twice as motivated raising Sholto. She's the finest police dog he's ever created. In her day she was probably the best in the world."

Spot agreed with Smudge's shoulder twitch that said, *And she is still one sharp cookie.*

"Christa started helping Hamish train dogs about the time she learned to walk," Lissa said. "She rose quickly in the ranks and in short order she and Sholto ended up running the canine training program. It kept her in Canada, and Hamish moved back home."

Harry signed and Lissa waved him off. "Hush," she said, "I'm getting there."

"Christa had less than six months left to her commitment when she found out Hamish had pulled every string he could with his friends to keep her in Canada," Lissa said. "Her name had been taken off several overseas deployment rotations, and all of their talks about how much she was contributing to the fight suddenly felt tainted to her. They weren't of course. The dogs and handlers she'd trained had easily saved hundreds of lives, but she wouldn't hear it."

Lissa walked to the glass wall and stood next to Ben, and they watched the double amputee wrestle with her dogs.

"Christa was angry," Lissa said.

Harry tapped the table. He shook his head and signed, *Christa was fucking pissed.*

Lissa nodded and said, "Well, she pulled a few strings of her own and she and Sholto were on the next plane to Afghanistan. In two months they'd earned two citations for valor, and the base commander assigned Christa a green platoon to show them the ropes. She told the new lieutenant not to follow a suspicious truck into what was known as 'the maze' in Mosul, but he wouldn't listen. A pair of IEDs took out the first and last vehicles in her convoy, and in an instant they were in the middle of a well-coordinated ambush. The enemy pounced, and her team was taking heavy casualties. Christa was wounded, but she returned fire and held them back long enough for Sholto to drag the survivors into a building."

Christa had seventeen confirmed kills that afternoon, Harry signed, *and Sholto had six all by herself. Their team told Hamish the real numbers were probably three times that.*

"As they pulled the last man through the doorway the enemy rained down enough concentrated rocket and mortar fire to bring the whole block down on their heads," Lissa said. "Christa grabbed Sholto, hugged her close, and they were thrown into what she described as a concrete washing machine.

When she woke up they were trapped in a small pocket under two slanted walls, buried under five stories of collapsed building. Her gear was gone, as was her radio and her sidearm. Sholto hadn't been hurt, but Christa's legs were trapped under one of the walls.

She heard a helicopter, and then reinforcements came pretty quickly. She could hear them faintly yelling, and then she could hear them taking more rounds of fire. All of the action was happening above them and she realized the basement must have collapsed and they were below ground level. She tried to yell but could only draw dust filled breaths and cough them out. Sholto barked but no one could hear them through the noise of the fight and thirty feet of twisted steel and concrete debris above them. After a while everything went quiet, and she was in tough shape. One arm was bleeding badly and she was drifting in and out.

For hours she watched Sholto trying to find a way through the rubble. The dog scrambled around in the dark and kept coming back to check on Christa. She brought back water bottles and two pistols. All of them were covered in blood."

Harry tapped on the table and signed to Lissa.

She nodded and said, "Sorry Ben. This may be a little heavy for you. Forgive me, we don't spend much time around kids, and you kinda don't act like one."

"It's okay," Ben said. "I've seen a lot for a kid, believe me."

He laughed, and added, "You know, being in Hamish's family and all. Please, don't leave anything out. It's important to me."

Harry nodded, and Lissa said, "Sholto kept hunting around in the dark, and each time she'd bring back a gun or a bottle of water, lick

Christa's face, and scrambled away through the debris again. She did that several times, and then one time she didn't come back."

"Sholto left her?" Ben asked.

"Yep, hours went by and there was no sign of her," Lissa said.

Ben looked at the pups, who stared right back at him.

"The next day came," Lissa said. "A little light filtered down into Christa's hole, and by noon it was hotter than an oven. She could hear faint voices and vehicles on the street but they weren't English, and the vehicles weren't Humvees. She decided not to yell for help. She heard helicopters pass close by several times and even hover for long minutes before they moved away.

And then night came. Christa had gone numb below the waist and one eye had swollen shut, but the bleeding had stopped and she could breathe easier in the cooler air. The next morning came and she heard more faint voices. She had run out of water and it got scorching hot again.

She told me at that point she did look at the pistol once, for a moment, but then decided to start yelling.

Just as she began to shout she was drowned out by helicopters, and then the distinct sound of a heavily armored vehicle. A Bradley, which is basically a tank big enough to carry troops. It shook the rubble around her and stopped right in front of what was left of her building. And then she heard the unmistakable Brooklyn accent of her base's colonel shouting.

A few minutes later she heard scratching, and Sholto popped out of a hole above her and landed in her lap. She had water bottles, a flashlight, and a radio. As Christa was hugging her she noticed Sholto's neck and thigh had been shaved and bandaged, and there were holes in her camouflage service vest. Hamish had made that vest and it was reinforced with layers of Kevlar. Sholto had been shot six times, and the vest had stopped the worst of them.

Their coalition airbase was seventeen kilometers from the collapsed building, and Christa could only imagine what holy hostile hell Sholto must have run through to make it back there. Taliban fighters had learned to fear and hate our dog soldiers, and they often targeted them.

After some back and forth on the radio Christa sent Sholto back up to the surface. She came back down through the hole a few minutes later with pain killers, two tourniquets, and a battery powered saw.

It took Sholto fifteen agonizing minutes to lead Christa through the debris. Mostly she did it by dragging her by a harness they had rigged up. Christa got stuck a few times and she told me if she still had both legs attached she never would have squeezed through.

When they dropped out of the last hole fifty hands pulled her into the back of the waiting Bradley, where a medical team pounced on her. Sholto was sitting next to her head when the Colonel climbed in beside them. He patted Sholto, and showed Christa his bandaged hand. The two little blood stains seeping through it were the same distance apart as Sholto's canine teeth.

'Warrant Officer Boucher,' the Colonel said to her with a smile, 'your Gunny is one mean motherfucking hero.'"

CHAPTER 39

"How do yeh know you're staying at a hotel in Glasgow?" Hamish asked loudly with cheeks that were flush and a tongue that was thick.

Tavish had tears streaming from his eyes and had just stopped pounding the table from the last punchline. "I don't know Hamish," he said. "How the hell do you know when you're in bloody Glasgow?"

"When yeh call down to the front desk to say yeh got a leak in your sink," Hamish shouted, "And they tell yeh to go ahead!"

Christa hadn't taken a full drink of wine all night. She coughed mid-sip and put the back of her hand to her mouth to prevent another leak. She laughed through tears and shook her head at Ben.

Ben was holding his stomach and couldn't remember when he'd laughed so hard.

Hamish and Tavish had been at it for more than an hour straight. A bartender and a lifelong bachelor, both Scots, they were a veritable encyclopedia of jokes. When the jokes weren't funny they were told loud enough that no one cared.

Christa and Ben tossed in a few of their own and it was an evening full of shouted laughter and table pounding.

Spot and Smudge's tails had gotten sore from wagging as they watched from the couch.

After dinner Ben volunteered for dish duty as the adults relaxed by the fire. Spot was curled up on the couch next to Hamish and Smudge was on the opposite couch with her chin on Tavish's lap getting deep head rubs. Sholto and the boerboels were snoring away on the rug in front of the fireplace.

Christa plunked down into a big leather chair, and everyone laughed when she put her feet on the hearth and wiggled them back and forth in front of the fire as she said, "Ooooh that feels good."

While she was explaining the ranch's history to Tavish, Hamish got up and joined Ben in the kitchen.

"Sounds like yeh had a good day lad," he said as he clamped down on Ben's shooting shoulder.

Ben fought back a grimace and a wince. His clavicle was indeed black and blue.

"Yeppers, it was pretty awesome," he said. He told Hamish some of the highlights, and then asked, "How's the elkie team doing?"

"Ach, my wee team," Hamish said with a sigh. "For the first time in my professional career I may have to admit defeat."

"They can't be that bad," Ben said. "Can they?"

Hamish walked over to the kitchen slider and wagged a finger at Ben to follow.

"What do you see down there boy?" he asked as he put his hand on Ben's tender shoulder again.

"What do you mean?" Ben asked through clenched teeth. "I see the barn, the corral, and the dogs huddled in their little igloos around the fire."

"Aye," Hamish said. "And have yeh ever seen me keep a fire going for them?"

Ben thought about it and said, "Never."

"Right," Hamish said. "And why do yeh think they'd be needing a fire? Those dogs eat frost and piss ice cubes, 'snot that cold out."

Ben shrugged.

"To dry them off lad," Hamish said. "Because that lot of idjets lost focus again today and chased a pine marten, while at a full run mind yeh."

Taking the bait, Ben asked, "How'd they get wet chasing a pine marten?"

"Because dear boy," Hamish said. "They chased the wee thing off the bank and into the fucking river."

"Oops," Ben said.

"Oops is bloody right," Hamish said. "I found a trout in my underwear."

He took a long pull from his drink, and then said, "We're out of here in two weeks, and next week we have graduation conference calls scheduled. One for Vuur and Rook, which after today we might just have a shot at pulling off. The other is for that lot out there. After a very long and very rewarding and somewhat profitable and soon to be cut-short career, I may have to push back a delivery date for the first time, and that's assuming I can turn them around at all. I don't miss commitments boy, I just don't."

Tavish excused himself to use the bathroom, and Christa came into the kitchen with their empty wine glasses.

Ben looked across the room to the pups, who shook their heads in sync.

Ben scowled at them, and said, "Unc, I think I may have a way to help you with—"

Hamish's cellphone rang and he raised a finger to Ben as he pulled it from his pocket.

He looked at the display before answering it, and then said, "Hey Blu, how's yer mammy?"

For the next two minutes he issued a string of apologies to the captain, and then hung up after mumbling a goodbye.

Christa gave him an inquisitive look, and when he didn't respond she asked, "Well?"

"Oh, that was Blu," he said.

"Uh huh," Christa said expectantly.

"She's got her knickers twisted over what I did," Hamish said.

Christa raised an eyebrow at him.

"Not about that!" Hamish said. "She's got nae' complaints there I assure yeh. No, she wants to skelp me 'cause I found a road kill fox that looked like a wee dog."

As Ben waited for Hamish to finish he noticed Christa's headshake. She seemed to have a pretty good idea what was coming.

"I put an old collar and leash on it," Hamish said. "And then I tied it to the tow hitch of her cruiser. She didn't notice until she pulled up in front of a grade school, where the bairns were queued for pickup by their less than pleased mummies and daddies."

CHAPTER 40

Did you finish the research I asked you for? Spot signed.

"Yes," Ben said as he pulled a USB drive out of his tablet and tossed it across the bed, "and my brain still hurts, thank you very little. Everything you'd ever want to know about subcutaneous shunting, vascular plexus, collagen migration..."

As he ran down the long list of things Spot had wanted Smudge groaned loudly.

She was sitting on the edge of the bed next to a small tub of Christa's foot wax. She was massaging the thick paste deep into the crevasses between her toe pads, and her eyes were rolling up into her head.

Ben smiled at her, and said to Spot, "You'll have plenty of time to read it in bed tonight."

We need one more night, Spot signed without looking up from his own small tablet.

Ben scowled at him, and when the pup didn't respond he turned it on Smudge.

She wiped her paw on a towel and then signed, *Which part of what we found last night didn't you understand?"*

"Don't get cheeky with me little girl," Ben said. "I remember wiping up your poopy accident from the kitchen floor, and that was only a few months ago."

Always with that one? Smudge signed as she looked to her brother for help. *It was one time, I had a hundred and two fever, and I was ready to pay the boatman. And I was four weeks old. When you were four years old you were still wetting your pull-ups.*

Enough you two, Spot signed. *C'mon Smudge, let's go.*

"Wait," Ben said. "Tavish might still be here, and Sholto may still be awake."

Spot gave him a disappointed head shake. His little boy Ben was one of the sharpest humans he'd encountered, even at eleven years old, but he still missed the obvious sometimes.

Sholto can still hear a mouse fart in the barn, Spot signed. *Of course she knows what we're doing and she's on board. Just like the elkies, and Rook, and Vuur.*

And Tavish left a half hour ago, Smudge signed as she slipped her back foot into one of the sled dog boots. *He made a valiant play, and Christa was interested, but she kicked him out without so much as a smooch on the cheek just the same. Hamish was sawing logs an hour ago. I could hear that man sleeping from Pembury.*

Spot could see Ben was unconvinced, and still very concerned.

He put his small tablet down and walked to the top of the bed, pushed Ben back onto the pillows, and then lay down on top of him and cuddled up under his chin. He gave him a lick as Ben put his arms around him and held him tightly.

Smudge jumped up onto the bed and dropped on top of them.

I know you worry about us, Spot signed, *and we appreciate it. But we gotta solve this thing. Something very wrong is going on out there at the mine. We have to figure it out before we get anyone else involved. You know what would have happened in Pembury if we'd gone to the police?*

"Nothing," Ben said.

Smudge nodded, and signed, *Probably worse than nothing. We'll be back in a few hours, and we promise we'll play this thing however you want tomorrow.*

Ben gave them both a big hug, and they all got off the bed. As the pups finished tying on their borrowed boots he turned out the bedroom light, pulled open the slider, and gave their heads a pat as they silently slipped past him.

They padded across the deck and down the back stairs, and as Ben slid the door closed he saw them nod to T'nuc and E'sra before they turned their coats white and sped off toward the mine.

What he didn't see was the figure hiding in the dark at the far end of the deck.

CHAPTER 41

"Oh, so you're turnin' this into an east-coast west-coast thing?" Jero asked as he stomped his feet to keep warm and rubbed his hands over his massive biceps. He was wearing his signature tight white thermal shirt and no jacket. He rarely wore a jacket, but he hadn't expected to be standing in the cold for a fucking hour tonight.

"No, not at all," Lucy said as he turned up the fur collar of his full-length leather coat and pulled his knit black cap further down over his bald head. "I'm simply saying Fiddy smacks the shit out of Cypress Hill, and everyone I've ever met from Cali is a punk,"

Jero snorted out a steaming laugh.

"Fuck *ese*," Lucy said, "how the hell can you live up here? Weren't you born someplace a little warmer?"

"They told me the mines shit gold up here," Jero said. "What they shoulda' told me is the fucking Cree bitches get pregnant if you smile at them. I got two kids, bro. I ain't going nowhere."

Lucy unzipped his coat just enough to get his big hand inside, moved aside the handle of his hand cannon, and fished out his wallet. He flipped it open and angled it to catch the light as he moved closer to Jero.

Rotty-wolf looked up for a second but then went back to his nap. He was sprawled out on his bed of cardboard on a pallet under the metal stairs the men were standing at the bottom of.

Lucy showed Jero a picture and said, "That's Anna, and the one in pink is Anita."

"Sweet," Jero said as he nodded and pulled his wallet from his back pocket. He slipped a worn picture out of a plastic sleeve and tipped it into the light so they could both see it. "Carlos, and Angelina," he said. "And that's my Nya behind them."

Just then the door to the office at the top of the stairs opened and Ty stepped heavily onto the metal grate landing.

Jero and Lucy dropped their hands and stepped away from each other.

Ty stared at them for a second before he said, "Get the fucking truck."

As Jero and Lucy turned and put their pictures away the four wolves in the large cages behind them stirred. One of them fixed a cold stare at Lucy and growled so low he felt it in his balls. The wolf had a series of puckered scars on its neck and face, and a deep one that ran down the center of its forehead. Mixed in with the scars were a few newer healing wounds, and Lucy noticed all of the wolves were similarly marked.

"Okay, yeah, so those things give me the fucking creeps," he said as he zipped up his jacket. "How much can you make on one fight? It can't be worth it."

Jero walked over to the row of cages and made an angry face at the four wolves as he flexed his muscles and banged on the metal doors. The wolves snapped at his hands as they paced and growled at him.

He turned to Lucy and said, "You get a hundred drunken loggers and miners together, fifty bucks a head, plus the booze and the drugs and the betting. Sweet money *hommes*." He hooked a thumb into one of his thick neck chains and held out the gold cross that hung from it.

The wolves tracked him with their stares as he walked past two empty cages and continued to the back wall of the maintenance building where there was a large sliding metal door. He flipped aside a latch and slid the big door open before walking out into the snow to get the boss's truck.

In the office at the top of the stairs Ty's heavy clomping rattled the coffee maker as his wet boots squeaked across the floor. He crossed the room to take Vic's fur coat from a row of hooks on the wall.

The big mine boss rose from his chair and slid his arms into the waiting coat as he grumbled, "*Madame*, those two abominations of yours had better start to reap some rewards or we may need another plan. A more direct plan, *sans ambiguite*."

"If there hadn't been a river between that skier and my abomination we'd have had the incident we need to proceed," Jia said as she warmed her hands on the office's hissing radiator. "There's only so many rivers."

"*Peut-etre*, but no one believed her," Vic grumbled. "Those imbeciles won't believe a wolf attacked someone until they see chunks of gory fur and human flesh together on the same patch of snow. We need something more significant than a little barking and growling. I could have done that with the regular wolves I have."

"Victor," Jia said with a smile as she gave his arm a gentle squeeze, "it's not an exact science, but I've been assured with that dosage they'll be raving mad by now and itching to tear open a few tree huggers for you."

Vic's furrowed brow softened and he started to nod, until he realized the sly woman was stroking his pole.

"*Tabarnack*," he cursed as he pulled his arm away. "What's stopping me from just sending the boys over—"

"Mr. LeClerc," the asset interrupted in a crisp voice that cut through the office. "You will get the wolf incident you need soon enough, and thusly we will get what we need. *Ne pas se inquieter*."

He was standing at a row of filthy windows looking down at the enormous garage, where Lucy and Jero were waiting by Vic's idling truck. Without turning around he said, "They are the perfect cover, and our orders were very specific about this appearing to have been an accident. We were also told we could count on your full cooperation."

He turned away from the window and subtly scanned Vic's desk as he crossed the room. Next to the half-empty bottle of booze was a stack of bills with Past Due and Second Notice printed on some of them. He also noticed a dusty framed picture with a round, homely woman standing behind two kids. The slack-faced boy was clearly a smaller version of Vic, as was his frowning teenage daughter, who sported a nose ring and overly severe black eye makeup.

The asset glanced at Vic's hand and saw the slight indent from the missing wedding band before he caught the mine boss's stare.

Vic found the man's smug, probing eyes to be as irritating as his arrogant British and perfect French accents.

He blocked his family from the asset's view by reaching for his glass, and as he downed the last dribble of whisky he glanced down at the man's odd boots.

They made absolutely no sound as he crossed the wet and cracked linoleum floor.

The asset closed the distance between them, and as he stood in front of Vic he shifted his weight to his left foot so his jacket opened just enough to quickly reach his silenced pistol.

He fixed the mine boss with a tight, chilling smile and said, "I assume we do still have your full support, *c'est ca?*"

CHAPTER 42

"Do it, or you'll nae' be getting any lunch," Hamish called up to Vuur, who was hesitating on a horizontal ladder mounted ten meters in the air. Icicles fell from the swaying rungs and hit the rope safety net before clattering on the concrete floor.

"Shush," Christa hissed without taking her eyes off of Vuur. "He'll get it. He's just a little afraid of heights."

The mastiff was crouched with his paws spread on the side rails of the ladder. The cold aluminum was slick with ice and his toenails were digging in to get purchase.

One end of the ladder was bolted to the landing of a third floor concrete stairwell. The far end of the ladder, where Vuur was teetering, was bolted to a wooden beam that was attached to an opposite concrete landing. The open span was about six meters, and with his weight quivering in the middle the whole rig bounced.

Ben was watching from between his fingers as an icicle spun away from the swaying ladder and splintered on the cement next to him.

They were standing on the ground floor of a huge abandoned saw mill complex. It was a kilometer downriver from the ranch at the head of another large valley that swooped down from the west. The Nellis's place was farther up that slope, and the river that ran past their sporting lodge fed into Christa's larger river where the valleys met.

Before her family closed their logging operation the mill site had been the main processing plant for their rough timber. It had sawed and planed trees from the slopes of six surrounding mountains that covered almost three thousand square kilometers. A mill had been in continuous operation for more than two hundred years on the site, and for most of those years the logs had been floated down the river in rafts. Remnants of the iron pike-pole tips used to maneuver the logs were still scattered at the rivers' edge, and there were ten-foot long double-handled saws rusting in the weeds. The nimble-footed River Pigs had danced on the log rafts until the late forties, when a surplus of cheap trucks left over from the war made it more effective to haul the logs down the mountain by road. Christa's great-grandfather had been a Jam Crew boss, and had lost his life in the crush of a log pile-up just upstream from the mill.

The original water-powered band saws had been updated to coal, and then to steam, and then to diesel-electric, and they'd been operational until Christa's parents retired. The offices were modern and still mostly weather-tight, but the processing equipment had been sold off and all that remained of the main building was a three story shell spider-webbed by catwalks. The outbuildings had fallen into decay, and they'd been purposely and carefully knocked over to create a city-block size area of twisted rebar and jutting concrete walls.

Christa and Hamish had turned the entire complex into their urban training ground, and it was Vuur and Rook's home when they weren't at the ranch. The dogs had lived in the abandoned offices for weeks at a time, and had learned to find food and water, both edible and not, that Hamish had hidden in places where they'd have to work to get at them. They'd been trained to twist door knobs with their mouths, pull off ventilation ducts, walk safely over glass, and find ways to navigate in the dark and find alternate routes around locked doors.

The old log staging area had been turned into an immense obstacle course. It started with low ramps and jumps for puppies to gain confidence and learn the basic commands, and ended with high thin beams and balance ropes a fully trained dog was expected to master. Along the way were teeter boards and a mix of different ladders, and there were timber structures of varying sizes and complexity. Some logs were cut off and stuck into the ground and some were mounted in grids and high catwalks. The end of the course was a hundred-meter long maze of collapsed buildings that had been carefully rearranged with tight spaces and dead ends. To successfully navigate it the dogs had to demonstrate patience and tenacity, and to complete it while finding hidden scents along the way they had to be world-class.

For Spot and Smudge the complex was like a big, serious Disney Land, and they loved testing themselves on the obstacles. They could smell the dozens of dogs who'd trained there, and agreed they'd have to be pretty talented to master every phase of it.

Which Vuur and Rook had almost done.

The police dogs enjoyed showing the pups around when Christa gave them a break. The boerboels had taught them how to navigate the course, and then the pups gave Vuur and Rook tips on how to do it faster.

Spot and Smudge had promised Ben they'd take it easy, which they took to mean making sure Christa wasn't watching too closely. They took turns riding in the sled with Ben when Hamish drove the elkies around the snow fields so one of them could coach the police dogs.

But there wasn't much they could do to help Vuur when he was stuck three stories off the ground.

He'd reached the transition from the ladder to the beam, but his hind legs had started to shake and Smudge was getting nervous. She was shifting on her paws as she looked up at Vuur, and then back at Ben, and then back up again.

Ben kept giving her subtle headshakes, but he was afraid it wasn't going to work for long. Even the sympathetic look Spot had been sharing with his sister had turned into a shoulder-twitch telling her to hang back.

Smudge sneezed.

And then she sneezed again even louder.

"Bless you," Christa said, not taking her eyes off Vuur.

Spot looked slowly back at Ben and shrugged slightly.

From his shaky perch high above them Vuur looked down, which he'd been trained not to do.

Smudge stared up at Vuur, and sneezed again.

Ben noticed she'd moved her body when she did it. She was communicating with the dog teetering high up on the ladder.

Vuur closed his eyes, steadied himself, and reached out a paw.

As he slid it along the wooden beam he knocked snow from it. He stretched out his front paws until his chest was touching the thin beam, and then he opened his eyes and slowly slid his hind feet off the end of the ladder.

Christa grabbed the shoulder of Ben's jacket and tugged it back and forth in time with each of Vuur's creeping baby steps.

He slowly straightened up, took a tentative full step, and then walked the rest of the beam without stopping. As he cleared the last meter he deliberately kicked snow down at the waiting spectators.

Smudge hip-bumped Spot as Christa called out, "Yes! That's my boy! *Onstagwekkende!*"

The huge brown dog with the black face and wagging tail bounded down the stairwell and shot across the floor. He knocked Christa down and was immediately pounced on by his proud brother.

They worked on agility for the rest of the afternoon and finished up with the collapsed building maze course. Ben helped Christa rearrange the plywood sheets used to blockade paths and create new dead ends so the escape route was never the same.

There were several ladders sticking up along the course so the humans could watch the dogs' progress from above.

Christa had chosen the run to be a speed test so the dogs weren't hunting for a scent. They'd just be navigating the maze as quickly as they could manage, and Ben could tell the dogs knew what was expected of them. They were dancing and stomping impatiently for Christa to give them the command to start.

Both dogs were sent into the maze, and Ben ran down the side to climb the ladder at the halfway point. He only got glimpses of a head or a tail as they twisted and turned and made their way toward him. Mostly they were deep in the cracks and crevices as they shot down paths only to get stuck and have to retrace their steps and try again. He could hear intermittent bursts of frustrated barks and reassuring yaps echoing up from deep in the maze.

When the dogs flashed by an opening just below him he raised his hand to mark their passing before he climbed down to run to the next ladder.

Crista was waiting with Hamish on a platform above the exit. She looked down at her stopwatch and smiled, and showed it to Hamish.

A few moments later Ben raised his hand at the next ladder and raced down the course to join them at the end.

"They're flying," he panted as he caught his breath with his hands on his knees.

The enthusiastic yaps were getting closer and they could see flashes of the dogs running side by side through the course.

Christa clicked down the stopwatch as the boerboels flew through the last doorway.

"One-o-eight point five," she said with a smile as she showed Hamish her watch. "A new record. Even Sholto the wonder dog couldn't have beaten that."

"I suspect not," Hamish said. He wasn't smiling.

He stroked his beard as he watched Christa and Ben wrestle with the proud mastiffs and the odd black pups in the snow.

"Right," he said. "That's enough for today I think."

CHAPTER 43

The rogue's first bite wasn't well placed, and it gave Alpha the chance to spin and catch the attacking wolf just behind the shoulder. His teeth had a good hold, and pulling hard allowed him to slip his neck from the deranged wolf's mouth and get onto its back. Alpha released his bite and with lightning speed clamped down again, hard, just behind the rogue's head. He tried to sink his fangs in deep but felt a sickening knot of bulbous, fetid muscle squish in his mouth.

The rogue howled in pain, and it came out as a gargled, distorted slur.

Both of the rogue wolves were vile. They smelled far worse up close than their trail had suggested, and their bodies were lumpy and twisted. They were also huge, and the chunky clusters of sinew under their matted fur was almost impenetrable. Bites weren't slowing them down any and Alpha was getting worried. The only bright spot was the rogues weren't very accurate, which Alpha felt had as much to do with their deranged behavior as it did their deformed bodies. They fought crazily and snapped at nothing as they clawed at the snow with odd, clubbed black paws.

Glasgow was pinned on her back beneath the second rogue, and she was having trouble breathing as it had her throat in a vise grip.

But it wasn't cutting off her windpipe completely, and that horrified her.

This lunatic wolf, with its disgusting slobber running over her snout, was saving her for some reason and Glasgow tried not to think about what that might be.

Her head was buried in the snow and it was hard to see but she'd twisted enough to watch one of her juveniles join the fight. He was her most confident son, and the one she was pretty sure would lead his own pack someday. He leapt over Alpha and pounced just behind him, clamping down on the rogue's hind quarters. Together they dropped the rogue onto its side as Glasgow's brother, the pack's other mating male, shot from the protection of the pines and went for its throat.

Bolstered by this renewed attack Glasgow kicked wildly at her attacker, eventually finding a tender spot in his groin and lifting him off her. She spun and bolted, narrowly missing a snap to the face. Once back on her feet she turned to attack and another yearling slid to a stop in the deep snow next to her. It was her daughter, the fastest one in the pack and the one most nurturing of her younger cousins. She lacked the aggression needed to rise to a position of leadership, but Glasgow wasn't disappointed.

Her daughter would make a great subordinate aunt, and as Glasgow had explained to her it was secretly the most important job in the pack, and the hardest, and the most rewarding.

The pack's nine-month old pups were being protected by the other breeding female under a nearby umbrella of pines. They were almost full height but still lacked the weight and skills to be effective in a fight, especially this one. They were as loyal as they were well-trained, and it was hard for them to watch their packmates being attacked. Their aunt was struggling to keep them in check and quiet, partly because she was itching to join the fight as well. They'd all been on some dangerous hunts and had seen a few hard family squabbles, but the noise and ferocity of this fight was making them shake.

Glasgow's brother had missed his attempt at the first rogue's throat and had paid dearly for the mistake. The crazed wolf had pulled back at the last instant and shot forward, tearing a large piece out her brother's chin and neck. He stumbled away a few steps spraying blood over the snow before he collapsed.

Alpha's teeth slipped off the rogue's greasy neck and he took away a mouthful of oily fur as the monster spun to face him. As it snapped crazily at him Alpha backpedaled into his son.

Glasgow and her daughter pounced together at the second rogue, driving it backward. She waited for the wolf to strike, dodged his bite, and used her weight to shoulder the lager animal into a snow bank. The rogue screamed in frustration, and the wild kicking of its feet only caused it to sink deeper into the snow. It shrieked a terrible howl, and then head-butted Glasgow hard enough for her to see shooting stars.

As the flashes pinged inside her head that horrific sound echoed in her ears. She'd never heard an animal make such an awful noise before. It was a painful, insane, tortured sound, and through her clearing fog she saw it had caused her young daughter to freeze.

The small wolf just stood there, staring down at the rogue wolf's large, lumpy, shaking-with-rage head. Glasgow could see what was coming, and she tried to make it to her daughter but it felt like her feet were swimming in the deep snow. The rogue leapt up from the bank and took her daughter's entire face into its jaws, and with one quick snap crushed her skull. Glasgow watched in horror as her daughter's ruined face looked at her for the last time before her eyes closed and she fell forward into the snow.

CHAPTER 44

"Thank you Ben, that was very informative," Mr. P said as the class clapped softly and a few of the kids waved goodbye.

Ben waved and tapped the screen to disconnect the video chat.

"That was torture," Christa said as she got up from the kitchen island to open the slider. The pups padded in from the back deck with Sholto and Rook.

"Yes it was," Ben sighed. "I wanted to do this one from the shooting range, with a grand finale of cutting off a target's head with a fifty cal shot and some Tannerite, but Mr. P wasn't so crazy for that idea. After that last call he said I had to run my presentation ideas past him first, and he vetoed anything that included dead woodland animals, or dogs, or wolves, or guns. Or Hamish."

"He's a poop," Christa said as Ben tapped a few buttons on his tablet and Mimi and Kelcy came on the screen.

"So how'd it go lad?" Mimi asked.

"Boring, boring, and oh oh wait! No, sorry, just more boring," Ben said. "It was a painful hour of Mr. P asking me every geography and sociology question about Quebec he could come up with, and then he added ten more minutes of who cares stuff to the end of each answer. Even the dogs were yawning."

"And how are my wee ones?" Mimi asked.

Spot and Smudge came over to the table and put their cold front paws in Ben's lap.

"Ach, there's my good boy and girl," Mimi cooed. "I miss you lot. Not so much the eating me out of house and home, or the barking, or the mess, or the dog hair all over, but everything else I miss."

The pups wagged, and the family chatted for a while, with Ben sharing a watered-down version of the highlights of his trip since their last call.

Kelcy told him about her job at the clinic, and said she'd been hanging out with Harriet and her buds, and everyone was cool. Harriet was their code word for One Ear.

Mimi asked Ben if he was staying out of trouble and helping with the chores, which Christa assured her he was.

As they told Ben about another nor'easter hitting Pembury, Hamish came down the stairs with Vuur trotting behind him.

"Hello sis," Hamish said as he detoured behind Ben to look down at the tablet. "Hope yer lum's reekin."

Ben knew he was wishing her well, which literally translated as hoping her chimney was smoking.

"Hamish, tell me you're keeping a limit on the cursing," Mimi said with a smile. "And I trust you're not shooting up the town and taking the boy around pubs and trollops."

Ben leaned in front of the screen, and with his hand on his chest he said, "Of course not Meem, perish the thought."

Hamish didn't respond beyond giving Mimi a wave.

He didn't look to be in a joking mood, and after the call Christa suggested they'd been hitting it pretty hard and maybe they should take the night off. There was a pizza place in the next town, which was an hour's drive away, but she thought they should celebrate as Vuur and Rook were doing so well.

Ben didn't need to be asked twice. He packed up his tablet and raced upstairs with the pups to wash up.

When they came back down Hamish was sitting at the head of the kitchen table with Christa seated next to him. They didn't look like they were ready to go get pizza.

"Who died?" Ben asked as he slipped into a chair with the pups at his side.

Hamish tossed eight dog snow boots onto the table, and he set a USB stick down on top of them.

CHAPTER 45

Glasgow dragged her beaten body into the river. She dropped into the cold water and let the chill numb her burning muscles. She lay there with her bleeding snout just barely sticking out from the freezing water and watched as the rogues toyed with her last surviving pup. They taunted the runt, the smallest girl from her last litter, taking turns nipping her rump as she spun in circles and tried to bite them.

Glasgow raised a paw from the water and the pup tried to run to her mother but one of the obscene rogues pawed her hard across the face with his knotted black paw. The girl fell backward and sat down in a heap as fresh blood ran from her nose.

Where do you think you're going? One of the rogues slurred. His body language and grumbling was almost unintelligible. It came out manic and frenzied, and far too loud as he added, *We aren't done with you yet little one, and she can't help you.*

As the second rogue male leaned in for another nip the little wolf feigned right and snapped up hard to the left, catching his lumpy face along the ridge of his forehead. Her bottom canine teeth sunk in just above his eye and her fangs dug into his ear.

The wolf howled and raised his head, taking the pup off the ground with him as the other rogue laughed ghoulishly.

The little wolf was attached to the rogue's face and she wasn't letting go.

Glasgow attempted to crawl from the water but her bloody, exhausted paws feebly scratched at the icy rocks. Her chin dropped back into the water as her radio collar banged softly on a boulder.

With one flick of his massive distorted head the rogue snatched the smaller wolf by the neck and snapped it. He dropped her lifeless body into the snow and walked toward the river with the other rogue following. It was still laughing in lunatic, snorting fits.

They walked past the torn bodies of Glasgow's sister and brother, and her mate, and the rest of the pack's juveniles and pups.

As they approached the riverbank Glasgow dropped her head into the frigid waters and let her feet go. Her body slid over the slick rocks and into the flow of the current. She dipped below the waves as the blood from her wounds swirled around her and she let the river take her.

One of the rogues wadded into the icy churn and dragged her wet body out of the river and onto the shore. They both stood over her as she coughed out water.

CHAPTER 46

"Aye," Hamish said as he nodded at the leather sled dog boots and thumb drive. "So, out with it lad."

Ben avoided his stare, and when he glanced down at Spot and Smudge they nodded in sync.

"We were going to tell you," Ben said as he looked up at his great-uncle. "Today in fact. We just needed to be sure."

"Be sure of what?" Christa asked. "That you could trust us? We don't do that here Ben. And who's this we?"

Ben could see there was more hurt on her face than confusion. He hated that he'd caused that hurt, and his eyes dropped to the table.

""We certainly donae' do that here," Hamish said. "I'm disappointed in yeh lad, but I think I understand."

"You do?" Ben asked as he looked up.

"Aye," Hamish said. "Yer pups are barmy wee things. I knew it when I first saw them, with their strange looks and their odd communicatin'. I suspect they've got something to do with Rook and Vuur becoming super cops overnight. Hell, even that dotty old cunt Sholto's got some new spring in her step. I thought I had it figured, but then I watched them head out for a stroll through the woods last night. There's something more going on here than meets the eye, isnae' there lad?"

"Yeah Unc," Ben said as he looked at the pups, "there sure is."

Spot put his front paws in Ben's lap so his head and shoulders were above the table. Smudge did the same in the chair next to them, and Ben patted both of their heads.

"And then there's this wee thing," Hamish said as he held up the USB stick. "I've been working with dogs for more than a half century and there's things on here even I donae' understand."

"Hang on," Christa said as she looked around the table. "I'm a little confused. I thought we were mad at him for stealing dog boots and going out at night without telling us?"

Hamish held out the USB stick to Ben and said, "Show her."

Ben took the little stick and tossed it into the air.

As it came down Smudge reached out with her paw, split it open, and caught the stick before it hit the table.

Both pups looked at Christa and wagged in sync.

"Fuck me," Christa whispered as her mouth dropped open.

Spot raised an eyebrow at her, and then lifted a paw and signed.

"Christa, language," Ben translated.

Hamish refilled his small glass, and after adding a splash of water to the scotch he did the same to Christa's. She didn't drink scotch often but she took a healthy sip, made a face, and then nodded for Ben to continue.

He was patting Spot and Smudge, who were sitting in their owns chairs on either side of him as he described their incredible first nine months of life to the riveted, frequently sipping Hamish and Christa.

He told them about their mother's escape from the kennels, Smudge's parvo, the goat pen fire and their paw surgery, and about their recruitment of the local coyote pack and Max. He told them about the pups studying everything they got their paws on, and how they helped him with his homework, and how far ahead he and Kelcy were in school.

He also told them about the family agreeing to keep the pups' gifts a secret.

Spot and Smudge helped him to answer Hamish and Christa's questions, and they stared mesmerized as Ben and the pups held full conversations in sign language.

Ben stopped short of telling them about the fate of the Dorschsteins, especially Jerry, or the demise of Dr. D the vet, or Liko, or Aaron, or the other bad guys the pups had taken care of.

At one point their silent conversation got a little heated.

Ben wanted to tell them about the smell the pups were currently chasing, and what they'd found so far, but Spot convinced him to hold off.

Just look at them, Spot signed. *I think we've given them enough to gnaw on for now.*

Hamish inspected Smudge's split paws, and laughed when she reached over the table and gave Christa a very firm handshake.

"So let me see if I got this right," Christa said. "You adopted these orphaned pups, and due to some genetic accident they turn out to be super smart. They surround themselves with a team of local wild dogs to secure their environment, and then they design their own hands, which they blackmail the local vet to install, so they can proactively interact within that environment. Is that about right?"

Spot and Ben both nodded.

"I must say," Christa said, "everything else aside, that's pretty fuc...freakin' cool."

She got up and went around the table to sit next to Spot, and as she took one of his paws in her hands she said to him, "I can see how keeping you two a secret makes sense."

Spot nodded.

"Apology accepted," Christa said to Ben. "I guess that also explains how you know sign language. Does your whole family sign with them?"

"Yeah," Ben said, "but they're a little slower at it."

Christa chuckled, and she could tell from Spot's nod that was an understatement. As she poked and prodded his paw she said, "The first of their kind. Think of the possibilities, and the responsibility."

"You should talk to my sister," Ben said. "She's seriously geeking out on that subject. She's studying to be a vet so she can help the pups figure out what makes them tick."

"Help the pups?" Hamish whispered more to himself than to anyone in particular. He let that thought run around in his head for a minute as he rolled the USB stick in his hands. Finally he asked, "Ben, exactly how smart are they?"

"Ask them yourself," Ben replied with a smirk.

So Hamish asked, and Spot answered using Ben as a straight translator.

As they chatted Hamish noted there was virtually no delay from the dog's signing to his grandnephew speaking it out loud.

Their rapid back-and-forth questions and answers went on uninterrupted for an hour, and along the way Hamish stopped referring to the pups as 'them', and started calling Spot 'you'.

They moved quickly through language, math, and the sciences, and whenever they went really deep into one subject Spot would pause their conversation to have a blindingly fast exchange with Ben.

When Ben noticed Hamish's puzzled look he said, "You guys are getting into stuff I don't understand, so Spot's giving me enough background so you don't think I'm an idiot. He's also phonetically spelling the bigger words so I pronounce them correctly."

Hamish and Christa exchanged a long look and a slow head shake.

They covered advanced animal physiology and communication, and by the time they strayed into humanities and philosophy Christa had refilled their glasses three times.

Eventually Hamish stopped asking questions, and as he leaned back in his chair he wondered aloud if Spot fetched his own newspaper before reading it.

Christa chuckled, and Spot wagged.

Hamish wondered if the wag had been a reaction to Christa's laugh, or if Spot understood humor.

Spot read Hamish's face and signed to Ben, but Ben didn't translate it.

Spot tipped his head down and gave Ben an obstinate stare until he turned to Hamish and said, "Spot says Scots wear kilts because sheep can hear zippers."

Hamish stared at the dog for a moment before he burst out laughing.

He grabbed Spot's head and gave it a firm shaking, and Ben said, "He was chomping at the bit to share that one when Tavish was here."

"Right," Christa said as she slapped her hands down on the table and stood up. "Who else is starving?"

Smudge wagged, and Christa gave her ear a tug before she went to the fridge.

"I'll admit I'm more than a little freaked out," she said as she pulled out ingredients to make a salad, "but I've known Hamish since I was six minutes old and I've never seen that look on his face before. We may need to start calling him Indiana Jones. It's like he's staring at the Ark of the Covenant."

Spot signed, and Ben translated in a deep voice, "You're meddling with powers you can't possibly comprehend."

"Yes!" Christa said as she pointed across the kitchen at Spot.

"Snakes," she said. "Why'd it have to be snakes?"

Spot wagged, and through Ben said, "We named the *dog* Indiana."

"Jones," Christa grumbled, "I always knew someday you'd come walking back through my door."

Spot said through Ben, "We have top men working on it right now."

Christa narrowed her eyes and asked, "Who?"

Spot wagged harder and narrowed his eyes back at her. Through Ben he said slowly, "Top, men."

Christa laughed and said, "Bad dates," at the same time Spot was signing it.

Not wanting to be left out Smudge raised a paw and signed, and Ben said, "This was no boating accident."

Spot and Christa looked at Smudge, and then at each other, and shook their heads.

Christa cut up vegetables as they continued quoting movie lines, and Hamish eyeballed them as he rubbed his beard.

When Spot and Christa's back-and-forth finally devolved into giggling and tail thumping she asked, "You alright over there partner?"

"Aye," Hamish said as he stared at Spot. "I was just thinking I'm looking at a dog that knows more about dogs than anyone walking the planet. Alf Wight's spinin' in his grave tonight."

"They're like canine Dr. Doolittles," Christa said. "So is Spot the brains of the operation?"

Smudge nodded as she answered through Ben, "He's way smarter, but I'm way stronger."

Christa chuckled as she grabbed her backside and said, "Us girls having a little extra padding doesn't necessarily make us stronger. I wish it worked that way sweetie."

Ben knew what was coming and he casually got up and moved the scotch glasses from the table to the island.

When Smudge asked his permission with an eyebrow waggle and a shrug Ben said, "Go ahead. Just make sure Sholto and the super cops know what you're up to so they don't pounce on you."

Hamish didn't have time to ask Ben what the hell he was talking about.

Ten seconds later Smudge let Hamish up from the floor. She shook her coat to return to her normal size as he stood and slowly put his tam back on.

"Cu Sith," Hamish whispered as he stared down at the deflating Smudge, who was looking up at him with the last of her added muscle shrinking from her wagging tail.

"Mimi calls her that too," Ben said.

To answer Christa's questioning look he said, "It's a mythical Scottish hell hound. Delivers the dead to the afterlife, has a big bark."

"Fucking fitting," Christa said, and then flipped off Spot before he could comment on her language.

"Alright then," Hamish said as he tipped his chair back upright. "Is that the lot?"

"Almost," Ben said.

Christa dropped the salad bowl when a pair of all white, medium-size dogs appeared where the black Spot and Smudge had been a moment earlier.

Hamish pounded the table and pointed at them as he said, "Yeh wee scunners! I thought my old peepers were playing tricks on me when yeh rounded the barn and just disappeared. Jesus, Mary, and Joseph."

Hamish sat down and called Smudge to him, and she put her front paws in his lap. He took out his reading glasses and carefully inspected her coat.

She closed her eyes for a moment, and changed back to all black.

"The army may want to have a chat with you two," Christa said as she picked up bits of lettuce and tomato from the floor.

"And thus the secrecy," Hamish said. "Dear God, the implications."

He held Smudge by the jowls and stared at her face, and she looked away for just an instant before she turned white again.

"Unc, Christa, I have a proposition for you guys," Ben said. "You saw how the pups helped Rook and Vuur? Well that was nothing. They were *trying* to be subtle."

He shot Smudge a dirty look, and Hamish easily read the surly, unapologetic crinkle of her white brows.

"You should see what they've accomplished with a scrappy pack of coyotes back home," Ben said.

Spot gave Hamish a confident nod, and as they held each other's eyes Hamish was pretty sure he knew where this was going, and who was behind it.

"We're listening lad," he said.

"Well, you're having issues with the elkies, right?" Ben asked. "And the conference call is in four days. Let Spot and Smudge work with you to train them. They'd love to roll up their paws and jump in, and I'm sure they could help fix the problem like super quick."

Smudge nodded enthusiastically, and Spot gave Hamish a single wag.

"And in return?" Christa asked.

Hamish answered for Ben as he continued to hold Spot's smart stare, "In return we teach these canny curs everything we know about top notch service dogs. Every technique, trick, strategy, the works. Is that about right?"

"Yep," Ben said as Spot slowly nodded. "You give us the secret sauce, and I'll promise not to breathe one word to Mimi about almost getting killed in a bar fight after dancing with a slut and blowing crap up at the shooting range and getting growled at by a potentially psychotic alpha wolf."

"I can see where Spot gets it," Christa said.

"Aye," Hamish said, but the look he gave Spot said he knew it was the other way around.

Damn yeh Jean, he thought, *what have yeh signed me up for?*

"Yeh numpties have got yourselves a deal," he said.

Spot gave him another wag, and extended his paw.

As Hamish smiled and shook it Christa asked, "So what exactly happened at The Grub?"

CHAPTER 47

Spot and Smudge paused to look down into the mine.

They were standing at the edge of a huge, reddish-brown and white bowl with a wide spiral road that wound down its sides and ended in a small lake at the bottom. They could see an identical bowl on the far side of a narrow slip of land that held a row of big buildings. The bowls were more than a kilometer across and the buildings looked like tiny sheds from the lip of the mine. From the perimeter gravel roads that circled the bowls a network of dirt roads radiated out into the thick pine forest and disappeared up the slopes of the mountains.

The mine was dark except for a few lights strung from crisscrossing conveyors that connected the large center buildings to smaller satellite ones. The conveyors ran above several large rock trucks that were parked in front of a long, three-story garage.

The pups picked their way down the steep, snow-covered road rings and cut over to the strip of land that held the buildings. They wound through the scattered piles of equipment and used the shadows to cover their approach to the garage, and as they crossed the icy gravel they changed their coats from all white to dark gray. When they got to the large sliding back door they listened for a moment with their ears pressed to the corrugated metal.

They exchanged a quick nod, and then Spot stood on Smudge's shoulders and balanced on her padded camo vest so he could flip open the latch.

He hopped down, and as Smudge shouldered the door open a huge furry block head appeared in the gap and barked right in Spot's face.

Relax! Spot barked back at Rotty-wolf. *It's just us, you half-breed idiot.*

The big dog's shovel tongue licked his own drooling jowls as his vacant eyes stared at the snow somewhere between the two pups. He huffed something unintelligible, and then backed away and returned to his cardboard-covered pallet under the stairs.

As the pups slid into the dark of the garage and pushed the door shut behind them the silently pacing wolves watched them.

Smudge passed the two empty cages, and when she approached the first wolf he brought his furry scarred face right up to the bars of the door. His head was twice as big as hers, and as he stared coolly down at her with his pale bronze eyes she reached a paw into the cage. She could feel his hot breath on her muzzle as she gave his thick neck fur a few scratches.

Okay killer, she grumbled in the best wolf-voice she could muster. *If I let you outta here you gonna play nice this time? If you can't get along with the rest of the group my kinda-wolfy buddy over there and I are going to shove you right back in here and you won't be able to hang with the pack.*

The big wolf's eyes darted from Smudge to Rotty-wolf, who was about as tall but thicker in the head and neck.

Sure, he intoned with a deep huff.

Spot and Smudge opened all of the cages and spent the next three hours with the wolves. They started out with some grooming and playful wrestling, which included rewarding them for being good with snacks from their vest pockets. Before long the four wolves were following basic commands. Their natural pack hierarchy and hunting instincts came roaring back quickly and Spot was able to get them to flush out Smudge from hiding places in the huge dark maintenance garage. In short order they were working together to set ambushes and coordinate proper hunts.

Rotty-wolf just chased after them and pounced on the victim once they were caught. He didn't really understand the hunting game or the reward process, but he was having a good time.

The pups were also having fun, and they enjoyed the wolves' accents. The Pembury coyotes' non-verbal and vocalized communication had always seemed rough to the pups, and felt peppered with a bit of Boston twang and attitude. Conversation with the Quebec wolves was more refined, but their huffs and grumbles were also sassy and a bit aloof in a decidedly French way. Spot wondered if it was coincidence, or perhaps just projection on their part, but either way it tickled Smudge to no end.

The wolves generally listened to orders and accepted the pups as a dominant pair. Only once did they have to reestablish the pecking order, which resulted in a brief time-out for the wolf who'd promised Smudge he'd play nice.

Otherwise the pups found them to be cunning animals. They were smart, and strong, but they had been physically and mentally traumatized. They were skittish and had strange quirks that the pups needed to be mindful of. They didn't like anyone walking behind them and they ran back into their cages if corrected too sternly, but once the pups worked through those issues the wolves were truly a joy to be around. They were funny in their own way and set traps and feigned attacks just like the coyotes did when they played, but Spot was starting to get the sense these wolves were innately more intelligent. Where the coyotes tended to react to situations reflexively the wolves were more deliberate and pensive.

As they played the pups asked the wolves about their lives before they were captured. Their stories were fascinating, and they started to understand the extreme nature of their environment. They appreciated the formidable prey the wolves hunted, and the harsh weather and tricky landscapes they had to cope with. They also faced competing predators equally as dangerous as they were. Coyotes had it easy by comparison. It was clear only a smart wolf could survive for long in their world, and they only really thrived when they were part of a dedicated pack. These wild dogs were very tough, but they were also complex and had a strong sense of self and their place in the range they felt they owned.

Unfortunately the stories of their lives after their capture were far less satisfying, and Smudge had to walk away in the middle of it.

Spot feared what his sister would do if they ever ran into Vic or Ty again.

When Smudge sniffed the four wolves for the first time she'd told Spot they smelled just like Vic's fur coat, and she wasn't talking about the bad smell. His coat was made out of wolf pelts, and it had the same dark gray coloring as these wolves.

Spot joined Smudge next to Rotty-wolf on his cardboard bed while the wolves continued to play in the garage.

We need to turn them loose, Smudge huffed as she fed Rotty another biscuit from her vest and barely got her paw out of the way in time. *I can't listen to any more of it brother. We can't let them get thrown into a dog fighting pit again.*

I know sis, Spot huffed as he stroked her upset face tenderly with his muzzle. *But we can't just let them run loose. I doubt they could fend for themselves out there anymore, especially in the dead of winter. They'd likely just run back here, or worse they'd run into town. That woman's crazed wolf story is probably floating around by now and these guys would end up shot. If they did escape into the woods they might bump into Glasgow's pack, and that wouldn't be good either.*

So we tell Hamish, Smudge huffed.

That's probably what we need to do, Spot huffed. *But not yet.*

As Smudge put the wolves to bed and latched the doors Spot checked out the two empty cages. The bad smell was very strong in them. They'd been hosed out but the stench still clung to the tiny bits of food, hairs, and scat that remained. It just didn't make sense, and Spot was gravely concerned about the fate of the two wolves that had been in those cages.

They had a few hours before sunrise and Spot wanted to take a longer route home.

From the mine he led Smudge to the high trail path. It took them up and over the ridge to the base of the mountain that separated the mine from Christa's valley.

They found a small mirror lake hidden in the trees on the plateau at the top of the ridge. It was fed by several rocky streams that flowed down from the mountaintop, and had been created by beavers who'd dammed the far end. There was a narrow channel in the dam that chugged water out in a fast moving chute that fell away over a tall cliff.

They paused at the dam's edge, and even in the moonlight the panoramic view of the valley and the mountains beyond it was amazing. They could see the tiny grid of lights from Piege in the distance, and the road that snaked down the bowl and split the town in half before it disappeared to the south.

To the east was the ore mine, with its brown rings surrounded by snow covered forest with dozens of white logging roads leading away into the mountains. One of the trails wound through the thick woods directly below them. It ran west from the mine through the forest, and would eventually come out behind Christa's barn.

Okay, Spot huffed as he slowly scanned the thousands of pristine acres. *I can see the appeal.*

It'd be beautiful if it wasn't for all this white stuff, Smudge grumbled as she let out a shiver. *And more's on the way.*

She nodded to the wall of dark clouds that was starting to obscure the canopy of stars and creep toward them from the northern mountains. They could feel the barometric pressure dropping, which indicated the break in the snow they had been enjoying would be short-lived.

They don't have bad weather in Quebec, Spot huffed. *You just brought the wrong clothes, according to Hamish.*

Smudge wagged, and huffed, *Parts of me that I hope to use someday are getting chilly. Let's head home.*

Be thankful you don't have hangy-downy bits, Spot huffed before they picked their way down the snowy ravine and followed the banks of the quickly dropping river. The pool at the bottom flowed out as a river again and dropped over a series of rocky falls.

The forest around the falls was tight and dark. The walls were too steep for logging so the Douglas fir and white spruce trees grew in natural tangles around the ravine's rocks. In a few places the river split and flowed around small islands and under fallen tree trunks.

The river widened and calmed at a clearing, and from the top of another set of steep falls the pups had a better view of the snowy trail below them that led from the mine to the ranch. The trail was a fire access road, but it was just barely wide enough for a truck. The river flowed parallel to it for a bit until crossing under the trail at a large culvert.

They paused at the top of the falls to watch startled trout splash away in the shallow water. Spot hopped across several large boulders and stared down into the spray where it narrowed and shot out over the steep wall of rocks.

As Smudge drank at the river bank and watched Spot pawing at the leaping fish she smelled an odd scent on the rocks.

She sniffed around on the muddy bank until she found its source.

It was a very large footprint.

When she put a paw in it she barely covered the base pad.

As she was comparing her split paw-fingers to the footprint's finger-size claws a small branch snapped in the woods on the opposite bank.

Spot didn't reacted even though he was closer, and Smudge guessed he couldn't hear it over the noise of the falls.

She heard another snap, and then branches crunching, and then crashing sounds that were getting louder and coming toward them, fast.

Just a she was about to bark a warning Spot finally looked up, and then they both heard the roar.

Two things saved Spot from being torn in half by the charging bear; not looking behind him to see what was making such a horrendous noise, and jumping the instant his sister barked for him to do so.

He launched himself from the top of the falls as the bear's dinner-plate size paw whizzed in the air behind his rump.

The big brown bear had blasted from the trees and crossed the clearing in a flash. It hit the river at the top of the falls, driving a wall of water in front of it as it pounded over the icy boulders. The water slowed it just enough to barely miss taking Spot's backside off when he leapt.

Smudge shook her snout and pumped herself up to full Cu Sith while her racing brain tried to come up with a plan. The huge snarling animal was blindingly fast. Trying to out run it through the thick woods and deep snow of its home turf wasn't an appealing option.

Smudge had seen the wound on the bear's shoulder as it was swiping at her brother's bottom. It was certainly the winter bear Greer Nellis had told them about, and she didn't want to consider what had been ballsy enough to wake it up and take a chunk out of it. It occurred to Smudge that Lissa had been right about winter bears as the animal looked less than happy.

While she was looking around for an escape she saw two little brown furry faces poking out from a rocky cave at the far end of the clearing.

Wonderful, she thought. *This bear is ornery, hungry, wounded, and protecting her young.*

Smudge also thought the bear may not be hungry for long.

As her brother flew away from the top of the falls she was worried it might go after him so she let out a medium bark. She was trying for enough volume to get the bear's attention but not enough to further piss it off, if that was possible. The angry mother bear locked eyes with her as it continued to charge across the falls, and Smudge's proud little moment of making sure it wasn't going to follow her brother was suddenly replaced by her kinda wishing it had.

She tried to make herself look as big as possible by hopping up on her rear paws as she moved back to the edge of the ravine.

The bear slowed as it came out of the water, cocked its head at the standing Smudge, and then stood up itself and spread its impressive paws as it stared down at her.

When it growled a ground-shaking growl Smudge thought, *Okay Momma, you win.*

She'd never seen an animal this large and she was struck by its amazing proportions. The bear's head was bigger than her whole body. Its thick neck flowed into powerful shoulders, and muscles rippled under the mass of moving brown fur. She confirmed its claws were indeed longer than her split paws, and when its jaws opened wide she thought, *I'm gone in two bites, maybe three.*

The bear let out another terrific roar, gave up trying to figure out why the muscular little black dog-thing was trying to face off with her, and decided to just pounce on it.

An instant before the bear hit Smudge she ducked and curled down onto the rocks in a tight ball. As the bear's weight dropped down on her she suddenly wasn't so confident about her plan. It didn't seem possible, but the animal felt a lot heavier than it looked.

Thirty meters below Smudge and the bear, Spot was realizing that he hadn't planned for a landing when he jumped off the falls. He was sailing high over rocks that were quickly falling away below him.

At apogee he let out a whimper, and as he fell he started to flail and twist to avoid the jagged tree limb that was speeding toward him. He managed to miss being skewered and grab the branch, but came away with just the broken tip as he spun down toward the churning water. As he rotated in the air he saw the bear drop on top of his sister like an attacking fur blanket, and then he hit wet rocks and bounced like a pinball down the falls. Barely on the edge of control, he danced on the slick boulders and tangles of fallen trees scattered throughout the sloping waterfall. He used his widened front paws to make course corrections at the last instant as he pushed off icy rocks and spun off slippery tree trunks. He had made several successful jumps until another broken branch sent him tumbling into the river.

The massive bear fell upon the curled-up Smudge, and as they rolled forward its huge head tucked and bit down, catching her by the back of the camo vest. Its big paws came in and its claws were heading toward her body.

Smudge got her rear feet under her, opened her front paws, and unfolded under the immense bear. She closed her eyes, and in a fraction of a second used Spot's focusing trick to manually activate her sympathetic system to flood her already pumped up muscle's adrenotropic receptors with a massive dose of adrenaline. Her back and shoulders responded, and contracted with incredible force. She flexed open like a leaf spring, popping up under the bear as their momentum carried them forward toward the edge of the ravine.

She found its rib cage with her split paws and shoved with all her might, lifting the seven hundred pound beast and launching it. The bear went airborne and let out a clenched teeth growl that Smudge felt down her spine.

Spot heard the roar from the river below just as he fell into a blender of spinning currents. He was pushed down to the bottom of the freezing river and ground against the sharp, hard rocks. His vest absorbed the blows to his sides and back, but his head was getting pummeled.

With his hind feet spread wide to find something to push against his nether parts slammed into a submerged tree trunk, and he groaned bubbles into the cold water as he came to an abrupt stop.

He scrambled up the trunk, popped out of the water, and grabbed a branch to flip himself out of the surging river and onto a rocky outcropping.

He heard another horrible, pained growl from high up on the ridge as he shook off the cold river water. He darted back up the falls, taking huge leaps and using his split paws to pull himself up and over the almost vertical jumble of tree trunks and rocks.

At the top of the falls the bear was flying over Smudge as it spun up and away. She felt a tug, and a heartbeat later she was yanked off the ground. The bear still had her vest clenched in its teeth and they were flipping through the air together.

The massive creature released Smudge and roared in disbelief as they fell into the ravine at tree-top level.

The bear crashed down into the branches with a tumbling Smudge following it down into the snapping tree limbs and explosion of snow.

Smudge caught a passing pine bough and swung around it, landing on her feet on a small ledge as the bear continued down the slope, bouncing off rocks and breaking thick limbs until it came to a hard stop at the base of a tree.

Smudge watched from her vantage point as the angry animal spun and got to its feet. It swatted a huge broken tree limb out the way as it roared up at her with spittle flying and its lips flapping over its huge fangs.

Spot left the river bank and shot across the slope sideways as he followed the crashing sounds. He found his sister's overhanging rock and dropped in next to her as the bear stood and let out another bone-shaking growl. It echoed off the ridge walls and faded away as it bounced down the valley.

Spot checked Smudge for holes or missing parts, and as he gave her a quick head-butt he huffed, *I thought you were grizzly chow.*

I bearly escaped, Smudge huffed with a wag as they both leaned over the precipice and saw the bear was hunting for a path up to them.

When Smudge took in a huge rush of air Spot covered his ears with his paws.

Smudge spread her feet wide, leaned far out over the rock, and let fly with an enormous bark. Her hind legs came off the ground and Spot grabbed her to keep her from pitching over the edge.

The bark shook snow off the trees and pounded back at them from far side of the ravine before chasing the bear's fading growl down the valley walls.

The bear froze. Its huge front paws had found the footing to climb but it just stared up at them and tipped its massive head.

The pups stared down at the bear.

The bear stared up at the pups.

So Dr. Doolittle, Smudge huffed to her wet, shaking, wagging brother. *Do you speak grizzly?*

CHAPTER 48

Hamish watched Spot and Smudge romping behind the corral with the elkhounds, and what had initially looked like play to him was starting to take on a definite logic. He was far from being able to speak elkie yet, but the basic patterns of communication he'd watched canines exhibit for half a century were starting to make sense in a way they never had before, and it had only been two hours.

Even as he was nodding his head he had to tell himself to sit still and watch. Giving up control of his training was harder than he'd expected, especially with their time crunch. He'd started out wanting Ben's pups to translate everything they were working on with his dogs but he knew the more pressing matter was to get the sled team whipped into shape in three days. To accomplish that he had to let Spot and Smudge work at their own speed, which appeared to be pretty bloody fast.

They'd each taken an elkie and run off into the snow, where they'd darted over open ground, blasted down the riverbed, and dodged through the trees together. They ran the dogs around the corral, where they alternated between simply trotting the perimeter and pounding as fast as they could around the igloos like barrel racers. The whole time they were exchanging little nods and twitches and huffs with their running partners. After a few minutes they'd drop that dog off, take out another one, and do it all over again.

Smudge spent a lot of time with E'sra. The two dogs had certainly developed a strong connection even before the training started and Smudge always ate alongside the powerful wheel, where Spot tended to move around at feeding time. As her brother worked with the rest of the team Hamish assumed Smudge was having the daft brute E'sra go deep into the finer points of following the team, picking up cues from the lead dogs, and farting.

From the far side of the corral Smudge read the look on Hamish's face. She huffed for E'sra to hang on a sec, and as she left the sturdy elkie's side she nodded for Ben to join her.

She stopped in front of Hamish, looked coolly up at him, and signed.

Ben translated, "Your face is speaking volumes right now Hamish, and these dogs are really good a reading simple things. That big dog at the back of your team, the one you're so quick to dismiss, is actually the second in command, and he's no dummy. T'nuc sets the pace and then relies on E'sra to keep an eye on the team while she navigates. They count on him for more than you know, and they trust him, completely. Which is more than I can say for you, you..."

Smudge didn't finish what she was going to say. She just dropped her paw, turned around, and went back to working with E'sra without looking back.

Hamish watched her walk away and then looked down at Ben, who said, "Mimi taught her if she can't say anything nice, well, you know."

Christa had been watching from the barn, and when Hamish caught her smile he said, "Stow it Boucher."

While Smudge worked with E'sra, Spot and T'nuc trotted around the snow field with the boerboel twins and Sholto. Ben told Hamish he wasn't sure what they were talking about, but he noticed T'nuc was doing a lot of positive acknowledgment like he'd seen the coyote's do when the pups taught them something new.

After another hour Spot and Smudge circled up the team in the corral, and asked Hamish to hook them up to their positions on the sled. Spot watched every move Hamish made with the harnesses, and stopped him a few times to ask questions through Ben. They connected Smudge to the rear harness next to E'sra, and the big dog showed them the different paces and ways to pull as they trotted around the corral with no driver. Spot took K'cuf's position next to T'nuc and she demonstrated some of the techniques she uses to supervise the team.

Hamish thought the musher-less sled just looked wrong, and his frustration really started to show when they had him undo and redo all of the harnesses three times.

He struggled to see the point of it, which the pups could easily see by his pursed lips.

Spot tapped him on the knee, and raised a paw for him to wait a moment.

Ben translated as Spot signed an apology to Hamish. He explained this was all very new to him and his sister, and they wanted to get it right. They'd found out each dog had a preference as to how they were rigged to the sled, and it made a big difference in how they pulled. He took the time to show Hamish some of the issues the wheels E'sra and R'ekcuf were having with the twisting of their inside rigging when they ran in silent mode.

And that's when Hamish realized he'd just been handled by a dog.

He tossed his head back and laughed a long, loud, howling laugh.

He grabbed Spot by the jowls, lifted his front paws off the snow, and stared into his wide, smart eyes as he said, "Aye, I got it yeh canny wee fucker. You're the boss here. Just tell me to shut it or we'll never get through this."

As Hamish turned the wagging mutt loose he noticed the elkhounds were all staring at him.

"Are yeh lot laughing at me?" he asked.

"Yes Unc," Ben said. "They sure are."

Spot had Hamish mount the sled and run the dogs around the snow field in a big circle while he and Smudge and Ben watched.

Every few minutes one of the pups would flash a sign, and Ben would call out for Hamish to mush the team at a different speed. A few times the pups had them stop completely so they could trot out into the field and have a quick yapped and huffed conversation with a single dog or the whole team.

At one point Spot had Hamish hike the team at a painfully slow pace as he walked next to the elkies. He signed something to Ben, who ran into the barn and came back with Christa.

She and Spot worked on the dogs' boots and harnesses, with Christa sending Ben back to the barn a few times to get tools and bits of hardware as she made adjustments. They shortened the distance between the double team leaders and the swing dogs, put K'naks into a larger pair of boots, and made other subtle changes that left Christa scratching her head.

Spot and Smudge exchanged nods, and waved for Hamish to drive the team around again at a double-pace.

The pups stood motionless for an hour watching from the middle of the circle with Ben and Christa.

Spot finally waved for Hamish to bring the team over, and when the panting dogs stopped in front of them Smudge hopped into the sled.

As Spot signed to Hamish, Ben translated, "Do a twenty-click loop with them, out to the log bridge and back on the other side of the river. We'll meet you by the saw mill. Go as fast as you have ever run a sled team before. Don't stop for anything, don't slow in the turns and don't brake down the draw. Drive them hard Hamish, let them find top speed."

Hamish stepped off the runners and walked past the wagging team.

He took a knee in front of Spot and said, "I'm nae' questioning yer sage wisdom, sansei Spot, but as this is the first day you've been a mush master, and I've only been doing this since before yer great great great great grandmother was latched to a teat, I just want to make sure I completely understand yer orders. Yeh want me to tell this winded team, the ones who two short days ago went swimming with a bloody pine marten, to run like the wind?"

Spot and Smudge nodded in sync, and so did Ben.

"That's how sleds break," Christa said. "And that's how dogs can come up lame. We've seen more than a few idiots do that to a team when they got caught up in the heat of a race, or when they panicked."

Spot stood on Hamish's knee so they were face-to-face.

He raised a paw and signed, and Ben translated, "They need to run. They need to show you what they can do together, and they want to take your directions while doing it. Their confidence problem was as much your issue as it was theirs."

"Was?" Hamish asked.

"Yes, was," Spot said through Ben. "They're as ready as they'll ever be to trust you. The real questions is, are you ready to trust them?"

Spot finished signing and held Hamish's stare.

"What'd yeh think lass?" Hamish asked without looking away from Spot.

Christa stuffed her hands into her pockets and said, "I can't believe I'm saying this, but I trust the annoying fifty pound genius."

Thirty minutes later Spot, Ben, and Christa were down at the mill watching Vuur and Rook cooperate in the maze. The police dog trainees were calling out dead ends and coordinating like they had done the day before, but they had shaved another two minutes off their maze time and were shooting for five.

"That's amazing," Christa said. "It's not just the cooperation, I mean that's cool, but look at their focus. Half of the concern when working in a stress environment with a dog is that they'll lose concentration, stop listening to commands or get spooked and do the wrong thing. Frankly, that's the same worry you have with people, but a poor dog can't tell you what's bothering them. Well, until now I guess. Oh my head hurts."

Ben chuckled and said, "My dad complains about that same thing when he sees the pups doing a new trick or whatever. He calls it mental whiplash. I've seen them doing it since they were pups so I just think it's normal."

"And you're eleven," Christa said. "You aren't a jaded skeptic yet."

Spot looked up at her and nodded as he wagged.

"Oh shut up," Christa said as she smacked his rump.

Vuur and Rook blasted through the exit doorway of the maze a full thirty seconds faster than their last record run.

Spot leapt down and congratulated them, and it quickly turned to rough housing. When Ben joined in they took turns attacking him.

The wrestling turned into the police dogs showing the pups ways to intimidate and take down perps.

After some trial and error Smudge figured out a way for the lanky police dogs to apply a choke hold after taking down said perp by using their powerful hind legs and locking them over their front feet.

'Cause sometimes you don't want to draw any blood, Smudge signed.

The way Ben casually translated that had chilled Christa, and when they tried out the choke hold on her it scared the hell out of her. Something deep down inside her freaked when Vuur started to squeeze.

As she rubbed her neck she said, "That'd put the poor scum bag in the looney bin, after they get out of the hospital."

The pups wagged, and then all of the dogs stopped playing and looked up river.

Spot flashed a quick sign, and then he and Smudge followed Rook and Vuur as they bounded off and disappeared around the corner of the maze.

Ben and Christa caught up to them on the bridge by the mill, and saw they were all tipping their heads at the mountain.

A few moments later they heard faint echoes of Hamish's booming voice bouncing down the valley from high up on the ridge.

Through binoculars they caught glimpses of the sled weaving through the thick trees as it sped down the slope. The team was flashing through the gaps in the trees so fast it was hard to track them.

"Whoa, they're moving," Christa said as she counted the dogs' cadence on her fingers. "That's an open-field triple pace, just shy of a flat-out run."

As her binoculars moved down the draw she whispered, "Absolutely nutty to be going that fast in there."

The sled blasted from the thick trees half a kilometer up from the bridge. T'nuc and K'cuf dove together over a small rise with the six other elkies chugging hard behind them. They turned parallel to the river bank, and Ben could see they were running in perfect sync. The sled launched over the large drifts, catching air as Hamish sunk down below the handlebar. Smudge's head popped up with each lurch of the sled, and then dropped back down into the fur blankets when they hit the next dip. She had the side rails in a death grip and Ben could see her bulging eyes.

The snow smoothed out at the valley's bottom, and as Hamish stood up straight he yelled, "*Ga rask,* you beautiful little fuckers! *Lope vind!*"

The sled sped up. The dogs were at full extension with their rear feet deftly passing their front paws as they coiled and stretched, and propelled the sled in perfect harmony. They looked like the cylinders of a finely tuned engine with their heads bobbing in unison. Even Christa could see the pride and elation on their furry snow-covered faces.

As they approached the little bridge Hamish shouted, "*Joss stoppe!*"

He jammed down on the foot brake and leaned hard as the team pulled in a tight circle and the sled slid out behind them sideways. The runners carved up a huge plume of snow that crested like a wave over the spectators as the team came to a skidding stop.

Hamish yanked off his snow-packed goggles, and with a huge smile creasing his frosted white beard he said, "Bloody brilliant!"

Smudge fell out of the sled, took a few wobbly steps, held a split paw to her mouth, and heartily barfed through her fingers.

CHAPTER 49

Ben was sitting on top of the workbench with his legs crossed. He was braiding long pieces of Kevlar strapping inside leather strips, and checking to make sure they were the precise lengths Christa and Spot wanted. Smudge was sitting at the far end of the bench feeding out strips from the spools when Ben tugged for more.

Christa was sitting up on the mechanic's roller at the front end of the sled, and she was shaking her head as she tapped a screwdriver to her lips. The gangline that connects the elkies to the front bridle of the sled was spread out along the barn floor. Spot had its middle component, the shockline, in his teeth and he was tugging on it. He was pointing at the mounting point where he wanted Christa to attach a limiting connector to restrict the lines' movements, instead of the standard clip carabiner she had in her hand. They'd been arguing for an hour about the changes he wanted, and Christa was smart enough to realize she was arguing mostly with herself.

She'd been building cutting-edge dog sleds for fifteen years, and now that she understood the dogs' points of view she saw her rigging had some basic flaws.

Ben was translating for Spot, and he'd been including the dog's cynical inflections and rude gestures without even realizing it. He'd stopped paying much attention to what was being said when the argument turned overly technical so he was interpreting Spot's paw signs and body language on auto pilot.

When Spot noticed Christa was getting testy he started taking it easy on the jabs and insults, which seemed to just annoy her more.

Hamish came through the back door of the barn whistling. He was imitating a tin whistle from an old Highland's tune about a lass in a lake as he tossed a stack of empty plastic pails into the sink and stomped the snow off his boots.

He joined the group in the sled bay, and finished the song with a stomp and a double toot.

"Coming down like the blazes out there," he said as he stretched under the heater with his fingers locked over his head. "Gonna be enough snow to drown the Wigtown martyrs by morning."

Smudge agreed with a nod.

As Hamish pressed his hands into the small of his back he looked down at the dogs, who were laying on the moving blankets under the heater.

"Sholto's dead," he said. "Oh wait, no. I see her breathing."

"Not funny," Christa grumbled from the front of the sled.

Hamish noticed both of the boerboel brothers were laying on their backs, and it looked like they were each trying to eat a tennis ball.

He scratched under his tam and asked, "What the Christ are those two numpties doing?"

Ben raised a finger for Hamish to wait a second as he said to Christa, "No, he said if you use a quarter inch Hiem's connector you can take twelve centimeters off the shockline's binding, which will eliminate the slapping problem. And yes, he knows that will only work if E'sra stops kicking the line." He turned back to Hamish and said, "It's an agility game and focusing exercise. The super cops are supposed to hold the tennis ball in their mouth, grab it between their front paws, pass it to their rear paws, and pass it back again."

Hamish watched his hundred and seventy-five pound mastiffs delicately balancing the balls between their meaty paws. He thought they looked ridiculous, but damn if they weren't completely focused on their bloody tennis balls. The balls hit the floor as often as they were held, but Hamish knew the completion of the task was only half the goal. He wasn't much for parlor pet tricks, but he couldn't argue with the concentration and dexterity it required.

Sholto was watching the police trainees with one eye open, but her tail thumped the blanket when Vuur successfully passed the ball to his back paws. If Hamish didn't know better he'd swear the old shepherd was encouraging them.

The past twenty-four hours had been a bit of a blur, and he was struggling with some of the same sensory drunkenness Christa was suffering from. Reality seemed to be on shaky ground, but he couldn't ignore the fact that Ben's special pups were unbelievably sharp and had the elkies heading in the right direction in just a few hours. Which was something he'd fought with for several months. He stopped short of admitting the pups had him moving in a new direction as well, but he freely admitted to being a bit thick-skulled.

He also couldn't overlook Ben. Jean had been right, the kid was brilliant, and he wondered if he just hadn't heard half of the things the annoying wee boy had been saying.

Hamish unzipped his jacket, rolled a stool over to the workbench, sat down with a heavy groan, and nodded at the front of the sled as he asked, "What are those two carrying on about?"

"They made a side deal," Ben said. "Spot helps Christa with the changes to the sled, and she agreed to modify the pups snow boots and vests."

"Aye?" Hamish asked as he picked up one of the booties. "You know she uses stingray leather? It grips better than leather when they're wet, and lasts ten times longer."

Smudge nodded an impressed nod that Hamish had no trouble understanding.

He tapped her snout with the boot, tossed it back onto the bench, and picked up one of the pups' vests.

He noticed the pockets Mimi had added to the inside, and when he unzipped one he saw it contained a few paper clips and a little red folding knife with a Swiss flag on it. His brow creased when he realized the knife was his. It had come from his junk drawer.

At the front of the sled Christa and Spot reached some agreement and fist-paw bumped.

"Look at the poor thing," Hamish said as tucked the knife back into the pocket and zipped it up. "That lass knows more about shaving ounces and seconds from a sled than just about anyone alive, but she's being shown an entirely new direction by a creature with four more legs than she has."

"Spot's in his element," Ben said. "Smudge calls it his professor mode."

Smudge agreed with a nod, and Hamish leaned back in the stool to watch his exceptional team of misfits work.

As Ben twisted the loops of leather he rocked back and forth a little and quietly sang a nursery rhyme his Mimi must have taught him when he was still a wee grandwean bouncing on her lap. Hamish hadn't heard it in almost forty years, but by the second verse every word came flooding back and he started to sing along under his breath.

"Yeh canae' shove yer granny auf the bus," Ben sang. "Yeh canae' shove yer granny auf the bus. Yeh canae' shove yer granny, 'cause she's yer mammy's mammy, no, yeh canae' shove yer granny auf the bus."

Hamish noticed Smudge was rocking in time with Ben's cadence as she fed out more Kevlar strapping. He could just picture his loving sister-in-law singing softly to the dog when she was a poor sick puppy, which was probably about the same time the pup's little brain was cooking itself into a neural network that was likely far more efficient than his own. He thought the swaying runt mutt probably remembered every word and was singing along with Ben inside her fuzzy dome.

He watched Smudge put down the roll of strapping and pick up a small glass jar. She carefully twisted off the lid, dipped in one toe, and came away with a small dollop of Christa's foot wax. As her dexterous paws smoothed it between her pads she sighed, and caught Hamish staring at her.

She held his stare as she gave her paws a sniff, and then wagged.

When she signed Ben translated, "I'm addicted to this stuff. It's better than being licked by a pack of coyotes."

Hamish stared at both of them for a long moment as he scratched his beard.

"Looks like this storm will last a few days," he said to Christa. "Perfect for the elkies' final test. I'll run them up into the mountains to check on the wolves, put on a few hundred kilometers on them, and be back in time for the conference calls."

"Sounds good," Christa said without looking up from the sled.

"Okay," Ben said. "Well, I guess we'll help get Vuur and Rook ready for their call."

"Yeh lot arnae' coming?" Hamish asked with a smirk.

"We get to go?" Ben asked as his eyes flashed to his pups.

"I need my team with me," Hamish said as he put his hand on Ben's knee and gave it a shake. "Who knows what those glaikit hounds will try to pull without you and the pups watching over them. Vuur and Rook are solid, and Christa can polish them up just fine for their call."

"Thanks Unc," Ben said as he dove off the bench and wrapped his arms around his great-uncle's wide shoulders.

"Aye lad," Hamish said as he returned the boy's firm squeeze.

He saw Christa was giving him an ear-to-ear grin from the front of the sled, and Spot's tail was thumping the floor.

Hamish stood and easily plopped Ben back down onto the bench, and the movement distracted Vuur enough for him to drop his tennis ball.

It rolled across the floor, Hamish kicked it back to him, and the police dog snatched it up, rolled onto his back again, and went back to passing the ball between his paws.

Hamish smiled down at him, and then closed his eyes and put a hand to his forehead like a magician about to guess a card.

"I see a warm beach and a drink with a brelly in my not too distant future," he said.

"Thanks to a pair of rescued orphan mutts," Christa said as she nudged Spot with an elbow.

"Aye," Hamish said as he agreed that was true enough with a nod.

He looked at the sled and asked, "How's the rig?"

Christa looked to Spot, and in a voice that had suddenly developed an Aussie accent she asked him, "The rig, how is she?"

Spot stared into the guts of the sled as he tapped a wrench on his snout and signed.

Christa nodded, and then looked up at Hamish and said, "It's got a cracked timing case cover and it's broken a couple of teeth off the timing gear."

Ben knew Christa wasn't really reading Spot's paw signs. They were doing a bit from 'The Road Warrior'.

Spot signed again, and Christa said, "The radiator's damaged at the core."

Spot signed again, and Christa said, "It's got a cracked water pump."

Spot signed again, and Christa said, "And it's got a fractured injector line."

Ben assumed Hamish wasn't going to play the role of Papagallo, the post-apocalyptic refinery camp's leader, so he asked gruffly, "Well, what does all that mean?"

Christa turned to Spot and asked, "Yeah, okay, but what does that mean?"

Spot signed, and Christa said, "Twenty-four hours."

"You've got twelve," Ben said.

Christa turned to Spot and said, "You've got twelve."

Spot wagged, and Christa turned back to Ben and said like a simpleton, "Okay!"

Both pups' tails spun, Christa and Ben chuckled, and Hamish shook his head at them.

"I donae' know which of yeh is more disturbed," he said as headed for the barn door.

He paused in the doorway to point at Smudge and add, "Eat some ginger. I don't want yeh bloody boking in the sled tomorrow."

And to Ben he said, "Remember to pack yer satphone lad, mine's soaking at the bottom of the raging burn somewhere."

CHAPTER 50

Spot and Smudge hid behind a large snow-covered piece of equipment at the mine. Spot had his ear pressed to the side of the metal garage while his sister paced nervously behind him. He could hear the grumbling of Vic's voice, and assumed he was in the office based on the glow coming from the second floor windows.

There was someone else with him, but with the blowing snow peppering the metal building and the wind rattling a loose corrugated panel somewhere above them it was hard to hear what their faint voices were saying.

We can't just leave them brother, Smudge huffed. *We just can't. I won't let them fight again. You promised we'd —*

Easy sis, Spot huffed. *We'll figure it out, but we need to hear what they're saying. Come on.*

They stuck to the shadows as they wove between huge buckets and dozer blades, and curved things that looked like dinosaur claws. When they moved around to the rear of the building they saw the sliding door was slid halfway open. A pair of big white pickup trucks were parked side-by-side just inside the garage. They were similar in size to Hamish and Christa's, but they were much older and a lot more beat-up. One truck was parked next to the metal stairs that led up to the office, and the other was parked next to the wolf cages. Dirty slush pooled on the concrete floor under them and dripped into the center drain.

The pups slipped out of their vests and hid them as they changed their white fur back to black. Part of the changes Spot had negotiated with Christa was to swap out the vest's body panels for winter camouflage. They worked perfectly with their white fur in the snowy dark of the woods, but would be no help inside the garage.

The pups moved into the gap between the far truck and the wolf cages. As the wolves stirred Smudge signaled for them to keep quiet with a shoulder-shake. The wild dogs paced silently behind the bars as she moved down the row of cages and reached in to give each of their snouts a rub. She left them to join Spot under the far truck, where he'd paused with his ears perked.

They both strained to hear, and with a quick nod they agreed they just weren't close enough to pick up what was being said in the office. They moved to the rear of the truck where they could see Rotty-wolf was snoring on his cardboard bed under the stairs. His thick leather collar was clipped to a rope that was tied to the handrail.

You keep him quiet, Spot signed. *I'm going up the stairs.*

They split up, and Smudge made sure no one was watching from the office windows before she darted through the pool of light to the sleeping wolf-dog. Her brother looped around the truck and waited at the bottom of the stairs.

Smudge tapped Rotty-wolf on the snout.

He farted.

She tapped him a little harder.

He opened one eye.

Shhh, Smudge huffed as she patted him gently on the head. *It's me.*

The massive half-wolf, half-Rottweiler looked at her for a moment and then shot to his feet and started barking his fool head off. He was standing with his paws spread wide and his tail wagging as his spittle and his questionable breath flew right in her face.

Smudge grabbed his muzzle and held his mouth shut, and he let out a few more stifled barks as he looked down his odd wolfy-rotty nose at her. As the barks devolved into grunted yaps she could see realization finally wash over his vapid face. He wagged at her, and when she let him go he turned once in a small circle and lay back down with his head hanging off the pallet.

He started to lazily lick his big paws as if she wasn't there.

Smudge shrugged to Spot through the open steps as the door at the top of the stairs flung open.

Spot quickly backtracked and slipped around the corner as the big thug Ty stepped onto the upper landing.

He looked down the stairs, and then leaned over the railing and yelled down at the wolf-dog, "Fuck are you barking at, you freak?"

The big dog turned his simple face up to him, and then went back to cleaning his paws.

Ty watched the pacing wolves for a moment before he went back into the office and slammed the door behind him.

Spot slipped back around the corner, crept silently up the stairs to the middle step, and leaned forward with his cupped ears perked. He could hear Vic's gravelly voice, but the mine boss mumbled so badly it was hard to tell what he was saying.

Smudge looked up at Spot through the grates of the steps and shook her head.

Yeah yeah, just one sec, Spot signed down to her before he continued up the stairs. He paused every few steps but couldn't make out what the mumbling mouth-breather was saying until he was almost to the landing.

"*Soucie pas,*" he heard Vic grumble. "Move the boys over to that second cut while we blast in the new basin."

Spot heard him shuffle some papers and then pound a glass down on a desk.

"*Sacre!*" he spat. "I forgot to order the new fucking planetary gear for the Terex. I tell you that creepy Chink bitch has got me all fucked up. She and that *fif* Brit are a real pain in my ass. After this storm clears I'm telling them to *va chier*. We'll deal with this shit ourselves."

Spot was pretty sure he was taking a long drink, and confirmed it when he belched.

"I'll give them fucking subtle," Vic grumbled, "and we're gonna clean some house around here at the same time, Ty. It's high time that bitch constable and that nosey sapper stop sniffing my ass. Make sure Jero is packing concealed at all times, and I don't mean in his ass crack. I don't give a flying fuck about his pachuco bullshit, tell him to wear a holster under a jacket. He may have to get rid of that big bodyguard on the quick."

He took another slug and grumbled with a slimy chuckle, "We'll see if our wolves like dark meat."

Spot heard Vic's chair squeak under his bulk, his boots scuffing in place, and the light tap of a bottle hitting the rim of a small glass. He assumed the mine boss was at his desk, which he guessed was on the far wall, and based on the little chirps of Ty's boots he was on a stool in the middle of the office.

When Spot caught a whiff of the warm air that was flowing from under the door he crept up onto the landing and brought his nose close to the crack. He picked up alcohol, beer, coffee, nasty cologne that was unsuccessfully masking body odor, propane heat, potato chips, and more of that vile smell that was all over the empty cages.

When Ty's chuckling subsided he asked, "With the weather coming in what should we do about this weekend?"

Vic took a drink and grumbled, "Those *guidoune* loggers won't leave their camp in this snow, and we'll be in the shit 'til the weekend. Push the fights back to next Saturday, we got other affairs to tend to anyway."

Spot listened for a while longer but they just rambled on about mine business.

Just as he was thinking about heading back down the steps Vic tossed what sounded like an empty glass bottle into a metal trash can and grumbled, "Go get 'nother from my glove box."

When Spot heard Ty's heavy footsteps crunching on the broken linoleum he realized he'd been wrong about his location. Ty's stool had been a whole lot closer to the door, and as Spot looked down at the well-lit bottom of the stairway he did some quick math and didn't like the answer.

He chose to dart forward instead, and his claws clicked on the metal grid of the landing as the opening door just missed hitting his rump.

Smudge watched from under the stairs as Ty stepped onto the small platform and swatted the office door shut before trotting down the stairs. He was five steps from the bottom when he stopped.

He turned around and looked back up the stairs.

Smudge could see her brother's lower half hanging down from the back of the upper landing. His rear paws were trying to get a hold of one of the metal support posts, and little rusty flakes were drifting down under him.

She quietly slipped around Rotty-wolf, positioned herself under Ty, reached up with her split-open paws, and hovered them an inch from the toes of his boots.

Ty stared at the top of the stairs as he tapped a ringed finger on the metal handrail.

It was impossible to tell if he could see Spot through the open stairs, but there was a flood light above Ty's head and Spot was mostly in shadow.

Long seconds passed, and then Ty turned and stomped down the rest of the way. He yanked open the truck's door, and as he pulled his bulk behind the steering wheel and pitched over to rummage in the glove box Smudge raced to catch her falling brother.

She went Cu Sith as she leapt and wrapped herself around him when they collided in mid-air. They fell through the dark together and slammed down on the concrete garage floor with Smudge twisting to break her brother's fall. They tumbled across the greasy floor until she caught the grate of a floor drain and brought them to a quick stop.

As they spun to their feet they saw Ty react to the noise with a spasm inside the truck. He hit his head on the dash, and his flailing arm grabbed the rearview mirror and yanked it off the windshield. He scrambled out of the truck with a bottle of booze in one hand and the mirror in the other, and in one quick move he tossed the mirror behind him and came back with a knife.

Rotty-wolf actually listened to Spot's quickly huffed instructions and turned his huge body away from them to stare at Ty. After drooling at the big thug for a few seconds he executed the second part of the instructions and sat down on the creaking pallet to lick his balls with gusto.

"You dumb fucking mistake," Ty spat as the knife disappeared behind him. He stomped up the metal stairs two at a time with the bottle as he added, "One of these days dog, one of these *Christo*-fucking days."

By the time Vic spun the cap off the bottle the pups were back outside the garage, where they were donning their vests and having an argument.

I know, sis, Spot huffed. *I promise you we'll rescue them, but there's nothing we can do for them right now. And there's more we need to do tonight. At least now we know there's time to figure out a plan before the next fight, right?*

Smudge reluctantly agreed with a nod as she peered around the open garage door.

The wolves were staring at her with their beautiful, tortured faces.

With a head bob she indicated to them she'd be back, and they replied with wags of their bushy tails.

Spot gently nudged her away from the door, and led her out of the mine and down a trail they hadn't yet taken.

An hour later they were standing at the back door of another garage. This one was about the size of Papa's barn, and when Smudge boosted Spot up to look in the window he saw a tidy, fully outfitted workshop. Parked in the middle of the workshop was a white truck with red stripes and two orange light bars.

This might be the dumbest idea you've ever had, Smudge huffed as Spot jumped down from her back and unzipped one of his pockets.

As a stiff blast of frigid wind ruffled their white fur and swirled snow around them Spot removed a paper clip and huffed, *I hope we never need this, truly I do, but I'm not walking into a gun fight with just sharp teeth again.*

As he straightened the paperclip and worked it into the door's padlock Smudge huddled against him and grumbled nervously, *Brother, we're going on Hamish's little field trip, and then we're going down to that mine and save my wolves, and then we're gonna deal with Vic and his arse-munching buddies and anyone else up here who's looking to fuck with us, and then we're getting the hell out of this bloody cold.*

Sounds good to me, Spot huffed as he clicked the lock open, and they were blinded by bright lights.

꙳⊰§§⊱꙳

Lissa and Harry Chogin were wearing fur hats, boots, and bathrobes.

They also had big flashlights and ever bigger handguns, and all four of them were pointed at the pups.

The couple were standing in the snow-covered footpath that led from their house to their garage, and they were staring, but not believing.

The two medium-size, all white dogs huddled at the back door of their workshop were wearing winter camouflaged vests. One of the dogs had its front feet up on their garage door, and in one of its strange paws was their padlock.

Which it had apparently just opened with a paperclip.

Harry nudged his wife and flashed a quick sign.

"It can't be," she said.

She turned to the white dogs and asked, "Spot? Smudge?"

Spot wagged, and Smudge lifted a paw out of the snow and signed, *We surrender.*

꙳⊰§§⊱꙳

Five minutes later Lissa was standing in her kitchen with a towel draped over her shoulders. She had her black Sig P226 pistol in one hand and a phone in the other.

Harry was sitting at the table with a fleece blanket wrapped around him, and he was holding a steaming cup of coffee that had two large shots of brandy in it. His matching pistol was sitting in front of him on the maple leaf shaped placemat, next to his little oxygen mask.

Spot and Smudge were sitting at the table opposite him, and they too had towels draped over their shoulders. Their wet vests were hanging on hooks by the back door, where they were dripping onto the boot pan along with the Chogins' bathrobes.

The pups had changed their fur back to black.

Put down the phone darling, Harry signed to his wife. *And the gun. Let's hear them out.*

Lissa put down the phone but she still tapped her nine millimeter against her hip as she paced.

"They're *loup-garou*," she said. "Harry, they're fucking *loup-garou*. They're real. My mom always said they were."

I'm pretty sure these two aren't shape-shifting werewolves, Harry signed. *Put the gun down before you shoot your foot off, or mine.*

He turned to the pups and signed, *Okay, give me that again a little slower. Why exactly do you need our explosives?*

CHAPTER 51

"Just when I thought it wasn't possible for this place to get more beautiful," Valerie said with her arms around Willie. She leaned down and drew him in for a deep kiss with her strawberry lip gloss sliding around his chapped lips as he fondled her bottom.

She straightened up again, and with his face planted firmly in her exposed cleavage she said from above his head, "Okay, I can see why you fucking idiots live here."

The group had just skied out of a stand of thick trees and into a clearing at the top of a ridge, and the vista below them was indeed truly breathtaking.

It was a postcard view of a river nestled in a white valley between snow-covered pine forests that swept up and away to the mountains.

From somewhere behind them a bald eagle cruised right over their heads and glided down to the river on widespread wings. It leveled out and seemed to hover for an instant over the water before it pounced and effortlessly flapped away with a fat trout wiggling in its talons.

"Wow," one of the skiers whispered to her husband as her camera clicked away. The majestic eagle disappeared over the trees, and she turned and said, "Cripes Willie, how much did that one cost you?"

The group chuckled, and Willie saluted them as though he'd arranged for the eagle.

He checked his watch and saw they were making good time even in the deep powder. He had fully expected Valerie to slow them down but her clumsiness was outweighed by the length of her stupidly expensive two and a half meter long skis.

The trekking had also gotten easier as the day went along. Once they were in the deep forest the wind died down and the driving snow turned to flurries. It was perfect skiing, and he figured the group should easily make it to the falls by lunch and the north lodge by sunset.

He had split the supplies for their spaghetti dinner among the backpacks, and he planned to let the others cook while he snuck Valerie away for her 'half-mile high club' initiation. If it was a repeat of last night he'd need a few extra servings of pasta to have the strength to keep up with her for round two. As he was the guide he'd taken the only separate bedroom in the south pass cabin, but he was pretty sure the whole group had still heard them going at it.

The shutterbug's husband was lagging behind them on the trail, again, and he was chomping on a granola bar, again.

Willie almost gave him shit, again, for just tossing the wrapper over his shoulder. The ignorant rich bastard had been told ten times already and Willie just couldn't be bothered to make it eleven, especially as both of his hands were busy with wonderful, chest-high ass.

CHAPTER 52

Glasgow had done all she could to sneak off but the rogues were vigilant, and they never slept. They ran everywhere they went, which was often just in big circles, and they hunted and killed every scent they picked up on. Sometimes they ate pieces of the kill, but most often the crazed wolf monsters just bounded off after the next scent. Even if they left her to give chase they'd always find her again after the kill, and sometimes they brought her back an organ or the animal's head, or they just regurgitated for her like she was a pup. What came up smelled far worse than their exterior, or even their scat.

She was exhausted. Her paws still hurt from the fight and she hadn't properly thawed-out from the swim in the river. Normally she would have cuddled up with the pack for a few hours until her extremities warmed, but she just shivered constantly and her feet and ears had gone numb. Although her body was about to give out she couldn't rest, even when the rogue's left her alone. She was haunted by the faces of her pack, and her daughter hovered in front of her whenever she closed her eyes. Even when she opened them that perfect little face lingered for long moments before fading away into the blowing snow.

The disgusting rogues had tried frequently to mount her but thankfully whatever affliction had turned them mad and lumpy had also prevented them from being effective at mating. She had been hinting to her Alpha recently that she was almost ready and these insane creatures were certainly picking up the smells of her heat. She didn't want to entertain the thought of these wolves being successful. Based on the deep bite marks and scratches they left on her neck and back the rogues could tell things weren't working. Frustration would eventually take over and they'd shove her aside as they growled and snapped at some unseen enemy.

Just when Glasgow thought things couldn't get any worse she had picked up hints of familiar scents, and she'd been working hard to steer the rogues away from them. She'd bounded over a narrowing in the river and had led the rogues up the far side of the valley after other prey. Her diversion had kept them distracted for an hour while they hunted and killed a snow fox and her young, but they eventually caught the scents she was trying to keep them from and bolted back across the river. She tried to pause at the water's edge but they just shoved her across and dragged her by the back of the neck when she stumbled.

The rogues stepped from the deep forest cover onto the trail made by the humans, and they could hear the small group was just around the bend. The humans had stopped and were communicating, and Glasgow tried one last time to convince the two male rogues to run the other way but she received a powerful swat to the face and was pushed forward down the trail.

They came upon a food item the humans had discarded. It was slick and unnaturally shiny, and the crumbs that were stuck to it smelled like nuts and roots.

The rogues nudged Glasgow forward again until they stopped at the head of a large meadow that sloped steeply down to a wide river valley.

The humans had left the rim of the bowl and were sliding away quickly on their slick sticks.

With a few shoulder shakes and gray-tinged mucus spraying grunts the agitated rogues devised their plan, and then split up.

Glasgow watched them darting through the trees on either side of the sloping bowl. She knew they would circle and attack from opposite flanks when the group of oblivious humans reached the narrow gap in the woods where it closed in again down at the river's edge.

CHAPTER 53

A hooting pair of twenty-something girls shot past Willie and Valerie. They crouched into a tuck to race down the steep slope after the rest of the group.

Willie thought they might be partners, but Valerie had disagreed with a head-and-chest shake, and assured him her gaydar was always spot-on. He thought that was a pity as things could get pretty freaky in the woods after a few bottles of wine and some weed, and a little molly, and maybe a line, or two.

Fuck em', all the more for us, Willie thought as he smiled, and remembered Valerie's panties basically flinging themselves off when they'd role-played 'bad cop frisk' with his emergency pistol.

He was tempted to spark up a little pre-game joint, but after this long downhill run and a quick lunch at the falls they'd be facing a long trek up to the north cabin. The trail gets steep in places were there aren't switchbacks, and they'll need to pole it most of the way.

Valerie sped off down the steep slope to chase after the young women, and Willie paused to check the forecast on his range phone. Most of the guides carried the same combo cell-sat-GPS-radio-emergency beacon unit. They were far from any cell coverage, and with the thick clouds there wasn't enough signal to even register one bar on the sat or GPS connection, but the mapping and weather app didn't need much reception as it would just accumulate data until it had enough to display. He'd left it powered on for the last hour and it had picked up enough signal to load the forecast and fix his approximate position.

The weather report showed the brewing storm was going to be a real dumper, but the worst of it should blow through overnight and they could hold off heading back down the mountain until noon. The snowfall was no problem of course, it was the high winds he worried about. It can make for a miserable trek at the higher elevations where the forest thins, but the ride down from the north cabin should be a cake walk as they can coast through the powder all the way.

Even with the earlier squalls everyone seemed pretty happy about the trip so far. The group had taken that shit at the bar in stride, and they gushed about Hamish and the kid more than they bitched about the food or the accommodations. They'd all brought good gear and were in okay physical shape, and none of them was a roaring pain in the ass like that crazy bitch in the last group.

But by far the biggest win had been the wildlife. After the eagle sighting they'd started a running joke about Willie having the critters on his payroll. He couldn't have planned it better, and they'd checked off pretty much every fur or feathered creature on their bucket lists.

Except for the big one of course.

They asked about the friggin' wolves at every stop, and even Valerie had been busting his balls over it.

Hamish's wolf stories and the kid pumping them up about the Alpha sighting had been pure gold, but it was doubtful Willie could actually deliver a glimpse of one of the furry beasts. He had to ride that fine line between optimism and promising with his guests. Of course they heard him promise regardless of what he actually said. He sort of understood Hamish's position on keeping the wolves' collar tracking signals a secret until the program matured and could be managed, but he and the other guides could also use the friggin' cash.

Still, even without a wolf sighting his tips from this group should be pretty good. He had saved the best vistas for the last, and he'd been dropping the 'Tipping ain't a city in China' line between hinting at his sister's upcoming kidney transplant.

Valerie had almost caught up to the girls, and they'd almost reached the rest of the group who'd clustered at the river's edge.

Willie tucked his range phone back into his bag, twisted his feet to make sure his bindings were secure, and as he shoved off hard with his poles he thought, *Time to show these city slickers what speed really looks like.*

CHAPTER 54

"*Stoppe gutter,*" Hamish called to the dogs.

They slowed together and brought the sled to a perfect stop in the deep snow.

He set the foot break, and from Smudge's perch on top of their gear she turned around and nodded her approval to him. She was wrapped up in a blanket to her chin, and she was wearing a pair of dog goggles.

Her muzzle and ears were covered in icicles, and Hamish gently brushed them off as he walked past her and said, "Aye, they're running pure magic."

He lifted his legs high to trudge through the thigh-deep snow, and as he passed Ben and Spot he said, "Give them a snack, check their boots, and break out the radio tracker." He didn't give the orders to anyone in particular as they'd just sort of figured it out throughout the morning.

Hamish was finding these pups and Ben pretty handy to have around. They added little weight to the sled, and they still noticed subtle improvements for the dogs he didn't. Even Ben was better at reading the elkies body language than he was. The lad wasn't as good as the pups of course, but he picked up on the ice in R'ekcuf's boot, and that T'raf had been uncomfortably gassy earlier. That last one wasn't too hard to figure out but Ben did notice something was off first, and not just because he was in the front of the sled.

As Hamish watched Spot and Smudge giving the sled dogs a treat, and Ben rolling in the snow with T'nuc, he wondered if he would ever be able to read dogs like that. Maybe that cocktail he craved with a brelly in it should be used for toasting his retirement. He had enough saved up and it was probably time.

Still, he wondered what a whole team of pumped-up Smudges would be like to mush. And then he pictured Spot mushing them, and that frilly drink was looking better and better.

He checked his stopwatch, and showed it to Ben and Spot.

Ben looked down at the GPS numbers on his tablet, did some math in his head, and said, "Seventeen kilometers an hour average, at almost a four hundred meter rise in elevation per hour."

"Aye," Hamish said, not overly surprised Ben's numbers were right. "In deep snow with a light headwind. Top speed of thirty eight?"

Ben and Spot agreed with a nod, and Hamish realized Mimi had been right about her wee grandson soaking up information like potato bread in barley soup.

To the whole team he said, "There's Iditarod teams that would kill for those numbers lads and lasses."

"So, do you have to change their names now?" Ben asked.

Hamish turned to put his stopwatch away, and to hide his smirk from Ben. As he zipped up his pocket he said, "Ach lad, what do yeh mean change their names? Why would I do that now?"

"Come on Unc," Ben said. "T'nuc? R'ekcuf? K'naks?"

The dogs looked up at him when they heard their names.

"*Backward* Norwegians?" Ben asked. "Don't you think the owner will be a little upset when he figures it out?"

Hamish was still looking at his pocket and trying hard not to laugh out loud. "Still nae' sure what you're driving at lad," he said.

"Unc," Ben said as he pointed at each dog. "You named his dogs Arse, Fart, Skank, Cunt, Fuck, Fucker, Dufus, and Ghost."

"I did?" Hamish asked as he bit back a smirk and threw Ben a bag of jerky. "Now that is one bloody strange coincidence. And watch the language, yer Mimi would nae' approve."

"Why Ghost?" Ben asked as he shook his head and tossed a biscuit to the wagging T'sohg. "Did you run out of swear words?"

Hamish sat down next to Spot on the front of the sled. The dog was wrapped in a blanket and using his dexterous little pads to tap away on his small tablet. Hamish had noticed whenever they crossed flat ground the dog had his nose buried in it.

"Yeh learning how to use the loo lad?" he asked as he gave Spot's ear a tug.

Spot held up the tablet to show Hamish he was studying a cutaway graphic of a pink cube with red and blue tubes running through it.

Hamish took off his gloves, pulled out his reading glasses, and looked at it more closely. It was a detailed diagram of skin, complete with the appendages of the dermis, nerves, and hair follicles. All the parts were labelled, and the graphic moved to show the hair growth as boxes with detailed descriptions popped up.

Hamish took off his reading glasses and said, "Lad, yer dog is lookin' at skin."

"Yeah, he's been obsessed with it since we got here," Ben said. "Hey Spot, what's next, zebra stripes?"

Spot's surly eyebrow raise was followed by him staring up at Hamish with a look that expected him to agree Ben was an annoying nuisance.

Hamish did with a nod, and as he and Spot shared a friendly stare he saw the depth behind those eyes. To all other canines on the planet direct eye contact for more than a few seconds was usually a sign of aggression. Hamish realized the pups' focused stare would help to establish them as the dominant player whenever they met other dogs, which would come in handy as long as the other dog didn't get its knickers in a twist about it. The casual human observer probably wouldn't notice their knowing stare, as he hadn't, but now he could see they looked into you as much as they looked at you. It was a strange experience, but it was one he was beginning to appreciate, and even enjoy. It was rewarding to get the kind of immediate visual feedback expected when communicating with humans from a dog. But it was still pretty bloody insane.

"Yeh are one knotty pine," he said. "Yeh know that, aye?"

Spot stared for a moment longer and then handed Hamish the tablet before he jumped down from the sled and walked off into the snow. He moved away from the team a few meters, stopped, and turned his head up to face the mountains.

Hamish chewed his sandwich and watched the odd dog stare off into space, as did the rest of the team.

Spot stayed perfectly still for several minutes, and then he shook off the snow that had accumulated on him and wadded back through the deep powder. He jumped back up onto the sled, turned in a circle, and sat down next to Hamish again.

Hamish looked down at the smart, crazy black dog who was staring up at him.

He looked again more closely, and slowly put his reading glasses back on.

"How in the bloody hell?" he whispered as he buried his hands into Spot's neck fur. It was much thicker than normal, and as Hamish ran his fingers through it he separated the hairs and picked out their different layers and thicknesses.

Spot had a full, dense winter coat any elkie would be proud of.

He raised a paw and signed, and Ben translated, "Simple modification to the same hypno-chromatophoric process we use to change our coat coloring, except I applied it to my existing awn hairs. By pulling in subcutaneous protein reserves and transforming them into alternating guard and down hairs I mimicked an undercoat. Of course, I don't have the exact combination of insulation and vapor expiration as a natural-coated cold weather animal, but it should do a satisfactory job of thermoregulation. I also reduced the hematocrit percentage to increase my blood's fluidity and reduce the risk of crystallization, and opened up the venules in my paws' pads for better heat exchange. I also wrapped them in a layer of fatty tissue for increased insulation, and made a dozen other small tweaks to my—"

Ben paused, had Spot repeat a sign, nodded, and continued, "—stratum spinosum and dermal papillae. Overall, the modifications yield pretty effective results, but I'm still trying to find the right amount to increase the capillaries in my cutaneous plexus. Henshaw cites wolves have a diameter that's eight times the size of a normal canine, but I really doubt that's accurate as my toes were burning up and they started melting the snow."

Spot finished signing, closed his paw, and returned it to the deck of the sled as he continued to stare up at Hamish.

Hamish chewed very slowly, and thought perhaps he was a little premature in admitting he enjoyed that immediate visual feedback. He swallowed, and said, "So, yeh can turn into a husky at will?"

Spot nodded, and added a little shrug and head tip that Ben translated as, "Isn't that what I just said?"

Hamish got up, finished the last bite of his sandwich, clapped his hands together and said, "Right. Let's be off then, shall we?"

He stood at the back of the sled, and as Ben and the pups packed up and got ready to move out he avoided looking at the fluffy Spot.

"*Ga hike*," he called to the team, and mushed them north along the ridgeline trail that took them higher into the park's mountains.

As they whooshed along through the trees Spot taught Smudge the thick-fur mantras, and at the next rest stop they didn't climb back into the sled when it was time to head off again.

They ran along with the team, and after pounding through the chest deep snow for hours on end they had an entirely new appreciation for the elkies' stamina and coordination.

Smudge even took a turn as a wheel, with E'sra running next to her to correct her mistakes. She quickly realized the same bonds that get strengthened while hunting with a pack are reinforced even stronger when running and pulling as a sled team. There was a greater dependence on the dogs running mere inches away, and the sense of not letting the team down was amplified in the precision of every step and tug. Even in half Cu Sith mode Smudge was getting a little winded, and when the novelty of running in the cold, deep snow wore off she relinquished her place at the back of the sled to the professional again. As she yanked off one of her front boots so she could reconnect E'sra to the harness she subtly gestured to him, *I'll never repeat this in public, but you're one awesome sled dog.*

E'sra snorted his agreement, and soundly cracked Smudge on the jaw with an appreciative head-butt.

When Spot wasn't running with the dogs he was checking the radio tracker with Ben. They had picked up a few pings of signal from Glasgow's collar, but they weren't sure they could trust the reading. The weather might have been messing with the tracker's reception as it showed the pack was pretty far to the southwest, which was an odd place for them to be. If they wanted to catch up to them it would mean finding a place to cross the river and backtracking, which wouldn't happen until well past sundown. Hamish decided they would run up to the next river crossing and find a good place to camp for the night. They could catch up with the wolves in the morning when they'd have a better fix on their real position. With the lingering low clouds it would get dark early and he wanted to get camp setup before the winds picked up.

He also planned to check in with Willie later to see if they had seen any sign of Glasgow or her pack, and to see if Valerie had found out why his nickname was Wee Willie Winkie.

CHAPTER 55

Glasgow was far past caring about hiding herself so she didn't bother staying in the woods. She would never normally follow a human trail but she walked in the ruts made by their sliding sticks to the lip of the steep bowl.

Even with her big paws keeping her from sinking into the snow the deep powder still came up to her chest.

All but one of the humans had made it down to the river's edge, where the forest closed in again at the bottom of the glade. The one that remained was a small male, and he was moving fast down the open slope. His bright covering was easy to spot against the field of endless white.

Might as well be a baby rabbit running straight toward them, Glasgow thought.

She normally had an ambivalence toward humans, unless they were hunters. The big one who observed wasn't a bother and she didn't mind him getting relatively close. His smell was familiar and he had a calm confidence about him Glasgow had learned not to fear, but he was still a human and she'd observed enough of them and what they could do to learn the lesson her elders had taught her well.

Run away, and stay away.

Still, she felt no animal deserved the fate that awaited these dumb creatures. She knew humans were powerful. They were the top predators in any forest, but they were also extremely stupid. She'd come across a few of them that had been killed by a bear or a moose, but most often they just drowned or froze. Usually it was simply from doing something dumb. Most humans shouldn't venture into the woods as they acted like lost whelps, and this group certainly didn't look to be the more formidable hunting kind of humans to her.

She had also learned that dead humans tended to just draw more humans.

Glasgow knew these humans wouldn't be able to hide from the two crazed rogues, but they certainly weren't doing themselves any favors either. They were all brightly colored and they were making noise and jumping around like foolish pups, and the one speeding down the mountain was taunting the rogues into a chase. Normally being seen and heard saved dumb humans more than it put them in jeopardy, but not this time. Not with these savage, ruthless hunters. They didn't care, they just killed.

She didn't want to watch. She wanted to run, but the rogues would just catch her and drag her back.

If she wanted to get out of this she'd have to do it herself. She couldn't wait for a Casanova rogue looking for a mate to come along and save her, and even if one did it wouldn't stand a chance. Watching these deranged creatures stalk, hunt, and kill was the only way. She had to catalog their habits and look for weaknesses.

CHAPTER 56

Willie raised his poles above his head and pumped them as he raced down the bowl. He had picked up a shit load of speed coming down the glade, in fact it was more than he was comfortable with and his legs were wobbling, but he thought, *Fuck it, give them a show. If I break a leg I can still get blow jobs with a cast on.*

The group was pointing at him, and the twenty somethings and the shutterbug were clicking away with their flashes popping in the snowy haze. Valerie was jumping up and down excitedly, and even with the powder flying over his skis and hitting his goggles he could see what an amazing feat of engineering her outfit was.

She hadn't made it all the way down to the others yet so she was the one he whizzed by first as he yelled, "God bless America!"

It was only as he passed the rest of the group that he noticed they weren't pointing at him. They were staring up the hill and snapping pics as he zipped by. He turned to look, caught the edge of a ski, fell hard, and almost tumbled into the river.

He got to his knees, and as he adjusted his package and lifted his goggles he followed their pointing fingers to see what the big deal was.

Standing at the top of the glade was a wolf. A big, light gray wolf. It was staring down at them from their ski tracks.

At that moment the snow eased some and the clouds thinned, and the top of the ridge lit up with filtered sunlight.

Valerie was still jumping up and down when she turned and whispered loudly, "It's so beautiful Willie, look at it!"

Shutterbug's husband stopped munching his granola bar long enough to flash Willie a big crumby smile and a 'we're both getting laid tonight' eyebrow waggle.

Without looking away from her rapidly clicking camera his wife smiled broadly and said, "That must have cost you a fortune Willie."

He snapped off his remaining ski and limped over to stand behind the group. He couldn't believe his fucking luck. He was adding up the tips and saw a new set of graphite Nordic's in his future, and a bag of BC gold weed.

The wolf was just standing there in a circle of sunlight, majestic as fuck and twice as pretty.

Fucking priceless, he thought. *I could kiss your big fuzzy cheek Hamish, you bloody brilliant Jock.*

"Behold, Mr. Canis lupus," Willie said in his best Attenborough voice. "Looks to be well over a meter tall at the shoulder and more than a hundred and fifty pounds. That's a male, you can tell by his ears. He's the alpha you heard about, and he's come out of the deep woods to check out us human interlopers. His pack will be back in that thick stand to the right. We went right past them without seeing them, but it's a sure bet they were tracking our every movement." He paused for the appropriate oohs and aahs, and as the group nudged each other he continued, "Looks like my choice of paths paid off. I was hoping we'd run into him here. See how he uses our tracks to avoid the deep snow?"

The group nodded, and Willie said, "He's got some crazy sharp senses. From three hundred meters away he can smell your perfume Valerie, and he can see your nips are hard."

"That's not overly impressive," Shutterbug mumbled not too quietly.

Everyone but the quiet Mormon couple from Vancouver laughed, although the husband did smirk until his wife shot him a look.

Valerie turned and stuck her tongue out at Shutterbug. With a hand on her hip and her head tipped to the side she asked, "So will he, like, fucking attack us?"

"No, certainly not," Willie said as he slowly unzipped his bag, slipped his hand inside, and grabbed the butt of his bright orange safety revolver.

He suddenly hoped that crazy bitch from Chicago really was a crazy bitch.

The way the big wild dog was standing in their ski tracks and staring down at them just didn't seem right somehow.

Shutterbug's husband dropped his empty granola wrapper into the fluffy snow. He was starting to peel open another when his question about how Willie could be so sure the wolf wouldn't attack was interrupted by a much larger wolf clamping down on the side of his head from behind.

Shutterbug turned to tell her wrapper-crinkling, loud-munching husband to shut the fuck up, but her pissy look turned to stone when she watched the wolf open up his chubby neck. He held out the granola bar to her like he was offering her a bite as the wolf's fangs sunk in deeper and a spray of blood shot out and painted a red trail up her front and over her camera.

Willie froze until another jet of blood pumped out, and then he started tugging on the pistol. The hammer caught in his bag and he just kept yanking as he turned himself around in a full comic circle like a kid who can't get their arm out of their coat sleeve.

The Vancouver couple panicked and turned to run but hadn't released their bindings. They went down together in a tangle of poles.

A beefy ex-marine in a bright green ski suit fared better as he'd silently unclipped before he tried to run in the deep snow. He pumped his knees high and gave it all he had, but in the end he only accomplished being the first one attacked by a second wolf that shot from the opposite tree line. The wolf was just as large as its pack mate, and it faked a lunge for the jar-heads' neck before taking him down by the thigh. It hit him so hard he spun like a football tight end, and the big wolf flung around with him as they twirled down into the snow. With one quick head jerk the wolf tore open the femoral artery in the marine's groin. From the flailing, growling, screaming mass of bright green and dark fur came an arcing spray of bright red that pumped out in a circle across the white snow like a sprinkler.

Shutterbug reached for her husband but only grabbed the granola bar as he fell backward from the weight of the massive wild dog on his back. The wolf leapt to the side as the dying man puffed down into the deep powder and flopped his arms and legs like he was making a snow angel.

The young non-lesbians hugged each other and screamed together, harmonizing as they invited the wolf to be its next logical target. It took a few bounding steps and leapt, and as they put their hands up the cuter of the two snapped one last killer selfie. The flash lit up the wolf's clubbed black feet and gore-smeared fangs just before it took a chunk out of Less Cute's face. They fell backward together, and the girls' skis and poles clattered wildly as the wolf pounced and bit.

Willie started to walk backward, stepping slowly and silently away from the growling and the screaming and the crunching bones and the spraying blood. He was still feebly tugging at his pistol as he backed up to the edge of the wide river.

The second wolf circled the not-so-quiet-anymore Vancouver couple as they swung at it with their poles and yelled obscenities. The big wolf pawed and snapped but held back as two pairs of poles jabbed at its snout. It decided to leave them for a mother-daughter team from Nashville with matching pink outfits. They too had unclipped from their skis and took two steps in the deep snow before becoming immobilized, mostly by fear. They had lost their matching ski poles so they balled their matching mittens into fists as the approaching wolf hungrily smacked its quivering, black-goo dripping mouth.

Shutterbug had stood perfectly still and quiet after her husband fell, and she hadn't make eye contact with the wolf that had been eyeballing her until the young women screamed.

She watched out of the corner of her eye as the two girls fell and lay side by side together under the wolf. Their skis were tangled and each had an arm trapped under the other in the deep snow. The massive wolf hopped to Cuter Girl's side as it opened its jaws wide, and when it shot forward and snapped down it covered her entire neck.

Shutterbug backed slowly away on her skis, pushing back with her poles until she slid next to Willie on the rocky riverbank.

Cuter Girl flailed at the wolf with her free arm as the mad animal lifted its massive head and her back arched out of the snow. Her wide eyes darted to Less Cute, whose teeth were showing through her torn-open cheek. Blood flowed freely into her snow suit, turning her white thermal top red. Less Cute was pounding on the wolf as well, but stopped when it fixed her with a cold stare from above her friend's neck. She watched helplessly from inches away as the wolf compressed its jaws. There was a snap, and as black goop and blood dripped into the snow below Cuter Girl's neck she stopped pounding too.

Willie found solid footing on the rocks at the edge of the water and freed his orange pistol. At the same time he yanked off the plastic safety cover from the emergency button that was clipped to the lapel of his snow suit. He pressed the button and felt it click, and then heard the slow beeping from his range phone that indicated his beacon had been activated.

As he raised the pistol with shaking hands he yelled at his brain to stop trying to figure out the chances that anyone would pick up his signal, or how long it would take them to reach him.

The wolf had finished tearing into the motionless non-lesbians. It raised its gore-streaked head, looked over to see its partner was circling the Nashville mom and daughter, and decided to give the Vancouver Mormons a go.

It charged them, ate a face-full of pole tips, and then leapt and retreated and shot forward again in random lurches. It was moving too fast and hovering too close to them for Willie to get a clean shot. He turned his gun to the Nashville mom and daughter, who were in worse shape.

They were a pink blur of yelling, growling, tearing death. One of them was below the clawing wolf, and her snowsuit had been shredded from her neck to her thigh. Willie could see naked flesh, and lots of blood, and what he could only guess were intestines wrapped around the crazed wolf's head. The gut's owner, Willie thought it was the mother, was clawing wildly at the wild dog's lumpy face as she watched her insides being pulled out. Her daughter was on top of the huge animal's back and she was raking ferociously at its dripping black mouth.

"Fucking shoot!" Shutterbug screamed.

"I can't get a clean fucking shot!" Willie screamed back at her. His scream was much higher pitched than hers.

"Just fucking shoot!" she screamed again.

Willie shot.

A hole appeared on the daughter's forehead and a red mist puffed out behind her. She slumped on the back of the wolf, and as she slid off it her mother grabbed for her hand but missed. Her red clutching fingers followed her daughter down into the snow, and then she stopped fighting and just lay back with her arms around the massive wolf's tugging head. She turned to look at Willie as the wolf nosed in deeper and her whole body shook. The growling animal grabbed something important inside her and she went slack.

"Shoot again, you fucking idiot," Shutterbug said as she tried to unclip her skis.

Willie just stared down the sights of his gun at the wolf as it raised its head and looked at him. Black drool and blood smeared its front. It dripped red slobber and pink intestine as it trotted over to join its partner, who'd gotten the Vancouvers' down to their last pole. The husband was kneeling over his wife while she held a badly bleeding hand.

Shutterbug threw her pole at Willie, and the effort put her off balance. As she tripped over her remaining ski she yelled, "Shoot!"

The pole caught Willie hard across the face and managed to break his paralysis.

He squinted, aimed, and pulled the trigger, and the revolver's tumbler spun the next shell into the barrel and spit flame as it kicked in his hand. He couldn't tell if he had hit anything. He capped off two more rounds and was pretty sure he caught one of the wolves broadside but it didn't slow down any. If anything it just became more enraged and pounced on the Vancouver husband. The man was able to jam the tip of the ski pole under the wolf and sink it in but the little round plastic basket at the tip stopped it from going in more than a few inches. The wolf crashed down on him as the other wolf grabbed his wife's leg and pulled her away.

Vancouver wife screamed and kicked wildly at the beast's face with her free leg. The huge attacker twisted its head and flipped her face-down in the deep snow. Her arms pin-wheeled in the powder as it stood over her, and just as she started to push herself up the wolf reared up on its hind legs and clamped down on her shoulder hard enough for Willie and Shutterbug to hear the snap.

Vancouver husband was on his back, and they could only see his arms sticking up from the snow. He was holding up a pole that the wolf had its jaws locked around, and they were playing a very serious game of tug-of-war.

Willie aimed for the wolf's chest, started to pull the trigger, and heard a scream.

Valerie was a little further up the trail, and she'd been silently watching the horror unfold with her hands clasped over her face. The wolf that was dispatching Vancouver wife stopped chomping, raised its red-smeared head, and locked eyes with Valerie.

The wolf tipped its distorted head as if it was confused, and then decided to drag Vancouver wife's still struggling body along with it. It gave up after a few meters after apparently deciding Valerie was a tastier target.

As is closed on her Willie noticed movement in the snow behind them. It was the third wolf, the lighter one they first saw at the top of the glade, and it was making its way slowly down the bowl in the trail from their skis.

The sun had disappeared behind the thick clouds again, and the snow started to fall in blowing sheets. A cold stiff breeze was being pushed into the valley from the approaching storm, but that wasn't the only thing chilling the shivering Willie to his core.

Without realizing it he'd stepped into the river and was standing shin deep in freezing water.

Shutterbug had watched what happened to the Vancouvers and quickly stomped the plastic basket from the end of her remaining pole. She held it like a sword as she unclipped her ski and moved closer to Willie on the riverbank.

"Shoot it," she whispered calmly.

She was tempted to take the gun but she'd never fired one and she was pretty sure Willie had hit the wolves at least once.

Willie tried to aim. He tried to hold the gun steady but Valerie's wail, Vancouver husband's desperate profanity, and the sickening growls from the wolves were making his vision spin.

The cold of the river crawled up his back. As it sucked the heat from his body it took his will to fight with it. His shiver turned into a constant hard shaking. He couldn't find both sights on the orange barrel, and the nose of the gun seemed to sway away just when he had it true. He shook his head and muttered. "I don't...no...no shot."

"Shoot it Willie," Shutterbug said again calmly. "Just pull the trigger. You can do it, you have to."

He fired, and the bullet slammed into the wolf that had closed to leaping-distance from Valerie. It went down, and the snow around it was a churning sea of grey fur and flying powder for a moment before the animal lay still.

The other wolf was still biting down on Vancouver's ski pole. Willie tried to get it lined up but it was tugging and bobbing too much. As he watched it closely he realized the animal was grotesquely disfigured, and it seemed to be getting far too much enjoyment from toying with its victim.

Willie suddenly wished he'd spent a little less time getting baked and more time with Hamish and his band of zealots learning more about wolves, and learning how to shoot. He'd only seen them in the wild a handful of times but he knew enough to recognize this was very fucking abnormal behavior. These huge wolves had been drooling and spitting black crap and yapping and snapping crazily. This one was also purposely biting and yanking on Vancouver's pole when it could easily shove it out of the way and go for a kill bite.

He looked at Shutterbug, who had just noticed the same thing.

"Fuck me," she said. "Willie, you have to kill it. Kill it now!"

"Fucking kill it!" Vancouver husband screamed his agreement from the snow under the pouncing wolf.

The insane animal paused and looked right at Willie.

It raised its lips at growled with the pole still locked in its huge teeth.

Willie had him, and he pulled the trigger.

As the trigger released and the hammer came forward Valerie screamed louder and Willie jerked the gun at the last instant. The bullet veered high but it still blew a chunk from Vancouver wolf's hulking withers.

Valerie screamed again. She had been knocked from her skis and gone down hard in the deep snow. The wolf Willie had shot was up, and it was now behind Valerie after having pounced and raked her front with its claws.

When Valerie got to her feet she had her arms crossed in front of her. There was blood on her face and running down her legs. She slowly opened her arms and they saw her tight ski outfit was ripped open down to her hip. She had several jagged wounds that started at her shoulder and crisscrossed down her front to her navel. Willie and Shutterbug could clearly see the white of her sternum and several ribs showing through, and the edge of one of her implants.

"Oh my God oh my God oh my God," Shutterbug stammered.

Valerie opened her arms wide and started to high step slowly through the snow toward Willie. She was saying something but they couldn't hear what it was.

Willie and Shutterbug saw the wolf that was tug-of-warring with Vancouver husband had apparently tired of the game after having been stung by the annoying flesh wound. It looked at Willie again and then pawed the pole away with one swat of its huge clubbed paw. The pole flipped end over end and stuck in the snow next to Vancouver wife, who was still groaning.

Willie staggered further back into the river with his boots slipping on the slick boulders until the current started to knock him over. As the freezing water passed his waist he held the pistol above the churning river and struggled to stay upright. His whole body jerked with freezing shakes and his teeth chattered loudly. He heard the pinging of the emergency beacon slowly muffle as his pack took on water and dipped into the swirling river behind him.

Valerie continued to walk toward him as she talked to herself.

The deranged wolf that had split her open came up behind her, and trotted past her as if she wasn't even there. Willie could see the bullet wound in its side, and the blood that was matting its fur, but it seemed unaffected. It walked over to Vancouver wife, who was now kneeling in the deep snow. Her neck was cocked at a strange angle and she had a puzzled look on her face. She seemed curious about the protruding end of her broken collar bone until the wolf stopped next to her and she seemed even more curious about it. She reached out and gently touched its snout before she fell forward into the snow.

Her exhausted husband was pinned down by a huge black paw on his chest. He was deep in the snow and could only see the red and black neck and chin of the drooling wolf above him.

"Sarah, can you hear me?" he called out. "Can anyone hear me? Help me."

Shutterbug gripped her pole and answered, "I can hear you, but no one can help us. You have to fight."

The wolf holding down Vancouver head-butted its fellow killer as it walked past and continued on toward the river.

Shutterbug exchanged a long look with Willie, who was standing chest deep in the freezing river and holding up the pistol in his trembling hand. The guide's normally smiling, pink face was ashen and slack, and she could hear his teeth rattling over the soft gurgling of the water flowing around him. She turned back to watch the huge, maniacal wolf walking toward her. Its powerful shoulders rolled with each step and its big head and dripping fangs swung back and forth, but it never looked away.

She looked down at the blood-smeared camera hanging from her neck.

As she slowly slipped off the strap she switched it from photo to video mode.

She put the lens cap on, pressed the record button, and as her eyes locked with the approaching wolf's she calmly said, "Colleen, your father and I love you more than anything in this world. You've been the best daughter a mother could ever want. Don't cry for us dear. We've had a long happy life, and we've seen and done wondrous things. You are a bright, special girl, and I am so very proud of you. Go find what makes you happy and don't hold back, don't ever hold back baby. Momma's loved you since the first second I held you in my arms, and I always will sweetheart."

She switched the camera off, and wiped off some of her husband's blood before she let the strap slip through her fingers.

She set the camera down on a tall rock, and as she raised her pole the wolf leapt.

Willie watched Shutterbug go down under the wolf as she cursed and stabbed wildly at it.

He saw Vancouver husband's hand desperately searching the other wolf's muzzle. He grabbed a handful of bloody, slimy lower lip before the wolf lowered its head and he let out a chopped scream.

Willie looked up the slope at Valerie. She had stopped walking and was just staring at him. She wasn't talking to herself anymore.

Vancouver wolf raised its head, and let some red part of the husband drop from its dripping mouth as it looked at Willie.

It turned back toward Valerie, and as it approached her at a trot she waved goodbye to Willie by rotating her arm and wrist like she was on a parade float.

Willie's shaking hand waved back, and then he noticed the other wolf, the light gray one that had followed their ski ruts all the way down the slope to stop a dozen meters behind the screaming Valerie.

It was just standing in the snow watching her get taken apart, and Willie thought it looked sad.

He looked away from Valerie in time to see the other deranged wolf remove Shutterbug's head with a hard tug.

Willie rotated in the water to face the far bank of the river, and looked up to see the snow falling from the waving tree tops and the breathtaking mountains beyond them.

As Valerie screamed her last scream Willie put the pistol's muzzle between his chattering teeth.

CHAPTER 57

Bill did his signature move of leaning back from the doorway to look both ways down the West Wing's hallway to make sure the coast was clear, and Kim smirked as she knew some gem was coming.

He leaned back into her office and said quietly, "Kimmy, us old Seabees pride ourselves on being able to bridge any chasm, but this unscalable thundercunt's colder than a well digger's scrotum in Anchorage. Come to think of it, she's more blue-blooded, and less fun to play with."

The president's press secretary laughed out loud despite herself. When she first met the National Security Advisor she thought him to be a boorish, sexist, homophobic, single-celled jar head, or whatever they called ex-navy anachronisms. Over the next eighteen months he proved her to have been totally right. He was also an unapologetic ultra-conservative, and he had wandering eyes, and he was a four-finger afternoon drinker like her dad had been. He was everything she despised, and yet Bill made her laugh harder and more often than anyone else in the White House. She included on that list the constant flow of ass-kissing posers who practiced their witty committee speeches on her, and fancied themselves a mix between Jay Leno and Walt Whitman.

In their eighteen months in the trenches together Kim had also come to understand Bill was the most genuine and least judgmental person on the senior staff. He honestly had no agenda other than expecting results. He would go to the wall for whomever performed best, even if that person was a green-skinned illegal alien with a short skirt and an Adam's apple. Those were his words, but she'd seen him back them up more than a few times, and he'd certainly protected her ass more than once.

"Well, you'll just have to find a way to charm her," Kim said. She wanted to add that she completely agreed that Bill's new Deputy National Security Advisor was exactly as he described, but her job was to avoid tossing logs on Bill's perpetually burning, non-PC fire. The big guy knew she and Bill were chummy, and he'd asked her to try to steer him to the middle of the river whenever she could.

"She's not that bad," Kim lied. "Go and have that beer with her, maybe you can compare war wounds."

She couldn't resist that one. She knew the closest Gloria Bekker-Myers had ever come to serving her country was throwing a posh fund raiser for wheel-chair bound vets. None of the vets were present at the black tie event of course, but they were supposedly the recipients of the donations. One of which was rumored to have been a new sand volleyball court for Gloria's foundation on Cape Cod.

Bill caught Kim's raised eyebrows and slight nod at the hallway behind him, and was glad he'd held his retort.

He turned around, and to the tall woman hovering over his shoulder he said, "Gloria, perfect timing. You ready?"

"Absolutely boss," Gloria said curtly while flashing her plastic smile. She nodded over Bill's bulk as she added, "Good afternoon Kimberly."

Kim waved, and as the two unlikely coworkers left her doorway to go have that friendly beer she so wanted to be a fly on that bar.

An hour later Bill tucked himself back into his pants, zipped up, and yanked down on the flush handle of the urinal, all with the same hand. He hadn't been on a ship in thirty years, but he still only used one hand to take a piss. Sailors learned quickly to keep one hand free to hang onto the boat, and it was a habit that never went away. He gave his fingertips a quick rinse, and as he picked up a sheet of paper towel he said to the mirror, "Well Master Chief, you haven't killed the snotty bitch yet. I'd say that's enough win-win socializing for one afternoon."

He returned to the bar of his favorite G-street hole in the wall. Three hours from now it would see a flood of aides and staffers seeking a cheap happy hour, but he and Gloria had the end of the bar to themselves. At least they had when he'd excused himself to go to the head. As he approached his new pain-in-the-ass underling he saw there was an extremely well-formed backside standing next to her.

The backside was attached to an even more appealing young woman in a clingy black dress, who turned and smiled a pretty smile when Gloria said, "Oh Bill, come say hello to a very dear friend of mine, Katia."

He shook the brunette's hand, and sometime later when Gloria wished them both a good afternoon and left the bar Bill barely noticed.

An hour later he was trying to keep up with the smoky young woman, and after they both belted back a third drink he loosened his tie and turned up his sleeves.

Katia nodded for the bartender to fill their glasses again, and took notice of the tattoo on Bill's thick forearm. It was a bumblebee holding a machine gun.

"My grandfather was a dirt sailor," Katia said as she moved closer and traced its outline, "He landed at Inchon with the First Marines, and then sweat blood to build Cubi Point."

Bill clinked his glass against Katia's, and with a proud nod said, "Well shit, to your grandad then."

"Can do!" they both said before tipping back their glasses.

Some early drinkers had started trickling into the dark tavern, and in a booth at the far end of the bar a big, brick-ugly man sat down and reached a hand into his suit jacket. He moved aside his pistol's handgrip and took out his cellphone and a small bluetooth earpiece. As he hooked the headset over his ear he thumbed the phone's screen to start recording from the micro-camera built into his glasses. He dragged his fat finger around the display and adjusted the zoom to better catch Katia and the National Security Advisor, who was losing his battle to not stare at her cleavage.

The man raised the volume from the remote mic in Katia's purse to better pick up her sultry voice whispering, "I just love tattoos. I have one as well, but we'd need to be a whole lot drunker for you to see it."

Bill laughed and summoned the bartender as he reached for his phone to text his wife he'd probably be missing dinner again. As he hit send he leaned back and looked both ways down the bar to make sure no one of any importance was paying attention.

CHAPTER 58

Smudge got up from Hamish's lap and gave him a dirty look.

Ben groaned and held his nose as he leaned away and said, "Jeez Unc, again?"

"Aye, that one was a little out of bounds, sorry mates," Hamish said with a chuckle as he pulled on Smudge's ear before she picked up her stuffed chicken toy and walked around the fire to cuddle up with E'sra and T'raf.

Ben waved away Hamish's foulness with his hat. The fire flared and they watched the embers get pulled up with the smoke. They drifted up through the gaps in the trees and quickly died away in the stars and the colorful northern lights. The wind had picked up after they made camp, but the snow had slowed to flurries and they enjoyed a rare break from the storm. Thick clouds were already starting to roll toward them from the mountaintops and the snow would start to fall again soon. Hamish expected tomorrow would likely bring another couple of feet.

Before his latest silent offense he'd been enjoying watching the boy and his pups take turns pointing up to pick out the shimmering constellations. Ben and Smudge knew most of them, and a few of the visible planets, and Spot filled in any they missed. As the pups signed their names Ben translated so Hamish could follow along. He knew his brother Duncan loved the stars and figured he'd taught Ben all about the night sky, but it also turned out to be one of Spot's many hobbies.

That didn't shock Hamish much, but he was surprised when the little know-it-all told him, through Ben, that the elkies liked to stargaze as well, and so did the pups' coyote pals back home. According to Spot, when the primarily nocturnal wild dogs were hunting the ambushers often sat for hours in the dark waiting for the drivers to chase prey their way, and while they were waiting they often watched the moon and the stars, and the bright strip of the Milky Way. It allowed them to zone out so their other senses could take over. Spot also told him, through Ben, that most dogs used the stars to orient themselves. They didn't name them as such, but they used the relation of the brightest star, Sirius, and the North Star, Polaris, to interpret direction, and even time. They understood how the moon and the stars rotated during the night, and shifted position relative to the horizon throughout the year.

Smudge sat up and signed, and Ben translated for her. She added that the stars were more than just clocks, maps, and focusing tricks to dogs. She said it wasn't only humans that drew comfort from being in an environment they were familiar with. The ever-present stars and their predictable positions were reassuring. The dog's excellent vision allowed them to see many more of the stars than humans, and the familiar blanket of white dots made the night sky feel like part of their home. She'd even seen the adult coyotes sharing their understanding of the heavens above with their young.

Spot's tail thumped the fur blanket, and when he signed Ben pulled him playfully into his lap and rubbed his knuckles into the dog's head.

"Spot says it makes perfect sense that Sirius is also called the Dog Star," Ben said, "because, you know, it's the brightest one."

Hamish chuckled, partly from the pup's pun, and partly as he wished his propeller-headed pals at the canine cognition center could be part of this discussion. Those arrogant brainiacs are barely scratching the surface of how a dog can get lost a thousand miles from home and show up on their own doorstep a month later.

"So yer telling me dogs have a built-in sextant?" he asked.

Spot nodded, and signed, and Ben translated, "Most of us are only familiar with our local hemisphere of course, but the stars are a key part of our internal positioning system, along with the earth's magnetic field, polarization of the light from the sun and moon, odor gradients from atmospheric circulation, and gravitational anomalies."

Hamish could picture those researchers' spinning propellers starting to smoke.

"Aye," he said, "and I suppose the idiothetic integration of these senses are advanced in you two curs?"

Spot nodded, partly to confirm Hamish was correct, and partly to convey he was impressed.

He could see Ben wasn't familiar with the term so he signed, *Idiotheic integration is the ability to use our internal inputs to accurately track our movement and position.*

Ben nodded, and Hamish asked, "So if you'd been blindfolded on the trip up here, how closely could yeh fix this spot?"

Spot signed, and Ben translated, "To within about ten meters."

Hamish shook his head, but not because he thought the pup was lying. He could picture those smoking propellers spinning off the researchers' heads.

"Ten meters, aye?" he asked with a big smile. "Well, here's a little atmospheric circulation to help yeh narrow it down."

A few seconds later Ben groaned and waved the air with his hat, and the pups wagged as the embers rolled up into the night sky.

They were camping under the umbrella of a large pine tree that formed a natural barrier to the wind and snow. Hamish had shown Ben how to cut snow blocks to close the gap between the drift at the base of their tree and the huge overhanging boughs. It effectively kept the heat from their little fire in, and the thick carpet of pine needles insulated them from the frozen ground. They'd stay cozy cuddled up with the sled dogs on the fur blankets as long as the snow didn't turn to rain, and with the temperature outside their little shelter hovering well below freezing there wasn't much risk of that.

When they were cutting the snow blocks the sled dogs had chowed down on a dinner of dry food, raw chickens, and lard. Ben was amazed at the staggering amounts they ate but Hamish said they had probably burned ten thousand calories since breakfast. He and Ben had split an orange, a big ham sandwich, a can of pork and beans they warmed up in the fire, and a bag of cheese and onion crisps. As the pups were eating alongside the sled dogs Hamish had asked Spot, "Do you prefer dog food or human food?"

Spot had looked up from T'nuc's bowl and signed as Ben translated, "We love the taste and textures of most human food, but we have to watch our figures. We're not puppies anymore, and our systems aren't built to process most of the things you eat. Neither are yours, by the way. If Aila saw how much crap we've consumed on this trip she'd send us all to detox. I'm still paying for the fries we scarfed at The Grub the other night."

Hamish had smiled, and in response let a loud explosion fly.

Ben took the can of beans from him, and Spot stared at both of them for a moment before he continued. Through Ben he said, "Smudge needs more calories than I do, depending on how often she goes Cu-Sith, and the modifications to our coats saps some of our strength too. Based on today, I'd say she needs about five thousand or so." He looked at his sister, and the bowl in front of her, and then signed again.

Ben translated, "Five, not fifteen."

Smudge had stopped gobbling from E'sra's bowl and looked up. She slowly licked a big smear of lard from her muzzle and gave them a wag before dropping back down to mow some more.

Hamish noticed the clouds were closing in on them again, and he said, "Give your Mimi a try before we lose our window lad."

The satphone's signal had hovered around one bar all day, and Ben had to try the call three times to get it to connect. His family was having dinner with Mimi, and they thought it was the coolest thing that he was speaking to them from the middle of the Canadian tundra. Ben had already told them about the pups getting busted by Hamish so they were free to ask Spot and Smudge how things were going. Through Ben they said they were having the time of their lives, and Hamish told them Ben and the pups had been a huge help.

The audio started to drop out so they sent out hugs and kisses, and cut the call short.

As soon as they hung up the phone's missed call and message indicator chimed. They could see that Christa had called several times but the message kept cutting out when they tried to retrieve it so Hamish just dialed the ranch.

"Hey," Christa said with some concern in her voice as she picked up on the first ring. "You get my message? Have you heard from Willie?"

"Nae', and nae'," Hamish said, and had to repeat himself after a blast of static interrupted him.

"Blu called," Christa said over the hiss. "The park station received pings from Willie's emergency beacon, but they've stopped and they can't raise him. There's no response from the north camp either, so we assume he's not there yet."

"Everything's going to be dodgy with this weather," Hamish said as he raised his voice over the crackles. "That Valerie lass probably hit the button by accident with her toe when Willie was, um, painting her nails. Still, if he activated it by accident he would let them know. We'll head that way and check it out, did they get the grids?"

Christa gave him the position of Willie's last ping, and as Ben and Spot mapped it on the little tablet she said the rangers were heading out and would stop at the north camp on their way.

Ben showed Hamish the location.

"Aye," he said. "The basin below the falls."

Christa had said something else but the phone cut out and lost signal.

"That's close to Glasgow's last collar reading," Ben said.

"Aye," Hamish said. "Let's pack up lad, it's a long hike."

Ben watched the phone's display read 'no signal' for a few moments before he turned it off and put it away.

"Tighten everything down and put the rifle in last," Hamish said. "Spot, please explain what's happening to the team."

As Hamish peed on the fire he thought through the possible scenarios that would lead to Willie's beacon having been activated, and then just stop transmitting. There was a chance it could be the weather, but the more likely explanations kept pushing their way into his head, and none of them were good. If Willie had hit it by accident, and if his sat and radio wouldn't work, he would have cycled the emergency beacon twice more at a set interval to let the rangers know it had just been a mistake. Willie was an odd duck, but he was competent enough and had lived in the back country most of his life. He wouldn't want anyone venturing out in this weather if they didn't need to.

Hamish tended to trust his gut, and it was telling him something was indeed amiss. It was also telling him to send down more crisps, so sometimes he had to take what it told him with a grain of salt.

The dogs had just refueled but hadn't had much of a break and he hated to be pushing them again so soon, especially in the dark, and in this weather. He also didn't like Ben being out here if something was truly wrong, but if Willie or his skiers really were in trouble he couldn't take the time to drop Ben and the pups off. Bad things tended to happen quickly in these winter woods, and minutes could make the difference between getting yourself home or getting yourself dead.

CHAPTER 59

As Mimi got up from the kitchen table to put the phone back in its charger they heard crunching on the snow outside. When she pulled aside the curtains headlights from a flatbed tow truck flashed through the kitchen as it turned in an arc and stopped in front of the pen.

She watched the truck's yellow rotating lights chase orange shadows across the snow as the driver's door opened and a bearded man wearing a fur-lined bomber's cap and thick coveralls jumped out. The stiff wind immediately grabbed the fuzzy ears of his cap and flapped them wildly. Mimi turned on the turnaround lights, and as the man approached the house another man jumped down from the passenger seat and followed behind him. The second man was wearing the same coveralls and hat, but a full ski mask covered his face. He also wore snow goggles and carried a thick clipboard.

The bearded man pulled open the storm door and wrapped on the window of the kitchen door.

Before Mimi pulled it open she gave Dan a nod.

He was casually leaning against the wall by the coat pegs with his hand resting on the barrel of the shotgun.

"Evening Jean," the man said as he tipped his head back into the light so Mimi could see his face. "Is it the jeep that won't start again?"

He put his finger to his lips and tapped the oval name tag sewn to his chest.

It was the FBI Director Douglas Barton, and he was wearing a convincing beard.

"Aye, the damn thing's a pain in the arse," Mimi said as she read his fake name. "Please, come in from the cold Arnold. Can I get you a cup of tea?"

"Yah," VB said. "That'd be awesome."

The other man followed him through the door and nodded to Mimi, and then to Dan, and then he paused until Dan stepped away from the shotgun and sat down at the table.

From the man's shape Mimi could tell he wasn't a man at all but a rather tall, sturdy woman.

As Mimi went to the sink to fill the tea kettle the woman quickly set her thick clipboard down on the kitchen table. She flipped it open and took out what looked like a small tablet. She tapped a button on the side, and as the screen lit up she held it at arm's length like she was taking a picture of the room.

"What's the problem with the Wagoneer this time Jean?" VB asked as his partner spun in a quick circle and swept up and down as she turned.

From over her shoulder the family could see what looked like an x-ray image of the walls of the kitchen, with various shades of blues and reds for the plumbing and electrical. There were numbers and arrows dancing around on the screen.

"Oh, you know Arnold," Mimi said as she set the kettle on the stove. "It's older than the hills, so I have no idea."

The woman completed her circle, set the tablet down in front of VB with a nod, and left through the kitchen door as she pulled it shut behind her.

"We're clear," VB said as he took off his hat and sat down. "There's been a development in Canada you need to be aware of, and I take sugar with a little milk."

CHAPTER 60

"Aye, we're crossing it," Hamish said over the howling wind as he slowed the sled team to a trot. "Unless yeh pups can grow wings."

Spot turned his disbelieving, icicled-covered face to look at the equally frozen and concerned Ben and Smudge, and they all squinted through their goggles at the comically narrow log footbridge they were heading toward.

The cliff trail they'd been following was precarious enough. It hugged the curve of a steep ridge before it made an abrupt jog over four large spruce trees that had been felled and bound together to span a deep gorge. The snow-covered bridge was barely more than a meter wide, and the thick, broken rows of icicles that hung down from it made it look like the upper jaw of a monster who'd been in a fight.

Hamish read their faces, and explained it was the only maintained crossing in the park's higher elevation, and detouring around it would take precious hours. He also said humans were its least frequent travelers. When he was doing the sustainability research for the wolf reintroduction he'd camped at the bridge, and in one night he'd watched fox, badger, wolverine, marmot, deer, and even a brown bear use the logs, sometimes at the same time and in opposite directions.

"So, what's your point?" Ben asked as the wind immediately pulled away his puffing breath. "If it'll hold a marmot it'll hold a shite-filled Scot and his lard-filled sled dogs?"

"Aye," Hamish said with a smile. "But I'm nae' so sure about the added weight of a useless city kid and his big-heeded mutts."

Spot's quick extrapolation concluded it was technically possible to cross the bridge as the crest of the outer logs were just wide enough for the sled's runners, with three centimeters on either side to spare. Smudge asked if he'd included in his calculation that the gorge was a natural wind tunnel, and Ben wanted to know if he'd factored in drowning in the frigid water or having his head cracked open on the rocks after they got blown off the bridge.

Hamish couldn't read their signing, but he said, "You're the ones who said to trust the dogs. So the real question is, do yeh?"

The sled dogs could certainly see the bridge, and they weren't slowing down.

Smudge yapped to T'nuc for her opinion about the icy logs, and the twenty-meter fall into the churning river they could hear but not see, and she wasn't surprised by T'nuc's curt response.

The team had been pulling hard from the moment Spot told them someone was in trouble. It seemed Christa had been right about elkies never quitting, and it was clear the team shared the same single-minded mechanism as Sholto and the boerboels when it came to protecting humans.

Smudge turned back and saluted Hamish with a quick paw swipe down her snout, and then pointed for him to forge ahead.

"You lot sure?" Hamish asked. "We can unload and go over one at a time if we have to, but it'll take time."

As if she could understand him T'nuc barked and the team gave the gangline and extra tug to bump the sled forward.

"Aye lass, there's the spirit," Hamish said. "Hold onto yer biscuits. *Ga hike!*"

The team pulled hard through the corner, pivoted around the wheel dogs to straighten out, and T'nuc and K'cuf hopped onto the bridge together. The rest of the dogs leapt up in perfect pairs, and spread apart a little so they could run down the center of the outer logs. They'd pulled the sled over narrow beams in the obstacle course, but it hadn't been in a blizzard, with a horizontal crosswind, in the dark, twenty meters above a raging river.

"Go *lett* now boys and girls," Hamish cooed. "*Forsiktig...* careful..."

T'raf took one look over the side of the log and closed his eyes. He followed his sister's feet slaps in front of him to stay in line as the sled's runners hit the logs. It skidded a little but the team pulled it true as they shot across the bridge.

Smudge leaned over the side of the sled and looked down as they passed the center of the span. The snow disturbed by the quickly sliding runners floated down and was quickly blown into the darkness. She could make out the churning spray and jagged rocks far below them, and when she turned her excited face back to the sled she saw her brother and Ben both had their eyes slammed shut.

She snaked a paw between their tightly gripped hand and paw and signed, *You have got to see this.*

Spot replied with a quick head shake, and Ben whispered, "All set thanks."

The sled abruptly dropped a foot when it shot off the end of logs, and Ben clutched both pups as Spot let out a yelp.

The fog of Hamish's relieved exhale slipped away with the wind, and as he turned the pounding team south toward Willie's last beacon ping he said, "There's really nae' need for yer Mimi to hear about that one lad."

CHAPTER 61

Lucy could barely see the tire tracks his headlights were following through the blowing snow. He was driving down into the mine, and he knew the unmarked shoulders of the dark access road fell off into the deep bowls so he didn't want to veer off course.

"You go any slower and I'm getting out and walking," Jia grumbled from the back seat.

"Sounds good to me," Lucy whispered under his breath.

"What's that?" Jia asked.

"We're almost there," Lucy said without taking his eyes off the tire tracks.

The faint ruts finally curved around to the back of the maintenance garage, and the Suburban's headlight beams shrank to little circles as he pulled up to the big sliding door.

The asset got out and held the door for Jia, who flipped up the hood of her long coat and joined him in the blowing snow.

They scanned the dark lot for a moment, agreed with a nod, and she waved for Lucy to lower his window.

"Park it behind that," she said as she pointed to a small outbuilding at the back of the parking area. It was connected to the garage by an overhead catwalk with large pipes running through it.

Lucy nodded, and squinted into the side mirror as he put the van in reverse.

As he backed away the garage door slid open and Jero appeared with Rotty-wolf on a leash.

He wore his typical snug, pristine white thermal and camouflage pants that were rolled up above his white socks and boots. He was also wearing an ill-fitting snow jacket that looked more like a vest on his massive upper body.

He watched Lucy back into the dark and cut the lights, and then shook his head at the paranoid little Asian woman and her stiff British companion.

Rotty-wolf let a stream of loud woofing barks fly as Jia and the asset passed them, and Jero yanked hard on the leash and shouted, "Shut the fuck up!"

He kicked Rotty-wolf hard in the side, but the dog didn't notice and continued to bark at the swirling snow.

The wolves coldly watched Jero from their cages, and their heads swung in unison to follow Jia and the asset as they passed Vic's truck and walked up the office stairs.

As they climbed the steps they noticed ten big men were standing around a rolling metal work table in the center of the garage. They were laughing, drinking beer, and fawning over their shiny new assault rifles.

Jero dragged the barking Rotty-wolf back under the stairs and clipped his leash to the handrail. He raised his thick arm like he was going to backhand him, and hovered for a few seconds to let Rotty-wolf pound out a few more barks.

"You really are a useless piece of *mierda*, you know that?" Jero asked as he let his hand drop.

Rotty-wolf looked up at him with his simple wolfish face and raised brown eyebrows.

In the upstairs office Vic saluted with the bottle as he grumbled, "Bravo *mes amis*. Sounds like your *fou* plan actually worked."

"What have you heard?" Jia asked as she stepped out of her coat and thanked the asset with a nod.

"That little faggot and his prancing yuppies are in trouble in the woods," Ty said, "and they're not far from where we released the wolves."

"That is good news," Jia said, "but it's hardly conclusive."

"Coincidence enough for me," Vic grumbled as he filled his glass. "*C'est bon*, I can sell it. The rest we can take care of ourselves."

"Wanna belt?" he asked as he hovered the bottle over an empty glass.

Jia nodded, and as Vic poured she said, "Are you sure about your hillbilly militia down there? It looks like you just gave a brick of fire crackers and a lighter to a bunch of fourth graders."

"The boys will be fine," Vic grumbled. "They're smart enough to not ask any questions and dumb enough to follow orders. We doing this or what?"

Jia looked to the asset for his input.

"This weather is a good omen," he said as he looked out at the blowing snow. "Radio communication will be chancy, and we can take out the cell tower on the way in."

He stared into the dark night for a moment, and then gave her a nod.

"Okay, we go," Jia said.

She took a sip of the strong whisky, grimaced, and turned to Ty and said, "Do I need to remind you and the tractor-pull convention delegates down there that I require the old man and the kid alive and unmarked?"

Ty stared down at her, and Jia added, "And I don't want any bullshit exceptions. Your boys already have little miner and logger hard-ons over my guns, and I'm going to take it out on you if I hear one of those idiots say 'we had to shoot him full of holes 'cause he called us daft'."

She had done a pretty good rendition of Ty's deep voice and Canuk-French accent.

"We should be able to handle a cripple, a geriatric, and a fucking kid," Ty said flatly.

The asset turned away from office windows and silently crossed the room.

When he stopped in front of Ty his cool stare made the big miner take a half step back.

"Was that cock-up at the pub your version of 'handling it'?" the asset asked as his stare turned even colder.

When Ty didn't respond the asset said, "The only thing I expect out of you, Thibault, is for you to keep those dozy prats in line and do your bloody job without hesitation or deviation. And your job is whatever Jia or I say it is."

Ty glanced at Vic but his boss just looked down into his glass.

When Ty turned back to the asset he tried his tough-guy jaw clench. It didn't work, so he smiled a not-so-confident smile and mumbled, "I'm all fucking over it."

He tore himself away from the asset's stare, and almost tripped over a stool as he crossed the office.

He stepped out onto the landing and yelled down the stairs, "Jero, stop humping that dog. You fuck-sticks put the beer away and get the trucks."

CHAPTER 62

The snowfall turned from heavy to a blowing freight train as the clouds dropped into the treetops and visibility fell to a few meters.

Booming rumbles rolled down from high up in the mountains and shook the forest as they echoed down the valley in waves. Hamish told Ben it was thundersnow, and it meant the storm was just getting warmed up.

The clouds strobed above the trail, and lit up the stopped sled and the still, panting dogs.

Smudge held up the broken ends of S'ufud's harness as the winds whipped its frayed tendrils, and Ben moved the light in closer so Hamish could inspected the damage. The tough, custom-wrapped cord had snapped where it connected to the gangline.

Spot signed, and Ben translated, "I'm sorry, that connection shouldn't have failed like that."

"S'not yer fault pup," Hamish said as he gave Spot's head a scratch. "We've been pounding through some thick shite and the old rigging would have shredded hours ago. This wrapped Kevlar was pure genius wee boy."

He ran his hands over S'ufud's icy fur and said, "I saw the branch it snagged on, and we're lucky it only shredded the line."

As he stood and looked at the team he added, "Nae' worries lads and lasses, we'll have this swapped in a tick."

The only direct route to Willie was through the deep forest, where the paths they followed were barely game trails. If they'd taken the easier valley route they wouldn't reach the skiers' last known location until well past sun-up.

The trees were protecting them from the worst of the winds, but the patrol sent out from the station won't have the same cover as they trekked up to the north camp. They'll be on powerful snow machines, but it'll be dangerous driving even for experienced rangers. The routes on the peaks were steep and treacherous, and rangers could be as pigheaded as elkies when someone was in danger, often at their own peril.

A few hours ago they'd gotten in a short call with Christa before losing signal again. There was still no word from Willie, and the rangers had missed their last check in. By itself that wasn't too odd in these conditions, but the combination was troubling.

Glasgow's signal was all over the place. She was probably generally in the direction of Willie's beacon near the river, but the storm was bouncing her radio pings randomly throughout the valley.

Hamish wanted to get down to the basin as quickly as possible but the dogs were getting beat up in the thick woods. The deep snow hid snapped branches and jagged rocks, and they were thumped and jostled as they bounced over logs and pushed through narrow openings in the trees. Even so, he had to keep slowing them down, and they had collectively insisted on skipping the last break. They just stayed in position when the pups unclipped them, and turned their noses up at the snacks waved in front of them. He'd been contemplating forcing a breather on them when the harness broke.

Ben swapped out the cord, and Smudge replaced K'naks missing boot, and Spot followed Hamish through the deep snow to the front of the sled.

He knelt and grabbed T'nuc by her chest harness, and she met his stare with her intelligent, intense brown eyes.

"I appreciate what you're doing lass," he said over the howl of the wind, "but we canae' save anyone if a few of yeh have to ride home in the sled instead of pullin' it. I canae' see all the obstacles so donae' let the team's stubborn weegie pride overrule their canine common sense."

Spot could tell from T'nuc's insulted head tip she'd caught the gist of that. The elkies were used to a Hamish lecture, and although they didn't understand the words they grasped a surprising amount of the message.

The sled dog leader looked back at her team, and when E'sra let out a sharp yap the rest of the dogs wagged.

T'nuc turned forward again and huffed a hard snort in Hamish's face.

Spot yapped to Ben, and when he swung his flashlight to the front of the sled Spot signed the human equivalent of what the elkies had intoned.

Ben raised his voice over the wind to translate, "You taught us well, so let us do our job."

Hamish stood and stared down at his wagging, stubborn lead bitch.

He gave her ear a tug, and as he walked back past the team through the deep snow he muttered, "Oh wee Willie, when I find yeh stoned out of yer mind with yer hand in that lass's honey pot I'm gonna feed yer damn liver to these lads."

Ben shared a smirk with his wagging pups as they crawled back into the sled and wrapped themselves up in the fur blankets.

Hamish stepped on the foot boards, pulled up the brake, and yelled, "*Ga hike!* Hike like the bloody wind, yeh baw-heeded pillocks!"

CHAPTER 63

"It was sweet of you to come all the way out here," Christa said as she poured hot water into two coffee cups and dropped a tea bag in each. Before she could stop herself she checked her hair in the kitchen window, where the snow was coming sideways and swirling around the dark back deck.

"How do you fancy it?" she asked, and upon realizing how that sounded shook her head and exchanged smiles with Tavish.

"Just a wee spot of milk please dear," he said as he unzipped his jacket and sat down on the couch next to Sholto. "I was out and about anyway. With the pissin' storm I promised Sally I'd check in on her mum."

Sally owned the small combo grocery-hardware store across from The Grub, and Christa knew her mother lived alone and was pushing ninety. She also knew the ornery old bat certainly didn't need or want anyone checking in on her, and her cabin wasn't exactly just down the street.

"Where's Hamish and the lad?" Tavish asked as he scratched Sholto's ears.

Christa grabbed a carton of milk from the fridge as she said, "They're out with the elkhounds for a final—"

She paused to answer her ringing cellphone, and held up an apologetic finger to Tavish.

"Hello?" she asked, "Jean?…Yes, how are you love?…No, it's not you. I've been having trouble reaching them as well. One second hun."

She put her hand over the phone and said to Tavish, "Sorry. Hamish's sister-in-law from Mass."

Tavish started to get up and motioned that he was going to leave, but Christa shook her head and waved for him to sit as she said into the phone, "No, it's the storm. The satphone's just having trouble connecting...No, the radio's useless up there in this, but I'm sure they're fine. I talked to them a few hours ago...No...Yes...Yes Jean, I assure you, they're absolutely fine. What's that?...Yes, I'm listening."

She brought Tavish his tea, and gave him a little smile as she sat on the arm of the opposite couch next to Vuur.

Tavish settled back and put his feet up on the hearth, and pretended not to watch her. He was pretty sure she had been glad to see him when he'd showed up un-invited, but her smiling face slowly turned dark and she was staring into the fire as she listened to the phone. He couldn't hear what was being said but he picked up enough of the caller's tone to get the sense it wasn't good news.

Even Sholto had sat up and was watching her intently.

Tavish checked his own phone while he waited, and fired off a quick text.

A moment later Christa held the phone away from her cheek and checked the display before she said, "Jean?...Jean, you still there?"

She checked the display again, and said to Tavish, "No signal. You have anything?"

Tavish looked at his phone, and held it up as he said, "Nary a bar."

Christa went to the wall phone in the kitchen, and after picking it up she said, "Hard line's out too."

"Happens all the time at the pub when it blowin' pure Baltic," Tavish said.

Christa nodded as she looked out at the blowing snow.

"I'm not meanin' to pry," Tavish said as he noticed her bunched brow, "but you seemed in a bit of a state on your call. Is everything alright then?"

"Yeah, fine," Christa said as she noticed the boerboels had raised their block heads and were staring at her.

Sholto slid off the couch and followed Christa as she crossed the kitchen.

"Better get some candles ready," she said. "Pretty safe bet we'll lose power at some point tonight."

As she opened the door to the walk-in pantry Sholto let out a low growl.

"Don't step through that door please love," Tavish said as he took his bespoke Mammut alpine boots off the hearth.

Christa turned to see Sholto was staring hard at Tavish, who was pointing a silenced automatic pistol at her face.

"Give whatever commands are needed to keep me from shooting these impressive dogs," Tavish said.

Vuur and Rook were still sitting on the couch, but they were staring at him with their heads lowered and their legs drawn under them for a leap.

"Vuur, Rook, *als heir*," Christa said, and both mastiffs slipped off the couch and walked over to stand next to her.

Sholto looked up at her, and she gave her the sign to just stand ready.

"Smart dogs," Tavish said. "Let's hope the rest of the family is as obedient."

Christa noticed his accent had gone from urban Edinburgh to snobby Surrey.

"They have leashes?" Tavish asked.

"In the front hall," Christa said.

"Get them," Tavish said, "and have the dogs sit where they are."

Christa motioned for them to sit, and as Tavish followed her with the pistol he removed a small radio from his coat pocket.

He clicked the transmit button and said, "We're set."

CHAPTER 64

"Ben, hand me that," Hamish said just loud enough to be heard over the wind as he stepped off the back of the sled and pointed to the rifle.

He patted the heads of the elkies as he walked passed them, and noticed they were staring downslope at the same thing that had caused him to stop the sled. He didn't need Ben or the pups to tell him the sled dogs were as curious about what they were seeing as he was.

He stepped past T'nuc and walked onto the packed grid pattern left by a pair of snow machines. With the toe of his boot he gently swiped at the two inches of powdery snow that covered the tracks and softened their outlines.

"An hour," he mumbled to himself.

The tracks headed downslope toward the valley floor. They were basically following the river, but taking a straighter path on the high berm as the water snaked back and forth in wide switchbacks.

He lifted his goggles, raised the rifle to his shoulder, flipped up the scope covers, and followed the tracks down the ridge line. It was hard to see with the dark haze and the blowing snow, but he confirmed what he'd seen from the back of the sled.

The tracks ended at the silhouettes of two stopped snow machines.

"Bugger," he whispered when he didn't see the silhouettes of any rangers.

He turned back to Ben and asked, "How far to Willie's signal?"

Ben held up the GPS unit and said, "About a kilometer that way, I think." He pointed past the ranger's machines and added, "It's still having trouble getting sync."

Spot showed him Glasgow's tracker and he said, "We're still getting funky readings from this thing too, but she's close, probably."

Hamish nodded.

He didn't like the looks of what he saw, especially as both of the snow machines' headlamps were on. If the rangers had trekked into the woods they may have left one of the lights on to help find their way back in the dark, but they wouldn't leave both on in case they were gone a long time and one of the batteries died.

Hamish looked down when he felt a tug on his snow pants.

"Aye," he said to Spot's concerned face. "We're going down there, but I canae' say I'm lookin' forward to it."

Spot motioned for Ben to translate, and then quickly signed his plan.

Ben did, and Hamish stared down at the pup for a moment before he said, "That's nae' half-bad."

Spot gave him a wag and a nod.

"That still leaves the other half lad," Hamish said as he grabbed Spot's snout and gave it a shake.

A few minutes later Ben was mushing the team in silent mode from behind the handlebars of the sled. He brought them down the ridge and halted them behind the ranger's snow machines by giving T'nuc the hand sign for, *Stoppe.*

Hamish was kneeling in the sled with the rifle socked to his shoulder, and he was sweeping it back-and-forth as he scanned the woods on both sides of the trail.

"It's clear," he said quietly as he stepped out of the sled and continued sweeping the rifle. "But yeh be ready to hike lad."

As he walked toward the snow machines with the rifle held at his hip Ben raised his gloved hand and flashed a quick sign.

Spot and T'nuc trotted out of the dark woods on the river side of the trail, and a few seconds later Smudge and E'sra appeared on the up-slope berm.

The pups had their winter camo vests on, and had changed their coats to husky-white. It was good camouflage, and Hamish saw his gray and brown elkies a few full seconds before he saw the outline of the pups.

Smudge and E'sra bounded down the rise to rejoin the team, and Smudge hooked him back up to the gangline before she hopped into the sled.

She signed, and Ben translated for Hamish, "It's quiet in the woods, and there's no sign of the rangers."

Hamish gave them a nod as he felt the snow machines' exhausts and confirmed they'd been there about an hour. There were some tracks in the snow around them, but as they were out of the trees they'd quickly faded to dimples in the stiff wind. Both machines had plenty of gas and there was more in their spare cans. One of them had a tow-behind sled with a large medical case, avalanche kit, and two stretchers stacked neatly on top of each other, but none of the equipment had been touched and both of their rifles were still strapped to the handlebars.

Hamish assumed their emergency backpacks, radios, and side arms would be with them, wherever that was.

He turned off one of the machine's headlights, and as he walked back to the sled he noticed T'nuc hadn't been clipped back into her place next to K'cuf.

She and Spot were still standing together in the deep snow near the river.

Spot had his nose buried in the lead sled dog's ear, and they were standing perfectly still. T'nuc's head was slightly tipped up and away like she was stargazing, but there was only hazy black and sideways-blowing snow above them.

Ben signed to Smudge, and Smudge nodded.

"Well?" Hamish asked as he climbed back into the sled.

"Spot's teaching her to focus," Ben said. "Elkies have almost twice the scent detection capabilities as the pups, so he's coaching her to remove nonessential smells and environmental distractions so she can zero in on the rangers."

"Twice?" Hamish asked with a skeptical brow raise. "Are yeh sure about that lad?"

Ben didn't answer, and Smudge looked up at Hamish like he was an idiot.

T'nuc left Spot's side and walked down the slope to pace back and forth at the river's edge. She walked carefully out onto the icy rocks, and then back to the snowy bank where she rooted around with her head buried below the powder.

After several long minutes Hamish was almost about to call her back to the sled when she stopped dead, and all but disappeared into the deep snow. Only her curved tail showed, and that had stopped dead too.

When her head popped back up she had something in her mouth. She trotted over to give it to Spot, and they had a quick vocal and physical conversation before she followed him up to the front of the team.

Spot hooked her back into position, and as she shook off a cloud of snow he trotted back to the sled and hopped up next to Hamish and Smudge.

Hamish clicked on a penlight, and Spot reached into the chest plate of his vest to remove what T'nuc had given him.

As Hamish examined the snow-clogged pistol Spot signed, and Ben translated, "T'nuc picked up the scents of two rangers. They were here about an hour ago, and they both fired their weapons at three adult wolves. Two males and a female. There is some wolf blood, but there's a lot more human blood."

Hamish nodded as he noticed the red smears on the gun's handgrip.

"There aren't any bodies," Ben said as Spot continued, "and the odd thing is there aren't any signs that the rangers left the area."

Spot looked down the slope to the churning black water, and when he signed Ben said, "T'nuc thinks they walked into the river."

Hamish watched the swift current roll around the wide bend and splash over the ice-covered boulders along the bank. Having recently been plunged into those frigid swells himself he knew if the rangers didn't get out and get warmed up quick they'd end up a frozen dinner for something. An hour was a very long time to be out in this cold, and he didn't see any fires downstream. He also knew no one would walk into that water willingly unless whatever was on the bank was somehow more dangerous. He sure hoped his lead sled dog was wrong, but he was quickly beginning to understand the elkies were far sharper than he ever imagined.

Maybe Ben had been right about their names.

Hamish watched Spot's paw twist and rotate as Ben said, "The rangers are male and female. The man sunk as far into the snow as you do, and the woman was—"

Ben asked Spot to repeat what he'd just signed a little slower, and when the pup did Ben nodded and said, "She was coming out of menstruation."

Hamish looked to the front of the sled and saw T'nuc was staring back at him.

"Did you know them?" Ben asked. "I mean, do you know them?"

"Aye, probably," Hamish said as he scratched his frosty beard. "There are two dozen rangers that rotate between here and Taillon and Valin, and I know most of them. And the lasses almost outnumber the blokes now."

"I'm sorry Unc," Ben said. "I hope they're alright."

"Aye lad," Hamish said.

He added a little forced chuckle as he said, "She might be happy she's nae' pregnant."

"T'nuc doesn't think the wolves are here anymore," Ben said. "At least they're not upwind."

"That's good news I suppose," Hamish said as he ejected the pistol's magazine and checked the chamber. It was a nine millimeter service Glock, and it had one bullet left in the magazine and one stuck in the slider. The gun must have jammed, and Hamish knew the only way to jam a well-maintained Glock was to bang it hard when it was firing.

"Let's get down to Willie's coordinates," he said as he cleared the jam and used a little snow to wipe off the blood.

"Unc, there's something else you need to know," Ben said as he watched the snow turn red. "T'nuc said the two male wolves smelled very wrong."

"Aye lad?" Hamish asked as he put the pistol in his pocket.

"Yes," Ben said, "and the pups are pretty sure they know why that is."

CHAPTER 65

"Naughty girl," Tavish said as he stepped into the neatly organized walk-in pantry. "I'm sure you have an automatic generator, and I don't see any candles in this closet. So let's see, what could it be that you wanted?"

He stepped backward out of the pantry holding a small metal box with a combination lock built into its top.

"Bitch was fucking strapped *hommes*," Jero said as he flicked his hands like they were wet. "That's some fucked-up shit right there."

Ty laughed, and said, "Yeah, looks to me like Peggy here had the drop on your fake ass from the jump, Guv'ner."

As Tavish walked past the kitchen island Sholto tipped her head at Christa, but she signaled for her dog to stay put.

Vuur, Rook, and Sholto were clipped to their thick leashes, and the leashes were tied to the island's heavy arched corbels.

Christa was seated in front of the fireplace in a large leather chair. She was taped to the armrests at the wrists and elbows, and her metal legs were taped together at the ankles. Tavish had taken care to roll her sleeves down so the tape wasn't stuck to her skin. She was securely restrained, but not painfully so.

"Now Christa," he said as he sat on the edge of the couch opposite her chair and picked up his cup of tea, "I have no interest in hurting you, or Hamish, or Ben. My employer simply wants to have a chat with the boy. We would have just asked nicely but it's a sensitive matter of some urgency and we need complete answers as quickly as possible. If everyone does what's asked of them we all go home happy. Do you understand?"

"Yes," Christa said.

Jero laughed and Tavish shot him a look that chilled the tough miner into silence.

When Tavish sent Ty a hard nod he pulled Jero down the hall to the ranch's front entrance, where there were more thugs talking and laughing with automatic rifles slung over their shoulders.

"So tell me love, where is Hamish, exactly?" Tavish asked.

"I don't know, exactly," Christa said. "Truthfully. He and Ben went to the east part of the park and I expect they'll be gone for at least a week. As you heard, I've been having trouble keeping in touch with them, but that's not rare in this weather."

"I see," Tavish said as he took sip of tea and leaned forward. "Perhaps I got a little ahead of myself. Just so we're clear here, if you omit a pertinent detail or tell me an untruth at any time I will inflict pain upon you. If you are still feeling uncooperative I will let Ty and Jero do whatever they want to you for a while. From there, it gets more creative and it doesn't look like you can afford to lose too many more pieces. Please don't put me in that position. I like you, and I don't want to see any harm come to you. Are we in agreement?"

"We are," Christa said.

"Brilliant," Tavish said, "and just in case you aren't understanding the gravity of this situation—"

He turned with lightning speed and shot Vuur without spilling a drop from his cup.

CHAPTER 66

Ben told Hamish what the pups had seen at the mine, and what they suspected about the male rogue wolves, and how that smell was connected to their struggles in Pembury.

He explained what had happened to Doug Dorschstein, and to Liko, and he described the white barrels, and the horror that was Jerry Dorschstein, and the effects that compound had on her and the dogs in her kennel.

If the wolves had survived being intentionally infected, Ben explained, it could result in hyper-aggression, significant muscle growth, and massive distortions to their bodies.

He also shared Spot's guess as to why the vile stuff had shown up in a small mining town in the middle of Quebec.

They sat together on the sled in the blowing snow, and Hamish watched Ben closely as he rocked slightly and told his story with his fogging breath quickly being whisked away. The lad had shiny smears of Christa's foot wax on his nose and cheeks to fight off windburn, and he looked just like his handsome dad, and his pretty mom and sister, all of whom had worn the same protective smears when they were out on the sled.

Hamish also thought he could have been looking as his brother Duncan from fifty years ago.

The brother he'd just learned had been murdered by that arse-hat Doug Dorschstein.

As much as Ben looked like his Papa, Hamish had come to understand the lad was an altogether different kind of kid.

Since they got the call about Willie's beacon Hamish had been watching for any signs that Ben was getting too rattled, but his grandnephew had kept his composure in a way that was both odd and fascinating. He worked the radio tracker and the GPS, and checked the satphone, and closely watched the sled dogs with the same frequency and attention to detail as he'd done the entire trip, but he was also intently scanning the woods and conversing with his pups in silent, urgent bursts of signing for hours on end. If Hamish didn't know better he would have thought Ben had been on patrol in a war zone before.

The factual way Ben relayed his horrific story had Hamish wondering if he was slipping into some state of desensitized shock, but then he noticed Ben was holding Smudge's paw as he spoke, and Spot was gently rubbing his knee. Hamish realized the kid was indeed scared shitless, but he was also fully processing everything around him, and he clearly drew a lot of strength and comfort from his unique dogs.

Hamish realized spending twenty four hours a day with his pair of smart curs might have altered the lad's perceptions a bit. He even wondered if the pups had taught Ben to control his fear, as dogs are known to do.

He handed Ben the rifle, gave his shoulder a gentle squeeze, and gave the pups a tender pat before he went to the back of the sled.

With a quick hand sign to T'nuc he mushed the team around the snow machines and down the trail into the dark gray haze.

As the lone headlight faded behind them and the woods closed in to form a tunnel another clap of thundersnow boomed and flashed dimly from high above the trees.

The sled slid quietly down the trail, and Hamish worked the rangers' wolf encounter and Ben's revelations over and over in his head. He tried to look at the situation forward and backward as he typically did when he faced a puzzle he couldn't solve, but answers were as hard to see as the haze ahead of them. He'd been in more than his share of scraps, and had gotten into and out of plenty of tight spots, but his adversaries had always been known. The dark strangeness Ben was talking about was hard for Hamish to buy into, but two days ago he would have bet big money he wouldn't be having a conversation with a dog.

He worried about his dear sister-in-law, and what she and the family had gone through this past year down in Pembury. He wasn't surprised Jean didn't say anything, and he didn't blame her for holding back about Duncan. She knew he would have been down there with a flame thrower and a rusty pair of pliers for those bastards. He also knew she was very capable of taking care of herself, and apparently Ben's pups were equally capable when it came to dealing with murdering Skippy McArsemunchers.

But clearly there were still a few more arsemunchers loose in the glen. Someone out there hadn't been dealt with, and there were too many pieces of that puzzle missing to solve.

He feared for Willie and the rangers, he wanted to touch base with Christa and Blu, and he didn't want to consider which female wolf was running with those rogue males. His racing brain tried to resolve all of these issues into a solution, but what weighed most heavily on him was making sure Ben got home safely.

The perfect rhythm and gentle bobbing of the team seduced his tired mind. He drifted, and started to see leaping wolves in the moving shadows of the trees and tortured skiers and drowning rangers twisting toward him in the snow blowing down from the overhead boughs.

And then he heard Duncan's warm, firm, cheery voice, *What's for you won't go by you, so keep your pecker up and get at it lad!*

Hamish called to his amazing elkies, "*Hike!* Pull strong, pull fast!"

Eventually the woods opened up at the bottom of the valley where the river widened. When the sled moved out of the trees the dogs could see they were facing a large, steep, treeless bowl. Hamish knew the spot well as he'd used its long sweeping incline as a grade test for his sled teams.

Ben lowered the rifle, checked their location, and turned to whisper, "We're passing Willie's coordinates."

It had barely left his lips when all of the elkies started to act up. They fell out of sync and were looking nervously from T'nuc, to E'sra, to Hamish.

Spot spun around and barked a quick warning yap at Hamish, who immediately stopped the team and swung the pistol around in a slow arc over Ben's head.

Smudge started to sign rapidly and Ben pulled her to him and said softly, "Okay, okay, calm down. I got it."

He turned to Hamish and said, "Lots of human bodies Unc."

As Spot pointed at piles of drifted snow Ben said, "There, there, and over there."

They had stopped near the convergence of two large stands of trees with the wide river at their backs, and Hamish's radar whispered to him that it was a great place for an ambush. He moved the team forward a dozen meters until they were away from the trees at the bottom of the slope.

The deeper snow in the glade had drifted into undulating peaks, and it suddenly felt like all of them were hiding bodies.

Hamish told Ben and Spot to stay in the sled as he kept the pistol sweeping along the tree line. He sent Smudge up to unclip T'nuc, and had her reattach the hanging harness to the gangline so they could move out quickly. If that happened T'nuc would still lead, she'd just run in front of the team.

T'nuc and Smudge waded through the deep snow to an oddly shaped drift, and when they both tucked in their chins and shook their heads Hamish could tell something was very wrong.

T'nuc hopped back a few steps, and nervously looked from Smudge to her team to Hamish and back to Smudge again.

With a huff Smudge told T'nuc to stay put, and then she stepped up to a small drift and carefully moved snow out of the way with her paws. She leaned in to sample the air again, and quickly pulled back like something had snapped at her.

She signed back to the sled and Ben translated, "Two human females, one younger, one older, wearing ski suits. It's the mother and daughter we met at The Grub. One of them is—"

He paused to check with Spot before he nodded and said, "One of them is disemboweled."

Smudge slowly dipped back down into the snow, and when she backed away again she paused for a moment before she signed.

"Oh no," Ben said.

"What is it lad?" Hamish asked as he continued to scan the trees with the pistol.

"Unc, the daughter's shot through the head," Ben said.

Through the blowing snow Smudge saw Ben's slack face, and was glad he couldn't smell what she and the rest of the dogs were being assaulted with. The stench of blood and corpses pervaded the air around them. Even with the crisp wind carrying much of it away she still felt like she was swimming in death.

She wouldn't have any trouble locating the bodies in the immediate area so she sent T'nuc to search the perimeter for more.

As the lead dog trotted away in the deep snow Smudge checked in with E'sra with a quick snort, and wasn't surprised to find he was way ahead of her. He and R'ekcuf had been keeping an eye on the tree lines that flanked the bowl since their first whiff of the place.

Smudge moved from body to body, and signed back to the sled the conditions of the corpses and their identities. The descriptions were horrific and Hamish hated that Ben had to translate, but he needed to know.

Further up the slope T'nuc found two bodies, and based on her descriptions Smudge figured out they were Valerie and the woman who'd tried hard not to laugh at Hamish's crude humor but couldn't help herself.

T'nuc circled to the river's edge and found another body that was only partially covered by snow. It was a woman, and her head had been removed.

With a quick yap T'nuc beckoned to Smudge, and when she joined the elkie she was staring down at a footprint frozen in the bank's mud.

It was a canine print, and it was huge.

Smudge's entire foot fit inside it with plenty of room to spare. She split open her paw and the two fingers didn't touch the print's widest pad marks. The marks also looked strange. They were bumpy and not symmetrical like a normal dog's.

Not far from the headless body Smudge found a camera. It appeared to have been set down deliberately on a taller rock.

She brought it back to the sled and Hamish wiped some of the blood from the display as Ben found the camera's power button.

The screen lit up and showed a picture of a cute teenage girl with braces. She was wearing a formal dress and standing next to a tall boy who was clearly her prom date. In the next shot she was standing between her mom and dad, and they recognized the woman and her heavy-set husband from The Grub.

Ben flipped through the pictures, and there were dozens of almost identical shots; the girl next to the boy, the girl in front of the boy, the boy pinning on the corsage, the girl wincing playfully, and a comically staged shot of the Dad glaring at the boy with a pointing finger. By the fiftieth shot her date had gone from looking bored to downright surly.

The pictures eventually showed a snowy highway, and then white landscapes that included mountains. There were a series of photos with Willie and the rest of the group, including several at The Grub that included Ben and Hamish and Sholto and Tavish and the pups. There were shots from inside a log cabin with the group drinking, and one of Willie sitting on Valerie's lap. There was a sunrise shot, and a few panoramic vista pics, and a swooping eagle, and two dozen other birds and animals.

And then there were three dozen shots of Glasgow. The majestic gray wolf was standing at the top of the same ridge they were facing now, but she was lit up by a shaft of sunlight.

The last picture was just a black box with an arrow in the middle of the screen.

Ben found the play button, and although the video was blank they heard the woman's last heart-wrenching message to her daughter coming from the camera's built-in speaker.

Spot had Ben play it again, and the pups and T'nuc tipped their heads and closed their eyes to concentrate. As the mother told her daughter she would always love her, Smudge raised a paw and signed.

Ben said, "They hear growling in the background."

Hamish saw the concern on Ben's face in the glow from the camera's display, and he saw Smudge's brow was similarly bunched. He searched for any words that would help them but none came. He just put a big hand on Ben's small shoulder and rubbed Smudge's white snout.

Ben nodded up at him, and then turned away to pack the camera into the sled as Smudge headed back out into the snow.

She and T'nuc found a total of eight bodies, and Smudge was able to identify all of them. It was certainly all of Willie's party, minus one.

Willie.

Smudge and T'nuc concurred about his scent. It ended at the river, just like the rangers.

Hamish didn't know what to make of it. The pattern of the bodies and their conditions just didn't make sense. Ben's theory about the poison formula sounded insane but Hamish struggled to come up with anything else that would do that kind of deliberate damage to people. He also wasn't ready to accept Glasgow or her pack had been involved with these new wolves, even though the evidence certainly pointed in that direction. The carnage would have taken some time given the destruction and distance between the bodies. Why wouldn't Willie have just shot the wolves? And why was one of the victims shot through the head? Willie should have been the only one with a gun, and the rangers never made it here.

As Hamish worked the problem he watched Smudge and T'nuc padding together through the deep snow as they inspected a wider circle around the sled. He didn't need Ben or the pups to tell him T'nuc was affected by the killings. He knew domesticated dogs don't like to be around human death. Cadaver dogs usually had the shortest working careers of any service dogs. Often they had to retire after one large incident like a plane crash or building collapse, and suffered from many of the same symptoms their human counterparts did afterward. They just don't handle the stress well, and they certainly couldn't be blamed for it. Their keen senses had to be a curse when immersed in a tragedy, and Hamish knew dogs could remember a hint of a single smell for their entire lives.

As he watched his team leader successfully ignore her instincts and stay on task he realized T'nuc was one of the finest dogs he had ever worked with, and she wasn't trained to deal with cadavers. She was a sensitive, smart animal and this was taking a toll on her. Running almost constantly for close to twenty hours probably wasn't helping either.

It was looking more and more like Hamish owed her and all of these elkies an apology. They were a solid team of dogs, and he had been wrong about them.

He also noticed Smudge was very tuned into the dogs' feelings. Spot may be smarter but Smudge was more intuitive when it came to reading them. She kept huffing to T'nuc, and nudging and caressing her, and he realized she'd been doing the same thing with Sholto. Ben's tough little dog was a perceptive wee thing, and she was clearly struggling with being around so much senseless death as well. He realized he was seeing it on her face as much as in her posture and actions, and wondered how much his awareness of the pups' emotions had increased. Their feelings just seemed to jump off their expressive little faces.

She was also checking in with each of the elkies with huffs and snorts, especially E'sra. The dogs had to be wondering what kind of monsters could do this, and if they could still be close by.

Hamish was wondering the same thing.

T'nuc and Smudge made one last quick sweep of the water's edge, and then Smudge signed to Ben, who said quietly, "I guess it goes without saying, but wolf smells are all around here too, and there's even some of their blood. The foul males were certainly here, and one normal-smelling female, but no others."

"Sorry Unc," Ben said as he read Hamish's dire face.

Spot showed Glasgow's tracker to Ben and he said, "She's around here somewhere, but we're still getting echoes off the storm."

They were able to get a few seconds of satphone signal but Christa didn't answer her cell and the ranch phone rang busy. They tried Blu but couldn't get the connection to stick before losing the signal again.

The clouds strobed and the valley shook with another rolling, grumbling round of thundersnow.

Hamish motioned for Smudge to come back to the sled. As she was hooking T'nuc up to the gangline he said quietly, "I say we get the fuck out of here."

Ben and the pups nodded, and T'nuc agreed with a snort.

As Hamish waved for the team to pulled the sled away in silent mode he thought, *I'm sorry, poor wee Willie, and sorry to yeh rangers. I'll be back soon with help.*

CHAPTER 67

From the dark of the trees at the side of the bowl Glasgow watched the sled pull away from the bodies.

No, turn around, she thought as she watched the running dogs charge up the slope. *Don't come this way.*

She recognized the strong little dogs, and the big male human. He was the one who watches, and she assumed the young human male in the sled was the one her mate had seen.

There were two other captive dogs in the sled with him that she didn't recognize, and she'd been watching them carefully from the shadows downwind. They wore human coverings, and they communicated with the humans and sled dogs in an odd way. She couldn't decipher the hierarchy of this odd human and dog mixed pack, or even which one was the alpha.

The rogues were confused by them as well, and they'd been watching since the odd group stopped at the other human killing site further up the river. The normally raging rogues had actually paused long enough to pay close attention when the dogs converged on the noisy sleds from three sides.

It had been a very smart way to approach the killing spot. This dog-human team weren't the same kind of stupid humans who slid down the slope on sticks. They were a well-disciplined pack, and they had weapons.

The rogues' behavior was becoming more crazed and aggressive with each passing hour, but they were being cautious with this group. They were licking wounds from the last two human attacks, and they were definitely learning from each encounter. Still, the senseless violence had also increased with each attack. It was sickening to watch them taunting their prey, and when these twisted animals finally did strike they tore madly at their victims long after they were dead.

At least she had eaten well and gained her strength back. Earlier in the day the rogues had taken down a family of white tail deer and Glasgow had an entire juvenile to feed on all by herself. She had never eaten alone before. She gorged, and the energy from the hot fresh meat and innards were now coursing through her body. It pushed out the cold and refueled her aching muscles.

Glasgow's body was repaired but she still felt sick.

She had taken a risk, and the two strong humans on the noisy sleds had paid a tragic price for her stupidity.

Those humans had come down from the north, riding down the ridge trail on their noisy sleds. Even with the darkness and the heavy snow she could see the color of their coverings and knew what they were. She'd seen several pairs of humans who wore those same colors and they'd never been a threat, but these two carried themselves like hunters and she could see their weapons. The male was as big as the one who watches and the female was sturdy, and they both conveyed a confidence she could see from across the ridge.

So Glasgow had taken a chance.

She'd goaded the rogues into attacking them.

When the confused rogues hesitated she whipped them into a frothing frenzy with taunts, and when they blasted away from the trees Glasgow had sped off with them. She could tell their plan had been to ambush the two humans when the woods constricted at the bottom of the draw, like they had done with the stupid humans. But Glasgow had intentionally sprung their trap early where the trees were loosely placed and the noisy sled humans had the high ground.

The rogues pounded through the snow ahead of her encouraging barks, and raced right into the oncoming lights of the noisy sleds.

She had successfully given the humans enough time to stop and grab their small weapons.

The rogues kicked into high gear, and Glasgow couldn't believe the speeds they attained going uphill through deep snow.

The humans fired, and when one of their shots flicked her ear she jogged away and slipped into the woods. She raced up the berm to get around and above the fight, and through the trees she could see the flashes and hear the reports from the weapons as the rogues attacked.

The pops slowed, and then stopped.

She had come out of the trees higher on the trail behind the noisy sleds, and watched in horror as the female human had one arm around the male and was dragging him slowly backward toward the river.

Their confidence had disappeared.

Glasgow could tell from the disturbed snow that one of them had been knocked off their sled and fled down the slope to the water's edge. The other had run through the deep snow after the fallen one, with the rogues darting all around them.

The large human was clutching his shoulder and Glasgow could see the blood. The rogues were still dodging back and forth and yapping and growling. They ran up and down the slope and around the sleds, leaping high and diving low in the deep snow. They were in constant motion and seemed to be successfully avoiding being hit.

The female hunter swung her hand-held weapon slowly, trying to zero in on one wolf at a time. Another shot flashed but in the dark it was impossible to tell if she had hit anything. The wolves didn't seem to react. As soon as she fired a rogue shot down the slope straight at her, faked a leap, and then darted away in the opposite direction at the last instant. The female fell on the rocks as she fired again. Glasgow assumed she missed as the wolf just continued to circle and jump in crazy zig-zags.

The female looked at her weapon and then dropped it as the male pulled out a small blade. They backed up into the water as the rogues closed in, and growled and snapped and drooled their black vileness.

Glasgow tried to shake away those terrible images as she watched the dog sled and the one who watches continue to fly up the hill in front of her.

The rogues had dashed off to set their ambush at the head of the glade, where the grade was steep and the sled would slow before it crested the lip.

Glasgow turned away and stared down at the river.

She felt helpless and so very alone, and she heard the screaming humans in the howling wind and her slaughtered pack calling to her from the churning black water.

CHAPTER 68

E'sra saw the wolf first and broke the team's silent mode with a quick warning yap.

The rest of the dogs and the pups saw the approaching wolf an instant later, and when Hamish followed their stares he had to shake his head to make sure his tired peepers weren't playing tricks on him.

Glasgow was racing through the deep snow, and she was cutting straight across the bowl right at them.

Ben saw the wolf a second later, and his shocked, confused head tip mirrored that of his pups.

The dogsled team hadn't received orders to change direction or speed so they continued to pound together up the steep hill as they watched the oncoming wolf. T'nuc looked back every few strides to check for signs from Hamish. None came, but she could tell by the bunch of his brow that he was working on a plan.

Hamish knew they couldn't outrun Glasgow, and he had to assume the rest of the pack's hunters were nearby and waiting to pounce. Stopping the sled while the team was facing upslope would make it hard for them to start up again, but at least the open glade gave them some maneuvering room.

Glasgow didn't appear to have any of the symptoms Ben had described, but she was plenty agitated. He'd never seen a single wolf approach a running sled team before, and it seemed to be a really dumb way to spring a trap. Hamish had observed Glasgow for days on end, and he'd seen her hunt, and he'd seen her with her pack. The mother wolf wasn't stupid.

All of this odd animal behavior irritated Hamish.

Unpredictable animals were dangerous animals, and he hoped only the two rogues were crazed human killers. But then why in the bloody hell was this normal wolf running toward them?

Spot had been watching Glasgow carefully, and he was convinced she was looking directly at him as she raced toward them.

He sat up in the sled and raised his head high, and the big wolf came to an abrupt stop in the deep snow.

She turned away and pointed her whole body uphill.

Spot followed her stare up the slope but didn't see anything other than blowing snow and the dark silhouettes of trees against the black of the night.

He turned back to Glasgow, who was looking at him again.

The big wolf pawed the snow, and turned again to look at the top of the ridge.

Spot quickly signed to Ben, who spun around and shouted, "It's a trap Unc! The killer males are at the top of the hill waiting for us!"

The utter confidence on the boy's face removed any question Hamish had about how Ben could possibly know that.

Hamish leaned hard on the handlebar and flashed the turn-and-run sign to T'nuc.

Spot and Smudge kept Ben from falling out of the sled as the elkies dug in hard and pulled the sled in a tight arc on the steep slope. The sled tipped up on one runner before the acceleration of the team yanked it flat again.

As they finished the turn Spot climbed over Ben and moved to the opposite side of the sled.

Glasgow gave him a wag from across the bowl, and then looked up the hill again.

When she stomped both front feet into the deep snow Spot climbed over Ben again and pulled himself up on the handlebar.

He leaned far out of the sled to look around Hamish's bulk, and his eyes went wide when he saw two massive dark wolves charging over the lip of the steep bowl.

Spot grabbed Hamish's snowsuit and tugged hard, and Hamish broke his stare away from Glasgow to look down at him.

Spot pointed behind them, Hamish looked back, saw the wolves, turned back to Spot, and turned to look at the wolves again.

When he turned back to Spot his eyes were as big as saucers.

"*Hike nesten!*" Hamish shouted as he shoved Spot back into the sled, and T'nuc pounded out a sharp bark at the team.

Ben and the pups fell into a pile as the elkies leapt against their harnesses in unison. E'sra barked the team into a pounding frenzy, and their reaching paws came fully out of the snow before coiling again and digging deep into the powder to launch the sled forward.

Hamish's head swiveled constantly as he kept an eye on Glasgow and the charging wolves, and searched their flanks for the rest of the pack. He thought the two who were blasting down the slope were darker than any of the wolves in her pack, but the flying snow obscured them and everything was moving too fast for him to be sure. They could just be the prey drivers pushing the sled to the waiting ambushers below, but typically the alpha would be leading the drive.

And if it was an ambush why was Glasgow just standing there in the deep snow staring at them?

He wanted to be on flatter ground when they stopped to make their stand, but he didn't want to be near the woods. Willie's slain skiers had grouped near the trees at the river bank, and Hamish's radar had been right about it being a perfect ambush spot.

He'd been chased by animals before, and had always found some way to get the upper hand. He'd been confident he could anticipate the way they'd attack, and even in the darkest situations he was sure he'd prevail. But never before had he felt this terror, or the helplessness that was creeping up his spine. He cursed himself for allowing it, but still the thought came, *This must be what prey feels like.*

As he bit the fingers of his right glove and yanked it off another thought pushed its way in, *Healthy wolves don't hunt humans,* and as he reached into his pocket for the pistol another thought came, *I've had a long happy life and have done and seen wondrous things.*

He told himself to piss off, and then his brother chimed in with, *You're not deed yet, you daft arse!*

Spot clung to the side rail of the sled and watched as Glasgow shifted in the snow and looked back and forth between him and the wolf pursuers.

Smudge was watching the same thing, but she saw something in the set of the big she-wolf's peaked brow and the quivering of her muzzle.

Smudge sucked in a big breath and pounded out a hug bark at the wolf, *HELP!*

Glasgow leapt straight into the air, and when she landed she sprinted toward the sled.

In an instant she was flying, and Spot couldn't believe her speed and the distance she achieved with each stride. He saw her toes had spread out wide to keep her long legs from sinking into the snow. In rear flight, when she pushed off with her hind feet, he calculated she covered more than three meters with each leap in the deep snow.

Spot looked over Hamish's shoulder, and as fast as Glasgow was he could see the rogues were faster. They were like a pair of zippers being pulled down the slope at incredible speed as they left a wake of split snow behind them.

As the grade eased and they approached the river Hamish did the math on the quickly closing triangle of the sled, Glasgow, and the charging rogues.

"Ben!" he shouted over E'sra's barks, "When we stop I want yeh to take the wolf on Glasgow's side. Nothing fancy lad, just get out of the sled, take a knee, aim, breath, and shoot it center mass. And donae' forget about that cold bitch after yer first shoot. Aye?!"

"Got it Unc!" Ben shouted as he readied the rifle.

"Steady now!" Hamish shouted. "In three, two...*Stoppe!*"

He stomped down on the foot brake, flipped around on the sled's footboards, and raised the pistol as the sled came to a quick stop.

In the instant before he fired he could immediately see there was something terribly wrong with the two wolves. They were huge, and lumpy, and bloody, and had thick streaks of black and red saliva streaming from the corners of their mouths. As they lunged through the snow on clubbed black paws he saw the look in their eyes was bloody demented.

Ben leapt out of the sled as it stopped and spun to a kneeling shooting stance with the rifle socked into his shoulder. He didn't bother with the scope covers, and he didn't even use the sights. He just aimed the barrel as Harry had showed him with the assault rifles so it was a little bit in front of the wolf. He didn't have time to recite his shooting mantra either, he just exhaled and pulled the trigger.

Spot leapt over the front brush bar and hopped from one set of elkies to the next releasing their harness carabiners as fast as he could, and the dogs pivoted and blasted back toward the sled as soon as they were free. T'nuc and K'cuf stomped the ground impatiently as Spot moved up the line toward them.

Glasgow was still several bounds away and coming fast. She was approaching broadside to the sled and heading right for Ben.

Smudge used the handlebar to launch herself over Hamish.

She shook her snout as she gained height, and her chest and shoulders swelled as she went full-blown Cu Sith.

CHAPTER 69

A cellphone rang, lit up, and vibrated on a dark nightstand.

The ringtone was Toronto Maple Leaf's announcer Andy Frost screaming about Mats Sundlin's five hundredth career goal.

Blu rolled over and hunted for the phone. Her roaming hand flicked it off the nightstand, and it took a bad bounce and ended up under the bed.

"Shit," she groaned as she rolled off the mattress and thumped down hard on her knees.

Her obese cat, The Beave, got annoyed and jumped off the bed, using Blu's back as a step stool. She waddled off to find a more hospitable place to nap.

"Pinard here, what's happened?" Blu grumbled after finally snagging the phone from under the bed and putting her hand down on an old but not completely dry hairball.

She listened, and made a face as she pulled a tissue from the box on the nightstand to wipe off her fingers.

"Okay, yes," she said, "put him through."

She got up and sat on the edge of the bed, and could hear the wind whipping through the eaves and the driving snow tapping on her dark bedroom window. The storm must have really picked up since she'd gone to bed.

"This is Captain Pinard," Blu said as she put on her reading glasses and looked at the clock on her nightstand, "I'm sorry, what was your name again?"

"I see," she said, "and what can we do for you Director Barton?"

CHAPTER 70

Ben knew he hit the wolf, but he hadn't led it enough to hit it center mass. He'd misjudged its speed, and although he didn't see the strike he guessed his bullet hit high on wolf's hunched back.

He cursed himself, and when he threw the bolt back to chamber another round and it chattered sloppily he heard Lissa's disappointed voice whisper in his ear, *Focus separates the real shootists from the panty crappers when the shit's flying around you.*

The rogue wolf barely flinched, but it veered away and dodge behind its killing partner in a crazed, bouncing run like a bucking bull coming out of a chute. Ben hadn't put it down, but he had hurt it.

Hamish fired the two remaining bullets in the ranger's Glock in rapid succession, and both hit his wolf in the chest as it leapt at him.

The monster's momentum would have carried its fangs into his neck if Smudge hadn't landed on its head. The huge wolf and the muscular dog tumbled and slammed into Hamish as one rolling boulder of fur.

They plowed into the sled, and it skidded sideways into Ben and knocked him off his feet. Most of the elkies hopped out of the way but the sled caught K'naks and T'sohg and sent them sprawling with a yelp.

The sled righted and slid away as a cart-wheeling Hamish hit the snow hard and all but disappeared into a drift.

Smudge and the wolf were a whirling ball of biting and snapping as they continued fighting toward the river bank. The deranged animal made horrible killer sounds as it lunged and spit black mucus at Smudge, who dodged its bites and beat it backward with fast strikes from her paws and shoves from her massive shoulder muscles. She pushed it away from Hamish and Ben and the elkies as she probed for softer places to strike. The rogue was pumping blood from its chest wounds but Smudge didn't think they had done anything other than piss it off even more.

Everything on the deformed animal felt too hard to make a good bite target. As the mad wolf snapped the air an inch from her nose Smudge got a face full of the vileness dripping from its snout. It had absolutely been infected by whatever horrible compound had been in the drums at the Dorschstein farm. The same stuff that had poisoned Jerry and turned her into a bloated raging monster.

The animal's howling war cry was shaking Ben's spine, and he thought it sounded more like a pack of wounded grizzlies than a wild dog. He fought the urge to put his hands over his ears as he got to his knees and brought up the rifle.

As Smudge and the rogue fought past E'sra he clamped down on the creature and yanked away a chunk of red, slimy fur. He spat out the foul meat, shook his head and sputtered like he'd taken a bite of hot shit, and raced after Smudge and the howling rogue with the rest of the elkies on his tail.

T'nuc and Spot leapt out of the way when the mass of fur and noise roared by, and neither of them gave chase.

They were watching the two other wolves.

The rogue Ben grazed had sped off bucking and hopping toward the far tree line like it was running away, but then it had stopped, shaken off like it was wet, and was tearing low through the snow straight back toward the sled.

And Glasgow was still coming fast from the opposite direction.

Spot flashed Ben a quick sign, and then barked for T'nuc to follow him. They turned away from the approaching she-wolf and bolted to intercept the rogue as fast as they could move in the deep powder.

Hamish had finally righted himself, and when he saw Glasgow was a few short leaps from Ben he tossed the empty gun and pulled his knife.

He flashed a glance to the river, where Smudge was pounding away at the wolf he'd shot with E'sra and the rest of the elkies in pursuit. He saw Spot and T'nuc were running toward the other approaching rogue, and then he turned back to Glasgow.

She was flying over the deep snow with her black radio collar bouncing on her neck.

Hamish tugged frantically to free a leg that was stuck deep in the drift as he watched Ben raise the rifle.

The boy had it pointed in the wrong direction.

Ben quickly assumed a kneeling sniper's cradle, and as he sat back on his heel and turned his body forty-five degrees to the target Lissa whispered in his ear, *Get your ankle directly under your spine, and turn your toe inward. Put the meaty underside of your elbow in the groove of your knee, reach under the rifle and lightly grasp your firing arm, and use your left shoulder as the contact point. This will keep your pulse from being transferred to the scope. Remember, you're not aiming the rifle, you're aiming your body.*

As he lowered his head Lissa added, *This was Teddy Roosevelt's favorite stance. The blind fool was a crap shot, but his form was perfect.*

Ben evened his breathing, lowered to look through the scope, and hoped Spot was right.

His dog had told him Glasgow wasn't a danger so he'd turned his back on the large wolf that was now only two big leaps behind him.

Hamish pushed helplessly against the deep snow as he yelled for Ben to duck.

§§

Ben ignored his great-uncle's warning as Glasgow's paws hit the snow less than a meter to his left.

She was past him in a flash, and he felt the change in the wind's swirl as she raced on toward Spot and T'nuc.

Hamish tried to process what he'd just seen, and was still shaking his head when Glasgow blew by the two smaller dogs like they weren't even there.

She was charging head-on at the approaching rogue.

Hamish pushed aside everything he thought he'd learned about wolves over the last half-century, and asked Ben, "You got it?"

"I got it Unc," Ben said against the stock of the rifle. He watched the blowing snow to gauge the wind's speed and direction, and estimated the distance to the insane wolf by working out the tree height behind it and factoring in its tracks.

He reached up to twist one of the scope's adjustments, put the crosshairs on the rogue, and saw the back of Glasgow's rhythmically bobbing head kept getting in the way of his shot.

"Move girl," he whispered, "just a little to the right."

With one big tug Hamish freed his boot. He sheathed his knife and waded through the deep snow behind Ben, and as he passed the sled he reached in and unclipped his axe before heading for the river.

When Smudge and the rogue hit the icy rocks at the water's edge they both lost their footing and tumbled.

Smudge didn't want to let any distance open up between them so she made a desperate lunge for the rogue's neck, and realized too late she'd just made a horrible mistake.

Her split paws slipped through its greasy, blood-soaked fur, and that left her face heading right for the rogue's opening maw.

The animal's fangs clamped down, tearing through neck muscle until it reached spine. It shattered bones with one huge twist of its massive, distorted head.

But it wasn't Smudge's neck the rogue had sunk its teeth into. E'sra had slammed into them and kicked Smudge clear of its lethal bite.

Smudge spun to her feet in the shallow, freezing water. She saw the rogue give E'sra one last violent shake before dropping his limp body into the river and spinning to face the closing half-circle of snarling elkies.

Smudge dove into the gap between the rogue and the sled dogs, and ordered the elkies back with a short but deafening bark over her shoulder.

The rogue took advantage of Smudge's looking away to leap forward for a bite.

Smudge heard the monster's claws scraping on the rocks, and in a tenth of a second she willed a massive shot of adrenaline into her right shoulder muscles. She spun back to the rogue and clocked the beast on the chin with a blindingly fast, teeth-rattling uppercut.

The rogue stumbled back a few steps on the slick boulders and tried to shake the shooting stars from its head. Blood poured from its mouth and from the bullet wounds on its chest as it stood panting out puffs of red and black. Its mad eyes darted from Smudge to the elkies as it hissed and growled at them.

Smudge could barely make out its twisted rantings. The slurring grumble was similar to the caged wolves, but with a choppy, truncated, non-French, non-silky accent. The intent was clear enough however, and she was pretty sure it was spitting out, *Kill you all, kill you all. I am going to rip all of you to pieces over and over and over.*

As Hamish stepped onto the riverbank he saw E'sra's body floating in the shallow water with a trail of far too much blood flowing away from his torn fur.

The rest of the team appeared to be unharmed. They were clearly enraged and lowered to pounce, but they were also stone quiet and looked to be obeying Smudge.

Hamish stepped in water, and saw every time the bleeding wolf stepped forward to snap Smudge would either smack it across the face or head-butt it under the chin hard enough to make the animal's hind legs buckle.

Smudge glanced back when she heard Hamish's boots kicking up water. Her eyes flashed from him to E'sra, and back to him again.

Hamish gave her an understanding nod, and hefted the axe.

When Smudge saw it she sent Hamish a quick wag before she turned back to face the wolf.

Her pumped-up forelimb flexed, and her cupped paw splashed frigid water in the rogue's face. She grumbled deeply in an accent she felt was close enough to its crazed vitriol, and it was clear the rogue understood her when she said, *You think I hit hard? Just you wait fucker.*

Hamish ran his hand over K'cuf and T'raf's heads as he stepped further into the water and stopped next to Smudge.

He buried his fingers into her fluffy, blood-smeared neck fur. Her incredible muscles rippled and flexed under his hand, and he saw the same bulked-up humps ran over her blocky head and formed a six-pack on her quivering muzzle. When she let out a low growl it vibrated his palm.

"Aye lass," Hamish grumbled as he fixed the wolf with the same hard stare Smudge was giving it. "The boatman's calling for this one."

The long shaft of the axe slid through his hand until the sharp blade stopped just above the water.

Back in the glade the other rogue skidded to a stop and backtracked a few steps in the snow.

He had fully intended to teach his insolent sub-wolf a lesson about loyalty before he tore open the little dogs behind her, but she had fixed him with a look that stopped him in his tracks.

The rogue had never seen such intensity from her. Her lips were pulled up in a high, snarling curl, and her fangs were chattering with rage. If he didn't know better he'd have thought she was trying to posture as an alpha.

Glasgow widened her eyes and raised her head above his as she growled, *This ends now.*

Spot and T'nuc exchanged a look as they fanned out and flanked her. They had clearly understood her growl and felt the power of it, and they were glad their paws were deep in the snow so the wild dogs couldn't see them shaking.

T'nuc lowered her head, bared her teeth, puffed herself up to full hackle-raise, and straightened her curled bushy tail until it stuck out arrow straight behind her. She added her own low growl, and Spot gave her an impressed nod. Their normally calm and composed lead sled dog was a certified elkie bad-ass.

Spot unzipped a vest pocket, pulled out the red folding knife, and flicked the blade out with one of his dexterous pads.

He thought it had a real 'West Side Story' vibe, but the other canines didn't seem very impressed.

T'nuc gave him a head-tip for the effort, and turned to snap a bark at the rogue.

Spot noticed the smart elkhound had changed her tone and accent to approximate that of Glasgow, and the rogue seemed to grasp the meaning.

Your killing days are over, T'nuc barked. *Time for you to die.*

The rogue couldn't fathom what was happening. The insubordination of his sub-female and the arrogance of these strange little owned animals was too much.

He clawed the snow and spat bile, and then shot forward and feigned a bite to the little sled dog before he lunged at Glasgow's throat.

She sidestepped deftly and let his mouth snap shut inches from its target. She'd been watching how the rogues attack and knew this one always faked and made a side lunge when he was most agitated.

Glasgow let the rogue's lumpy body move past her as she slid around him and came in behind his ears to clamp down on the back of his neck.

Spot lunged low and came up under the wolf's chin, biting its throat as he thrust underneath it with the blade. He was trying to open up its undercarriage but his forelimbs weren't long enough and he only hit ribs. As he stabbed at it rapid-fire he tried to slip the knife into something important.

T'nuc shot past them and wrapped herself around the wolf's hind quarters to force its back feet into the snow. When she noticed Ben's bullet wound on its rump she reared back and bit down hard on the gash.

The wolf let out a horrible, raving howl as it twisted and tried to attack.

Glasgow's bite slid over rocky muscle and she only managed to take away a chunk of slimy fur.

The rogue got one of its big clubbed paws behind her, shoved her down into the snow, ignored the frantically stabbing Spot, and moved Glasgow into position for a face bite.

Just as the rogue opened its jaws to sink them down into Glasgow, Spot released his bite and let go of the knife. He shot up with both split paws and wrapped them around the huge wild dog's bloody throat.

His searching finger pads slid over tough, slick, fur-covered lumps, and he realized there was no way to strangle the animal.

The rogue wolf looked down at the pathetic little dog and let out an awful, crazy, arrogant, dripping growl.

Spot clearly made it out as, *Now what runt?*

He planted his rear feet on Glasgow and used her as a base as he pushed her down into the powdery snow. He flooded his system with adrenaline and pushed the rogue's head up as high as he could. As his paws clamped down on its neck he stiffened his whole body, locking his muscles and holding the struggling rogue's head perfectly still.

Fifty meters away Ben slowly let out his breath as his shooting mantra played in his head.

Yeh canae' shove yer granny auf the bus, he thought as he squeezed the trigger in one smooth motion.

He watched through the scope as one of the rogue's eyes split and the top of its head sprayed out in a puff of black and gray and red.

The rogue at the river glanced up the glade when the crack of the rifle split the air, and he flew into a rage when his assassin partner fell.

It was time to end this big human's pitiful posturing, these controlled sled dogs taunts, and the feeble blows from this odd, swelled runt.

He needed to finish this. He needed to kill every warm-blooded thing in this glade, and he needed to go discipline his sub-female.

As he sprung forward he roared at the runt, *I'm gonna snap you in half like that other pitiful little bag of fur.*

He pushed off hard, faked a snap at the dog, and picked a spot on the human's furry neck to tear into.

Just as the insane animal leapt, dripping a trail of black spittle and blood on the rocks, Smudge opened her paws and grabbed its clubbed front feet. She twisted under it and pulled down hard.

The rogue's chin smacked down on a boulder in front of Hamish, and as it looked up at him with disbelieving eyes it scrambled to get a rear foot hold on the icy rocks.

Hamish stepped forward and swung the axe in a huge overhand arc. His feet came out of the water, and when he drove the blade down into the rogue's skull it drew a spark from the rock below its chin.

CHAPTER 71

T'nuc pulled the dead wolf off of Glasgow, and as the she-wolf sprung to her feet and shook off a cloud of snow Spot looked back across the bowl.

He shared a quick nod with Ben, and then looked down to the river bank. His tail dropped when he read Smudge's fallen face and the deflated posture of the elkies.

He turned to tell T'nuc she had better go check on her team but she was already blasting toward the river.

Glasgow gave the dead rogue a sniff, and then took a few steps back and turned toward the woods.

Wait, Spot huffed. *Please don't go.*

Glasgow stopped. She turned and stared down at the curious captive dog.

Thanks, Spot huffed with a shoulder shake and head bob he hoped was universal.

Glasgow cocked her head at him, and then looked down the glade to watch the humans and the rest of the dogs at the riverbank.

Spot turned and saw Hamish was carrying E'sra's body out of the water as Ben arrived with a fur blanket from the sled.

As they walked through the snow with the line of elkies following them Smudge left the procession to join Spot and the big she-wolf.

Smudge chin-rubbed her brother, and then slowly approached Glasgow just as the caged wolves had first approached her. The wolf accepted her introductory head-butt, and returned it with a stiff snort the pups read as a sign of peer hunter respect.

Smudge thanked her for her help, and they weren't exactly sure if Glasgow's paw stomp was 'you are welcome' or 'you are idiots'.

Probably a bit of both, Spot huffed with a wag.

After a few minutes of the pups tweaking their growls, yaps, and body language, they were covering ground pretty quickly with the big wolf.

They answered her questions about their odd mixed pack, and they explained the rogues in terms they thought she could grasp.

She snorted a rude snort, and told them she'd seen rabid animals and these rogues weren't rabid.

The pups agreed with conciliatory ear flicks, and then Smudge asked Glasgow about her pack.

She stared at them for a long few seconds before she explained what had happened, and how it had started with the rogues' sudden appearance in the forest and the senseless animal killings. With her tail tucked and her ears down she told them about her pack's slaughter at the river, and Smudge found her story harder to listen to than the wolves at the mine. With every pained yap and tormented grumble Smudge pickup more of the subtleties in her accent, and she could feel the raw hurt flowing from the sensitive wolf. Glasgow had lost everything in a flash of insane, senseless violence, and she'd tried to let the river take her but the rogues had pulled her out.

Smudge grasped everything Glasgow was communicating, but she knew she couldn't fully appreciate a mother's heartbreak.

I am so very sorry, Smudge grumbled as she stepped up to Glasgow and delivered a tender rub. *Your poor family. That's an awful, painful thing for you to bear.*

Glasgow said it wasn't only her family she couldn't save.

She told them about her horrible mistake with the rangers, and about the tragedy with the skiers. She said she understood the decision of their leader, who had walked un-assailed into the river and used the weapon on himself.

And then Glasgow surprised them when she asked about E'sra.

It was obvious she identified with the depth of Smudge's grief, and Spot watched in awe as the huge wild wolf approached Smudge to share their hurt through gentle touches and low vocalizations.

As Smudge rotated her head under Glasgow's chin Spot agreed with his sister's look of utter guilt for having brought their troubles to this place. E'sra, Willie, the skiers, the rangers, and this sincere and majestic creature's pack had been slaughtered by something they never should have been a part of.

Spot stepped forward and huffed to Glasgow, *There may be more of those rogues coming if we don't stop the humans that are making them sick. We need your help, and we need to stick together, and if we do I think I have a way for you to be part of a family again. You can lead your own pack, and you can control your future. In time, things can be good here for you again, I promise.*

Glasgow thought about that for a minute as she watched the other captive dogs and the humans caring for them. This strange mixed pack had saved her life, and they had killed these rogues, which wasn't an easy task. She could never have a safe family if there were more coming, and she couldn't hope to stop them herself.

I will join your pack, she grunted, and punctuated it with a firm stomp. *We will do what must be done. What is my place here?*

Oh, we'll fit you in somewhere, Smudge huffed with a wag. *Probably just under the big human, but definitely above the runt human.*

The she-wolf thought that was acceptable, as long as mounting wasn't part of the deal.

CHAPTER 72

The sky lightened at sunrise, but not significantly. It was January in the mountains of Quebec in the middle of a snowstorm, and the thick clouds still reached down past the treetops. Shadows started to form and they could see a little farther into the woods, but the snow was still falling heavily and everything beyond the immediate swirls was light gray instead of dark gray.

After they secured E'sra's body in the sled Hamish decided to backtrack to the rangers' machines to take their rifles before heading off again.

As they followed the river down the mountain to the ranch's valley Ben kept trying the satphone and the radio. For the few seconds he did get a signal there was still no answer from Christa.

T'raf took over E'sra's vacant wheel position, and Smudge ran in her place as a swing dog next to T'nuc. The elkies had been running for almost twenty-four hours, and the last eight of those had been non-stop.

Every hour or so Hamish shouted over their heads to ask Smudge if they wanted a break, and after a quickly huffed conversation with T'nuc she would bark the same reply every time without looking back.

Spot would sign it anyway, and Ben would translate, "Get to Christa."

Spot tried to get his sister to switch off with him but she wouldn't reply, and he didn't push it. He could tell she didn't want to be in the sled, and knew she just wanted to run with the team. She'd been in full Cu Sith mode longer than she ever had before, and he could see her hot breath puffing out as fog as she ran in perfect sync with the elkies.

Glasgow mostly stayed in the woods, but every so often she would show up out of thin air to run alongside the sled. She'd eyeball

Hamish, check in with Spot, and then dart off into the thick brush again. The wolf didn't appear to be winded, and even though she stuck to the heavy forest she had no problem overtaking the elkies who were running at almost full pace down the established trail. Ben couldn't figure out how Glasgow appeared on either side of them without him having seen her cross their path. She must be moving way ahead or behind them as she patrolled. He also noticed the elkies had stopped scanning the wood to focus on their running, and Spot confirmed they were happy to have the wolf's protection. The sled dogs knew there wasn't much chance they were going to get ambushed again with her watching over them.

What felt like painfully slow hours passed, but eventually they arrived at the back of the large snow field behind the ranch. It was a flat, treeless white blanket that stretched to both sloping valley walls, with the river running down its west side.

They scanned the back windows of the house through their rifle scopes and with keen dogs' eyes, but they weren't close enough yet to make out any details through the blowing snow. They could see the kitchen and great room lights were on, and there was smoke coming from the chimney.

When Hamish lowered his rifle he flinched hard.

Glasgow had trotted silently out of the trees behind them and stopped at his side.

Being arm's length away from the huge and utterly wild wolf triggered that pucker he'd told Ben about.

Glasgow picked up on Hamish's pucker, or more specifically the sudden constriction of his bronchi, the rise in his heartrate, and the tensing of his muscles.

She turned her big head to look up at him, and gave him a single wag. Although she'd agreed to let the human be the top dog, and found herself drawn to him for some reason, the proper amount of wolf-human respect was still warranted.

As Hamish stared down into her beautiful, deadly amber eyes he said, "Could someone ask her to quit staring at me like I'm a wounded woodchuck?"

"Sure Alpha," Ben said with a smirk, and then he asked Spot, "Did she see anything out front?"

Spot and Glasgow chatted with huffs and grunts, and when Spot signed to Ben he translated, "There are five vehicles in the driveway."

As he raised his rifle again he asked, "What do you think Unc?"

"I'm nae' thinking Christa's having a barn burner and forgot to invite us," Hamish said as he scanned the house. "I donae' like it lad, nae' one wee bit. And I donae' think we should just go waltzing on down there."

He rubbed his frosty beard as he considered their options. If they snuck into the east woods they'd come out unseen behind the barn, but they wouldn't be able to see inside the house until they were pretty close. They could cross over the river and loop around to the west as Glasgow had just done, but the front entrance wouldn't offer any views into the house. The only way was to head into the blowing snow of the open meadow and hope they could get close enough to see what was going on before being seen.

He slung his rifle, and then clapped his gloves and rubbed them together as he said, "Right, lads and lasses. Here's what we're going to do…"

CHAPTER 73

Christa could see well enough from her good eye to check her hand. It had stopped bleeding so she relaxed her cramped fingers.

Tavish had cut down between each of them on her left hand, starting at the webbing and splitting it an inch past the knuckle.

He had done it slowly whenever he didn't like her answers to his questions.

Initially he'd been convinced she knew more than she was telling, but he'd never seen anyone keep a secret by the fourth knuckle, especially after he held the knife to their other hand.

It was pretty clear she didn't know shite about what they were interested in.

Christa wasn't sure if the blood had stopped flowing from the back of her head. She'd hit it on the back of the chair when the big thug Ty had gotten frustrated with Tavish's apparent lack of progress. He'd decided to help the interrogation along with a punch before Tavish stuck his silencer in the big miner's nose and backed him off.

For as big as Ty was Christa thought he hit like a little girl. Still, his ring had torn open her eyelid and the cut had flowed for a long time after her eye swelled closed.

She sent another reassuring smile to her dogs.

They were the smartest, bravest curs on the planet. Especially Vuur, who was bleeding from a graze wound to his cheek. The quick dog had turned away fast enough to miss most of Tavish's intended head shot. There was a horrible few seconds when Christa thought he would shoot again, but Tavish must have been satisfied with the terrorized look on her face.

She had signaled for the dogs to stand down, and that's exactly what they'd been doing for hours without so much as a twitch. There was no way they could break free with one tug, and if they struggled they'd get shot. So they had sat silently and watched as Christa got cut, and screamed out in agony, and took a beating. They were staring at her attackers with simmering rage, but they hadn't moved.

An Asian woman who was dressed in all black, Tavish called her Jia, had arrived at some point after the interrogation.

She wasn't very pleased to hear Hamish and Ben were away for a few days, and as her bodyguard removed her coat she became very vocal about wanting this business, whatever it was, finished before the storm broke. She apparently didn't give a flying fuck about the weather but Tavish got her to agree they shouldn't leave before first light. He explained they could ride right past Hamish in the dark and not see him, and he would hear the snow machines coming long before they got close to him.

Christa watched Tavish and Jia stand at the back slider talking quietly until the sky lightened.

At some point there was movement and mumbling from the miners and loggers who were waiting in the front hall. Christ couldn't hear what they were saying, but she heard Vic's unmistakable grumble cutting in and out over their radio.

The thugs came and went through the back slider a few times, and Christa could feel the cold breeze and snowflakes land on her hot skin whenever they passed her. They crunched up and down the icy back deck stairs, and she heard her snow machines starting up in the barn.

The massively muscled Latino man they called Jero, and Jia's big dark bodyguard she called Lucy, were standing at the family room slider not far from Christa's chair. They were watching the men in the barn filling the snow machines with gas and checking their weapons.

"Well Lucius," Jero said as he put on his jacket, "don't get your nails dirty waiting for the men to bring home the prey."

He looked down to start the zipper of his jacket, and added not very quietly under his breath, *"Mayate."*

"Shut your midget ass up, paragraph," Lucy said, "and go do my bidding."

"Paragraph?" Jero asked as he puffed up his formidable chest.

"Yeah fool," Lucy said as he smiled a full white smile down at him. "Paragraph, cause you aren't even a full essay."

Jero couldn't help but burst out laughing, and he was still chuckling when Ty came from the front hallway and said, "Quit sucking each other's dicks and come here."

They joined Tavish and Jia at the kitchen slider, and Ty said, "We'll head east to the mine trail and then south to the logging range, where Peggy said Hamish and the runt should be camped."

"If she's telling the truth," Jia said.

Ty looked over at Christa, and as he rubbed his knuckles he said, "You wouldn't lie to me, would you sweetheart?"

"Get your men ready," Tavish said as he stepped in front of Ty and fixed him with a cold stare and a tight smile.

Ty backed away, and as Tavish zipped up his coat he said to Jia, "We'll bring them to the mine."

"And I'll finish up here," she said with a nod.

Tavish handed her a radio and said, "I'm on seven, but doubtful you'll get much until this lightens up."

Jia started to ask a question when Jero stepped in front of them and pointed at the snow field behind the ranch.

"*Mira alli*," he said. "What the fuck is that?"

CHAPTER 74

Tavish stepped through the kitchen slider and out onto the porch with his pistol hidden behind his back.

"Hey there my wee boy," he called out to the snow field. "Come on, come along now."

He'd changed his accent back to friendly Glaswegian.

When he whistled and clapped his thigh with his free hand the black dog that was limping through the deep snow looked up at him.

Spot sent him a wag, and picked up the pace as he angled toward the house.

As he hobbled past the corral he glanced over to the barn and saw two of the sliding doors were open and the four snow machines were idling just inside. Two men with automatic assault rifles were standing near them, and they turned to watch him limp past.

As Spot entered the path to the house he pretended to slip, and flashed a quick update back to the snow field.

Ben was somewhere out there in the white haze following him through his rifle scope.

Spot hopped up the back steps, and as he crossed the icy deck he slipped again to relay what he was seeing inside the house.

He really did slip as he limped into the house, and almost swallowed the small red lock blade he was carrying in his mouth.

Tavish closed the slider behind him and said to Jia, "That's one of the lad's dogs."

"I let Ben's pups out last night," Christa croaked in a weak dry whisper without looking up. "I saw them chasing a deer. They must have gotten lost in the storm."

Spot limped over to her and nosed her good hand before hobbling across the room to thump down heavily on the floor next to Sholto.

Jia dismissed Christa's comment with a wave as she said to the men, "Get going."

Tavish lead Ty and Jero through the slider, and before Ty slid it closed he called down the hall to the three other thugs who were waiting in the front foyer, "Tell Vic we're heading out."

The loggers grumbled a reply, and Jia and Lucy watched Tavish and the two miners cross the deck and head down the steps.

Spot got up, stretched like a cat, and nosed and sniffed each of the tied-up dogs.

That drew a quick look from Lucy before he turned back to the conversation.

Spot walked around the kitchen table and drank from a water bowl in the corner, where he was out of sight of the bad guys.

Christa subtly flashed him three numbers with her good hand.

When she nodded at the lock box that was sitting on the island Spot wagged, and looked up at the kitchen clock. He touched his wrist, and then tapped the floor five times.

CHAPTER 75

Glasgow trotted through the deep snow, and when she paused to look back over her shoulder Smudge's barely visible outline popped up from behind a drift in the blowing haze and waved her on.

When Glasgow was exactly two hundred meters from the back of the ranch Smudge gave her a wave to stop and execute the plan.

Glasgow raised her head high and pranced and stomped and ran around in circles.

After a few turns she paused to glance at the men in the barn, and saw they hadn't noticed her.

When she looked behind her Smudge gestured with a deep head-bob, and Glasgow turned back to the ranch and shot out one big bark.

The men in the barn were just about to mount the snow machines when they all stopped to look out at the field. A logger with a gray ponytail stepped off a machine and walked out into the blowing snow.

When he saw the wolf he waved for the rest of the men to join him at the corral fence.

"Is that one of ours?" Ty asked as he put a boot on the lowest rail and brought up his assault rifle.

"No *jefe*," Jero said as he looked through his scope. "Ours are much darker."

"Right," Ty said like he'd known that.

Jero could tell Ty was relieved. His boss put up a good front around their caged wolves but Jero knew he didn't care to be close to them. He wouldn't go near Jia's infected pair after they had started to bloat and turn aggressive. Ty had refused to go with Jero to release them, even after he'd eaten a fist from Vic for his insubordination.

Lucy and Jia had heard the bark from inside the house.

As they watched the wolf through the slider the three loggers came running from the front hall and rushed out onto the icy deck.

Lucy went to close the glass door behind them. As the cold blast and swirling snow cut off he wondered why anyone would actually be excited by the sound of a bark enough to run toward it.

One of the loggers, a chubby man in a red suspenders, raised his rifle and said, "That's a big damn wolf."

"How would you fuckin' know?" an even bigger man in a black quilted vest snorted as they all raised their rifles to get a better look.

Down in the corral Tavish joined the men at the fence. He watched the prancing wolf for a moment, and then asked, "Might I assume that is not normal wolf behavior?"

"Fuck no," Jero said. "*Es locochon hommes.* Is that shit we gave our wolves contagious?"

Lucy had just asked Jia the same question inside the house as they watched the animal dance around in circles far out in the snow field.

"No," Jia said. "They told me it only infect—"

"Put your hands up," Christa said quietly from behind them.

Jia and Lucy heard the unmistakable double click of a hammer being pulled back on a pistol, and they put their hands up.

"Turn around, slowly," Christa said.

Jia and Lucy turned around, slowly.

What they had assumed was a beaten-down and bloodied crippled girl taped to a chair had somehow become a standing muscular woman. She had a calm, chilling look in her good eye, and she'd spoken with the quiet grit of an ex-military officer.

Christa had pieces of cut duct tape hanging from her sleeves and pants legs. She was holding a large revolver in her bloody hand and a little red pocket lock blade in the other.

"How the fuck?" Lucy and Jia whispered at the same time.

Lucy didn't think to call jinx this time.

They noticed the lock box on the kitchen table was open, and Ben Hogan's wagging black dog was standing next to Christa.

And then they noticed the much larger dogs weren't tied to the island anymore. They were spread around the room, and they were silently closing in on them with equally chilling calm stares.

At the corral fence the man with the gray ponytail looked through his rifle scope and asked, "Should I cap it?"

"No, this fucker's all mine," Ty said as he lowered his head and started to track the wolf's movements.

"Ty, wait," Tavish said as he raised his assault rifle to scan the gray silhouettes of the trees at the far end of the snow field.

Ty wasn't waiting, and he started to pull the trigger just as Tavish yelled for them to get down.

They heard a chopped whistle and a simultaneous thump.

The camo jacket of the logger standing next to Gray Ponytail puffed out and he dropped to his knees.

The crack from the rifle echoed around the valley as he fell backward in the snow.

Before the man had hit the ground Tavish was already darting away. He rolled and came up behind a small metal igloo, and tapped on it to make sure it would deflect a bullet.

He looked at the back deck of the ranch and confirmed what he thought he'd heard.

I hadn't been one rifle shot, it had been two simultaneous shots.

A chubby man in red suspenders grabbed his neck and fell forward over the deck railing. He tumbled down the slope behind the house spraying blood across the snow each time he rolled.

Tavish swung the assault rifle to scan the snow field. He had seen the flash of a scope just before the shots, but he didn't want to raise his head too high to locate the shooter. He had guessed the flash was four hundred meters out, and that matched the time between the bullet hits and the rifles' reports.

Whoever it was out there knew what they were doing. The assault rifles they had supplied to Vic's men were intended to pump out a lot of rounds, but were barely effective to three hundred meters. And that was in experienced hands on a clear day with no wind. The shots Tavish heard were from big rifles, and a hunting rifle in the right hands could be deadly accurate at four hundred meters. If these shooters were practiced in winter shooting in blowing snow they could mean real trouble for Ty's cowboys.

Tavish watched as the gray wolf darted away and ran low and straight for the river bank where it met the misty woods at the back of the clearing. Using a wolf to spring an ambush was a new one for Tavish, and he'd seen his share of ambushes. It had to be Hamish, and it appeared he wasn't the drunken old Scot he'd thought he was. The wolf had been dancing around just close enough to be seen, but far enough away to be tough to hit.

It also occurred to Tavish that if Ben was the only one out there with Hamish the lad was a hell of a shot as well.

Jero, Ty, and Gray Ponytail opened up from the corral fence with their assault rifles.

Gray Ponytail was shooting at the wolf, who was barely a ghost outline and too far away to ever be hit by their rifles. Tavish didn't think the man could hit the barn the way he was spraying lead, and as the reports from their rifles popped and echoed around the valley he shook his head. Their muzzle flashes were making them perfect targets.

Tavish thought about the wolf trap, and about Ben, and about his black dog limping in from the white of the blowing snow field at an opportune moment. They hadn't tied up the dog, and he couldn't recall if it was wearing a collar. He looked at the deck through his scope, where the three remaining idiots at the railing were shooting bursts into the field, and then he noticed Jia and Lucy were inside the house with their backs to the closed slider.

Their hands were raised.

CHAPTER 76

Christa saw the neck of the man in the red suspenders pop open and blood spray on the slider a second before they heard the shot and the glass spider-cracked and fell in a shower of little tempered glass blocks.

Red Suspenders fell over the railing, and the rest of the thugs on the back deck balcony started shooting into the field. She could tell they hadn't acquired targets and were just spraying and praying.

Jia jumped behind Lucy as Christa took aim.

Just as she pulled the trigger the other glass door of the slider shattered and a bullet whipped past her ear close enough for the concussion to painfully flick her swollen eye. She flinched and pulled her shot. It went high, taking a small chunk out of Lucy's leather jacket collar and missing his neck by an inch.

Tavish squeezed off another round, and was impressed Christa could move so fast. His shot went just under Lucy's armpit and missed Christa as she disappeared from view.

Tavish smiled, and tipped her an impressed nod as he realized a few hours ago she had looked him in the eye and convincingly lied to his face as he split open her knuckles one at a time.

You're one tough girl, he thought. *Pity.*

He waved to the men on the deck but they were busy shooting at nothing. He grimaced, and fired a round into the wooden railing next to a heavy-set man in a black vest.

Splinters sprayed Black Vest's face and he looked around, saw Tavish pointing, and seemed to take forever to understand what a point meant before he spun around.

Black Vest saw Christa flying stiff-legged through the room, took a moment to understand that she was no longer taped to the chair, and sprayed bullets in her general direction.

When she returned fire at a run and grazed Black Vest's shoulder he panicked and didn't look where he was pissing bullets as he jogged his bulk across the deck.

Christa took a few large hops and tumbled over the couch. As she shoulder-rolled across the floor behind the kitchen island the couch and the granite countertop exploded with a line of torn holes.

The dogs had spread out around the room and taken up positions to strike at the deck as snow and wind whipped into the house through the blown out sliders.

When Spot and Vuur saw Lucy reach into his long leather coat and pull out a hand cannon they both dug their hind claws deep into the thick family room rug. They lunged together at the big bodyguard as wind flapped the tails of his jacket and puffed at the flames in the fireplace.

Vuur crossed the distance in two leaps and went for Lucy's gun hand.

Christa had dropped the small red lock blade when she'd bolted, and Spot picked it up before he launched himself. As he gained height he split his other paw open and reached for the big bodyguard's fat neck.

Both of Lucy's arms shot straight out. One aimed the big gun at the black-faced dog's block head and the other caught the smaller black dog in mid-air. His fist closed around a big hunk of its neck fur.

As Spot dangled in the air he brought the blade up in a sweeping arc and drove it through Lucy's leather coat. It sunk deep into his thick forearm and he dropped Spot as Vuur slammed into him, and in one motion clamped his mouth down hard on Lucy's gun hand and shoved away with his paws.

Lucy howled and stumbled backward as Jia launched herself out of the house. She danced across the icy deck and half-fell down the stairs behind Black Vest.

Lucy staggered back through the doorway and skidded across the deck with his eyes wide. He was trying to understand why there was a knife sticking out of his forearm and how'd he lost his gun and three fingers.

Spot shot up again and his hind paws landed on Lucy's belt as his opened front paws wrapped around Lucy's thick neck.

They thumped into the deck's railing between the two remaining thugs as Spot sunk his grip in deep and his strong toe-pads found the rapidly pulsing targets he was hunting for. He concentrated, and growled, and his forelimbs straightened as he sent a shot of epinephrine down to his paws to help him compress the bodyguard's carotids.

Lucy's vision quickly darkened around the edges until all he saw was the dog's too-knowing stare. He panicked, and flailed wildly as he pounded at the vice grip on his neck and slapped at the disbelieving men next to him who were staring with their mouths hanging open.

Spot felt the ebbing of the big man's blood supply, and realized he'd have to admit to his sister that she'd been right. He recalled an argument they'd had about the best way to strangle someone. Smudge had been convinced her method of carotid compression required much less pressure than his preferred tracheal asphyxia, and she'd said it was faster and more controllable. Based on the dark man's eyes rolling back into his head and his arms dropping to his sides Spot would have to concede that she'd been right.

Damn, he thought as he added another growl.

As Lucy went slack he started to fall back over the railing, taking Spot with him.

Vuur spat out the hand cannon and the fingers and rushed forward. He chomped down on Lucy's groin to pull them both back onto the deck.

For a few long heartbeats the two thugs tried to make the sight of Lucy being choked by one dog and having his balls ripped out by the other work in their heads. As they stared dumbly at Spot's opened paws two more big dogs raced low and fast toward them from inside the house.

A tall thug with a big brown beard and a white knit skull cap backpedaled and slipped as he swung his gun up. He pulled the trigger as he fell and the stream of bullets drew a curved line of holes across the deck from the toe of his boot to the slider. The deck in front of Sholto splintered and she dodged right as Rook pounced on the man from the left.

White Cap steadied and tried to raise his gun but Rook pawed the barrel out of the way as he bit down and yanked off the man's entire trigger hand at the wrist. As White Cap gaped at his stump Rook lunged again and took his entire beard into his big mouth. He snapped the thug's jaw with a lightning fast head twist as Sholto shot past them.

Jia caught up to Black Vest at the bottom of the stairs and used his bulk for a shield as they ran down the snowy path toward the barn.

From behind his igloo shield Tavish watched the dogs on the deck attack. Lucy and the bearded man were flailing under a barrage of moving fur, and he saw the remaining man take a few steps away and raise his assault rifle at the German shepherd who was quickly closing on him.

An instant later the man's shoulder puffed out in a spray of red and down stuffing, and a heartbeat later Tavish heard the rifle shot from the field. The man spun and the back of his jacket puffed out twice more as another kitchen slider blew out. The last two shots must have been Christa firing from inside the house, and Tavish watched as the man fell under the pouncing shepherd.

He cursed himself for having underestimated this family, and their dogs.

As he turned back to scan the field he thought, *These 'soft targets' of Semion's are quickly tipping the balance of power in the wrong direction.*

He caught movement in the trees on the right side of the glade. There were two shapes, and they were barely a different color than the shadows they were speeding through. They had to be dogs, but dogs shouldn't be able to move that fast in the deep snow and thick woods. Regardless, he assumed they weren't on his side and probably wouldn't help his quickly diminishing advantage. He raised his rifle, found center mass on the first target, led it for distance and speed, and the igloo under his elbows shook as a jagged hole opened up in the metal right next to his cheek. An instant later he heard two rifle cracks in quick succession.

He ducked, and saw Gray Ponytail was looking down at a jagged hole were his shoulder had been a second earlier.

As a red flood started to flow down his arm Ty and Jero stopped shooting, looked at him with wide eyes, and then looked at each other before they dropped down behind the fence. They quickly realized the skinny wooden posts would offer them no cover, so Ty picked up the man's rifle and they dragged him howling and kicking through the corral toward the snow machines.

Black Vest and Jia had made it to the barn, and he slung his assault rifle as he swung a big leg over the first idling snow machine. Jia jumped on behind him and barely held on when he roared out of the barn. They spun in a tight arc as they raced out of the corral and headed east toward the mine.

Ty and Jero launched out of the barn right behind them on two of the other snow machines, with Gray Ponytail half-slumped and facing the wrong way on the back of Jero's seat.

Tavish ran low to the barn and jumped on the last idling snow machine, and as he raced out of the barn he scanned the glade.

A sled appeared from the blowing snow and gray fog at the far end of the snow field.

It was being pulled by a team of running dogs, and one man was standing behind the sled and one was kneeling in it. Just as Tavish reminded himself one of them was an eleven year old boy he saw a pair of muzzle flashes. An instant later the corner of the plastic windshield of his snow machine shattered and he felt the whisper of a concussive wave blow past his ear.

And then he heard the double crack of the shots.

He ducked, and yanked the throttle, and followed the other snow machines as they growled loudly away from the corral.

They were heading for the mine trail, but the path behind the barn climbed away along a low slope and there were a few hundred meters of open snow to cover before they reached the relative safety of the trees.

Tavish hadn't been around snow machines since he was a little kid, and these were far sleeker and much bigger than the ones he remembered. They were all black with a purple stripe, and they were either brand new or had been pristinely maintained. The engines were powerful and the machines ate up the snow.

They quickly reached top speed and were doing better than a hundred kilometers an hour. It wouldn't take long to reach the woods and they would easily outrun the dog sled, but not a well-placed rifle bullet. Or two. He leaned down low over the engine behind the little broken windshield, and noticed Ty and Jero were doing the same.

Gray Ponytail looked strange sitting bolt upright behind the hunched-over Jero. Based on his grimace he was in a lot of pain, but Tavish gave the tough miner credit for holding his rifle with his good arm and firing ineffective bursts at the field.

They caught up to Jia's sled, and Tavish could tell she was freezing as she clung to Black Vest's back. She wasn't wearing a coat and her black hair was flying around her wind-reddened face like Medusa's snakes.

He saw her flinch hard and assumed she'd seen muzzle flashes when two more cracks came a second later. They were barely audible over the roar of the snow machines' engines and he didn't see or feel any hits.

He risked a quick look back over his shoulder as he didn't want to slow or lose control, but the glimpse was enough for him to see Hamish's sled was still far back in the field and it seemed to be crawling compared to them.

All four machines reached the woods and veered closer to each other when they entered the trail. He assumed it was some manner of fire road as it was wide enough for the sleds to run side-by-side.

None of them wanted to let off the throttles as they blasted their machines down the trail. The engines hummed loudly as rooster tails of snow flew from their tracks, and when they rounded the first bend Tavish shared a tight smile with the shaking Jia. They were both glad to have a wall of trees between them and the sled.

But when he looked down the trail his smile faded.
A large white dog was waiting for them.

CHAPTER 77

With the snow whipping his face Tavish had to blink several times to confirm what his wind-torn, watering eyes were seeing. The dog perfectly matched the snow around it. It wasn't pure white but a shade of gray-blue that mimicked the shadows of the trail. It was a medium-size dog with a fluffy coat, and it was about the same size as Hamish's sled dogs, but it was much thicker through the neck and shoulders and it had a block head like a pit bull's.

And it was wearing a military style winter camo vest.

It cocked its head as it stared at them for a moment, and then broke into a full run straight at them.

The four roaring snow machines quickly closed the distance to it, and even with the dog charging them no one wanted to slow enough to shoot at it. They hadn't moved far enough down the trail to remove Hamish's sled as a potential threat so they hadn't let off the gas. Their rifles were slung over their backs, and with the trees zipping by so close no one dared trying to drive with only one hand.

The sleds moved apart a little as they reached the dog, and Tavish wondered what the animal was trying to accomplish. Even though it moved quickly through the deep snow it couldn't hope to pounce on them as the sleds would easily maneuver around it. For a moment he thought Ty was going to run the dog down but he must have realized it looked beefy enough to cause a proper wreck, and it was jumping high enough out of the snow to come over the handlebars. Tavish thought about slowing to pull his pistol but didn't see the need, and he didn't want to get too far behind the rest of the group.

As Ty's sled roared around the dog it pounded out a bark that was so loud Tavish jumped in his seat.

The bark was far too loud. They should have never been able to hear it over the roar of the four engines but he felt it shake his bollocks. He was surprised by how badly the bark rattled him, and he had to work to push away a voice in his head that wondered what the fuck was going on with this family and their strange canines. He'd been trained not to entertain unproductive thoughts that wouldn't help his current situation, but he didn't argue with the voice when it suggested they finish this business and get the bloody hell away from Canada.

Gray Ponytail almost dropped his rifle. He hadn't seen the dog, and when it barked right next to him he flinched and looked at it with wide, confounded eyes.

Jia hadn't seen the dog either, and its bark made her reflexively cower into a ball behind Black Vest.

As Jero careened around the dog a tree branch brushed Gray Ponytail's good shoulder and left a trail of falling powder behind them. At that moment Tavish realized the sleds separating to avoid the dog had brought them close to the trees, and he remembered there had been two shapes flashing through the snow behind the barn. This was another ambush using a dog, and again he'd caught it too late.

Just as Jero started to steer his snow machine back to the center of the trail a big gray wolf leapt from the thick pines and knocked him and Ponytail off the machine's bench seat.

His throttle lever sprung back to idle when he let go of the handlebars and the engine went from a screaming roar to a low purr. The machine veered slowly into the center of the trail and came to stop as it sunk down into the powder.

Jero pin-wheeled across the snow and came to a hard stop on his back. He sprang to his feet, brushed the snow from his face, and swung the rifle around from his back.

Tavish's sled sped around the wolf so close he could have grabbed it. He passed Jero before he came to a stop next to the now empty sled.

He turned to see the huge wolf had Gray Ponytail's good shoulder in a vise grip and was growling deeply and shaking him violently. It let him go and looked up for a second before it took another bite and tugged him over Tavish's tracks and into the woods on the far side of the trail.

Ty had covered a lot of ground before looking back and noticing the empty sled. He slowed to a stop and spun on the seat as he unslung his assault rifle.

Tavish unzipped his coat and pulled his pistol with blinding speed. His first target had been the wolf but out of the corner of his eye he saw the white dog was right behind him. He got off one round just as the dog disappeared in a flash into the woods. He swung back to the wolf but he could only hear Gray Ponytail screaming from behind a thick umbrella of snow-covered pines.

Jero opened up into the woods, alternating between the last places he'd seen the white dog and the wolf as he high-stepped through the snow toward his sled. He shot in bursts between each big step.

Tavish raised his hand and Jero paused. They heard Gray Ponytail give one last scream, and then the bushes rattled and snapped loudly.

Jero swung his gun toward the sound, but Tavish swung in the opposite direction and saw the white dog running fast behind the trees on the slope above Jero's sled. The damn dogs were coordinating their attack in a way Tavish wasn't sure even the best trained dogs could do, and he didn't see any humans around to command them. He tried to push that aside as he knew Hamish would be coming around the bend any moment and he wanted to be gone when that happened. Confined by the trail, and at these distances, they were sitting ducks for a talented rifle shot. And the Scot and his grandnephew had talent.

Ty must have thought the same thing. He yelled over the idling machines for them to move it, and started to lay down bursts of suppressing fire into the woods on both sides of the trail. Tree trunks sprayed bark and bullets buzzed past Tavish and Jero as snow fell from the boughs.

Jero slung his rifle and moved quickly to his sled, and Tavish saw the wolf and the white dog had split up and were coming fast from higher up the steep sides of the trail. Ty was shooting way too low and too far downrange to be a deterrent.

"Gun it!" Tavish yelled to Jero, who was smart enough to listen and immediately shot away on his sled.

Tavish hesitated before hitting his throttle. There was a gap in the trees and he saw an opportunity for a clear shot. He raised his pistol and followed the running white dog, leading it enough so his bullet would hit just behind its head.

As he started his trigger pull the speedometer on his handlebars exploded.

CHAPTER 78

Tavish didn't wait to figure out what had happened. He'd seen too many colleagues and enemies waste their last second on earth trying to figure out where a shot had come from. He had survived in this business by letting his flight instinct take over when he saw a shot, and he liked to be gone before he heard it.

In one motion he slapped the pistol into his belt and yanked back hard on the throttle. The powerful sled jerked away and rose out of the snow just as the dog and the wolf blasted onto the trail.

The wolf thumped off the side of Tavish's sled as he sped past. It clamped onto his snowsuit leg for an instant before it tore off a piece of the fabric and tumbled away behind the sled.

The white dog missed a bite for Jero and bounced off the back of his sled, only it didn't fall away as Jero sped off.

Tavish thought for a second the dog was running behind Jero until he saw it was holding onto the bar above its rear fender.

Jero looked back and saw the dog that was clinging to his sled, and then he looked at Tavish with uncomprehending eyes.

They were flying down the trail toward Ty, who flicked his assault rifle to single fire and tried to get a clear shot at the white dog but only had Jero in his sights.

Jia and Black Vest hadn't stopped. Their tail light was receding down the trail and fading into the haze.

Snow swirled around Jero's speeding sled and the white dog, and Tavish couldn't tell exactly what he was seeing. He fought to not stare at the dog so he didn't crash into the trees, but he was pretty sure the muscular canine was holding onto the bar with its paws, and they were wrapped around it like hands.

When another shot took off Tavish's rearview mirror he stopped worrying about Jero and the crazy white dog who appeared to have hands, and held the throttle tight as he ducked down over the growling snow machine.

There was no way the shot was from Hamish. Another shooter had to be in the woods behind them, likely at a high angle, which would mean they came from the road that wound along the ridge to the ranch. As Tavish shot straight down the trail he slid over so he was hanging off the side of the snow machine to put its bulk between him and the shooter. He was actually drawing a little comfort from the fact that another human was close by until the voice in his head whispered, *Even if that is the dogs' handler they're still way too fucking coordinated, and one of them's a wolf for fuck's sake.*

Jero whipped his sled back and forth wildly across the trail as he tried to shake off the dog. When that didn't work he ducked low and fish-tailed hard into the dense snow-packed pine branches along the side of the trail. He almost flipped the sled over as the heavy boughs snapped and whipped at him. He disappeared into a cloud of snow and branches for a second, and when he blasted back onto the trail the dog was gone.

Tavish and Jero caught up to Ty, and the three of them exchanged dumbfounded headshakes as they crouched low over their machines and sped off after Jia.

CHAPTER 79

"You're going to get a lot of mileage out of eye shadow for a while," Blu said as she finished dressing Christa's swollen eye.

Christa smiled, and then winced as she said, "Ouch."

As she touched the tender red lump on her temple Blu gave her an apologetic shrug.

"And so will Vuur," Ben said as he gently cleaned the crusted blood from below the angry row of stitches on the wagging mastiff's black cheek.

Lucy was seated at the kitchen table with his big black leather jacket draped over the back of the chair next to him. His hand with the missing fingers was bundled in a thick wad of bandages, and the puncture wound on his other forearm had been stapled shut. His good hand was stuck down his unzipped pants, where it was holding an ice-filled kitchen towel to his well-bitten man parts. Even with his dark skin the bright red bruises on his neck were clearly visible.

He sat very still as he stared at the black dog seated across the table from him. He only had a vague recollection of the dog stabbing and choking him, but he no longer had any doubts about its dexterous paws as it was using some kind of sign language to communicate with the kid. He was pretty sure the dog was talking about him as it was signing to the kid but staring right at him.

Ben laughed and said, "Yeah right Spot. He might need some neck makeup, but he won't be needing a condom for a while."

There was a stack of curved ammo magazines in front of Ben. He'd collected them from the attackers' assault rifles, and he was thumbing out shells from the half-empty ones to make a few full ones.

Blu's radio crackled and she grabbed the mic on her lapel and said, "Yes Dave, that's my car on the ridge, just come on down to the ranch."

After speaking with Director Barton she hadn't been able to reach Christa or Hamish so she'd driven to the ranch. When she saw the miners' vehicles parked out front she'd stopped at the top of the ridge road and decided to come down on skis with her rifle. And that's when she'd heard the shots. She saw the four snow machines racing away from the barn and she recognized Jero and Thibault, and then she saw Hamish's sled out in the field. When it appeared the miners had started a fire fight with a dog and a wolf on the trail she'd assumed the canines were the good guys.

She'd missed her shot, the dogs had chased off after the fleeing sleds, and she'd come down to the ranch. She was still trying to wrap her head around how the white dog was actually one of Ben's black dogs. It was hard to grasp, even after Spot had demonstrated changing colors as she stared at him, and the white dog she saw bolting down the trail was a hell of a lot bigger than Spot.

Blu wondered if she had the same befuddled look on her face as the bloodied bodyguard.

Deputy Dave pulled his cruiser into the ranch's parking circle and stopped behind the large pickup trucks. As he walked to the front door he noticed a pair of sturdy furry dogs were standing on the covered walkway like sentry statues. They just stared at him with swiveling heads as he walked slowly past them.

The front door was open a crack, and he looked at one of the dogs and asked, "So, do I, you know, go on in?"

The dog just stared at him, and he decided to slip into the house.

He stepped into the foyer and stopped dead when he came face-to-muzzle with a massive black-faced dog. It didn't move as it scanned him with a hard stare, and Dave noticed its huge front paws were smeared red up to its elbows. He really hoped that wasn't blood as he backed against the wall and crept slowly around it. He wasn't a big fan of dogs, especially ones that came up to his chest and weighed more than he did. He hugged the wall and tried not to return the dog's stare as he hurried into the kitchen.

When he saw Christa's face he flinched, and grimaced when he noticed her bandaged hand and the blood on the floor and the bullet holes that ran across the island and up the wall.

He turned away from Christa and almost ran into another black-faced dog. For a second he thought it was the same one from the front hall until he noticed its bloody chest and stitched-up cheek.

He saw there was a huge black man sitting at the kitchen table across from the kid and the black dog from The Grub, and at the far end of the table there was a neatly laid out row of rifles and automatic weapons. When he felt a cold breeze he turned and saw the sliding glass doors had been shattered. The glass and snow spread across the floor and continued out to the deck, where he saw more blood and two bodies covered in jackets. Hamish's large German shepherd was standing between them, and she was staring out at the barn and the snow field. There was another fluffy dog like the ones out front standing next to a sled by the barn, and it was standing perfectly still as it watched the woods. There was another covered body by the corral fence, and Hamish was walking fast toward the house from the barn.

"What in the frickin' happy heck went on in this place?" Dave asked as he put his hands on his hips.

"Grab some tarps and tape from the garage and cover up these broken windows," Blu said. "Sweep up all the glass, and don't forget the deck. After that I want you to stay on station in your cruiser. Stay clear of the dogs, don't touch any of the weapons, and stay off the radio unless there's an emergency or you hear from me. Don't touch the bodies, I'll call the coroner once I'm out of the valley. Christa's the most experienced officer here so I'm putting her in charge until I get back. You got that?"

Dave nodded, but he was staring at Christa's angry swollen eye.

"Deputy," Blu said with some force. "You reading me?"

"Yes captain," he said as he broke his stare and looked up at her. "I, I got you, sir."

"So get to it," Blu said as she pushed him gently toward the hallway.

Dave stepped wide around the staring dog as he left, and Blu gave Ben's back a little scratch as she said, "Maybe you should try to get some rest."

"I'm good, thanks," Ben said without looking up from loading the magazines.

Spot did look up, and he gave Blu a nod she couldn't help but read as, *He's alright.*

Hamish came up the deck stairs zipping up a white camouflage jacket. He briefly paused at the railing to give a red-smeared Sholto a pat as he said, "Gunny's last firefight."

Christa laughed, and then touched her cheek and said, "Oww, ass."

Sholto licked Hamish's hand, and he stepped into the house with his boots crunching on the broken glass. He tossed Spot his white camo vest, grabbed one of the assault rifles, and Ben started handing him the full magazines.

As he stuffed them into his pockets he looked down at Spot and asked, "You ready Einstein?"

Spot nodded as he finished clipping on his vest, and then he turned and signed to Ben.

"Don't worry about us," Ben said as he knelt to zip up one of Spot's vest pockets and kiss him on the head. "You just be careful, and take care of Unc and your sister."

Spot licked his face, and then shot Lucy one last cold look.

Ben stood and turned to face Hamish, who wrapped his big arms around him and gave him a long, tight squeeze. He drew back and held Ben's shoulders, and smiled down at the young handsome face that could have been his brother's.

Hamish had been in places where boys Ben's age had to grow up fast and hard. He'd seen young men forced to become adults before they should, seen them forced to defend their families, and forced to pick up a gun, and forced to kill. He didn't like his grandnephew being tossed into this shit pile but he couldn't ignore how amazingly brave this annoying spoiled little city brat had been. The lad hadn't a trace of stubble, but Hamish thought he had more brains and hairier balls than any bloke he'd ever fought next to.

"Yeh did one belter of a job out there lad," he said. "I'm honored yer part of my clan, and yer Papa and yer Mimi would be right fucking proud of yeh."

Ben smiled and handed Hamish the last full clip as he said, "You did a good job too Unc, and I promise not to breathe one word of this to Mimi."

Hamish turned to Christa, and she slapped the revolver into his palm as she said, "Go kill those fuckers for me Hamish, and bring all of our pups back safe."

"Done," Hamish said as he tenderly covered her bandaged hand with his own. He took the pistol, and then slung the assault rifle over his shoulder and picked up his hunting rifle.

When he noticed Blu had picked up her rifle he moved in front of her and asked, "And just where do yeh think you're going Captain Pinard?"

Blu smiled, and poked him in the chest as she said, "Listen to me, you thick-skulled Jock. I know I can't stop you, but you're not shooting anyone on my watch unless I'm there. I can lend you some legitimacy, and maybe a vest, and I'll arrest anyone left standing."

CHAPTER 80

Glasgow appeared from the trees and trotted across the trail to join Smudge, who was shaking snow from her fluffed-up coat and flexing her cramped paws.

They exchanged head-butts, and Glasgow licked her cheek.

I'm fine, Smudge grumbled as they watched the snow machines disappear around the bend in the trail.

Glasgow snorted a short huff, and Smudge cocked her head at the big wolf.

I know how to set an ambush, Smudge huffed.

Glasgow didn't respond, and Smudge grumbled, *I'd like to see you do better.*

They rotated their ears to follow the slowly fading screaming engines, and Smudge huffed, *They have to go around the ridge, so we're going over it. C'mon.*

They darted across the trail and Smudge was back up to full pump by the time they hit the trees.

The muscular gray-white mutt and the huge gray wolf pounded hard up the steep wooded slope as they took big leaps through the deep snow together.

CHAPTER 81

Jero and Ty and Tavish caught up to Jia and Black Vest, only he wasn't wearing the vest anymore. It was big enough to wrap all the way around her twice, and the heavy man was shivering in just his red plaid flannel shirt.

After following the trail from Christa's ranch they had picked up the pike route. It would take them around the base of the east ridge, and eventually to the mine. Although still technically a fire road, it was barely wide enough for a truck and wound between steep walls of rock and tangles of trees that crowded the trail.

Tavish caught glimpses of a series of steep rocky falls high above them. The river they fed followed the curve of their trail for a few hundred meters before it passed under them through a culvert and dropped away between a slice in the gorge.

When Tavish looked away from the falls to see what was waiting for them in the middle of the trail he groaned, "You abominable twat."

The huge gray wolf was staring right at them with its head held high and its tail swishing like an invitation to come get eaten.

The four men realized they couldn't just zip around it on the narrow trail, and their snow machines' screaming engines quieted to an idle as they settled to a stop in the deep powder.

Jia stood up to see over the wide shoulders of Red Plaid, and was immediately locked into the wolf's stare.

"What the shit is that?" she whispered.

"That, *jefa*, is no fucking good, that's what that is," Jero said. He and Ty were similarly caught in the wolf's stare, but they were slowly swinging their assault rifles around.

Tavish had pulled his pistol but he was leveling it at the woods. He moved in quick arcs as he turned his body all the way around to scan both steep walls above the trail.

When Jia saw he was completely ignoring the wolf she whispered to him, "Just what the fuck are you doing?"

Without looking at her Tavish said, "I'm afraid the boys are correct. That wolf happens to be a harbinger."

Jia looked into the thick woods where Tavish was sweeping his gun and asked, "A harbinger of what exactly?"

Jero and Ty pulled up their rifles and took aim at Glasgow through their scopes, and just before Tavish could tell them to forget the bloody wolf and watch the woods the muscular white dog shot silently from the trees and darted low and straight across the trail.

It ran right between their machines.

It blasted behind Ty and Jero and passed in front of Tavish and Red Plaid before launching off the rim of the culvert on the far side of the trail and disappearing into the snowy pine boughs with a white puff.

Tavish had whipped his pistol around to follow the dog, and he'd squeezed off two rounds. His silenced pistol huffed and the shots puffed snow near the feet of the miners, but both shots missed the fast white dog.

When the shots kicked up snow next to Ty and Jero they spun their guns toward Tavish and gave him hard looks. They hadn't seen the white dog.

Before they could ask the crazy fucking Brit what he thought he was doing a crunching came from high above them. It was loud enough to be heard over their four idling snow machines, and it was coming fast down the slope toward them.

As Tavish aimed up at the rumbling sound and saw shaking trees and falling snow he thought, *How can a dog start an avalanche?*

In a panic Red Plaid tried to pull his assault rifle around his bulk but only managed to knock Jia off the back of his idling snow machine.

That ended up saving her from the swiping paw of the massive brown bear who exploded out of the trees in a cloud of snow and branches.

It slammed into Red Plaid and sent him and the machine tumbling as it let a deep grumbling growl fly.

Jero and Ty turned and got off one hurried shot each before the roaring bear continued through them as well. It plowed into Jero, flipping his snow machine over and tossing Ty into the woods like a doll.

Tavish didn't hesitate, he slammed the pistol into his belt and raced away on his snow machine. He slowed between the two wrecked sleds just long enough to grab a handful of Jia's hair and black vest and pull her onto the running boards of his sled. He squeezed the throttle all the way and the snow machine screamed as it lifted high out of the snow and shot them straight toward the wolf.

Red Plaid sat up in the deep powder when he heard them roar past, and he watched the British man and Asian woman speeding away with his black vest flapping in the wind.

Strips of skin and hair hung from the side of his head between the deep claw slices. The wound dripped blood over his plaid shirt and speckled the white snow around him. When he heard the bear's horrible growl and saw Jero's feet kicking wildly from below the animal's brown bulk he fumbled for his assault rifle.

Ty stumbled out of the woods next to his still upright and idling snow machine. He was covered in snow and pine needles, and the shoulder of his jacket was torn and hanging, but the bear's claws had barely grazed his skin and left only two thin red lines.

He mounted his machine, but when he saw Jero struggling under the bear he hesitated to squeeze the throttle.

He let go of the handlebars and raised his rifle, but his head was still spinning and the immense animal was a mass of whirling brown fur. Every time he started to pull the trigger it moved and he almost shot Jero.

The bear had raked Jero down his front and split his jacket open. There were four long red stripes down his ripped white thermal top and his gold chains had been torn off. He was missing a nipple and a big piece from one of his bulging pectoral muscles, but he was still pounding away at the bear's face with his big fists.

Ty tried one shot to the bear's rump in a spot he felt was safely away from Jero.

The animal pounded a huge paw down into Jero's bloody chest and bounced up on its hind legs. It stood and turned its massive head toward Ty, and howled down at him through its finger-length, blood-tinged white fangs.

Ty let go of his rifle, and his bladder. He stared at the bear as his shaking hands reached out and grabbed the handlebars.

"Sorry," he mumbled as his bloodied friend looked up at him with terrified eyes from under the bear.

Ty squeezed the throttle hard and looped in a wide arc around them as he shot off down the trail toward Tavish and Jia.

Smudge had leap from high above the trail at Ty, but she ended up landing in the trail left by his roaring sled. When she saw he and Tavish were speeding toward Glasgow she darted down the trail after them, giving the bear a wide berth and using the packed snow left by Ty's tracks to gain speed.

Glasgow dipped low and then sprang high as Tavish's sled zipped past her. Her snap caught his elbow, but he jerked his arm free and only left some flesh behind as the handlebars twisted and the front skis bit into the snow at a hard angle. The front end of the snow machine dove wildly and the back end bucked, and Jia's body came off the sled completely. She threw her arms around Tavish's waist to keep from falling off as the black vest flapped around her. Tavish overcorrected and the sled banged down hard and canted in the opposite direction, whipping Jia to the other side of the sled. She clung to Tavish, and barely missed being chewed up by the spinning track as the sled bounced and flipped her back the other away.

Glasgow landed with her feet spread, spat out the chunk of jacket and elbow skin, and shot off after the violently wobbling sled.

With a frozen, straight-ahead stare Ty roared past Red Plaid and ignored his raised and bloodied hand.

Red Plaid watched him go, and then looked down at his assault rifle as more blood trickled down and mixed with the snow that covered it. He wiped at the red that was seeping into his eyes, clicked off the safety, and raised the weapon. As he tried to blink away the blur he aimed at the bear, who was stomping down on Jero's chest with both front feet. The animal's forelimbs were straight from its shoulders to its paws and every time it pounded down Red Plaid could hear Jero's ribs snapping under the hundreds of pounds of shaking fur.

Jero huffed painfully with each hit, but he was still pummeling away with his red-smeared, cannonball biceps pumping.

As Smudge raced through the snow toward Glasgow she saw Red Plaid was staring down the barrel of his rifle. She picked up as much speed as she could on the packed trail and veered at the last second to launch herself at him. She knocked the rifle away just as he pulled the trigger and the gun spat fire and sprayed a stream of bullets across the snow and up into the trees. Smudge grabbed the man's bloody head with her split paws, and as her momentum carried her past him she snapped his neck with one great flex and a sharp twist.

She landed on her feet and raced back to the packed trail as Red Plaid collapsed sideways into the red-flecked snow.

As Ty's snow machine screamed past Glasgow she made a leap for him, and when her snap to his bare shoulder missed by a whisker he didn't so much as blink. He stared straight ahead as he flew past her, and she could see the stain on his crotch and smell his mess, and she heard him stammering to himself.

Tavish's sled finally straightened out and slammed back down on both front skis. A battered Jia sat up behind him, and they roared off with the machine spitting out a tail of snow as they caught up to Ty.

The machines pulled away with their whining motors slowly fading as Smudge joined Glasgow on the packed snow left by their tracks.

From behind them Jero let out a scream, which was followed by a series of loud snaps, and then there was silence.

Before the powerful sleds disappeared around the next bend Tavish slowed and angled his machine across the trail. He and Jia looked back at the two odd canines, and the huge brown bear in the background.

Smudge saw them exchange a headshake, and then Tavish turned back to the handlebars and they sped away to follow Ty toward the mine.

When the bear let out a deep growl Glasgow and Smudge turned around to face her.

Smudge bobbed her head in as close an approximation to a bear thank you as she could remember from her brother. She motor-boated a deep grumble she hoped came out as, *We owe you one big mamma.*

The bear swatted a paw-full of bloody snow at them, snorted out a puff of red-tinged, foggy breath, and then picked up the top half of Jero and ambled back into the forest toward her den.

Smudge and Glasgow rotated to stare down the trail again, and Smudge noticed the wolf was giving her a sideways look with a slightly raised eyebrow.

Don't give me that, Smudge huffed. *I'd still put this one in the win column.*

Glasgow held her sideways stare and swapped brows.

And what happened to you? Smudge huffed. *You can take down a running elk but you can't stop a human on a sled? I know a coyote who's tougher than you are. You sure you're not a Cantis lupus?*

Glasgow growled.

Alright, I'm sorry, Smudge huffed. *Don't get your furry knickers in a bunch. Let's just let it go and focus on the task at hand.*

They rotated their ears to listen to the fading whine of the two snow machines, and Glasgow asked a question with a shoulder twitch.

We sure are, Smudge huffed as she turned to the south, *but we have another stop to make first.*

CHAPTER 82

Blu's cruiser crunched quietly down the icy, tree-lined gravel road with its lights off. She slowed as she entered the clearing, and then stopped on the rim road that ringed the mine's west bowl.

Hamish pulled up next to her in his truck. They got out and slung their assault rifles before picking up their hunting rifles and stepping to the edge of the pit.

The boerboels appeared out of the trees a few meters to their left and crossed the road to look down into the mine as Spot came out of the woods to their right. He checked in with Rook and Vuur, and then nodded to Hamish that all was clear in the woods behind them.

Hamish waved Spot over, and as he trotted over to them he noticed they were standing between a pair of grid tracks. They were fresh and crossed over each other as they followed the access road down into the mine complex.

Spot sent the police dogs to patrol along the ring road as Hamish and Blu looked through their scopes at the jumble of buildings. Nothing was moving in the snowy, early morning haze and there were no lights on in the compound. Aside from the wind whistling through the trees behind them everything was dead quiet.

Hamish turned around with his rifle to follow the tracks down the pike trail. The trail that ultimately led to the ranch.

Blu noticed Spot was staring down the trail as well with his ears pricked and swiveling. Even though his expressive face was harder to read when he was all white, she would have sworn the smart dog and Hamish had the same concerned look.

She knew they were thinking the same thing she was, that there were only two snow machine tracks, and no dog or wolf prints.

"I'm sure they're fine," she said. "Those machines were flying and they probably didn't even catch up to them."

"Looks like they caught up to two of them," Hamish said quietly as he rubbed Spot's head.

"Didn't you say she's the toughest dog you've ever met?" Blu asked. "I expect that's saying something, and she's with a big damn wolf."

"Aye," Hamish said as he turned back to the mine, "but they should have beaten us here."

They scanned the complex through their scopes for another minute before he said, "I got nothing."

Blu nodded her agreement as Spot checked with Rook and Vuur, who agreed from a hundred meters further down the mine rim road.

Hamish was familiar with the dozens of logging and fire roads that connected to the mine's two big bowls, but he'd never been down into the complex itself. The narrow isthmus of land housed a dozen huge processing buildings surrounded by smaller outbuildings, and the two access roads were only ways in or out. Wide gravel roads for the huge rock trucks led from the cluster of buildings and spiraled down into the tiered mine bowls until they ended in pools of water at the bottom.

The snow machines had gone down the north access road. The south access road was the wider one, and it ran parallel to train tracks that would eventually run past Piege and take the mine's ore pellets to the steel mills in the south.

Spot yapped a few commands to the boerboels, and they tore off at a run along the rim of the bowl before turning to head down the south access road. When the road leveled out they took turns leapfrogging past each other, with one brother racing ahead as the other brother kept watch. They alternated until they found a hiding spot among the car-sized, snow-covered boulders that rung the perimeter of the complex.

When they were set they signaled the all clear to Spot, and he led Hamish and Blu down into the mine. They crouched in the steep shoulder of the north access road to stay out of sight of the buildings as much as possible until they came to the boulders.

They worked their way toward the closest building in dashes and stops, with Blu and Hamish waving each other on as they took turns scanning the mish-mash of dark rectangles. The corrugated metal buildings were all different sizes and shapes, and there were doors and windows in no logical order. A maze of conveyors and catwalks spider-webbed between them, and hundreds of other obstacles were scattered around the complex. There were huge rock trucks dwarfing the regular sized work vehicles, mining equipment, parts wrapped in plastic on pallets, and large electrical panels. Any one of them could effectively hide a shooter.

There was also fifty meters of open icy gravel between them and the closest building, and Blu didn't like their tactical position. Even in the blowing snow they'd be exposed as soon as they stepped out from behind the rocks. She thought about suggesting they just hold the compound and call in backup but she knew that stubborn look on Hamish's face. He wasn't in a waiting mood, and she could easily see Spot had the same impatient look.

"Why am I suddenly picturing fish and a barrel?" she whispered.

"Aye," was all she got out of Hamish.

Spot sent the boerboels to patrol the far side of the complex with instructions to stay out of sight and report if they saw anything on two or four legs.

He and Hamish moved down a few boulders so they'd have the shortest sprint to the closest door.

Blu saw Hamish set down his hunting rifle and unsling his assault rifle, and she did the same. She cursed herself for not taking him up on his offer to join the damn shooting club. Although she wasn't a bad shot she knew the hobbyist nuts at the range could tell her where her assault rifle had been manufactured and how many joules of muzzle energy it pumped out. She'd watched that crazy Harry Chogin shoot a smiley face in a wooden target with a fully automatic burst at a hundred meters. He'd also drawn a circle around the target's groin before he cut its smiling head off.

She took one last scan of the complex, flicked off her rifle's safety, flashed Hamish the all clear sign, and then whispered to herself, "Please let it be all clear."

She was struggling to comprehend Vic's gambit at the ranch. He'd been an asshole since the first day he arrived, and he liked to play Mafioso with his boys and throw his weight around town, but until recently he'd just been a petty thug. She knew he'd dug his fat fingers into most of the nefarious action in the eight mines and forty logging operations in her jurisdiction, but in the past he'd been smart enough not to cross the unspoken line most jerk-water police captains had with their local troublemakers. She understood boys would be boys, and as long as they kept it to their own partying and no one got hurt she mostly turned a blind eye. She would make enough busts to keep the drugs in check without affecting production and pissing off the owners down south, but this was an escalation of a disturbing trend. Over the past year she'd been building a pretty solid case as Vic dabbled in additional revenue streams after the price of steel took another big dip. His bonuses must have been taking a nose dive, and in addition to the typical back-country trifecta of meth, weed, and tax-free booze she'd caught wind he'd recently added prostitution, trafficking, and even dog fighting. And now he'd added the local logging thugs to his payroll, and some of those boys were the real deal. It wasn't difficult to find bad-asses on logging crews as it was a pretty common job for recently paroled hardcore head cases, but Vic wasn't normally so ambitious.

He'd become a first class *tabernac* that needed to be dealt with, but what annoyed Blu most was the idiot had been keeping a step ahead of her whenever she was close to catching him red-handed.

She suspected Barton may be right about Vic having gotten himself mixed up with a bigger player. It sure would explain his boys' new weapons.

Even so, she wouldn't have thought him ballsy enough to try to fuck with Hamish. That stupidity might just earn Vic the very bad day he had coming. Although her big Scottish part-time lover could be a little blustery she knew he actually had to be pushed pretty far before he cut loose. When it finally happened Lord help the idiot, or more often idiots, who were doing the pushing. She'd interviewed more than a few big, bloodied loggers who were reluctant to admit they'd had their recently paroled asses handed to them by a gray-bearded old man.

Blu also knew how Hamish felt about Christa, and messing with her would earn someone a lesson they'd only be taught once. It was obvious he felt the same way about his grandnephew, and she was starting to think he felt the same way about the boy's smart damn dogs too.

CHAPTER 83

Ty picked himself up from the mining office floor and held his jaw, which was already starting to show the red knuckle marks.

"No," a crimson faced Vic grumbled as he stood in front of Ty with his fist still clenched. "You aren't going anywhere. You're going to grow a pair and go open the garage door, and then you're gonna grab those two remaining idiots down there and post them in the west windows. I don't want any fucking shooting unless I say, and I don't want to hear any *merdi fou* shit about white dogs and imaginary wolves and bears. Did I not tell you to lay off smoking that crap today?"

He scowled at Ty long enough to see if his underling was going to be stupid enough to answer that question.

When Ty didn't Vic went to his desk, and as he yanked open the side drawer and took out a bottle he rubbed the scar on his face.

"We're going to finish this," he grumbled as he spun off the top and filled his glass. "Now *foutre le camp* so I can think."

Ty stared at his boss for a moment before he snatched up his assault rifle and skulked out of the office.

As Vic took a long drink he heard Ty stomping down the metal stairs, and Rotty-wolf start up with another round of big barks. He heard Ty kick the dog before he yelled at the two loggers who were waiting in the garage.

"Jesus *Chrisse*," Vic grumbled to himself as he rubbed his scar again and picked up his radio.

"Where are you?" he grumbled into it.

Through hissing static the barely audible response said, "I'm on my way."

"Hurry the fuck up," Vic grumbled as Jia and Tavish came up the stairs and stepped into the office.

They'd returned from the Suburban, which was still parked behind one of the outbuildings at the back of the complex. Jia was wrapped in Lucy's spare leather coat, and even with the sleeves rolled up she was swimming it. Tavish was carrying a first-aid kit, and as he removed his jacket and wrapped a bandage around his elbow he looked at his watch.

"Don't get your kilt in a tizzy," Vic mumbled as he set an empty glass on his desk. "It takes time to get down the mountain in this snow. He'll be here."

Jia nodded for Vic to pour as she removed a huge pistol from the coat. It was one of Lucy's hand cannons, and it looked huge in her small hands as she popped out the magazine to make sure it was full before clicking it home again.

As Vic was filling the glass Rotty-wolf let another round of barks fly, and a second later Ty came pounding up the stairs.

He opened the door and leaned into the office, and just as he said, "They're here," cracks of automatic fire rang out from the far side of the garage.

"*Saints en crisse,*" Vic grumbled as he downed his drink and grabbed the rifle off his desk. "I thought I told you *connards* no shooting."

CHAPTER 84

Spot was trying to check every window and every shadow but there were just too many places for a bad guy to hide. He didn't see the men in the windows until he and Hamish were halfway across the icy gravel.

The men noticed Hamish at pretty much the same instant, and they immediately pushed open the sashes and aimed their assault rifles.

Blu saw them a second after Spot and sighted on the closest man. He was still mostly covered by the second floor window and she barely saw his outline through the glare and the falling snow.

Spot turned, saw Blu taking aim, and launched himself at Hamish.

Hamish saw him coming and whispered, "What's the matt—"

Spot slammed into his feet sideways and tripped him.

The man in the third floor window fired first, and he was looking to cut Hamish in half but the snow chipped and sparked two meters behind him as he and Spot tumbled out of the way. The rifle's pops bounced around the mine and reverberated out into the valley as Hamish came up on one knee and brought up his assault rifle. He tried to find a target but the snow was blowing in his face and he hadn't seen the muzzle flash.

Blu had seen it, and she quickly adjusted her aim and sent out a short burst that shattered the lower pane of the shooter's window and splintered the casing. She thought she'd hit him until he spun and sprayed in her direction. His partner joined in and she was showered with snow and rock chips as she dropped back behind the boulder.

Spot saw Blu crouching behind the rock, and Hamish swinging his rifle up to aim at the shooters' flashes. He wanted to grab him and dash for cover but wasn't sure if that'd be the right call. They were exposed in the middle of the lot but it was still more than twenty meters to the nearest door and a running Hamish made for a big target.

When Spot saw the men rotating their rifles away from the boulder to take aim at Hamish he bolted. He ran to the front of the building, stopped in clear view of the shooters, and started to bark as he leapt wildly around in circles.

When both men glanced down at him he changed his fur from white to black. The color change started at his snout and flowed quickly down his neck and over his whipping tail, and before he'd changed to all black he started the change again. White flowed over the black, and he started flipping his coat colors back and forth as fast as he could. He also pulsed his fur's thickness, and the changes sped up until he looked like he was flashing under his white camo vest.

Both men paused. They stared at the strange dog chasing its own tail around in the lot below them. The odd thing was hard to follow, it looked like it was fading in and out against the blowing snow like an optical illusion. The men tipped their heads like that was going to help make sense of what they were seeing, and they then shook their heads and forced themselves to look away.

Hamish willed himself not to stare at Spot, but when he swung his rifle back to the building he had lost the shooters' positions. There were just too many shadows and windows and everything had started to look like a gun or a shooter in the waves of shifting snow.

Spot snorted out a frustrated huff and stopped in his tracks. He barked, and pointed his whole body like a hunting dog at one of the third floor windows.

Hamish drew down on the window and found the man was aiming right at him. He saw a muzzle flash, and bullets sparked and kicked up puffs of snow and ice as they sped across the frozen gravel toward him.

One punched through his thigh and he flinched as he fell back and pulled his trigger. The shooter ducked when the bullets pinged off the metal wall near his window but he popped right back up again.

As Spot raced back toward Hamish he saw the third floor shooter was aiming to finish him, and the second floor shooter was firing short bursts to keep Blu pinned down.

The third floor shooter squinted into his scope, and then he just vaporized.

He was there one moment and the next he was just a cloud of red mist and chunks of spraying meat as his rifle tumbled out of the window and crashed onto a stack of pallets.

At that same instant the neck of the man shooting at Blu puffed red and his head came off. It spun up and away, bounced off the window, and fell back into the garage along with his body and his rifle. All that remained was a red trail on the window pane.

The mine boomed a second later with the thunderous claps of two nearly simultaneous rifle recoils. They echoed loudly off the building and around the valleys of the bowls before chasing each other away into the mountains.

Hamish grabbed his leg and pinched down hard on the wound as Blu came running low and fast over to him. She grabbed him by the collar and dragged him behind the nearest pallet of plastic-wrapped equipment.

She swatted his hand away and felt around the red hole in his pants, and then pulled her belt off and wrapped it around his leg. She grabbed his beard, turned his face to her, and said, "This might sting."

He nodded, and when she cinched it down tight he lifted off the snow and sucked in a sharp breath. Blu found the exit wound on the back of his leg and determined it was an in-and-out shot through the outer meat of his thigh, so as long as they kept pressure on it he shouldn't bleed out. She quickly stripped off her bulletproof vest, jacket, and uniform shirt, and then pulled her thermal top over her head.

"Here now lass," Hamish said between deep pants as he gave Blu's formidable bra a look. "We donae' have time for any of that."

When she wrapped her top around the wound and tied it tight he sucked in another hard breath.

She quickly put her shirt, jacket, and vest back on, and gave him a quick kiss before she pulled him to his feet.

They hobbled past Spot, who was scanning the rim of the bowl.

He'd recognized both of the distinctive large caliber sniper rifle shots, and he was wagging as he knew who must have brought their sniper friends to the mine.

CHAPTER 85

Lissa looked through her spotter's scope at her husband, and shook her head.

Harry was half way around the rim of the west mine bowl with his ridiculous fifty caliber cannon. He was looking back at her from his spotter's scope and grinning like he did the first time she let him round second base. He gave her a wave with two fingers as he took a pull from his little oxygen mask and turned back to his scope.

They were five hundred meters from the complex, and from their high vantage points they could cover both access roads and everything but the very rear of the buildings.

After dropping Harry off she'd parked her utility truck under a stand of trees at the head of the south access road. She was sitting on its hood with half of her large rifle covered in her winter-camo hooded poncho. It was tucked under her backside to form a teepee that flapped gently in the wind.

She signed an all-clear to Smudge, who was standing a few meters away at the lip of the bowl with the big wolf Hamish called Glasgow.

Smudge gave Lissa a nod, zipped up one of her vest pockets, and darted off down the south access road with the wolf galloping next to her.

Lissa turned back to her scope to watch Hamish limp to one of the large buildings with an arm around Blu. They paused at a door, Blu poked her head in, and then held it open for Spot. He darted into the dark building and reappeared a moment later to wave them in.

Lissa swung her rifle to the bottom of the access road, where Smudge and Glasgow had met up with one of Hamish's huge police dogs.

As they disappeared around the back of the complex Lissa tried to push away the lingering whiplash she was feeling.

Her doorbell ringing just after dawn was pretty odd, but it didn't hold a candle to seeing Smudge and her big wolf pal standing on the front stoop. On the way to the mine Harry had to keep her from driving off the road as she kept looking back through her rear view mirror at Smudge, who had shrunk back to normal size right before their eyes, and the wild wolf who was riding next to her in the back seat of the truck.

She willed herself to focus on her task, and checked on Harry again with another quick look. She could see the glow in his thick glasses change as he toggled from thermal imaging to night vision and back to normal optics while moving his huge rifle from side to side.

He put his eye to his spotter scope briefly, and after seeing she was looking back at him signed, *Just my luck, doesn't look like Vic's dumb enough to poke his big stupid head out.*

She flashed him smile, and they went back to covering the buildings. She had the same multiple mode sniper scope, and she toggled through the settings as she scanned the shadows and windows from one end of the complex to the other and back again.

When she heard crunching on the snow behind her she drew her sidearm, spun, and had Deputy Dave dead in her sights.

His cruiser rolled to a stop next to her truck, and he lowered his window and said, "Hey Lissa, where's Harry?"

"Jesus Dave, you tryin' to get shot?" she asked as she pulled out an earplug and holstered the pistol. As she turned back to watching the buildings through her scope she said, "Harry's a ways around the rim road."

Dave got out of his cruiser and stepped up next to the truck as he said, "I was patrolling Christa's ranch but the place is ten twenty-four. She and the boy are secure. Figured it was more imperative for me to report in down here."

He looked down at the mine and put his hands on his hips as he asked, "What's our current sit rep?"

Lissa drew a patient breath and held the retort she had on deck. She'd known Dave since he was ten and he just never seemed to grow out of being a snot-nosed imbecile. He was the one Lissa pointed to when people asked why she and Harry never had kids. Before his equally moronic parents somehow got him to stop smoking pot long enough to get into the police academy, they had forced him to take a shooting class at the range. He couldn't hit a moose if it was standing on his foot and he bitched and whined the entire time. The targets were too small and the range was too cold and the guns were too heavy, and too loud, and not calibrated properly, and were obviously defective. Harry had never been so thankful to be half deaf.

"We're covering the access roads and the front of the buildings," Lissa said without looking away from her scope. "If they try to hike out the back we'll see them. We can't shoot effectively that far in this wind, but Harry can pin them down until I drive—"

"Is Hamish down there?" Dave interrupted curtly.

"Yeah Dave," Lissa replied, no longer trying to hide her annoyance. "He and Blu just went into the crusher building on the north side."

"I guess that's acceptable, for now," Dave said with a nod. "I'll let you know when we need to recalibrate."

When Lissa turned to suggest Dave go back to whatever crossing guard duty Blu had assigned to him she noticed there were three parallel red marks running down the side of his neck. They looked angry, and very fresh. They looked like a scratch from a dog.

She went for her sidearm again but it was too late.

Dave shot her three times with a silenced pistol, and then twice more after she tumbled off the hood of her truck.

CHAPTER 86

The huge, dark crusher building was filled with dirty bus-sized gray metal vats connected by a network of conveyors and yellow walkways. Below the vats were several rows of open top train cars.

Blu helped Hamish hobble over the tracks to a metal workbench, and as he dropped on top of it she scanned the shadows of the big building with her rifle.

Spot had darted away to patrol the immediate area and appeared every so often from behind a train car or a catwalk to nod an all clear to them.

"Okay cowboy, you're out of this rodeo," Blu said quietly. She handed Hamish his pistol, and checked his radio by blowing softly into her lapel mic. The speaker of his handset crackled softly, and she put a hand on his shoulder and gave him a firm look as she said, "Stay put. We can't have you leaking all over this clean mine. I'll send Vic your regards."

"Aye," Hamish said as he looked down at his blood-soaked pant leg. "I'll just hold down this bench so it canae' get away."

Blu gave him a smile and a tug of his beard, and then walked off low and fast with her rifle held high as she moved between the train cars toward Spot. He was at the far wall, waving her over to a door that led to the big maintenance garage.

Smudge and Glasgow followed Vuur to a small outbuilding, where Rook was standing guard in the shadows near a snow-covered black SUV.

Well done lads, Smudge huffed to the boerboels as she saw there were recent footprints in the snow that led from the SUV to the garage's big sliding door.

When she tried to step closer to the SUV Rook blocked her path and huffed for her to stay back.

Bad smell, the mastiff grumbled.

Smudge gave him an understanding head-butt, and slipped past him to approach the van's back door.

She was five steps away from the bumper when the terrible scent lit up her nose. It was even stronger than it had been on the rogues, and Glasgow read her reaction and let out a whine as she started to backpedal.

Smudge calmed her with a soft huff, and fought to keep her own apprehension buried as she assured the dogs everything was going to be okay.

She held her breath and stepped forward to try the rear hatch's latch. When it popped open and swung up she stared at what was inside with her tail sinking between her legs.

She backed away and trotted over to Glasgow.

Hold still, she huffed to the wolf. *I have an idea.*

Two minutes later the four dogs weaved through the pallets of equipment and stopped just out of sight of the open sliding garage door.

They could see Vic's work truck was parked next to the stairs.

Smudge could also see Rotty-wolf's snout poking out from his cardboard bed under the metal stairwell. The office lights were off, as were all of the lights in the immense building, and she could see the two snow machines were parked far inside the garage behind one of the big yellow rock trucks. Several of the massive trucks were lined up in the repair bays, and they were in various stages of disassembly with their huge engine parts hanging down from gantry cranes. In front of the trucks were catwalks that climbed up the front of the building, and spaced throughout them were filthy windows.

Smudge could see blood spray on two of them, and what was left of the two shooters' decimated bodies.

There was no sign of anyone else in the nearly pitch black building.

Glasgow tipped her head up as she sampled the air. She could smell the four male wolves in their cages and she could smell hints of the same vileness that covered the rogues.

When Smudge picked up on Glasgow's nervous shifting she huffed, *Relax lass. These guys aren't rogues, they're normal wolves. Well, mostly normal. I'll introduce you but we have some business to take care of before you get too distracted with bad boys.*

Just as Smudge was going to slip into the garage the deputy's cruiser came around the corner of the building and sped quickly toward them.

The dogs shrunk back under cover as the car swept past them and curved around Vic's truck with its wet tires squealing on the concrete floor. The cruiser turned past the corner of the office stairs and its lights came on as it continued out of sight into the dark of the cavernous garage.

CHAPTER 87

As Blu reached for the door handle of the rusty metal door Spot tugged on her pant leg and raised a paw for her to wait.

He hopped onto a workbench and tossed her a can of spray lubricant.

She gave him a little headshake, doused the hinges, and tossed the can back to him before slowly cracking open the door. It let out a tiny squeak before opening the rest of the way without a noise. She held it with her foot, gave Spot a nod, and he darted into the maintenance building.

He stopped behind a fork truck under the front catwalk and gave the room a quick look and a sniff before waving her in.

Blu scanned the dark building with the assault rifle, and just as they started to move toward the office Dave's cruiser pulled into the building. She and Spot ducked back as its lights came on and it disappeared into the darkness behind a wall of racking.

Spot and his sister had played hide and seek in the dark at the back of the garage with the wolves. It was a maze of racks and shelves stacked haphazardly with equipment and parts of all sizes. The garage's filthy front windows let some light into the bays where the rock trucks were, but everything behind them was black and Dave's car could be anywhere back there.

Spot read the confusion and concern and anger on Blu's face, and although he shared her feelings he gave her a wag.

"I'm okay," she whispered as she gave his head a rub.

He nodded for her to follow him along the front of the building. He stuck to the shadows under the catwalk and they kept an eye on the office and the dark back of the garage as they skirted the pools of blood from the shooters.

Spot motioned for her to wait before he shot off low and fast across an open empty bay toward the first disassembled rock truck.

When he stopped behind a two-story tire he patted himself to indicate no one had shot at him. Blu shook her head, and moved quickly in a crouch to join him.

As they slipped under a huge hanging transmission the headset of her police radio crackled to life.

"*Salut* Hamish and Captain Pinard," Vic grumbled smugly in her ear.

⤞⧉§§⧉⤝

Blu crouched in the shadow of the rock truck with her rifle, and Spot pointed to indicate the rough direction Vic's voice was coming from. It was somewhere in the dark behind the racks.

"*Allons* Hamish," Vic grumbled over the radio. "I know you can hear me. Not feeling chatty, eh? *Bien*, let's try this."

There were some muffled thumps and then Vic grumbled, "Say hi, *mon cheri*."

Christa's voice said calmly, "Five total with ARs, three local, twelve meters rear center. Ben is wi—"

There was another louder thump, and then Vic grumbled, "Pick her up."

"Hamish," he said, "I know you're in the crusher building. If you and Captain Pinard aren't standing in the middle of the maintenance garage with your hands up in the next ten seconds Peggy-of-Arc here gets her other eye poked out."

Spot leapt up onto a work table next to Blu. He heard more whispered voices coming from the back of the garage, and he pointed out their number and direction.

Blu nodded, and could tell the smart black dog was as frustrated and unsure as she was.

"I'm sorry boy," she whispered as she stroked his head. "I'm not sure what to do either."

"Seven, six, five," Vic grumbled. He paused the count to add, "Did you catch Peggy mentioning I also have *petit*-Hamish to bargain with after she's used up?...Four, three, two..."

Blu was reaching for her lapel mic when Hamish replied over the radio, "Wait Vic. We're coming."

Blu quickly set her rifle down, undid the top button of her uniform trousers, untucked her shirt, and then reached down to quietly unstrap her ankle holster. She removed her backup pistol, tucked it deep down the back of her pants, picked up the rifle again, patted Spot, and walked out from under the truck.

"I'm here," she called out loudly as she stepped into the middle of the garage. She held the assault rifle out by the barrel and her sidearm pistol swung from her outstretched finger. As she turned in a slow circle to show them her back she noticed Spot was no longer on the work table.

Tavish slipped out from behind a tool rack in the back of the garage, not far from where Dave's cruiser had gone. He had his silenced pistol pointed at Blu and his rifle slung over his shoulder. "Where's Hamish?" he asked as he stepped forward. He waved the end of his gun, indicating Blu should send hers over.

"He's injured. Took one in the leg," Blu said as she set her weapons down and kicked them across the concrete floor toward him. "He went back up the north access road to go for help."

Tavish stepped over her guns and motioned for her to turn around. He yanked the handcuffs from her belt and cuffed her hands behind her back, and then fished in her pockets for the keys and dropped them into his vest pocket.

"Help?" Vic grumbled as he stepped from the shadows with Christa in front of him. He cracked a big terrible smile as he added, "From the Chogins?"

Blu saw Christa's eye had started to bleed again, and whoever had taped her wrists together hadn't bothered to roll down her sleeves.

Vic had Dave's radio in his hand and a pistol pointed at Christa's back.

"*Mon Dieu*," he grumbled. "How I wish it was me who'd gotten to shoot that sapper *chienne*."

He clicked the radio and grumbled, "Hamish, *ecoute*? You there buddy?"

Blu had wondered how Dave could have driven down into the mine without Lissa stopping him. She was having trouble deciding if she wanted to rip his traitorous, pimply face off with her bare hands or arrange for him to be gang raped in prison for the next twenty years. She decided both would be fitting.

"Aye Vic, I'm here," Hamish said over the radio.

"I need you and Harry down here in the next three minutes," Vic grumbled as he beckoned behind him with a wave of his pistol, "or your annoying little bastard here is getting a new hole in his head, *comprenez vou?*"

Jia walked out of the dark holding Ben by the shoulder. His wrists were taped and he had a bad scrape on his chin that bled a thin trail down his neck.

With her huge coat and hand cannon Jia looked like a kid playing a sick game of thug dress-up.

"Aye, I got it," Hamish said. "Don't hurt them, we'll be right down." The radio clicked and went silent.

Over his shoulder Vic spat, "You two idiots go watch for Hamish's truck."

Ty and Dave stepped out from the shadows behind him carrying rifles.

As Dave walked past Blu she spat, "You little piece of shit. I always knew you were a stupid fucking punk."

Dave changed course and came up in front of her. He tried a tough guy look but the effect was lost as he had to stand on his tiptoes. He reconsidered and hit her hard across the face with the butt of his rifle.

The blow rocked Blu's head back and she fell to one knee.

Dave danced on his toes as he yelled, "Boo yah! I've wanted to do that for a long fucking time!"

Blu spat blood on the concrete floor, and Dave laughed as he tried to high-five Ty. The big thug just stared at the short deputy's hand as it hung in space. Dave shrugged, and was still smiling as he pranced to the windows at the front of the garage.

As he ducked into the shadows under the catwalk he spun to shoot Blu one last middle finger and slipped in an oily slick. His feet flew out from under him and he landed hard on his back with a wet thump and a huff. He flailed in the puddle, struggled to stand up, and flopped onto his back again. He had to crawl to the stairs and use the handrail to pull himself back to his feet.

Everyone in the garage watched as the deputy rubbed his hands on his uniform pants and cursed while trying to wipe the gloopy oil from between his fingers.

When Dave moved into the light of the window he noticed it wasn't oil.

He'd slipped in the pool of bloody remains from the shooter that Harry had decimated. Gore dripped from the catwalk and ran down the wall next to him, and as he dry heaved and fought hard to keep down the contents of his stomach he groaned, "What in the happy hell?"

"Quit fucking around you two and pay attention!" Vic shouted surprisingly clearly from across the garage before he shook his head and grumbled a string of profanity, *"Criss de calice de tabarnak d'osti de sacrament de trou de vierge..."*

Tavish and Jia exchanged smirks.

Blu was still down on one knee, and she was slowly slipping her cuffed hands under her vest and down the back of her pants.

She winked at Christa, and then caught Ben's eye as he looked up at the top of the rock truck.

Blu snorted and tipped her head back like she was attempting to stop her nose bleed, and saw Spot running along the top of a gantry cranes. He leapt to the next crane, and then split open his paws to climb down one of the chains that supported the massive hanging transmission.

Dave's pale face grimaced and his shoulders lurched as he continued to pick clumps of red flesh from his uniform.

"Protégé of yours?" Tavish asked as he looked down at Blu. "Doesn't speak well for your branch of the service I'm afraid. I despise working with non-professionals."

"Yeah," Blu said, "me too."

Tavish smiled and said, "I would offer you my handkerchief for that bloody pecker of yours mum, but I doubt you'd need it for long."

Blu spat blood at Tavish's too-clean custom boots, and then nodded at his bandaged elbow as she said, "Looks like I'm not the only one who got a boo-boo."

Ben rolled his shoulders and stretched his neck so he could look up at Spot.

From his perch on top of the transmission Spot was nodding and signing at the big sliding door at the back of the garage.

He looked down at Ben, and when he signed a quick string of signs Ben bit back a smile and gave his smart pup a wink.

Ben said loudly to Tavish's back, "That is a big bandage you have there, little red riding hoodlum. What happened? Did you have a run-in with a WOLF!?"

Tavish turned around to look at the boy, as did Ty and Dave from the front windows.

Ben scanned each of the men as he said, "No wait, let me guess. Was it a wolf and a white dog? Yeah, you Nancies got your asses kicked by a girl wolf and a little white mutt in a sweater. Ha! My uncle was right, you are a bunch of poof-buggering wankers."

He looked at Ty's crotch and said, "And what is up with that stain on your pants, chug?"

"Shut up!" Ty yelled back. It was much louder than was necessary and his booming voice echoed in the huge garage.

Ben raised his bound hands and pointed at the angry red scratch on Dave's neck as he said, "You know how it feels, don't you Deputy Dip-shit? I bet you leaked more than a trickle into your Batman underwear when our gray-muzzled old shepherd almost took your pussy-ass backstabbing head off, didn't you, Skippy McArsemuncher?"

Dave yelled across the garage, "Fuck you...you...you little fucker!"

Ben laughed out loud and said to Ty, "And what happened to that midget Cro-Magnon lover of yours, *ese*? I didn't know my bear even liked Mexican food. I bet my big brown furry buddy tore his goddamn roided throat out. That unlucky number thirteen is a little more messed up looking now, isn't it?"

"How the fuck do you know about the bear you little asshole?!" Ty shouted.

"*Fermer!*" Vic shouted. "All of you shut the fuck up." He pointed a fat finger at Ty and grumbled, "And quit with your fucking delusional bear bullshit already. Just watch that fucking window!"

Jia said to no one in particular, "It really was a bear that attacked us."

"Well, isn't that funny," Ben said as he turned around to face her. "'Cause while you were getting bear-whooped deputy dog fart over there was executing your bodyguard."

When Jia's brow twitched Ben said, "Oh, wait, he told you Lucy died in the firefight?"

Ben turned to Dave and said, "You're just lying to every motherfucker up in this bitch today, aren't you DEPUTY DOUCHEBAG!?"

Dave swung his rifle around and pointed at Ben as he yelled, "I thought we told you to shut the fuck up!" His eyes darted from Ben to Jia, who was nervously tapping Lucy's big gun against her leg.

Ty's face twisted and his eyes got wider, and he shouted across the garage at Ben, "It was them, wasn't it? Those fucking dogs of yours. I knew it was them that attacked us at The Grub!"

"That's right, pants-wetter boy," Ben shouted right back at him. "Are you just now putting this together? Aren't you part Inuit? I'm sure you've translated the sign that hangs above our ranch. Even your drugged-out brain must have figured out why it's called Amaruq Irriq."

Christa flashed Ben a nod and a little smile.

Ty's brow bunched as his mind raced back to the deranged aunt he was sent to live with when he was ten. He could see her rocking in her chair by their little fireplace, drinking herself into oblivion as she beat the clicks and guttural notes of their Inuktitut language into him. Her harsh voice spoke the words and he could still feel her crisp backhands making sure he parroted them back correctly. His eyes widened even more as the translation of Christa's ranch washed over his strained face.

He mouthed the words silently to himself in English.

"Well done, eskimook," Ben said. "Are you finally understanding what's happening here?"

Ty actually nodded to Ben.

Dave didn't like the trembling lips he was seeing on the normally tough First Nations miner's broad face.

"Well?" he yelled to Ty. "What the fuck does it mean?"

Ty just shook his head.

Ben laughed out loud and said, "Ty's not home right now, leave a message at the beep."

He turned to Dave and said, "It means Mountain of the Wolves."

Ty started to back away, and as Ben looked at all of the gaping faces he shouted, "Don't you people get it?! All of our dogs are *Loup-Garou*! They can turn into a bear, or a wolf, or a fucking fanged ghost if they want to!"

He pointed at Ty, and in the best Hamish and Papa voice he could muster he added, "Yeh've really stepped in the shite, Thibault Lavoie. Yeh done gone and gotten the pack bloody pissed off!"

Ty continued to back away with the rifle swinging and his eyes darting around the dark garage.

"Where are they?" he whispered.

Ben ignored him, and said to Jia, "And what the fuck were you thinking poisoning those poor wolves? Are you batty, you daft bitch? Those abominations were nothing but a light snack for my WEREWOLVES!"

Jia let go of the strange boy's shoulder and took a step away from him. She was standing right under Spot.

"*Ta gueule!*" Vic screamed. "Stop this shit everyone, just stop this shit right now!" He stepped around Christa as he shouted across the garage, "Dave, is that fucking truck coming yet?"

Dave ignored the window and asked, "What's this about *Loup-Garou*? That shit's not funny, seriously."

Blu worked her hands all the way down the back of her pants as she watched Tavish, who was still staring at Ben. It looked like even the professional assassin was getting a little rattled as he touched his elbow and took a few steps away from the boy.

Ben cackled a crazy laugh and shouted, "You want to know where my killers are?! Well you won't have to wait long to find out. They're coming for you. They're coming for all of you motherfuckers. You'd better have some silver goddamn bullets in those guns or you might just want to drop them and run."

When Ben slowly raised his hands and pointed in the direction of the big metal sliding back door Rotty-wolf started barking his head off from around the corner of the office. At the same instant the door started to bang loudly, and everyone jumped as the dog's bellows and the booms echoed through the garage.

Jia swung her gun toward the slamming and the roaring barks. She yelled over the noise, "What the hell is that?"

"Ty, go check that out," Vic grumbled as he raised his rifle at the door.

"Fuck that, and fuck you!" Ty yelled. He swung his gun wildly back and forth as he backed away. He was moving toward the door Blu and Spot had come through earlier.

"ALRIGHT MY BEAUTIFUL WEREWOLVES!" Ben screamed. "COME GET YOUR BREAKFAST!"

A huge gray wolf and an improbably muscular white dog bolted around Vic's truck and charged into the garage.

Jia and Dave screamed, and his was higher-pitched.

Smudge and Glasgow zig-zagged across the floor toward Ty and Dave.

Ty turned and pulled open the door to the crusher building, and his forehead ran into the muzzle of Hamish's pistol.

"From Christa," Hamish said as he pulled the trigger.

Ben ducked as Spot leapt from the chain. He landed on Jia and her scream cut off as they crashed into a rack of huge metal parts. The rack canted, and as its heavy shelves collapsed Jia dove away into the shadows and Spot jumped forward to knock Ben out of the way.

Christa swept out with a hard kick and caught Vic across the knees. As the big miner fell he pulled the trigger of his assault rifle. The bullets cut across Christa's legs and danced a row of sparks across the floor between Blu and Glasgow until the red-smeared window behind Dave shattered.

Dave dove onto a metal table, tumbled over it, and slammed into a large tool chest before he hit the floor.

Blu rolled onto her back as Tavish spun and leveled his pistol at her.

She flung her legs open wide and pointed her crotch right at him. The move distracted him for the second she needed to get her hand around her backup pistol's grip. When he looked at the bump in the seat of her pants he barely had time to raise an eyebrow before flame shot from it. The bullet tore through his square jaw, and he reflexively pulled his trigger as he fell face-first to the concrete floor. His pistol huffed and spit flame, and Blu felt the shot thump her hard in chest.

Ben got up and saw one of Spot's paws moving under the pile of parts. As he started to lift one of the heavy pieces Jia appeared from the shadows and pointed the huge handgun down at Spot. She pressed a finger to her lips and whispered, "Come with me or I'll shoot everyone you care about in this room, starting with Houdini here." When Ben raised his taped hands she yanked him away into the dark of the garage.

Vic got to his feet and limped quickly toward his truck. He spun as he walked, and was just about to shoot Christa when he saw Hamish coming through the door with his pistol raised.

Vic sprayed bullets in that direction as Smudge dove over Ty's body and hit Hamish in his wounded thigh. They fell back through the doorway as the metal wall and concrete floor pinged and sparked around them.

Dave got up and knelt behind the metal table. He brought his rifle up, sighted down the barrel at Blu, and looked up when something huge thumped onto the table above him. A big paw stomped down on Dave's already blood-smeared hand, and the claws raked him as it shoved the rifle away.

Glasgow growled down at him as she stared deep into the trembling deputy's eyes.

Dave saw a thousand generations of killers in the wolf's confident stare, and he felt the helpless desperation of their prey. His lips quivered but he couldn't get the scream in his head to come out.

Glasgow's muzzle curled up, exposing her large fangs as the deep drumming of her growl finally managed to pull a soft whimper out of the terrified traitor.

Smudge rolled off of Hamish, saw the bleeding wound and the shirt that was tied above it, and gave him a worried look.

He grabbed her neck fur and pointed her at the garage as he said, "I'm fine yah numpty. Go make sure they're safe."

Smudge nodded, raced back through the doorway, jumped over Ty's body again, and saw Dave pounding on the metal table under Glasgow.

The big wolf had clawed his face and clamped down on his neck in one smooth move.

Glasgow was enjoying the gurgling sounds coming from the struggling human's compressed windpipe, and as she closed her eyes and bit down even harder her daughter's beautiful face appeared.

Her precious little wolflet was wagging as she bound around in the snow in front of her. She yapped happily, and it was Spot's message she was conveying to her mother, *Everything will be good again.*

Blu saw Dave flailing under the wolf, and she yelled to Smudge, "Don't let her kill him!"

As Smudge raced through the garage she huffed a quick snort at Glasgow.

The wolf's eyes opened and she let go of Dave. As he dropped screaming to the floor his hands flew to his face. He was trying to put the thick red flap of skin that was his cheek, upper lip, and nose back into place.

Smudge saw Christa and Blu were on the ground. They didn't look happy, but they were moving and he didn't see blood leaking from anywhere important. She didn't see Ben or Jia, but she saw Vic was aiming right at her.

And then she noticed Spot's legs kicking below the collapsed pile of parts.

She changed direction and ran for Spot, but as she charged across the garage she sucked in a huge rush of air and let a massive bark fly at Vic.

The big mine boss staggered back a few steps as the too-loud bark punched him in the gut. It echoed through the building and shook the corrugated metal door. Vic abandoned all thoughts of shooting the dog and let out a string of French curses as he lunged away toward his truck.

Smudge was happy to see she'd rattled him, but the bark hadn't only been meant for him.

Vic paused at his truck to dig his keys out of his coat pocket, and his grumbled curses tapered off when he heard a pair of yaps.

He looked up to see two massive black-faced guard dogs were staring back at him from the blowing snow.

As he slowly brought up his rifle both dogs tipped their block heads at him, wagged their whip tails, and then looked at the row of wolf cages.

Vic turned and saw their doors were open.

He froze with his paralyzed finger on the trigger as he stared at the hackle-raised, muzzle quivering, scar-faced wolves.

The dogs let another quick yap fly, and the four wolves were on Vic in one leap.

Rook and Vuur were content to hang back while the talented wild killers worked.

The wolves stripped off Vic's wolf-fur coat, almost gently, before they exploded in a violent flash of dark fur and spraying blood. The big mine boss was quickly separated into gory pieces by the boiling knot of his pit-fighting, savagely snarling wolves.

His head rolled under the truck and bumped into Rotty-wolf's cardboard bed. The simple mixed breed dog wagged, and licked the red smears from the scar on Vic's face. A face that was permanently frozen in a terrified mask.

Smudge opened her paws and grabbed the big gear plate that was pinning her brother. Her back muscles shook and bulged as she yanked it off him with one great pull.

Blu was flat on her back with her hands still down the back of her pants. She groaned as she gingerly moved her shoulder around in a circle, and guessed Tavish's shot had cracked a rib. There'd certainly be a nasty bruise under the vest as well, but she was pretty sure it had stopped the worst of it.

She smiled at Christa, who was also on her back and trying to bend her leg. There was a rip in her pants and one of her titanium knee joints was hanging in pieces. She returned Blu's smile, and raised an eyebrow at the black charred circle in the police captain's crotch.

As Blu scooched toward Tavish's body to retrieve her handcuff keys she said, "Hamish is going to have a field day with this one."

"Definitely not a place a lady should ever get powder burns," Christa said as she crawled across the floor to grab Blu's rifle and service pistol.

Smudge tossed another large truck part aside and pulled Spot up from the floor.

Where's Ben? he asked as he spun in a circle.

Smudge sniffed the air and growled, *This way.*

They darted off together and disappeared into the shadows as they ran in perfect sync.

The pups flew through the dark maintenance garage, rechecking the path of Ben's scent with every breath as they ran between the rows of racking until they came to a back door and crashed through it together.

Smudge had guessed Jia's destination and the pair of footprints they saw in the snow confirmed it. Her huge coat was flapping in the wind as she dragged Ben toward the outbuilding, and the black Suburban it hid.

Spot turned white and they sank down into the snow as they slid to a stop. Jia had heard the door slam and swung the gun around toward them. She paused for a moment, sweeping the big pistol back and forth over the seemingly empty lot before yanking Ben toward the van again.

As the pups popped back up from the snow Vuur and Rook peeked out from the shadows of the equipment on the far side of the outbuilding. When Spot motioned for them to stay put Vuur looked up and pawed at the snow.

Spot followed the mastiff's stare, and then tapped Smudge and pointed to the raceway above them. A bundle of large gray conduit pipes exited the second floor of the garage and ran overhead all the way to the outbuilding. The pipes were bolted together inside a frame that was held up by several thick metal support posts equally spaced across the lot.

Smudge took two running steps and launched herself off of Spot's back. She landed deftly on the overhead pipes and raced off toward Jia and Ben.

Spot signed to the boerboels and then shot off along the edge of the parking lot, darting through the cover of pallets and equipment.

As Jia reached the outbuilding she put the gun in one of the large coat's pockets, and when she fumbled for the van's keys Spot stepped from the shadows behind her and signed to Ben.

Ben nodded, looked up to see Smudge was poised for a leap from the overhead catwalk, and ripped his arm from Jia's grasp.

When she turned he swung his taped fists up as hard as he could and caught her square on the jaw.

Her head snapped back and she got a good look at Smudge's split paws just before they closed around her throat.

They fell back into the snow, and as Jia screamed and beat on Smudge's muscular, steel-trap fore-limbs Spot and the police dogs bolted from their hiding places.

Rook and Vuur knocked Ben down and helped Spot to snatch him away. They each took a limb and dragged him protesting through the snow. They tossed him down behind a dozer blade and the boerboels sat on him as he struggled to get up.

Spot spun, kicked hard, and left a trail of flying snow as he shot away from them.

Do it sis! he growled as he watched Smudge sink her hold in deep. *Strangle that bitch!*

Smudge flexed her shoulder muscles as her paws found Jia's carotids, noting one was nicely labelled just below her left ear by a triangle-and-tree tattoo. It was the same tattoo she'd seen on Liko's neck, and Mina's, and they all shared the same strong jaw and high cheeks.

What's the deal with this fuckin' family? Smudge thought as she focused all of her strength on her tightening grip. She released a flood of adrenaline into her paws, and growled, *This one's for E'sra.*

Jia gurgled, her back arched, and she twisted and struggled wildly under the strong dog as she dug in her coat pocket and found the grip of the pistol. Her sleeves were pinned but the jacket was so large it gave her room to point the huge handgun up.

She fired it right into Smudge's side.

Smudge tumbled away into the snow, turning from white to black as she fell.

Spot roared and added a burst of speed as Jia got to her feet and unloaded the clip at him. He darted from side to side as the snow-covered gravel exploded all around him.

Jia scrambled into the van and yanked the door closed just as the white dog bounced hard against it. She locked the doors and started the engine, and when she pulled away the dog was still clinging to the door handle. She spun the van in an arc as the dog smashed his head into the window right next to her. The window spider cracked and he was rearing back for another hit as she aimed the van for one of the support poles.

Spot leapt away just as the van sideswiped the pole. It tore off the side mirror and showered sparks as it screeched down the side of the van.

The engine roared and its tires spun in the snow as it swerved and clawed across the complex's gravel lot and sped up the access road.

Spot rolled to his feet and snorted out a nose full of blood. He ran back to join Ben, who was kneeling in the snow next to the boerboels.

They were staring down at Smudge, and the charred circle in the side of her vest.

When she wagged Ben said, "That Kevlar's some amazing stuff. We owe Christa big time."

Excuse me, Spot signed, *but it was my idea, and design.*

I can't believe that bitch shot me, Smudge signed as she rolled to her feet.

She poked at the hole and added, *Ouch. That really, really hurt.*

CHAPTER 88

The Suburban's windshield finally defrosted as Jia crested the upper ridge of the mine.

She passed a white utility truck, and saw a round man with thick glasses was sitting next to it in the snow.

He was rocking as he cradled a large white camouflage bundle in his arms. Jia noticed there were streaks of red smeared across the bundle, and the man didn't even look up as she flew by.

The SUV spit gravel as it turned down a fire trail and sped away from the main road. As much as Jia didn't like that smug shit Tavish she had to admit he truly was a professional. He had mapped two dozen routes out of this horrible, frozen little town, including a dozen from the logging roads and fire trails around this horrible, frozen mine.

The skies were beginning to lighten and the snow was starting to let up as she turned on the GPS unit. After a few minutes it got enough signal for her to randomly choose one of Tavish's zig-zagging routes out of the maze of mountain roads.

It would take a few hours but she had a full tank of gas. Lucy may have been a smart-ass, but he too had been a professional.

CHAPTER 89

Fourteen minutes before Jia was selecting one of Tavish's routes, Lissa Chogin had gotten her last kiss from her husband.

She dropped Harry and his big cannon off at head of the north access road, and as she pulled away she said with a wink, "Shoot that big thing straight my dear."

She drove back around to the head of the south access road, where Smudge and Glasgow were waiting for her at the rim of the mine. As she unlocked one of the tool boxes on the side of her truck Smudge left Glasgow to join her.

"Are you sure you know how to use this?" Lissa asked as she held up a little orange detonation control box.

Smudge nodded, and before she took it she signed, *It's just insurance. I'll give it back if I don't use it, maybe.*

Lissa laughed, and as she taped a radio detonator to five tubes of ANFO she said, "The range is only about a hundred meters so you have to be close, but not too close."

Smudge zipped the items into her vest, and then signed, *How about the collar tracker?*

"Oh, right," Lissa said as she opened one of the truck's other toolboxes. "This is the smallest one I have. Range is only about five clicks." She turned on the small device and held it up, and the signal level meter pegged when she pointed it at Glasgow.

Lissa was still getting used to being close to the huge wild wolf. She'd seen her from across a valley on one of Hamish's excursions, but now that they were less than three bounding leaps apart Lissa was as scared as she was in awe.

Glasgow picked up on Lissa's shiver and swiveled her big head around to stare at her.

"You are such a pretty girl," Lissa cooed.

To Smudge she whispered, "Can you ask her to stop looking at me like I'm a steak?"

꙳ᨆ§§ᨆ꙳

Six minutes after Smudge zipped the explosives, detonator, and tracking device into her vest pockets she was telling Glasgow to hold still. They were standing at the open rear door of Jia's black Suburban as the boerboels kept watch.

Smudge nosed into Glasgow's thick neck fur to bite down on her radio collar. She grabbed it with her powerful paws, and when she yanked hard the metal rivets popped out of the thick plastic.

After carefully sliding the collar off of Glasgow's neck Smudge took it to the back of the SUV and tucked it behind the small white drum.

The drum was the exact same kind that held the vile crap at the Dorschstein's kennel, and it smelled just as bad. It also had the same FLAMMABLE and EXPLOSIVE warning symbols plastered all over it.

Smudge unzipped her vest pocket and removed the bundle of ANFO vials and the little orange radio detonator. When she turned them on their green IN RANGE lights lit up, and she tucked the ANFO bundle behind the drum next to the collar.

꙳ᨆ§§ᨆ꙳

Twenty-five minutes after Jia's van left the mine, Glasgow burst from a stand of snow-covered trees.

She came to a sliding stop at the edge of a small rise that looked down on a logging road.

Her paws knocked snow from the curled lip of the overhanging drift, and the balls it formed rolled down the slope and onto the pristine snow that covered the road.

A few seconds later four darker male wolves charged from the same cluster of trees and came to a stop beside her.

She wagged and rubbed against her new pack, having thoroughly enjoyed running through the woods again with mostly normal wolves at her side.

She yapped over her shoulder, and a fluffed-up Spot shot from the trees to join them at the small precipice.

A moment later Smudge trotted out of the woods. She was panting hard as she stepped to the edge of the rise and pushed in between her brother and Glasgow.

Glasgow gave her a surly look that asked, *Trouble keeping up with the pack, domesticated runt?*

Smudge shook the snow from her vest and thick black coat, and huffed, *Easy Balto, I was recently shot.*

Glasgow closed her eyes and raised her head to the wind. Her ears tipped forward and she grumbled, *She's just over that hill, and she's coming this way.*

Smudge unzipped her vest and took out the little radio collar tracker.

Its signal level meter pegged when she pointed it in the direction Glasgow was staring.

When the big she-wolf gave her a sideways glance she put the tracker away and huffed, *I believed you.*

She swapped it for a small orange box. It looked like a long thin pack of cigarettes, and she put one end in her mouth and pulled it to extend a short silver antenna.

With a flick of her toe-pad she slid down a protective clear window, and slid a small switch to the ARM position.

The light above it lit up red.

All of their heads swiveled when they heard the crunching of the SUV's tires.

When it appeared over a hill the IN RANGE light on the little box started to flicker yellow.

When the SUV crested the next hill the light flashed green a few times and then turned solid.

Smudge held the little box out to her brother, and Spot hovered a toe pad over the DETONATE button.

Three hundred meters away Jia checked the GPS's display.

The route she was following would put her on paved roads in less than seven kilometers. In another two hours she'd be on the main highway, and if all went well she'd be at the airport in three hours, and back in New York by midnight.

She smiled, and looked out through the passenger window as the sun peeked through the clouds just above the mountains. It lit up the tops of the pines and the white valley below her.

"You were right Lucy," she said. "It is actually rather pretty up here."

She turned back to the windshield and saw a row of large wolves standing next to the road at the crest of the hill.

As she got closer she noticed two of the wolves were smaller.

And as she got closer still she saw they weren't wolves at all.

They were Ben Hogan's two black dogs.

The dogs were staring at her, and they were wagging in sync like wiper blades.

As Jia grabbed the big pistol from the passenger seat something in the back of the SUV beeped, once.

CHAPTER 90

Ben waded into the knot of wrestling dogs and smacked T'nuc hard on the rump. The lead sled dog released Spot's leg, spun to chomp down on Ben's, and tugged him down into the snow with a playful growl.

R'ekcuf bit Ben's hood, and the two elkies played tug of war with him as the rest of the team joined in.

Christa walked out of the barn with the boerboels trotting behind her. She had her tablet under her arm and a tripod over her shoulder, and to the helpless flailing Ben she said, "Quit bullying my dogs, Skippy McArsemuncher. Next call's in twenty, let's shake a leg."

Ben shoved and kicked the pile of elkhounds off of him, and called them to attention with a raised hand.

"You guys did totally *utmerket* today," he said as they wagged and stared attentively up at him. "I'm proud of every one of you numpties, and it looks like your new boss was pretty impressed. He said you're going to be celebrities in Norway, so don't forget your humble roots and the little people you peed on to get to the top."

He gave each of them a vigorous rubbing before he waved them away. The sled dogs went back to rough housing as Ben and Spot padded through the snow to join Hamish and Smudge and Sholto.

Hamish was leaning on the corral fence, and they were all watching Glasgow and her four subordinate males disappear into the woods at the far end of the snow field. She had a new tracking collar on, and Smudge said she'd taken a shine to the cheeky lead male with the big scar on his forehead. Hamish thought it was typical that a wolf named Glasgow would fall for a bad boy, and also fitting that she be the only female alpha wolf he'd ever heard of. The pups had established her as the pack's leader, and her new harem of males were fine with it. Hamish could tell they'd been down a hard road, and Smudge assured him their wounded psyches would thrive under Glasgow's firm TLC.

Smudge closed up her little jar of Christa's foot wax and wiped her paws on the leg of Hamish's cover-alls. She'd rubbed a generous amount into each of the wolves' feet, and Hamish hadn't needed any translation of their wags and deep happy groans.

"Help a bloke out lad," he said as he waved Ben over and put an arm around him.

Hamish was using a cane, and they hobbled through the snow to Christa's idling pickup. He wasn't the only one who was limping. Dave had grazed Sholto's rump when she tried to stop him from kidnapping Ben and Christa, so her backside had been shaved and bandaged.

"Figures Gunny's last bullet wound would be in the arse," Hamish said as he gave the shepherd's ear a tug.

Christa's smirk caused her to wince, and as she touched her tender eye she said, "Sure, but Sholto didn't whine for an hour after she got shot."

They drove to the old saw mill, and as Christa setup the tripod, tablet, and satellite tether Ben gave the boerboels a pep talk while Spot and Smudge brushed their coats.

After listening to the way Hamish peppered his speech with Afrikaans when speaking to the boerboels Ben had studied up.

"Okay my brus," he said as he paced in front of them with his hands behind his back. "It's all *lekker*. Let's just have a *jawl* of a time with this thing. The elkies made it look easy enough, right? It's not a big deal. We've practiced, we're ready. I'm not nervous, and you shouldn't be either my *chommies*."

Ben shook his shoulders and flopped his arms, showing the dogs how to get loose. Rook and Vuur shook like they were wet, and their big black jowls slapped and sent out little sprays of spittle.

"That's *befuck* boys," Ben said. "Good. Breathe, always remember to breathe."

"Would yeh please cut that out," Hamish said as he limped into the building. To the boerboels he said, "And you two ignore that duf, *Kom heir honden.*"

The mastiffs bounded over to him as the last of their shaking flowed off their tails.

Christa raised her hand to shush them as a handsome dark man in a periwinkle dress shirt appeared on the tablet's screen.

"Theo, can you hear me?" she asked as she stepped back and Rook and Vuur walked into the picture with a stiff-legged Hamish.

Theo smiled broadly, and said in a South African-accented voice, "Hallo! Yes I can hear you fine." He leaned closer to the screen and said, "Christa, what in the good name of the maker has happened to your beautiful eye? And Hamish why are you limping brah?"

"Training accident," Christa said. "Theo, I'd like you to meet our young dog whisperer, Ben Hogan."

Ben joined them, and waved.

He saw Theo was seated at an outdoor table in the shade of a neatly trimmed thatched roof. The patio behind him was ringed in bright flowers, and the sun was setting between steep green hills in the background. A thick gold chain with a cross hung around Theo's neck, and he held a fat sandwich in hands that sported several large gold rings.

"Are those my *kliene honds*?" he asked with a smile. "My how they've grown, they look proper *sterke.*"

"Strong they are," Hamish said. "And they're smart as the blazes. Just yeh wait and see."

Theo leaned in again and looked at the dogs as he asked, "Why does one of my beautiful boerboels have train tracks running down the side of his face?"

"Training accident," Ben said.

Theo stared at his dog for moment, and then at Christa's eye, and Ben's chin, and Hamish's cane.

Hamish quickly asked, "Theo, how are things in the KZN?"

Theo waved his hand as if brushing something out of the way and said, "*Eish* Hamish. We are still having a hang of a problem with the poachers. They took another rhino this morning and it's getting worse every week." He paused, and seemed to waved that away too before his smile returned and he said, "But I'm enjoying a sarmie in the boma, it's twenty eight degrees, and life is lekker brother. How can I complain?"

"How's your mum, and your cousin?" Hamish asked.

"Mum says thanks for the puzzle," Theo said. "She's pulling her kinky damn hair out over it. And my stroppy cousin is still plenty mal in the head man. The king talks about taking a sixth wife. He may need Vuur and Rook more than I do. Speaking of crazy women, did you get my gift?"

"Aye," Hamish said with a big grin, "but I donae' think I'll have an opportunity to use it anytime soon."

"A coupon for a Joburg brothel is hardly what he needed Theo," Christa said.

Theo tipped his nearly bald head back and roared. He leaned forward and said, "Tell me one Hamish, I know you have one."

Without a pause Hamish said, "Have I told yeh about the young Zulu warrior and his chieftain father who went to Joburg city for the first time?"

Theo was already chuckling as he replied, "No Hamish, you certainly have not."

"They were amazed by everything they saw," Hamish said. "The buildings were impossibly tall and their lobbies were adorned with the finest stone, but the bushmen were truly in awe of the shiny walls that moved apart and back together again. 'What is this, father?' the son asked. His father shook his head as he responded, 'I have never seen such a thing in all of my years my son'. Just then a round old woman with a surly puss waddled past them and got into the elevator. The doors closed, the numbers above the doors counted up, stopped, and then counted back down. The doors opened and a smiling young choty goty blonde with big anties strolled out. 'Son, go get your mother' the Zulu chief said."

Theo pounded on the boma's table and shook his head as he said, "That's top kif, Hamish, pure riches!"

For the next hour Hamish took Theo through Rook and Vuur's training and abilities, with Christa and Ben helping to set up the demonstrations and move the tablet when needed.

Although they laughed and busted each other's balls a lot Theo was very serious about understanding the details of each test. He thoroughly grilled Hamish on any limitations to the dogs' skills, and was quickly realizing there weren't many.

Christa and Ben watched the exercises from the sidelines, and she quietly told him about the huge trust Theo managed for his cousin the Zulu king, who was a direct descendent of King Shaka himself. Theo oversaw almost a third of the king's land, including several gold and diamond mines. He also ran the king's game reserve and the KwaZulu-Natal wing of the South African Police Service. Hamish had trained all of the king's top staffer's protection canines for decades. They were usually shepherds, but the South African boerboel mastiff was Theo's breed of choice for his personal guard dogs.

At the end of the final demonstration Vuur and Rook darted over to stand at Christa's side, and they each had a handgun in their mouth. When she raised a hand they set the guns down at her feet.

Ben and Hamish hobbled into the picture showing off their untorn jackets. They had been disarmed without a scratch.

As Hamish stopped in front of the tablet and folded his big arms across his wide chest Ben could see the pride on his ruddy face. He smiled broadly and said, "Well Theo, what'd yeh think mate?"

Theo had stopped chewing a half-hour earlier. In fact he hadn't moved, and most of the meat had fallen out of his sandwich.

He leaned forward in his chair, pointed at the screen and said, "Hamish you must not show these animals to anyone, and we need to talk about an exclusive contract before you take on any more work. I want your team down here training my rangers, no *grapje*."

Christa joined Hamish, and as she clapped him on the shoulder she said, "Hold that thought Theo, we've got one more thing to show you."

For an encore Rook and Vuur easily took Hamish to the ground and disarmed him as they had in the earlier exercise, but in the blink of an eye Vuur pinned his arms while Rook looped a paw around his neck and under his bearded chin. The mastiff then hooked it with his front paw locked in the crook of his hind hock, and arched his strong back to sink in the choke hold.

Hamish quickly tapped out as his head was pulled painfully backward. The big dogs let him go, and when Hamish grabbed their collars they backed up and pulled him to his feet.

"Thank goodness the guards at Number Four prison never met you," Theo said as he stared at the screen. "You are truly a dog *fundi* my *chommie*. All of you are." He wiped his hands on a napkin and said, "My friends I need to go, but all kidding aside Hamish, we need to talk again soon. Name your price and clear your calendar."

They said their goodbyes and closed the call, and Hamish put an around Ben as he smiled a big smile and said to Spot and Smudge, "So partners, when does yer summer vacation start?"

CHAPTER 91

Kelcy walked into the office and the frosted glass doors closed behind her with a soft whoosh.

She put a tablet down on the corner of her boss's desk, and Dr. Martin Osipoff smiled and held up a finger for her to wait as he spoke into his cellphone.

"Of course not, it's never a bad time for y'all," Marty said warmly to the caller. "I can make the conference call, give me three minutes. Yes…Okay…Thank you."

As he put the phone down he reached across the desk and retrieved the tablet. He flicked around the screen for a moment, and in his charming slight drawl said, "This is perfect, thanks Kels. How you getting on with the golden?"

"Hunkey-dorey boss," she said with a big smile. "We set her leg and Lindsay's showing me how to change the drain after school tomorrow. She should be chasin' cars again in a week."

"That's just fine, nice work kid," Marty said as he stood up. "Go ahead and knock off a little early."

Kelcy gave him a nod, and as she turned to leave he asked, "When's your brother coming home? I have something he might be interested in."

"He'll be back this weekend," Kelcy said. "I can bring him by next week."

"That'd be great," Marty said.

The teen bounced out of the office with the doors whooshing open ahead of her and closing behind her.

Marty tapped a remote panel on his desk, and looked across the office to the large monitors that had switched from the clinic's logo to show the security camera feeds.

As he watched Kelcy walk to the lobby he tapped the panel again, and a solid panel slid over the frosted glass doors. There was a click, and a strip of green light appeared along the top edge of the jamb. A second later the window shades shut and the lights dimmed a little.

He tapped again, and the security feeds were replaced by a small padlock icon and a green spinning status indicator.

As he came around to the front of his desk and leaned on it a very large man appeared on one of the monitors, and a fit, pretty brunette appeared on the other.

"Good evening Katia," he said. "*Privyet* Semion, I trust you are both—"

"You're aware of our setback in Canada?" Katia interrupted.

"Yes," Marty said as he looked down at his trousers. He brushed away a dog hair and Katia's all-to-frequent rudeness.

"What's your status?" she asked.

"Both sites are fully operational," Marty said as he looked up. "We're ready to begin testing."

"Dah, that is good," Semion said with a nod. His eyes shifted to Katia as he said, "So we do it the hard way. Start your program, dear daughter."

Afterwords from your author

Late January, a little south of Boston...

I curse the winter. I truly despise the cold and am so very ready to be done with shoveling snow. If I never have red cheeks or blue fingers again that would be just fine. After many (many) years of living in the north alongside the other nutty people who struggle through the dark months to keep their cars running and their pipes from freezing, and in February start to consider wrapping themselves in their electric blankets and jumping into a hot bath, I am so ready to celebrate however many New Year's Eves I have left by raising a carved pineapple cup with my toes in the sand somewhere warm.

But I sure would miss watching my dogs play in the snow.

I would miss it a lot.

If you've spent a winter where appreciable amounts of snow and dogs are both present you've likely experienced canines' love for the white stuff. My pups happily dive face-first into it like furry Tony Montanas snorting un-cut Columbian.

Regardless how far south the thermometer needle points they scramble over each other to be the first one through the door whenever there's fresh snow to run through. It doesn't matter that they just ran through it a few hours ago, and every day for the past week, or month. Even in the coldest New England winters, when the snow is so high they have to be let out through the garage, the pups can't wait to be neck deep in it. They bound off in great leaps to chase some unseen thing into the woods and return hours later with icicles hanging from their wagging tails. Not that they won't be shivering and ready to come in, but after an hour napping in front of the fire they'll be begging to go out and do it all over again. A fresh new inch of snow will have fallen, and for some reason it will be imperative that they run around like idiots all over again with their noses buried in it.

I can watch them for hours. They play tag, they dig, they pounce, and they help me shovel the driveway by fighting in my neat piles of snow and pushing them back down onto the driveway. And they usually invite the neighbor dogs to come join in, just to make sure no pile is left un-toppled. (The very dogs this book is dedicated to).

I do envy having that much enthusiasm for the cold, but I think red cheeks should be from sunburn, and blue fingers should only come from stirring an icy beverage.

Yet here I sit, typing away as another nor'easter howls through the eaves and the white stuff falls horizontally, and I try to ignore the two medium-size black dogs who are wagging (sort of in sync) by the back door as they stare at me.

They're letting me know a fresh inch has fallen, and it's not going to sniff or pee on itself.

As I get up and put on my coat and gloves I realize I can't bitch too much. We'll be back in front of the fire soon enough, and the pups will expect me to tell them what happens with the rogue wolves, the crazed bear, and those murderous miners who are chasing our protagonists through the great white north.

Not a bad way to pass a snowy afternoon, but I still wonder why the hell I live where it gets this damn cold.

All the best,
RU

꒰꒱§§꒰꒱

I hope you're enjoying cuddling with the Spot and Smudge books as well, hopefully by a warm fire. If you are, the best compliment you can ever pay me is to recommend them to a friend, or to leave a good review, or to vote for one you agree with. I realize it takes a few clicks and a few minutes of your time but it truly does help and is greatly appreciated.

Please let me know if you have so I can thank you.

RU

Visit Spot and Smudge's website!
See the real Spot and Smudge
See the cool Spot and Smudge art gallery
Get our Special Deals
Grab some Spot and Smudge gear
Find out about the books
See the charities the pups support
Say hello, and learn a little bit about your author
SpotandSmudge.com

One million eye rolls, and counting…

There is an amazing group of creative, sharp, patient people who save me from myself. I'm convinced dogs learn loyalty from people like them…and they could teach coyotes a few things about rending flesh, too, and I mean that in the best possible way. These stories simply wouldn't happen without their many talents.

Thanks, Alphas.

Allison Caputo	Chelsea Watt	Morgan Watt
Elaine Onoyan	Kristi Hornickel	Paul VanOpens
	Paul LeClerc	

THE STORY CONTINUES...

LET SLIP THE PUPS OF WAR
SPOT AND SMUDGE - BOOK 3

OF ROGUES AND REVENGE
SPOT AND SMUDGE - BOOK 4

A WEE INFESTATION OF JERRYS
SPOT AND SMUDGE - BOOK 5

DAWN OF THE CANICENE
SPOT AND SMUDGE - BOOK 6

WANT MORE WONDERFULLY TWISTED DOGS?
GET THE **ONE PAW IN THE GRAVE** SERIES OF SHORT STORIES:

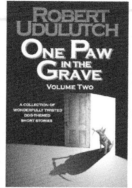

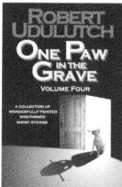
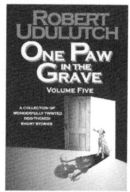
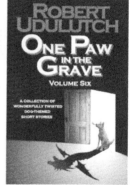

Made in the USA
Monee, IL
19 November 2024

70653499R00282